# SPECIAL MESSAGE TO READERS

**THE ULVERSCROFT FOUNDATION**
**(registered UK charity number 264873)**
was established in 1972 to provide funds for
research, diagnosis and treatment of eye diseases.
Examples of major projects funded by
the Ulverscroft Foundation are:-

- The Children's Eye Unit at Moorfields Eye Hospital, London
- The Ulverscroft Children's Eye Unit at Great Ormond Street Hospital for Sick Children
- Funding research into eye diseases and treatment at the Department of Ophthalmology, University of Leicester
- The Ulverscroft Vision Research Group, Institute of Child Health
- Twin operating theatres at the Western Ophthalmic Hospital, London
- The Chair of Ophthalmology at the Royal Australian College of Ophthalmologists

You can help further the work of the Foundation
by making a donation or leaving a legacy.
Every contribution is gratefully received. If you
would like to help support the Foundation or
require further information, please contact:

**THE ULVERSCROFT FOUNDATION**
**The Green, Bradgate Road, Anstey**
**Leicester LE7 7FU, England**
**Tel: (0116) 236 4325**

**website: www.foundation.ulverscroft.com**

Katherine Webb was born in 1977 and grew up in rural Hampshire before reading History at Durham University. She has since spent time living in London and Venice, and now lives in rural Wiltshire. Having worked as a waitress, au pair, personal assistant, book binder, library assistant, seller of fairy costumes and housekeeper, she now writes full time. Her novels have been translated into 24 languages.

You can discover more about the author at www.facebook.com/KatherineWebbAuthor

# THE NIGHT FALLING

Puglia, Italy, 1921: Leandro returns home, now a rich man with a glamorous American wife. But how did he get so wealthy — and what haunts his outwardly exuberant wife? Boyd, a quiet English architect, is hired to build Leandro's dreams. But why is he so afraid of Leandro? Clare, Boyd's diffident wife, is summoned to Puglia with her stepson. At first desperate to leave, she soon finds a compelling reason to stay. Ettore, starving, poor and grieving for his lost fiancée, is too proud to ask his Uncle Leandro for help — until events conspire to force his hand. Tensions are high as poverty leads veterans of the Great War to the brink of rebellion. And under the burning sky, a reckless love and a violent enmity will bring brutal truths to light . . .

KATHERINE WEBB

# THE NIGHT FALLING

*Complete and Unabridged*

# CHARNWOOD
Leicester

First published in Great Britain in 2014 by
Orion Books
an imprint of
The Orion Publishing Group Ltd, London

First Charnwood Edition
published 2015
by arrangement with
The Orion Publishing Group Ltd
An Hachette UK company, London

The moral right of the author has been asserted

A catalogue record for this book is available from the British Library.

ISBN 978–1–4448–2641–8

Published by
F. A. Thorpe (Publishing)
Anstey, Leicestershire

Set by Words & Graphics Ltd.
Anstey, Leicestershire
Printed and bound in Great Britain by
T. J. International Ltd., Padstow, Cornwall

This book is printed on acid-free paper

*This blind urge to destruction, this bloody and suicidal will to annihilation, has lurked for centuries beneath the patient endurance of daily toil. Every revolt on the part of the peasants springs out of an elementary desire for justice deep at the dark bottom of their hearts.*

*Christ Stopped at Eboli*
Carlo Levi

# Clare, afterwards

They must all change trains at Bari and the platform fills with shambling people, creased and surly like sleepers newly woken. Mostly Italians; mostly men. Clare takes a breath and tastes the sea, and suddenly she needs to see it. She goes alone, leaving everything she owns and not caring; walking unhurriedly when once she might have been anxious — fearful of theft, of impropriety, of the next train leaving without her. This new fearlessness is one of the things she has gained. Everything she's seen and felt over the summer, every wild thing that has happened has purged the fear from her; but she doesn't yet know if gains like this one will balance out the loss.

Bari's city streets seem alien after so many weeks in Gioia and at the *masseria*; they are too big, too wide, too long. But there are the same knots of restless men, and the same feeling of waiting violence. Clare draws some curious looks as she goes, with her worn-out foreign clothes, her fair hair, her air of detachment. This could well be the last day she ever spends in Puglia — if the choice is hers, it will be. After today, after she rejoins the train, she will leave it and every second, and every passing mile, will carry her closer to home. This thought slows her steps. Home is not home any more. That, like everything else, has changed; home is another of

3

the losses, stacked up against the gains. But as she continues to walk she wonders about it, and decides it could also be a good thing. A part of her release.

The pavement is lustrous, worn by use, polished by salt spray; gradually the light in the sky changes, and seems to lift and widen. Her gaze is drawn upwards for a moment, but then the street opens onto the quayside and the sea is there in front of her, with the early morning sun still soft on its surface, and the colour of it is a revelation. Clare walks to the very edge of the land, until all she can see is the blue. A blue that seems alive, that seems to breathe. This is what she was looking for, what she'd hoped to see. She lets the colour soak her, like it soaks the sky, and even though it's painful it's somehow still a comfort. A reminder to go forwards, and not look back. She stays there for a long time because she knows that when she turns away this colour — this exact blue — will be just another memory, the best and bitterest of all.

# Ettore

He has heard another man say, on the long, dark walk before dawn, that hunger is like a stone in your shoe. At first you think you'll just ignore it — it's an irritation, but it doesn't really hinder you. But then it makes you limp, and makes it hard to walk. The pain grows. It cuts deeper and deeper into your flesh, crippling you, slowing your work, catching the corporal's cruel eye. When it reaches the bone it grinds in and becomes a part of you, and you can think of nothing else. It rusts your skeleton; it turns your muscles to rotten wood. The man warmed to his theme as they trudged, and felt their bones rusting. He kept thinking of ways to embellish it, hours afterwards — the comments coming apropos of nothing and puzzling the men who hadn't walked within earshot of him that morning — as their arms swung the scythes to cut the wheat, as the sun rose and burnt them, as blisters swelled beneath their calluses. Over the squeak and clatter of wooden finger-guards on wooden handles, his embellishments kept coming. *Then it turns your blood to dust. Then it fells you. It creeps up your spine and lodges in your brain.* And all the while Ettore thought it was a stupid comparison, though he said nothing. Because, after all, you could always pull off your shoe and kick the stone away.

He can't kick his hunger away, any more than

he could wake up if Paola didn't shake him. She's rough as she does it, and punches him if he doesn't wake at once; her knuckles are sharp against the bones of his shoulder. She moves as briskly and abruptly in the pre-dawn darkness as she does at day's end, and he doesn't know how she manages it. How she has the energy, or how she sees so well in the dark. Other men, conditioned from childhood, wake of their own volition at three, at four, at five at the latest, but by then the chances of work are slipping away — it's first come, first served, and the queues are long. Other men don't need their sisters to rouse them as Ettore does, but without Paola he would slumber on. He would sleep the day away soundly, profoundly. Disastrously. For a few seconds he lies still, and asks nothing of his body. Just a few seconds of rest, in darkness so complete he can't be sure whether he's opened his eyes or not. There's a smell of tired air, of earth and the rank stink of the *prisor*, which needs emptying. Even as Ettore notices it, the collector arrives outside — the slow plod of mule hooves in the small courtyard, the creaking of wheels.

'*Scia' scinn*!' the collector calls, all weary and hoarse. '*Scia' scinn*!' *Hurry up! Come down!* Sighing sharply, Paola checks that the wooden lid is tight to the ceramic *prisor* pot, then hefts it up and carries it out. The stink gets stronger. In the dark, Paola says, at least your neighbours can't see as you tip it into the collector's huge barrel. But as the little cart moves away, jolting on the uneven stones, there's always a trail of

6

human waste on the ground behind it, slippery and foul.

Paola shuts the door gently behind her, and keeps her footsteps soft. It's not her brother or Valerio that she doesn't want to disturb, but her son, Iacopo. She likes the men out of the room before he wakes, so that she can nurse him in peace, but this rarely happens. With the scratch and flare of a match, and the growing glow of a single candle, the baby is awake. He makes a small sound of surprise and then mewls quietly in protest, but he is sensible and doesn't cry. Crying is hard work. Part of the ammonia stink in the cramped room is coming from the child. Without water to wash him, or his blankets, it's hard to get rid of the smell; there's the sourness of vomit, too. Ettore knows that once she is alone Paola will wet a rag to clean him, but she's careful not to let Valerio see her do so. He is fiercely jealous of their stock of water.

*Livia.* Ettore shuts his eyes on the candle flame; sees its red imprint on the inside of his skull. This is the order in which his thoughts run each day, every day: hunger, then the reluctance to rise, then Livia. Impulses really, rather than thoughts; Livia is as visceral, as connected to his body and his instincts rather than to his mind as the other two things. *Livia.* It's less a word and more of a feeling, irresistibly linked to memories of smell and touch and taste and loss. Good losses as well as bad — the loss of care, for a moment; the loss of all responsibility, of all fear and anger, washed away by the simple joy of her. The loss of doubt, the loss of misery. The way

7

her fingers would taste after a day spent cleaning almonds — like something green and ripe you could eat. The way she seemed to feed him, so that when they were together he forgot to be hungry. Just for that while. He can picture the exact grain of the skin on her calves, soft as apricots at the backs of her knees. And then there's the loss of her, like a slash with ragged edges. Like the onslaught of ice a summer hailstorm brings: bruising, freezing, killing. The loss of her. The muscles around his ribs pull tight, and shake.

'Up, Ettore! Don't you dare go back to sleep.' Paola's voice is hard as well — it's not just her face and the way she moves. Everything about her has gone hard, from the flesh on her bones to her words and the contents of her heart. Only when she holds Iacopo is there softness in her eyes, like the last remembered light after sunset.

'You're the stone in my shoe that I can't ignore,' he tells her, standing up, stretching the stiff cords of muscle that run down his back.

'Lucky for you,' Paola retorts. 'If it wasn't for me we'd all starve while you lay dreaming.'

'I don't dream,' says Ettore.

Paola doesn't spare him a glance. She crosses to the far side of the room, to the recessed ledge in the stone wall where Valerio sleeps. She does not touch him as she wakes him; she only speaks, loudly, near his ear.

'It's past four, Father.' They know Valerio is awake when he starts to cough. He rolls onto his side, curls up like a child, and coughs, and coughs. Then he swears, spits, and swings his legs to the floor. Paola glares.

'Vallarta again today, boy, if we're lucky,' Valerio says to Ettore. His voice rattles in his chest. Paola and Ettore share a quick, meaningful glance.

'Best hurry then,' says Paola. She pours them both a cup of water from a chipped amphora, and the ease with which she does it shows that the jar is already less than half full. Paola must wait for their appointed day before she can go to the fountain for more — it's either that or buying it from a dealer, which they cannot do. Not at such prices.

★ ★ ★

Masseria Vallarta is the biggest farm near Gioia, some twelve hundred hectares. It's one of the few, even now at harvest time, that has been hiring men every day. Before the war this was the one time of year when work was guaranteed — weeks of it. The men would sleep out in the fields rather than bothering to walk back and forth every morning and night; waking with soil in the creases of their clothes and dew on their faces, and the bite of stones underneath them. The debts of the winter could finally be earned back, and paid off — the rent on their measly apartments, bills for food and drink and gambling. Now, even the harvest is no guarantee of work. The proprietors say they can't afford to hire the men. They say that after last year's drought, and the vacuum of the war, they are going out of business. If they are hired to

Masseria Vallarta today, Ettore and Valerio will walk ten kilometres to reach the farm, and start work at sun-up. There's no food from the night before; they ate it all. There might be something at the farm for them, if they are hired, though it will come out of their wages if there is. The men stamp their feet into their boots, button their battered waistcoats. And as he goes out into the cool of the morning, into the ageless shadows of the little courtyard and the narrow streets that lead to Piazza Plebiscito, where they will queue for work, Ettore makes his promise. He makes the same promise every morning, and means it with every fibre of himself: *I will find out who did it, Livia. And that man will burn.*

# Clare

It's always a shock to see how much Pip has grown during term time, while he's away for weeks on end, but this time it seems like something more fundamental has changed. Something more than his height, the length of his face or the width of his shoulders. Clare studies him, and tries to put her finger on it. He has fallen asleep with his head against the dusty window of the train and his dog-eared copy of *Bleak House* resting against his chest. Fine strands of his hair have fallen forward onto his forehead, and shake with the movement of the carriage. With his eyes shut and his mouth drooping slightly open, she can still see the child he was. The little, lonely person she first met. His face is more angular now — the jaw stronger, the brows heavier, the nose slightly longer and more pointed. But his light brown hair is as flyaway as ever, and he doesn't need to shave yet. Clare looks closely, checking. There's no shadow of whiskers on his chin or top lip. Her relief at this is profound, and makes her uneasy.

She turns to look out of the window. The landscape is unchanging. Mile after mile of farmland; wheat fields, for the most part, interspersed now and then with orchards of faded olive trees, and gnarled almond trees with their trunks twisted and black. When Pip is a man, an adult, when he finishes all his schooling, when he leaves home for good . . . Clare swallows, fearfully. But she can't prevent it, of course. She can't cling on to him. She won't let herself. Perhaps this is what has changed, this time: he's become enough like a grown man that she can no longer deny it's happening, and that one day soon he will separate himself from her, and start his own life. She's not his mother, so perhaps she should feel the wrench of this a bit less. But a mother has an unbreakable bond, the bond of blood and heritance, of knowing that her child was once a part of her, and in some ways always will be. Clare doesn't have that. Her bond with Pip feels more breakable, more delicate; perhaps every bit as precious, but also with the potential to melt away without trace. She fears that most of all. He is only fifteen, she reassures herself. Still a child. The train gives a lurch to one side, and Pip's head bangs against the glass. He starts awake, snapping his mouth closed, squinting.

'All right there, Pip?' Clare says, smiling. He nods affably.

'We must be nearly there.' He yawns like a cat, unashamedly. His teeth are just starting to crowd at the front, jostling for space.

'Pip,' she protests. 'It's like staring into the abyss.'

'Sorry, Clare,' he mumbles.

'We are nearly there.' Clare gazes out at the bleached grass of a field, blurring past. 'We *must* be nearly there.'

Her mouth feels as stale as her crumpled clothes and her sticky skin. The train is stuffy, airless — it's no wonder Pip keeps nodding off.

12

She might have done so herself, but Boyd cautioned her about the Italians and their light fingers, so she's too worried about their purses and possessions, and what Boyd would say if they were robbed after he'd warned her. She wants to stretch her legs and wash her hair, but at the same time, as a few scattered buildings come into view, she suddenly doesn't want to arrive at Gioia del Colle. There's something wonderful about travelling — about being moved across the long miles of the earth with no sense of responsibility, their aim achieved purely by waiting patiently. And, because she and Pip are alone in the compartment, there's only the ease and pleasure of his company. No manners to be minded, no struggle to find small talk. Their long silences are thoughtful, companionable, never uncomfortable. And she's also nervous about what waits at the end of the journey.

Boyd has committed them to spending the entire summer with people she has never met, and knows precious little about. No amount of protest would sway him from the plan; and she couldn't even write down her reluctance in a letter to him, as she preferred to — to make sure she kept her argument straight and her tone of voice even. Not when he was already out in Italy, and the instruction for her and Pip to join him came faintly down a rustling phone line. In desperation she'd suggested a fortnight, rather than the whole season, but Boyd hadn't seemed to hear her. And just like that, the restful summer at home she'd been looking forward to — alone with Pip, watching the sweet peas climb

13

their bamboo canes and playing whist in the shade of the high garden wall — had vanished. The Italians who will be their hosts are clients of Boyd's; Cardetta, an old acquaintance from New York, and his wife, who is charming. Beyond that, she knows only that they are rich.

The train has passed cone-shaped huts built of rock, like strange hats discarded by stone giants. It has passed fields full of working men, swinging scythes; dark, thin men who did not look up as the train clattered by. It has passed small carriages pulled by donkeys, and farm wagons pulled by oxen, and not a single motor car. Nothing, beyond the train itself, to betray that the year is 1921, not 1821. Clare is struggling to picture what rich might look like, this far south; it worries her that there might not be electricity, or indoor plumbing; that the water might make them sick. In the north they say that the country south of Rome is best avoided, and that the country south of Naples is a barren no-man's-land, peopled by sub-humans — a godless, under-evolved race too base to drag itself out of poverty and dissolution. Pip's school had been happy to release him early for the summer break when she wrote to say that they would be taking him to Italy. *What better way for Philip to finish the academic year than by visiting the very treasures of art and civilised thought he has spent the recent months studying?* wrote the master. Clare let him picture Rome, Florence and Venice, since that was the conclusion he'd leapt to, and left it at that. She herself has never heard of any of the major towns here in the

14

south: Bari, Lecce, Taranto. And the town where they are headed, Gioia del Colle, was difficult to find on the map.

Just half an hour later the train creeps into the station, between two near-deserted platforms. Clare smiles at Pip as they stand and stretch and gather themselves, but it's she who wants reassurance, not Pip. Hot, heavy air is the first thing to greet them, and it has the smell of blood on it. The unmistakable metal reek of gore. The deep, fortifying breath Clare had been taking sticks in her throat, and she looks around, repulsed. The sky is an immaculate blue, the sun low and yellow in the west. They move away from the hissing train, and the buzz of insects fills their ears.

'What's that smell?' says Pip, holding the creased sleeve of his blazer to his nose. But then they hear a shout, and see a figure waving from the window of a car.

'Ahoy, dearly beloveds!' Boyd's voice is tight with excitement. He waves his hat and laughs, and when he emerges from the vehicle it's with an unfolding of long limbs, the unfurling of a long spine. He is tall and narrow and, ever fearful of appearing clumsy, he moves with exaggerated grace.

'Ahoy!' Clare calls, relieved. She has brought them this far, and has the soothing feeling of handing control back to her husband. She and Pip cross quickly to the car, and Clare turns to wave the porter over with their luggage.

'Make sure you've all your bags. I wouldn't put it past them to miss one and carry it all the way to Taranto,' says Boyd.

'No, this is all of them.' Boyd hugs Clare, hard, then turns to Pip and hesitates. This is new, too — this slight awkwardness between them. It tells Clare that Boyd can see his son's encroaching adulthood just as clearly as she can. They shake hands, then smile, then bashfully embrace.

'Philip. You're so tall! Look — far taller than Clare now,' Boyd says.

'I've been taller than Clare since the Christmas before last, Father,' Pip points out, slighted.

'Have you?' Boyd looks troubled; his smile turns strange, as though he ought to have known or remembered this. Clare is quick to deflect him.

'Well, you do spend most of your time sitting in a chair, or on a bicycle, or in a boat. It's hard to tell your height,' she says. Just then the breeze blows and brings the tang of blood and violence anew. Boyd pales; what's left of his smile vanishes.

'Come on, climb in. The slaughterhouse isn't half a mile south of here, and I can't bear the smell of it.'

The car looks brand new, although there's a fine veil of dust dulling its crimson paintwork. Pip examines it at appreciative length before they climb in. The driver, dark and inscrutable, barely nods at Clare as he and the porter secure their bags, but his eyes return to her, again and again. She tries not to notice. He would be handsome but for a harelip; a neat divide in his upper lip, and in the gum behind it, where his teeth are twisted and uneven.

'You might get a few looks, dear girl,' Boyd tells her in low tones, as the car pulls away. 'It's the blond hair. Rather a novelty down here.'

'I see,' she says. 'And do you get looks, too?' She smiles, and Boyd takes her hand. His hair is also fair, though now it's filling with grey it looks more silvery, and seems to have an absence of colour. It's thin across the top of his scalp; his hairline has crept back and back from his forehead and temples, like an ebb tide slipping from a shore. This is what Clare notices about him when they have been apart for a while, though this time it has only been a month: that he is growing old. He asks how their journey was and what they saw, what they ate and if they slept. He asks how their garden in Hampstead looked, before they left it, and when Pip's school report is due. He asks all this with a strange desperation, a kind of manic neediness that immediately puts Clare on edge, at some bone-deep level where memory and experience reside. *Not again*, she begs silently. *Not again.* She sifts hurriedly through her mind for something she's missed — some sign, something he might have said on the phone, or before he even left; some hint of what the problem might be. She has done as he asked, and brought herself and Pip all this way to him, and yet there's something wrong. There's clearly something wrong. They leave the station behind in a cloud of pale dust, and though fresher air comes pummelling in through the windows, Clare is certain she can still smell blood.

17

# Ettore

Piazza Plebiscito is full of men dressed in the typical black. These are the *giornatari*, the day labourers; men with nothing to their name, and no means to feed themselves but the strength of their backs. In the shadowy dawn they are a dark scattering against the pale stones of the pavement. The murmur of voices is low; the men shuffle their feet, cough, exchange a few low words. Here and there an argument starts, shouts ring out and there's a scuffle. Once he and Valerio are in their midst Ettore can smell the grease in their hair, the sweat of all the days before on their clothes, the hot, stale fug of their breath. It's a smell that has been with him, all around him, since the first days he can remember. It's the smell of hard work and scarcity. It's the smell of men as animals, muscle and bone made hard by graft. The overseers are there, on their horses or standing holding them by the reins, or sitting in little open-topped carts. They hire five men here, thirty there; one shepherd wants a pair of men to help trim his flock's feet. It's easy work but he can pay next to nothing, and the men eye him in disgust, knowing that one or other of them will have to take his low wages.

This is how it was always arranged, until the Great War. Those that want work come to the piazza, those that want workers meet them there.

18

A wage will be offered, and men selected. There is no negotiation. Then, after the war, things changed. For two years, things were different — the worker's unions and the socialists won some concessions, because during the war men like Ettore and Valerio, who had so little cause to fight, were promised things to keep them in the trenches. They were promised land, better wages, an end to the unending hardship of life, and afterwards they fought to make the landowners and proprietors keep those promises. For a few febrile months, it seemed like they might have won. They established a closed shop of labour, in which only union men could be hired, and no one from outside the county. Wages and hours were fixed. The labour exchange kept a roster to make sure each man got his fair share of work, and there was to be a union representative on each farm, to make sure conditions were met. This was only the year before, towards the end of 1920. But somehow it's all coming unravelled again. The tide in this simmering feud, which is generations — centuries — old, has turned again.

It's a strange conflict — one around which everyday life keeps moving like a river around rocks. It has to, because the men must eat, and to eat they must work. So life must go on, even when the rocks in question are things like the massacre at Masseria Girardi Natale, the summer before, when workers armed with only their tools and their anger were shot down by the proprietor and his mounted guards. Now the contracts all the proprietors signed are being ignored, and men who protest aren't hired. There are rumours of a new type of brute squad: teams of thugs led by veteran officers — captains and lieutenants tainted by the madness of the trenches, who remember the peasants' reluctance to fight, and despise them for it. The peasants are used to hired gangs — *mazzieri*, named after the *mazza*, the cudgels they carry — but these new ones are something else. They are being armed and abetted by the police, unofficially of course. And they have a new name — they are the *fasci di combattimento*. They are members of the new fascist party. And they have a single-mindedness that's scaring the men.

Some nights Ettore goes to a bar and reads the newspapers out loud to the unlettered. He reads from the *Corriere delle Puglie*, and from *La Conquista*, and from *Avanti!*. He reads of attacks on syndicalist leaders, on chambers of labour, and on socialist town halls in other towns. In Gioia del Colle, the old way of recruiting has slowly crept back into the piazza, and the two sides stare at one another across this bitter divide — workers and employers. Each waiting to see who will blink first. In February there was a general strike in protest at the massing and arming of the new squads, and their brutality, and the breaking of the contracts. The strike held for three days but it was like a finger pressed to a widening crack in a dam; a dam behind which the tide is rising inexorably.

Ettore and Valerio push their way towards the overseer from Masseria Vallarta; a man well into his sixties with drooping white moustaches and

20

an immobile expression, as solid and unreadable as the trunk of a tree. Pino is already there; he catches Ettore's eye and jerks his chin to greet him. Giuseppe Bianco; Giuseppino; Pino for short. Pino and Ettore have lived shoulder to shoulder since they were in the cradle. They are the same age, have seen the same things, suffered the same hopes and hardships; they've had the same patchy, soon-curtailed education, and had wild times at Saint's Day festivals more pagan than holy. They've been to war together. Pino has the face of a classical hero, with enormous soft eyes, warm and brown rather than the usual black. He has curved lips, the upper protruding slightly over the lower; curling hair and an open expression far out of place in the piazza. His heart is open too; he's too good for this life. There's only one thing the two men do not share, and it's driven a wedge between them this year: Pino is married to his sweetheart, but Ettore has lost his. All the girls used to quarrel to catch Pino's eye. They knew a soft touch when they saw one, and fancied waking up next to that face for the rest of their lives. Now that he's wed some of them try just as hard, but Pino is faithful to Luna, his wife. Little Luna, with her buoyant breasts and her hair hanging right down to the broad spread of her buttocks. Pino is the only man Ettore knows who can find a real smile before dawn in the piazza.

He smiles now, and thumps Ettore's upper arm companionably.

'What's new?' he says.

'Nothing at all.' Ettore shrugs.

21

'Luna has something for the baby. For Iacopo,' says Pino, and looks proud. 'She's been sewing again — a shirt. She's even stitched his initials into it for him.' Luna works in fits and starts for a seamstress, and carefully collects whatever scraps of thread and fabric she can spirit away. There's never enough to make clothes for adults, but Iacopo now has a vest, a hat and a pair of tiny slippers.

'She should be setting such things by for when you have your own baby,' says Ettore, and Pino grins. He longs for babies — a herd of them, a flock. How or whether they'll all be fed is not something he lets worry him. He seems to think they'll be self-sustaining, like hearth spirits or will-o'-the-wisps, like *putti*.

'Iacopo will have outgrown them by then. I'm sure Paola will lend them back.'

'Don't be so sure.'

'You mean she'll want to keep them, to remember how little he was?' says Pino. Ettore grunts. What he'd meant was that he's not so certain Iacopo will outgrow the little things so soon. His nephew is reedy and too quiet. So many babies die. Ettore frets about him, frowns over him. Whenever Paola sees this she shoves him away, and curses. She thinks his anxiety will coalesce and bring some grim prophecy down on her son.

The man from Masseria Vallarta takes a sheaf of paper from his pocket, unfolds it. The waiting men focus their attention on him, watching with steady expectation. It's a strange ritual — the farm has a harvest to bring in and the men all

22

know it, but even so, they do not trust the man. They do not trust that they will have work until they are standing in the field, working. They do not trust that they will be paid until the bailiff puts the coins into their hands the Saturday after. The overseer catches Ettore's eye and gives him a hard stare. Ettore stares right back at him. He is a union man, and the overseer knows it; knows his name, and his face. Some have led the strikes and the demonstrations while the others followed, and Ettore is one of the first kind. Or he was — in the six months since he lost Livia he's done nothing, said nothing; he's worked with a steady, mindless rhythm, ignoring his hunger and his exhaustion. In all that time, he has spared not a single thought for the revolution, for his brothers, for the starving workers or the ever-present injustices, but the overseers don't seem to have noticed his change of heart. The absence of his heart.

So there's a black mark by his name that nothing will shift, but he also works without pause, and attacks the ground with the heaviest mattock; he presents them with a conundrum: a troublemaker who works like a Trojan. The corporal with the white moustaches hires him with the merest nod of his head, marking down his name. Then he flicks his gnarled finger at the others he's chosen, including Pino, and those men file away to begin the long walk to the farm. Valerio is not chosen. Years of wielding the mattock have shaped his spine, bending him like an overblown tree, and though he's tried not to cough since they got to the piazza, you can see the effort of containing the spasms in the way his body clenches and shakes from time to time. He cut about half as much wheat as some of the other men yesterday, and the immovable overseer has an infallible memory for such things. Ettore grips his father's shoulder in parting.

'Go now to the shepherd, over there. Go now, before others take his lire,' he says. Valerio nods.

'Work hard, boy,' he says, then gives in to his cough. Ettore doesn't bother to reply. There is no other kind of work, after all.

The sun is rising in a gentle riot of colour by the time they reach the farm. Pino turns his face to it for a minute, shuts his eyes and takes a deep breath, as though, like a plant, the sun will give him the energy to work that day. When the sky is alight like this Ettore thinks of Livia, shielding her black eyes with one hand. When it rains, he thinks of Livia squinting up at the clouds, and smiling as the water hits her skin. When it gets dark he thinks of the times they met beneath the arches of Gioia's oldest streets, when they would know each other by touch and smell alone, and she would take his questing hand and kiss his fingertips, and send thumps of desire straight to his groin. He knows that his thoughts of her show on his face, and he can tell from Pino's expression that he sees it — that subtle sinking, a creeping mix of sorrow and frustration; he can see that his oldest friend doesn't know what to say to him, as long as the moment lasts. They are each given a drink of water and a chunk of bread before work starts. The bread is fresh, which it normally isn't, and the men tear into it like dogs. The water has the stone grit taste of the cistern. They start work straight afterwards, wriggling their fingers into the wooden hand-guards that are meant to protect them, but which the farmers really like because they extend a man's grasp, and mean he can gather a bigger sheaf of wheat each time. One man wields the scythe — the taller, stronger ones, with the longest reach — and behind him comes another man, tying the cut stalks into sheaves.

For hours there's nothing but the swing of blades, the crunch of the cut stalks as they fall and are gathered up. High above their heads black kites ride the hot air, circling; curious about the smell and movement of the working men. From a distance it looks as though the harvest will be good: field after field of golden grain, rolling in the scorching *altina* wind from the south. But up close the men see that the stalks are sparser than they should be, shorter, with too few grains on each ear and too much space between them. The yield will be less than hoped for, and their wages to match. At midday the sun is debilitating; it crushes the men, it weighs them down like chains. The corporal's horses wilt, hanging their heads and letting their eyelids droop, too fagged to even shake the flies away. The overseer calls a halt and the men rest and have another drink of water, just enough to wet their parched throats. As soon as their shadows have crept two hand spans to one side the overseer checks his watch, rouses them, and work continues.

Pino and Ettore pass each other, working within earshot for a short while as their lines coincide.

'Luna is trying to buy beans today,' says Pino, conversationally.

'I wish her luck. I hope the grocer doesn't rob her.'

'She's smart, my Luna. I think she will get some, and then we'll have a fine dinner.' Pino does this a lot — talks about food. Fantasises about food. It seems to help him beat his hunger, but it does the opposite to Ettore, whose stomach writhes and mutters at the thought of fava beans boiled with bay leaves, and maybe some garlic and pepper, and mashed up with strong olive oil. He swallows.

'Don't talk about food, Pino,' he pleads.

'Sorry, Ettore. I can't help it. That's all I dream about: food, and Luna.'

'Then dream quietly, for fuck's sake,' says the man working behind Ettore.

'I don't mind if he talks about his wife as long as he doesn't spare us the details.' This is from a lad no more than fourteen, who grins lopsidedly at Pino.

'If I catch you dreaming about my wife, I'll cut your prick off,' Pino tells him, angling his scythe towards the boy, lifting its wicked tip; but he isn't serious, and the boy grins wider, showing them his broken front teeth.

The *altina* picks up, smelling of some distant desert, humming over the grey stone walls of the field and through the leathery leaves of a fig tree in one corner. The ground is dust-dry, the wheat parched, the sky mercilessly clear. The men lick their lips but can't keep them from cracking. Flies buzz brazenly around their heads and necks, biting, knowing that the men won't spare the effort to swat them away. Ettore works and tries not to think. He comes across a patch of wild rocket leaves, bitter and mean. He picks all he can find and eats them when nobody is looking, feeling his throat clog with saliva and the hot taste of them. The guards are extra vigilant at this end of the day — eyes sharp for signs of the men slowing down, of surreptitious rests being taken, of the scythe being leant upon, not swung. The man gathering the wheat Ettore cuts has dropped far behind — he keeps straightening up, pressing his fingers into his spine and wincing. The overseer has a long leather whip, coiled at his hip. His hand strays to it, time and again, as though he'd love to use it. Ettore's stomach clenches even tighter after the snack of rocket leaves; his head starts to feel light, strange, as it often does towards day's end. His body keeps working, regardless; shoulders swinging the weight of the scythe, back muscles tensing to stop its momentum, twisting him from the waist, hands gripped tight. He can feel every tendon as it rubs over bone, but his thoughts drift away from him, away from the heat and the toil and the suffocating wind.

He has heard about a hole in the ground at a town called Castellana, twenty-five kilometres from Gioia, towards the sea. This hole in the ground is wide and nothing that goes into it ever comes out, except bats — streaming millions of bats, like smoke. Sometimes it belches up shreds of a chilly white mist, which are said to be the ghosts of people who have gone too near and fallen in. It is the mouth of hell, the locals say; it plummets right down into the core of the earth, into a blackness so heavy it would crush you. Ettore thinks about this hole as his body keeps going, and his back burns like there's a knife stuck in it, and his guts cramp from the leaves he ate. He thinks about jumping into it and falling through white mist and then cool, clammy darkness; he thinks about curling up in the ancient black depths, in the world's stony heart where no man belongs, and waiting there. Not waiting for anything, just waiting; where it is cold and still and silent.

He's suddenly aware that his name has been spoken. Ettore blinks and sees Pino off to one side, his face wide with concern. He realises that his scythe is still, that he has straightened up and let it come to rest on his boot. He can't seem to make his hands tighten on the shaft. Behind Pino, he sees two guards exchange a word and a nod, sees them kick their sluggish horses to life and set out towards him. He can't seem to make his thoughts come back from that hole in the ground and his sudden yearning for it. With all the will he can find, he grips the scythe and lifts it, turning his body to the right, angling the tip of the blade to catch the right number of wheat stalks. But he is too far from the edge of the crop, and the weight of it throws him off balance. His body uncoils, the way it must. It has moved this way thousands of times, on thousands of

28

days; he can no more stop it than he can stop his heart beating. But he will fall if he doesn't correct his stance, and though falling would be better than the alternative, he has no choice in this either. His body drives itself, is its own master; it keeps its own counsel, as he has trained it to do. Ettore teeters, and lurches forwards. His left leg lands in the path of the scythe as it swings, and he can do nothing to stop what will happen, though he sees it clearly enough. The metal bites easily, cleanly. He feels it hit the bone and lodge there. Pino shouts, and so does the man behind him. A bright spray of blood splatters the wheat stalks, looking too glossy and red to be real, and then Ettore falls.

# Clare

Gioia del Colle is quiet. Low sunlight pools in the street corners, reflecting from smooth stone slabs and streaked walls. Though they pass along avenues of elegant villas, four storeys high, with painted render and symmetrical shuttered windows, the road is crusted with manure — the fresh and fly-struck scattered over the old and dry. There are women out walking with huge urns or baskets on their heads and shoulders, but they do not speak. The only car is the one they're riding in; it creeps along slowly behind a dray cart loaded with barrels. Clare sees almost no men, and when she points this out to Boyd, he shrugs.

'They're all out working on the harvest, darling,' he says.

'So early in the year?' she says, but then remembers all the teams she saw from the train, their scythes moving with the steady rhythm of metronomes. She opens her mouth to say something about the lack of tractors, or harvesting machines, but shuts it again. The south is poor, she has been told. Everywhere is poor after the war, but the south was poor to begin with. They have gone from destitute to something less than that.

In the rear-view mirror she catches the driver's eye, flicking over her as though checking something. She shifts her weight and turns to

30

smile at Pip. The car turns onto Via Garibaldi and drives down between the tall, ornate fronts of the best houses Clare has seen yet. Some might even be described as palaces, she thinks. *Palazzi*. Slowing, the driver sounds the horn, and a set of carriage doors in the wall of one building swing open for them to drive through. They pass beneath a wide, dark archway and into an open courtyard. 'Oh, look!' says Clare, surprised. Boyd seems pleased by her reaction.

'A lot of the grander houses are designed like this — a quadrangle around an inner courtyard. But from the outside you wouldn't expect it, would you?' he says. The sky is a perfect bright square above them.

'I had no idea that there would be places like this here. I mean . . . ' Clare pauses uncomfortably. 'It's obviously a very poor region.' In the mirror, the driver stares at her.

'The peasants are poor, the gentry are rich, same as anywhere,' says Boyd. He gives her hand a squeeze. 'Don't worry, darling. I wouldn't bring you to darkest Africa.'

A few watchful staff appear around the cloistered edges of the courtyard, ready to take the luggage, and as the three of them exit the car Clare feels her heart bumping with nerves. Their hosts appear through double doors in the far side of the building — a couple, the man holding his arms out wide, as though to greet old friends; the woman with a smile to rival the sun.

'Mrs Kingsley! We are so delighted to finally have you here!' says the man. His hands come to rest on her shoulders, heavy and warm, and he

31

kisses her on both cheeks.

'You must be Signor Cardetta. How do you do? *Piacere*,' says Clare, using the Italian word self-consciously, uncertain of her accent.

'Leandro Cardetta, at your service. But — you speak Italian, Mrs Kingsley? This is wonderful!'

'Oh, hardly at all!'

'Nonsense — she's being modest, Cardetta. She speaks it very well,' says Boyd.

'Well, I hardly understood a word the driver said to the porter at the station. It was very disheartening.'

'Ah, but they probably spoke in the local dialect, my dear Mrs Kingsley. Quite a different thing. To the peasants down here, Italian is as foreign a language as it is to you.' Cardetta turns her gently towards the radiant woman. 'May I present my wife, Marcie?'

'How do you do, Mrs Cardetta?'

'Oh, I'm Marcie — only ever Marcie! When people go around calling me Mrs Cardetta I don't even know myself,' she says. Marcie is striking, elegant, with the narrow hips and shoulders of a boy, and disproportionately full breasts sitting high on her chest. Her eyes are blue and her hair the colour of ripe barley, set in a wave that grazes her jawline. Her American accent is unmistakable and Clare tries not to show her surprise. 'What — neither one of these fellas warned you I was a Yankee?' says Marcie, but she doesn't seem displeased.

'Warned isn't the word, but no — I had assumed you were Italian, Mrs Cardetta — Marcie. Do forgive me.'

32

'What's to forgive? And who is this highly distinguished young man?' She holds out her hand and Pip shakes it, and though he is polite and confident as he does it, a touch of colour brushes over his cheeks. Clare thinks of the way she herself used to blush when shown the least attention by a man — or any new person — and feels a rush of tenderness towards him. He waits, as he should, for Signor Cardetta to proffer his hand and his name, then he does the same — deferentially, but not too much so. She's proud of him, and glances at Boyd, hoping that he will have noticed. But Boyd is watching Leandro Cardetta, the way a person might watch an animal suspected of only feigning sleep.

'Thank you for sending your wonderful car for us, Mr Cardetta — it's an Alfa Romeo, isn't it? It's beautiful, but I don't recognise the model,' says Pip enthusiastically. Leandro grins wolfishly at him.

'*Bene, bene.* You're a young man of excellent taste, I see,' he says. 'But you wouldn't recognise it — it's brand new, and only a few have been made. Rarity, you see — that is the key to true value.' The pair of them saunter over to the crimson car, to peer at it from all angles. Marcie Cardetta smiles and takes Clare's arm; she is all ease and familiarity, and Clare can't imagine how that must feel. Marcie is dressed in white, like a bride: a long skirt and tunic in some fluid fabric that ripples and follows her every move, belted low around her hips. As they walk into the house Clare catches the scent of her — musk and lilacs, and somehow the suggestion of

33

moisture. It's an oddly intimate aroma, at once compelling and intrusive. There's scarlet lipstick on her mouth, and powder on her cheeks; up close Clare can see the fine lines at the corners of her eyes. She is maybe forty, or a little older, but has such glamour that she seems far younger — younger than Clare, even, who suddenly feels just how very thirsty and unwashed and tired she is. Only as they step into the shadows inside does Clare realise that Boyd has been left alone, hesitating, in the centre of the courtyard. She looks back at him to smile but he has his hands in his pockets and is staring down at his feet, frowning, as if displeased by the dust on his shoes.

Marcie walks her onwards, and talks.

'My dear Clare, I cannot tell you how *thrilled* I am to have you here — you and Philip, of course, but mainly you — poor Philip! No, it's all right, he didn't hear me. Just to have somebody to talk to, you understand — other than a man, and what woman can really talk to a man? I mean with *words*, you understand, not that other language we all speak.' She dips her head towards Clare, gives her a conspiratorial little nudge with her shoulder. 'I mean just to talk about *everything*. The Italian women — well, I should say the Puglian women, because you could hardly compare the specimens down here to those in Milan or Rome — well, they look at me like I fell from outer space! Not a word of English, any one of them. And I've *tried* to learn Italian — believe me I've tried, and I've managed it a bit, but when they don't want to understand you, by golly, they'll make sure they don't. Staring at you with those black eyes of theirs — have you seen their eyes? Did you notice their eyes? Like jet buttons on a sackcloth waistcoat, with their faces all so brown. We must make sure you don't get too much sun, dear — your skin is just delightful . . . And how funny is it that you can go six months without seeing a blonde down here, and now we have two under one roof!'

On and on Marcie talks, as she leads Clare up to the room she'll be sharing with Boyd. The house is warm and shadowy, and full of echoes. The light is barricaded out — on the sunny west side of the quad the shutters are all closed, so that only thin, bright shafts get through here and there. Clare's smile begins to ache in her cheeks but she feels some of the tension that has clenched her guts since the train left Bari begin to dissipate. Inwardly, she's still as uncomfortable in new company as she has ever been, and she'd been dreading the conversation drying up, dwindling into silence while she floundered for a way to replenish it. At least it seems that there will be few such awkward silences to contend with. Few silences at all.

Once they reach the room Marcie clasps Clare's hands for a moment, gives a happy little shrug and leaves her to change. A steady quiet settles in her wake. Clare turns around, sees the book Boyd is reading and his glasses, placed neatly by the bed. The room is large and square, and faces south, and Clare opens the shutters to a rush of hot air and the slanting yellow light of evening. The walls are a rich ochre colour, the ceiling a high spread of dark wooden beams, the floor terracotta. There's a painting of the Madonna above the fireplace, and one of Paris above the bed, which has an ornate brass bedstead and a mattress sagging visibly in the middle. When a servant brings in the luggage, the door howls in protest. It's made of the same aged wood as the ceiling, and has massive hinges to cope with its own weight. Like a door in a castle, Clare thinks. Or a jail. She leans over the window sill and looks out at the clustered red rooftops and the narrow streets. Immediately behind the Cardettas' house is a small, neat garden with more paved walkways than flower beds. There are fig and olive trees for shade, and a vine-covered veranda where a long table waits, covered with a linen cloth. There are herbs but few flowers, and no grass. One of the fig trees is alive with small birds — Clare can see them all, rattling the leaves, hopping about like fleas. They chatter rather than sing, but it's still a nice sound.

The door moans again as Boyd comes in. He has a way of moving, a way of standing slightly curled in on himself, that looks faintly apologetic. Clare smiles and crosses to him, to be folded into him, against the smooth fabric of his shirt and the slight give of flesh underneath. He is that much taller than her that her hair gets caught up with the sharp points and buttons of his collar. He has a faintly sour scent about him that she doesn't remember smelling before. Or perhaps once before. It makes her uneasy.

'I'm so happy to see you,' he murmurs into the top of her head. Then he holds her out at arm's length, studies her intently. 'You didn't mind coming?' Clare shrugs. She can't quite bring herself to deny it, not completely, because she did mind. She likes the unhurried habit of their home life in Hampstead, and taking Pip to their favourite places in London during the holidays. She doesn't like to admit to herself that she'd been glad when Boyd announced he would be going to Italy, but it's true nevertheless. It was better for him to be working, to be occupied; it was better for her and Pip that they had the house to themselves, and could keep their own hours and counsel. That they could make as much noise, and be as silly as they wanted. Say what they wanted. For a brief while the summer had stretched out ahead of her, wonderfully long and serene, until his phone call from Italy curtailed it.

'I was surprised. You wouldn't normally ask me to travel — not all this way. But I had Pip with me for the journey, so of course it was fine.' This much is true, at least.

'I know it might seem a bit peculiar. But Cardetta wants me to stay for as long as it takes to finish the designs, and I can't . . . it's too good a commission to turn it down. I mean — I'm happy to work on it. It's an interesting project.' He kisses her forehead, one hand on her cheek. 'And I couldn't bear the thought of so many weeks without you,' he says. Clare frowns.

'But when you first telephoned you said that it was Cardetta who wanted us to come out — Pip

37

and me? Why would he? To keep Marcie company?'

'Yes. Probably. Anyway, he only suggested it, and it gave me the idea. He had to offer the invitation first, of course. I couldn't just ask and oblige him to accept.'

'I see.'

Clare disengages herself from his arms and goes over to open her bags. It hadn't seemed like that when they first spoke about it, soon after Boyd's arrival in Italy. Even thin and buzzing along the telephone wire his voice had sounded tense and beleaguered, and almost fearful. She'd heard it in the clipped way he spoke, and straight away she'd felt the familiar dread sinking into the pit of her stomach, solid as wet sand. They've been married for ten years, and she is minutely attuned to the least sign of distress in him. She knows well enough what can come of it. It's there now, of course — she saw it the first moment she set eyes on him, as he waved from the car. But sometimes it comes to nothing. She doesn't want to acknowledge it too soon and risk it coalescing when it might not necessarily.

Born shy, the only child of parents who never raised their voices, never argued or ever spoke of their feelings, Clare longs for peaceful accord more than anything else; nothing jarring or unexpected, no awkwardness. Over the years, Boyd's episodes have honed her fear of confrontation to a point of excruciating finesse. For days, weeks, sometimes even months, he is transformed; silent and precarious, unreadable. He drinks brandy at any hour, he doesn't work, he doesn't go out, he barely eats. His silence thickens like a black cloud around him, which Clare is too scared to penetrate. She walks on eggshells around him, dogged by her own inadequacy, her inability to bring him out of it. Sometimes, during such spells, the sight of her makes him collapse into violent sobbing. Sometimes days pass and he doesn't seem to see her at all, and she remembers what happened when she persuaded him to go to New York, years before, and what *might* have happened, had she not prevented it. Then she can't sleep or eat herself. She's a prisoner to his mood, too frightened to make a sound. The relief when it's over, when Boyd finally rises from his chair and sinks himself into a hot bath, and asks for a cup of tea, is so immense she has to sit until her breathing slows.

Boyd watches her as she hangs her skirts and dresses in the giant wardrobe that looms along the far wall of the room. He sits on the edge of the bed with one long leg crossed over the other, his hands laced over the uppermost knee.

'I'm sure we could find a servant to do that for you — Cardetta seems to have hundreds of them,' he says. Clare smiles over her shoulder at him.

'I can manage well enough without a ladies' maid,' she says. 'He must be very rich, then?'

'I should say so. This is one of the oldest and biggest houses in Gioia — well, of those that he could get his hands on, anyway.'

'Oh?'

'Cardetta wasn't always rich — and he was

away in America for twenty years. I get the impression that the *signori* here — the upper crust — treat him as a bit of a Johnny-come-lately.'

'Well, I suppose that's understandable,' she says. 'Especially if he was away for so long. How did he make his money?'

'In New York.'

'Yes, but — '

'Do stop that and come here,' he says, with mock severity. Clare looks at the crumpled silk shirt in her hands, and the way the pale yellow of it perfectly mirrors the light-filled sky outside. She wishes she wouldn't hesitate but she can't seem to help it. But then she smiles and does as he says, sitting gingerly in his lap. He wraps his arms around her waist and buries his face in her chest, and somehow it's not sexual, but as though he wants to hide. 'Clare,' he breathes out her name, and she feels the heat of his breath on her skin.

'Is everything all right, darling?' she says, trying to sound bright, trying for offhand.

'It is now that you're here.' He tightens his grip until Clare can feel his watch digging into her ribs. 'I love you so much, my dearest Clare.'

'And I love you,' she says, and just then notices how very dry her lips feel. Dry and miserly. She shuts her eyes for a moment and wishes that he would stop there, say nothing more. She wishes that his grip would loosen. But he doesn't stop there, and he doesn't loosen his grip.

'I would die without you, you know. I swear it.'

40

Clare wants to deny it — she has tried to before. She has tried, in the hope that he will realise how onerous his words are. 'My angel,' he whispers. She can feel his arms shake from the strain of keeping hold. Or perhaps it's she that shakes. 'My angel. I would die without you.' She wants to say, *no, you would not*, but when he says such things something gets hold of her throat and squeezes it, and no words will come out. She can't tell if it's guilt, or fear, or anger. She reminds herself that most women would be grateful for such devotion in a husband; she reminds herself to be grateful.

'I should go and check on Pip,' she manages to say, sometime later.

★   ★   ★

When the sun has set they join their hosts for a drink in the garden, at the long table beneath the vine-covered veranda. A silent girl with her black hair parted in the middle, wearing an old-fashioned, high-necked blouse with a frill, brings a tray of glasses and a jug of some dark drink, and begins to pour. Small round fruit plop out into the glasses with the liquid, like soft pebbles.

'Oh, good — *amarena*,' says Marcie, clapping her hands. 'This is just the thing you folk need after your long trip. Wild cherry juice — we can't always get them, but when we do, one of the kitchen girls mixes up a batch of this stuff. She keeps the recipe all to herself, mind you — she absolutely refuses to show me! There's some herb she adds that I just can't put my finger on.

She says it was her grandmother's secret. Isn't that just hilarious? To guard something as silly as a recipe?'

'It's not silly at all,' Leandro tells his wife serenely. 'She has precious little to call her own.'

'Well, fine then.' Marcie doesn't miss a beat. 'Try it — go on. There's sugar there if you want it, but I think it's delicious as it is.' She beams at Pip, and he does as he's told. He's changed into a clean shirt and tie and his stone-coloured linen blazer with its matching waistcoat, but somehow his clothes still look wrong in their surroundings. He looks like a hastily spruced schoolboy, when at home he'd worn the new outfit into town with the hint of a proud swagger in his step. As if he realises, Pip stays at the edge of his chair and looks embarrassed. Clare sips her drink.

'It is delicious,' she says automatically, and then realises that it's true. She steals a long glance at Leandro Cardetta.

He looks to be approaching fifty; he has copious iron-grey hair, swept back from his temples and from a high forehead, deeply lined. He is certainly not beautiful, but perhaps he's almost handsome; his face has a certain gravitas, a kind of heft to the sculptural features — jaw and nose and brows. His skin is bronze and has the thick, smooth look of good leather. There are deep creases at either side of his mouth, and pouches under his eyes, and those eyes are so dark it's hard to see the pupil against the iris — it looks instead as though his pupils are enormous, dilated far beyond the norm. Perhaps it's this that makes his resting expression one of

42

warmth and approachability. He is not overly tall, not nearly as tall as Boyd; his shoulders are strong and square, ribs like a barrel; a slight paunch, a mark of good living, fills out the space behind his shirt. He leans back in his chair, the small glass of *amarena* held in the fingers of his left hand with surprising delicacy. He is watchful without being disconcerting; elegant not but effeminate.

Catching Clare's surreptitious gaze, he smiles. 'Whatever will make your stay with us more comfortable, you must only ask, Mrs Kingsley,' he says smoothly.

'Unless it's music or shopping or cinema, or a blaze through a casino — in which case you're bang out of luck!' Marcie declares.

'Marcie, *cara*, you must not make it sound as though Gioia is completely devoid of fun. We have a very fine theatre — do you care for the theatre, Mrs Kingsley?'

'Oh, very much so. And Pip too — he is proving to be a fine actor, in fact,' says Clare.

'Philip — is it true?' Marcie leans across and grasps his forearm, staring avidly.

'Well, I . . . ' Pip's voice breaks and he clears his throat, flushing. 'I was in a play last term, and people said I did well. I was Ariel in *The Tempest*.'

'And you were quite brilliant, actually,' says Clare.

'But — *I'm* an actress, didn't you know? Well, I was, back in New York. Not much call for it here. But, oh, I *love* the theatre! I love acting . . . It's something in the blood, don't you think

43

— it's a calling you can't ignore. Do you feel that, Pip? Does acting make your heart soar?'

'Well, I . . . I do think I should like to be in another play, certainly,' he says. 'But it's not something one can really make a career out of, is it?' These are Boyd's words, coming out of his mouth, and they give Clare a sinking feeling. Pip's heart did soar during that play. She saw it happen.

'Well, why ever not? *I* did.'

'Pip's a good scholar. He'll go up to Oxford, and then to chambers,' says Boyd. He sips the crimson drink then rolls his lips back slightly.

'Add some sugar, if it's too sour,' says Leandro, passing him the sugar bowl. Boyd smiles thinly without looking at him, and spoons some into his glass.

'Chambers? You mean law? Ugh, why not say mausoleum? Poor boy!'

'Not at all. My father always intended me for the law, but I hadn't the mind for it. Pip has. It would be outrageous to waste such natural good fortune.'

'And what about what Pip wants?' Marcie asks this lightly but Clare can see Boyd taken aback to be challenged; she wishes Marcie would drop it.

'He's only a boy. He can't be expected to know what he wants,' he says. Marcie pats Pip's arm, then gives him a jaunty wink.

'I'll work on them, don't you fret. What's the law compared to applause?' she says. Clare is relieved when Boyd chooses not to reply to this question.

44

Dinner is an array of dishes, some of which arrive together, some on their own after a suitable pause. Fresh white cheeses, breads, vegetables dressed in lemon and oil; pasta with broccoli; rolled strips of veal; soft focaccia bread oozing olive oil and the smell of rosemary. Pip eats as though he hasn't for days, but even he is defeated in the end. He shifts uncomfortably in his chair and Leandro laughs — a deep, sudden bark.

'Philip — I should have warned you. Forgive me. In this house they will keep bringing food as long as you keep clearing your plate.' Pip has had a glass of wine, and looks far more relaxed.

'I think I shall be very happy here,' he says, and Leandro laughs again.

'Perhaps a short walk, to look at the town and to let the meal settle before bed?' says Clare. She too has overeaten; the smell of the fresh food woke a hunger gone dormant from being so long ignored. Marcie and Leandro share a quick glance between themselves. 'Isn't that the thing to do, here in Italy? *La passeggiata?*' says Clare.

'Yes, Mrs Kingsley, that's so. However, here in the south we take our *passeggiata* earlier in the evening — around six, as the sun is setting. The gentlefolk, I mean. Now, this late, the streets are . . . more for the working men, lately back from the fields. There's no law, of course, but perhaps tomorrow, at an earlier hour, might be better for you to walk,' says Leandro.

'Oh. I see,' says Clare. Leandro inclines his head smoothly at her acceptance, and she wonders about the black-and-whiteness of this, the idea that people are either peasants or gentry, with none of the middle strata to which Clare and Boyd belong at home.

Marcie suggests a tour of the house to Clare instead, when the food is cleared away. Boyd and Leandro stay at the table, drinking a bitter fennel liqueur that Clare can't stomach, and that makes Pip grimace. Leandro fills and lights a long pipe, made of some pale wood and banded with ivory. Its blue smoke hovers in the air like a phantasm. Pip dithers for a moment, half out of his chair. He's not child enough to follow the women, not man enough to want to stay with the men. His eyes are pink and sunken with fatigue.

'You look done in, Pip,' says Clare. 'Why not turn in? I shan't be far behind you.' She guesses he will like the time alone, to read and explore his room, and she sees she's right in his relieved expression.

'Perhaps you're right, Clare,' he says. 'If you'll excuse me, Mr Cardetta? Father?'

'By all means, Philip.' Leandro nods, gives a benevolent smile. 'Rest well. Tomorrow, we will talk motor cars, you and I — I have something to show you that I think you'll like.'

Marcie leads Clare away, passing from room to room, flicking the light switches on as she goes, leaving them for the servants to switch off behind them. The leather soles of her sandals make almost no sound as she walks; her narrow figure is sinuous beneath her clothes. They pass through a library and some stern, masculine rooms that have huge desks and severe-looking chairs, through a cavernous sitting room more

46

lavishly done, and then another, and then a dining room with a table in the middle that could comfortably seat twenty-four diners, and a ceiling festooned with painted plasterwork. The floors are of polished stone or colourful, intricate tiles; the windows all have heavy shutters, and their voluminous curtains are held back by twisted silk ropes. It is all grand, with a kind of solid splendour, but Clare finds it oppressive, stagnant, as though it froze in time fifty years earlier. She begins to imagine the air creaking as they push through it. The place smells of stone and parched wood, and the prickle of dusty damasks.

Marcie turns to face Clare as they reach the foot of a marble stair.

'Well, what do you think?' she says. Her accent runs the words together: *whaddyathink?*

'I think it's very lovely,' says Clare, after a fractional pause. Marcie smiles delightedly.

'Oh, you Brits are always so damned *polite*! How could anyone not love you? It's a *museum*, I know it is; a gentleman's club from eighty years ago. Deny it — I dare you!'

'Well . . . some of the decorations are perhaps a little dated.'

'Ain't that the truth. I'm working on him, honey, I'm working on him. My Leandro isn't all the way used to the idea of a woman's touch yet, but I'll get him there, you'll see.'

'Now is the perfect time, surely? If Boyd's here to redesign the façade, why not update the interior at the same time?'

'That's my *exact* argument, Clare. My exact

argument. Can I say something rather personal?'
The question comes so suddenly that Clare
blinks. In the half shadow of the staircase it's
hard to read Marcie's expression. She's smiling,
but then, she's always smiling.

'Of course,' says Clare. She hopes the question
is not about Boyd. *What has he said?*

'Well, it just seems to me that you can't even
be *thirty* yet. I can't figure that you're that
charming boy's real mother?' Clare's heart thuds
in relief. She exhales slowly.

'I'll be thirty at my next birthday, and you're
right. Pip's mother was Boyd's first wife, Emma.
She was an American — a New Yorker, like you.
She died when he was four years old.'

'Oh that poor child. And poor Emma,
knowing she had to leave her tiny boy behind!
But lucky him to have such a thoroughly lovely
and *un*wicked stepmother.'

'We're very close. I was only nineteen when I
married Boyd . . . ' Clare trails off, unsure what
she intended to say. Marcie's eyes are alight, her
curiosity plain, and Clare wonders how long she
has been alone in this house, and how lonely
she has been. 'Well. I suppose I've been more
like a big sister to him than a mother. He
remembers Emma, of course.'

'How did she die?'

Clare hesitates before answering. Soon after
she met Boyd she asked her parents the same
question, since they had mutual friends and a
closer acquaintance with him then. She was told
Emma had died in childbirth, while they were
living in New York; that Boyd's grief had been

all-consuming, and she should avoid all mention of it. She'd accepted this unquestioningly, until a few months after her wedding when she'd come to know Pip a little better, and discovered that he had memories of his mother. Then her curiosity had been uncontrollable. It would have been too cruel to ask Pip, still a small boy, the true cause of her death so in the end, on an evening when Boyd was calm and happy, Clare gathered her courage and asked him. And he'd looked at her with such profound shock it was as though she hadn't even been supposed to know Emma's name, or that she had existed, let alone shown any interest in her. His pained expression had chilled her; it made her regret her words at once. She tried to take his hands and apologise but he disengaged her, stood and went to the door as if he would leave without answering. But then he paused, not looking at her.

'It was a . . . a sudden fever. An infection. Sudden and catastrophic.' He swallowed; his cheeks were pale and drawn. 'I do not wish to speak of it. Please don't mention it again.' And that night in bed he hadn't touched her, not even with the sleeping length of his limbs, and Clare had cursed her own insensitivity, and vowed to do as he bid.

Shaking off the memory of that night of lonely self-recrimination, Clare uses Boyd's exact words to answer Marcie.

'It . . . was a sudden fever. Boyd has never been able to talk about it to me; not properly. It's too painful for him.'

'Poor man, I'll bet it is. Men are so less well

equipped to deal with things like that, don't you think? They have to be strong, and they're not allowed to cry, or seek comfort in friends, so they just bottle it all up and let it fester. My Leandro has things he won't talk about — scars he won't show me. I don't know, maybe it's because I'm an actress, but I just think let it *out*, you know? Let it out. Look at it in the light of day, and maybe it won't seem so bad. But he won't, of course. That man is a damned fortress when he wants to be.' She runs out of breath, takes a gasp as if to go on, but doesn't. She smiles instead. 'Well, I suppose it's up to us to just be there if they ever do want to talk about it.'

'Yes. But I don't think Boyd ever will. Not about Emma. He . . . he loved her very, very much, I think. Sometimes I think he's afraid to tell me about her, because he doesn't want me to be jealous.'

'And are you? I would be — I am most *definitely* the jealous type. I had it easy, since Leandro's first and second wives created such a stink when he divorced them that he can't stand either one of them now. They both hate me, of course; and they have three sons between them who are none too keen either. Nothing much I can do about that. But the ghost of a beloved first wife — ugh! Who could compete?'

They turn and start up the stairs together, shoulder to shoulder, one slow step at a time, and Clare doesn't answer straight away. She thinks of the time she found Boyd in his dressing room, holding a pair of ladies' silk gloves that were not hers and running his thumbs over the fabric with a slow, hard intensity. He didn't notice her standing there, and in that moment Clare saw an expression of such acute anguish on his face that she hardly recognised him. The gloves trembled in his hands, and when he spotted her he dropped them as if they'd burnt him and his face filled up with blood in such a rush that a vein bulged out at each temple. As if she'd caught him in bed with another woman; but in fact that came later. She said *It's all right*; but he didn't manage to reply.

'I've made a point of never to try to compete. Love isn't a finite resource, after all. He can love me as well as still loving her,' she says now, in a low voice.

'What a wise and wonderful thing to say! You're far more of a grown-up than I am, Clare,' says Marcie. Clare says nothing, not sure that Marcie means this as a compliment. 'And you married him at nineteen? Goodness, you were just a girl!'

'Yes, I suppose I was.'

'Me, I wanted to live a little before I settled down. I wanted to, you know, try a few of them on for size before I chose. But perhaps I was a little wild back then.'

'I grew up in quite a rural part of England, so there really weren't that many eligible men to choose from. My parents actually met Boyd first, through some friends of theirs, and thought he'd be a good match for me.' At this Marcie's eyes go wide.

'You let your *parents* choose your husband for you?'

'Well, no, it wasn't quite like that — '

'No, sure, sorry — I didn't mean to pounce. I left home at thirteen, that's the thing. I can't imagine what having that kind of guidance was like.'

'It was very . . . ' For a moment, Clare can't think of a word. She was a child, and then she married Boyd and became a wife; these are the only two incarnations of herself she has ever known, and at the moment of transformation she'd been happy — relieved that things were settled and certain.

She was the only child of parents who'd almost given up hope; her mother had been forty when she was born, her father well past fifty. By the time Clare was eighteen her mother was frail beyond her years, worn thin and increasingly vague, and her father had pains in his chest for which he took tablets — five or six a day, ground vigorously between his molars at regular intervals — though they did little to alleviate his symptoms. In much the same way as she can now see Pip growing, her terms away at school allowed her to see, clearly, how age and infirmity were stealing a march on her only family. More than any of her classmates, she was faced with the thought of not having them any more, of being alone in the world, and the empty spread of an unknown future frightened her. But that makes her settling on Boyd sound like an act of dry calculation, or of knee-jerk desperation, which it hadn't been. 'I was glad that they approved of him. And they were glad that I did, too, of course.' Marcie says nothing for a while, and Clare realises how bloodless this sounds. 'And I loved him, of course. I grew to love him.'

'Well, of course you did. He's a sweetie. So gentle! I can't even imagine him having a temper, and he obviously adores you. You must get away with murder. Me, I have to be careful. When Leandro goes off it's like a volcano!'

'No, well . . . I've never seen Boyd go off, I don't think,' says Clare. Instead he implodes, into a distant, silent place where she can't reach him, and then the world seems flimsy and unsafe, and she and Pip cling to each other, cast adrift, waiting to see how and when and if he will come out of it again. It's been five months since the last time it happened, and now she's sure she can sense the gathering pressure of the next time. She hopes she's wrong. 'How did you meet Leandro?' she says, changing the subject because Marcie's expression is quizzical and almost pitying.

'Oh, he saw me on stage one night. He says he fell in love with me before I'd even sung a note.' Marcie smiles again and loops her arm through Clare's as they climb.

★ ★ ★

Alone, Clare knocks softly on Pip's door and opens it. The door has the same sepulchral groan as the one to her room. Pip is sitting on the wide window ledge, looking out at the night. The sky is a deep indigo, freckled with stars.

'All right there, Pip?'

'All right, Clare. I was trying to work out

53

which different constellations you can see this far south, but I didn't bring a chart and I'm completely lost.' He turns to face her. He's in his pyjamas with a green tartan dressing gown tied tight around his middle. Both pyjamas and gown are too short for him already, and Clare smiles. She goes to stand beside him and looks out. He smells of toothpaste and the lavender sachets she packed in with their clothes.

'I'm afraid I can't help you there, Pip. You know I'm a complete dunce with astrology.'

'Astronomy. Astrology is horoscopes and things.'

'Well, that rather proves my point, doesn't it?' she says, and Pip grins.

'And you're not a complete dunce at anything. You just pretend to be to make me feel better,' he adds perspicaciously.

'Oh, I don't know. A star's a star as far as I'm concerned, as long as they sparkle and look pretty. What else ought I to know, then?' Pip begins to tell her about how long the light has taken to reach their eyes, and how many different types of stars there are, and how some of them are planets, and how there might be people on them, looking at the pinprick glimmer of Earth from light years away. He rambles on for a while, as he does when he's exhausted. Outside there are few lamps lit in the streets, or behind the closed shutters of other houses. There's no more noise of people, or *passeggiata*. Gioia dell Colle is early to bed.

Pip's room is much the same as Clare's, but smaller, and facing west. She looks to see if he's

54

unpacked, and finds his trunk more or less intact, hidden away in the wardrobe, which is all she's come to expect, really. She glances at the bedside table, already knowing what she'll see there — the one thing he always unpacks, no matter where they go: a photograph of his mother in a silver frame. The picture is a studio shot; Emma is standing alone next to a tall jardinière full of some extravagantly trailing plant, with her thin, pale hands clasped in front of her. The picture was taken in 1905, the year before Pip was born, and she's wearing the fashionable high-necked dress of the time; Pip claims to remember the very one, and says it was a gorgeous colour, the crimson of a Virginia creeper in autumn, but in the picture it merely looks dark and severe. Her face is serious but not sombre, a thin oval with light eyes and a mass of curly hair, piled high and spilling down over her right shoulder. Though her expression is fixed for the photographer, Clare has always fancied that she can see a trace of mirth in her lips and the arch of her brows. She picks up the photo and studies it, made curious anew by Marcie's questions. This is the only picture of Emma she has ever seen. It might be the only one that exists. Emma is every bit as frozen in time as the house in which they're staying. She can clearly see the ways in which Pip has taken after her, and it's only this that makes her seem like a real person to Clare: a woman who laughed and sneezed and got angry and made love; not just a face in a photograph, a ghost who haunts her husband.

Pip looks around at her, and sees what she's doing. He's never acknowledged any awkwardness between Clare and the memory of his mother, and Clare is grateful for it. He has never compared her to Emma; he has never said, in anger: *You're not my real mother.* Some things don't need saying. He has never blamed her for his mother being dead, as other children in their grief and confusion might have done.

'I think she would have liked the dinner, don't you?' he says.

'Oh, absolutely. Particularly the fried zucchini flowers — I remember you telling me how she liked to try new things. They were so light. Delicious. Would she have liked Mr and Mrs Cardetta, do you think?'

'Yes, I think so.' Pip thinks for a moment. 'I think she was inclined to like most people. And they're very welcoming, aren't they?'

'Very.' They do this sometimes, particularly in times of stress — guess at Emma's opinion of things; her likes and dislikes, how she might have behaved in a particular situation. It's a way to keep her alive, a way for Pip to feel that he knows her, when in fact his memories are the fleeting sensory impressions of early childhood: the colour of her dress; the length of her hair; her voice and the warmth of her hands; that she loved oranges and her fingers often smelled of the peel. Sometimes this is also how Pip lets Clare know his own opinion of things — difficult things that he would stumble to speak openly about. Sometimes he declares that Clare and Emma would have got on, and been good friends, and this is another generous fiction — that the two women could ever have been in his life at the same time.

There's a measured pause as they both look at the picture, then Clare puts it back in its place. She is always careful never to leave her fingerprints on the glass.

'Is . . . is Father all right?' Pip asks, with painful nonchalance. 'Yes. I think so, yes,' says Clare, with equal bluff. Pip nods, and won't quite meet her eye. 'He'll be better now we're here, anyway. Don't you think?'

'I suppose so.' Pip keeps his eyes on the picture of Emma. He suddenly looks defeated; unhappy, and far from home. Clare searches for the right thing to say.

'I know this is a bit strange, our coming out here like this. And I know it . . . it could be a bit of a lonely summer for you, not seeing any of your friends,' she says. Pip shrugs again. 'But we'll have fun, I promise. And I bet you'll make some new friends, too . . . Have a good sleep, and tomorrow we can go exploring. And Mr Cardetta might take you out again in that car you liked so much — the Alfred Romeo.'

'It's Alfa Romeo, Clare,' says Pip, with a smile.

'See. I told you I was a dunce.' She hugs him for a moment, quickly kisses his temple. 'Sleep. I'm about to.'

Boyd is still outside with Leandro. From the bedroom window, two storeys up, Clare can see pipe smoke rising in the light of the oil lamps on the table; she can hear the soft roll of their voices, but not their words. She listens for a while all the same, then closes the shutters as noiselessly as she can, not sure why she feels she must be quiet. The bed sinks as she climbs into it; the sheets smell a long time unused — clean, but stale. The room is warm and still, and as soon as she shuts her eyes she hears the whine of a mosquito near her ear. Then she hears two more. She hasn't been entirely honest with Marcie, because there is one way in which she is jealous of Emma: Pip. Not because she wants to be his mother — he wouldn't be who he is without Emma — but because she wants a child of her own; she wants to carry it and know the strangeness of a separate life inside her; she wants the shock of labour, and the perfect satisfaction of nursing. She wants to be a mother, as well as a stepmother and surrogate older sister. Love is not a finite resource — she could love her own child and love Pip just as much. And then, of course, there's the fact that Pip is nearly grown, and will soon leave her by herself.

But Boyd doesn't want another child. Boyd is afraid to have another child. Boyd can't quite put his fear into words but it exists, and it's bone deep. Whenever she and Boyd have made love it has been with the rubber sheath between them, and the lights out. Sometimes, Clare feels that they have never actually made love at all, since they could not see each other, and did not touch. She'd wanted to talk again about a baby during this trip, but Boyd is already tense so now she's not sure. There's already that undercurrent that she dreads to see in him, and she knows it has something to do with Cardetta, so she guesses that it's also to do with New York. The mosquitoes whine in Clare's ears, and beneath the sheets she starts to overheat. Her skin prickles. The first and only time she and Boyd were in New York together was one of the worst times of her life; her memories of it are like a strange and sickening dream. She's wide awake even though she's exhausted, and she knows it's because she's waiting. She's waiting to find out what it means, and what will come of it.

# Ettore

Ettore is eleven years old. It's March and the sky is flat grey, an unbroken swathe of cloud which makes it look as though rain will fall, but it won't — the sky has hovered like this for days, and come to nothing. The work gang is weeding, pulling up any wild plant amidst the young shoots of wheat now sprouting from the grain sown last October. Right now, the fields around Gioia are more mutedly, softly green than they will be for the rest of the year. Since this is one job that doesn't require great strength, boys as well as men are employed. In years when there are more weeds — after a damp spring, for example — boys as young as eight and nine will be out in the fields, paid so little money it barely warrants the term wages. But little is not nothing — only those men who have built up such debts that they must work for free to recoup the losses get less. It is dull work, endlessly repetitive. When Ettore's back gets tired from bending over, he bends his knees instead, as his father has taught him. To give the one set of muscles a break. After a while, he switches back again. His hands are stained and the skin is stinging and split from pulling at the tough stems, pitting his weight against deep roots knotted in the stony soil. Each boy has a canvas sling around his shoulders, and the number of times it's been filled and emptied will dictate what he is paid come Saturday.

Along the edge of the field his father Valerio and some other men are breaking rocks. The smack of their picks, arrhythmic, echoing like gunshot, is all anyone has heard all day. They will all hear it in their sleep that night. Ettore gravitates towards the men, hovers as near as he dares. It's *tufo* stone they're breaking, the same stone that covers the county, coughed up from the ground as though the earth has an endless supply. Gioia dell Colle is built of the stuff. When newly cut or dug up it's a soft buff colour; with time it weathers to grey, and the rain carves holes through it like worms through cheese. But what fascinate Ettore are the shells. The *tufo* stone is full of seashells. Sometimes just fragments, sharp little edges, but sometimes whole ones, their ridges making perfect, undamaged fan shapes, millions of years old. Pino laughed when the schoolmaster told them that — that the shells were millions of years old. He couldn't fathom it, nor how they'd got into the stone, so he laughed. Ettore tried to explain it to him afterwards, because to him it held all the allure of proven magic, but Pino's attention was like a gnat, weaving here and there and never quite deciding where to land.

Ettore keeps edging closer to the stone-breakers. He casts a furtive look back at the overseer, to make sure he's not watching. They are at Masseria Tateo, and the overseer is Ludo Manzo, the corporal most feared and hated of all around Gioia for his cruelty, his arbitrary dispensation of punishment and his loathing of the *giornatari*, which has all the vehemence of one who has walked in their shoes, and never wants to do so again. The punishment that the men fear most is that they will not be hired again. They must work, or starve, and Ludo Manzo dismisses men for the least slackening of their pace, the least expression of displeasure, with his famous catchphrase ringing in their ears: *There's no work here for ungrateful* cafoni. *Cafoni* means ignorant redneck, it means bumpkin, it means peasant scum. They are also beaten or lashed, sometimes; but it's the boys who fear him most. The boys seem to attract the worst of his attention — and it is attention, not temper. In fact, when he notices a transgression Ludo actually seems pleased rather than not — pleased to have cause to punish. Perhaps it relieves his boredom. The men mutter to each other that he has sold his heart to the devil for a life of ease. But the day is long and the hours even longer, and the minutes stretch out into aeons to a boy of eleven, and so Ettore edges over to the newly broken stone, making some charade of picking weeds as he goes, and tries to see any perfect shells, newly come to light. If there are any, bedded into rocks of a size he can conceal, he will try to spirit them home for his collection. Once or twice Valerio has tried to cut a shell free for him, but they always shatter.

There's a minute flutter of raindrops then. Across the field, weed-pullers and stone-breakers pause and turn their eyes briefly to the sky. But that's all there is; those few drops.

'You're not paid to watch the weather, you fools,' Ludo Manzo shouts at them. As one, the men go back to work. All but Ettore. There, facing the sky a few metres away, is the perfect specimen. A scallop shell as wide as the palm of his hand, turned upwards like a bowl and now with one spot of rain marking it darkly, as though it was meant to be. It's embedded in a chunk of *tufo* that he might just be able to carry home, wrapped in his cap. He crouches over it and wriggles his fingers underneath it, hefting it to check the weight. It's at the top end of what he can hope to conceal, and he lingers in indecision, wondering if it's worth asking Valerio to try to cut it smaller, though he's unlikely to under Ludo's watchful eye; wondering if he could come back for the shell later, if he hides it now; wondering if he should just grab it and hope for the best at the end of the day.

'Ettore, what are you doing? Are you crazy?' says Pino near his ear, in the loudest of whispers. Ettore leaps up in alarm, knocking Pino's chin with the top of his head so that both of them wince.

'Mother of God, Pino! Don't sneak up like that!'

'I just didn't want Manzo to see you! What are you doing? Oh . . . not another shell. It's a nice one,' he concedes, crouching. 'But how many more do you need?'

'I like them,' Ettore mutters. He shrugs, and his friend looks at him with his head on one side, squeezing the soft flesh under his chin into a little roll. Against all logic, Pino, at eleven, is almost chubby. The neighbours all pinch his cheeks in delight, and say that he has a lucky angel watching him, feeding him honey in his sleep. They ruffle his hair, when it's not shaved off for lice, hoping that some of his luck will pass to them, and to their own weedy, infested children.

Pino stands up, grabs Ettore's sleeve and pulls him away. They walk a few paces, then he bends and scrabbles at a thistle in a desperate show of industry. Ettore gazes back at the rock, trying to fix its location in his mind for later.

'Come *on*! *Please*, Ettore!' Pino begs. They all fear Ludo Manzo, but Pino fears him more than all the rest, because Ludo seems to hate him for some reason. Maybe it's his ready smile, or the way he laughs at things that others can barely find a smile for; maybe it's the way he looks well fed, though he is not. Maybe it's because, however harshly Ludo treats him, Pino is never crushed. Before long, he will be smiling again.

'All right, all right, let go! You're the one who'll catch his eye!' Ettore casts a glance in the direction of the corporals, and sees that they are all watching them. Three of them, including Ludo, mounted on wiry brown horses. They are on the far side of the field so he can't see their faces, but he feels their eyes on him and it turns his knees to water. He crouches down, wants to disappear; he grabs at weeds and begins to pull them up with feverish vigour, stuffing them into his canvas sack. Fear churns in his guts. 'Pino, don't look up,' he whispers, and Pino turns pale. His eyes are wide enough to fall out of his head; his mouth hangs slightly open as he too begins to work as though his life depends on it. They keep

64

their heads down, hoping that nothing will come of it. Ettore aches to look again, to see if their attention has moved on, but he daren't. Then they hear a horse approaching, and Pino gives a small, wordless mutter of fear.

Only when the horse is so close that they must move or be stepped on do the boys stand up and scurry back. They look up into the black eyes of Ludo Manzo. He has a long, skeletal face, with the exact round shape of his eye sockets plain to see, and scarred, gaunt cheeks. His beard is a scribble of black wire, and he stinks of stale wine.

'Do you boys think I'm blind or stupid?' he says conversationally. 'Well? Which is it? Speak up or I'll beat it out of you.'

'Neither one of those, Mr Manzo,' says Pino. Ettore glances at him incredulously. Pino always seems to think that people will do right, if he does. When Ludo speaks, Ettore stays silent. Without fail.

'You've always got an answer, haven't you, fatso? Well then, you tell me — if you don't think I'm blind or stupid, why do you think I can't see you from over there, dossing instead of working? Or do you think I won't mind paying you for wasted time?' This time there's silence from both boys. The stone-breakers work on, making their fearful din. Ettore snatches a quick glance across, but Valerio's head is down. He wishes his father would notice his trouble, even if there's nothing he could do to help. Ludo crosses his arms over his horse's withers, tips his hat back slightly on his head, peers down at them and thinks for a while. 'Did you just forget what you were supposed to be doing? Is that it — are you too stupid to remember to work?' he says at last. *Shut up shut up shut up*, Ettore thinks, even as he hears Pino take a shaky breath, and open his mouth.

'Yes, sir,' he says. Ettore gouges an elbow into Pino's ribs but it's too late. Ludo sits up with a gleeful twist of his lips.

'Well then, let's see if we can't do something to help you remember.' The other guards have come to watch; one grins and chuckles to himself, knowing there's some spectacle to come; the other frowns at Ludo and pauses, as though he might say something. But in the end he only turns his horse away and walks it slowly to the far end of the field. Ettore wishes he would come back.

A short while later there's another sound amidst the breaking of stone: the sound of Pino crying, and yelping in pain. Ettore tries not to look; he doesn't want to witness his friend's humiliation, but his eyes flicker back, treacherously, just once. He catches a glimpse of Pino's bare behind; his trousers are round his ankles and he's shuffling between the watching guards. Ettore can't tell exactly what he is being made to do. Pino stumbles and falls down a lot, his cheeks blaze with pain and embarrassment, and Ludo laughs so hard he has to blow his nose; a kind of hard and silent laughter with no joy in it.

Ettore looks away. He is left alone to listen as this goes on — that's his punishment. Ludo is an uncanny judge of character, and seems to know that this is worse for him, that his guilt will eat him because it was his interest in the shell that started it. Across the field, the other workers try not to see. Only the boys glance over occasionally; some of them look sick, others fearful, others blank. Ettore is put back to work with the other corporal close by him, cussing at him if he looks over his shoulder towards Pino. But it's not Pino he's watching, in truth; it's Ludo Manzo. He wants to memorise Ludo's face — every line of it, every whisker, and the way the muscles seem to writhe in his cheeks as he laughs. He wants to be able to picture it in his mind's eye as clearly as he is seeing it now, because it will most likely be dark when he kills him.

★   ★   ★

Anger wakes him from this dream-memory with his teeth grinding hard together, his jaw aching and his breath flaring his nostrils. It's the kind of anger that can't be suppressed, or ignored. It causes an impulse to destroy that will turn on him if he doesn't satisfy it. Ettore opens his eyes and lurches to his feet, ready to tear into Ludo Manzo with fists and nails and teeth, but he is at home, and he is alone, and bewilderment stops him. Then the room lurches and chugs into a sluggish maelstrom all around him, and he sits back down, shaking. Only then does he remember cutting his leg with the scythe, or rather, his leg reminds him. The pain seems to fizz peculiarly, like the prickles of a thousand hot needles, then it clamps its teeth in a tight, unbearable grip like a steel trap. Ettore stares down at it in horror but there's nothing much to see. The leg of his trousers has been rolled up over his knee and the exposed skin is caked in dried blood. There's a cloth tied across the wound itself, and he recognises it as one of Iacopo's wraps. Wincing, he pulls it off. The wound is a dark gaping slice, clean but deep; he can see the grey-white of bone in there, and lumpish black clots of gore. Immediately that the cloth is off, fresh blood begins to well and drizzle onto the floor. Ettore watches it stupidly. His throat is so dry he can't swallow.

The door swings open and Paola comes in with Iacopo in a sling on her back. She hesitates when she sees him sitting up, and for a moment relief floods her face. Then she sees his leg and rushes forwards.

'For God's sake, Ettore — I just got it to stop bleeding and the first thing you do is start it up again?' Ettore tries to say sorry but he can't make his voice work. Paola drags a small stool across to him and plonks his leg up on it. She ties the cloth back over the wound, and then squeezes it. Ettore chokes a little, coughs in shock at the pain, and Paola looks up at him. 'Sorry,' she says. 'Sorry for your pain.' His blood squeezes up between her fingers and he sees her pale, and her lips press tight. Over her shoulder Iacopo gazes at Ettore with an inscrutable expression, and Ettore reaches out his finger. The baby grasps it at once, with his whole hand, and opens his mouth to suck it. The strength of his grip makes Ettore's stomach clench in pleasure. Some days Iacopo's grip is weak, some days strong; some days he doesn't even reach for the finger. Today the baby has a calm, businesslike demeanour, and his grip is steadfast.

'I'll be all right. It'll be all right,' Ettore manages to say.

'Will it?' says Paola. She pushes him back onto the straw mattress, then lifts up his damaged leg and lays it out. She wipes her hands angrily on a rag and won't meet his eye. She wears a scarf over her hair, like always, tight to her head and tied at the nape of her neck. Her hair is rolled into a knot there so that no stray strands escape. It makes her look severe, older than her twenty-two years; it accentuates that hardness she's had since Iacopo's father died. She shakes her head. 'If you can't work, we're finished.' Ettore can't remember when he last heard his sister sound frightened, but she does now.

Lying down makes the room spin again, and Ettore shuts his eyes to still it.

'Of course I'll be able to work. How did I get back here?'

'On Pino's back, of course. All the way from Vallarta.'

'Pino always was a big ox. I could go back now and finish the day. I'm fine.'

'Go back now?' Paola is trying to clean the blood out from under her fingernails.

'It's still light. There's still time. I worked nine hours or more before it happened, I think . . . '

'Yesterday. That was yesterday, you idiot; you've been asleep since then, nothing would

69

rouse you. Who knows if they'll pay you for an unfinished day . . . You were bleeding so much when you got here . . . You needed to rest.' Paola can't help but sound a tiny bit resentful. They all need to rest, after all.

'I've lost a whole day's work today, then?' says Ettore, his eyes snapping open. Paola gives a curt little nod. Never once, since he was ten, has he missed a day's work when work was available. He feels like a man left stranded; he feels traitorous and betrayed all at once. He sits up again but Paola stops him with a curse.

'It's too late now! You might as well rest. Luna is trying to borrow a needle and thread, to close the wound.' Paola undoes the sling and deftly gathers Iacopo into her arms. She smiles wearily at him, and his little face broadens in delight. 'How did it happen?' she asks.

'I don't know. I . . . I lost my balance. I was thinking about . . . something. I just lost my balance, I think.'

'Didn't you get a meal?'

'A little bread, but no wine.'

'Those miserly *bastards*!' Paola suddenly barks, and Iacopo's eyes go wide. She quickly puts him over her shoulder and sways him, rolling her eyes anxiously to the ceiling.

'Paola, please don't worry. I can work. It will be fine.' But Paola shakes her head.

'You must go to our uncle. Ask him for an easy job while you heal.'

'I will not.' They glare at one another, and Paola looks away first.

Ettore stays still for a few hours, taking in the

strangeness of seeing their one room in daylight. He watches the beam of light from the single window as it glides slowly across the floor. Paola comes and goes. She brings him a cup of water and then a cup of *acquasale*, thin soup made by boiling up stale bread with salt in water, with a little olive oil or cheese added in times of plenty. There is mozzarella in the soup she gives him; Ettore glances up but doesn't ask how she got it, because he knows she won't answer. A man called Poete has a crush on her; he works at the small mozzarella factory at the far end of Via Roma. He has hands like paddles, a chinless face, and always smells of milk. The workers at that factory are allowed to eat as much mozzarella as they like inside the factory, but they aren't allowed to take any home for their families. That way, the workers gorge themselves once or twice, but are then too sick of the stuff to want it any more. A few months ago a man tried to smuggle home a whole mozzarella — a knot the size of his fist. When it looked as though he would be caught he stuffed it into his mouth and tried to swallow it, and choked to death. Poete got his job, and there's not much he wouldn't attempt, it seems, for the things Paola will then do to repay him. She chose him carefully. Poete has subverted one of the lads who brings the milk from the farms every morning, in heavy pails swinging from the handlebars of his bicycle; so Paola regularly gets pilfered milk for Iacopo, since her own is never quite enough for him. Clearly, Poete has also found a way to smuggle out cheese sometimes. It tastes impossibly good, impossibly rich. Ettore shames himself by wolfing it down, and not sharing it with his sister.

It's hard for Paola to get paid work because of the baby, and because of her reputation. If there is an outbreak of violence in Gioia, a protest — like the stoning of a shop where the baker has been mixing dust into the loaves and selling at high prices — Paola is at the front. She makes her voice one of the loudest, and she does not defer to authority, or to the Church. When she was fifteen there was the scandal of the priest who had been discovered interfering with the little orphan girls in his care. Paola claims to have thrown the torch that finally set his house on fire. The peasants have little enough use for the Church, anyhow — the priests say the droughts and hardships are the result of their godlessness, and they continue to charge for funerals, weddings and christenings, when none can pay. Last year, when the government ordered rationing to help with the post-war shortages and women were frequently made to grant sexual favours to officials in return for their flour, oil and bean coupons, Paola took steps to protect herself. On the day one such randy official made his intentions plain, she let him lead her to a quiet place then she put a knife to his scrotum, got all the coupons she was due and some extra ones as well. She laughed about it, and said the man would be too embarrassed to tell anybody, but Ettore worried for her, then and now. The officials know her face, and he fears that they will mark her out, and make a point of finding her.

Sooner or later. She goes about with Iacopo strapped to her back like a talisman, but that won't deter them when it comes to it.

By afternoon Ettore is on his feet. He can't put any weight on the cut leg so he hops, using the walls for balance. From their door a short flight of stone steps leads down to a tiny courtyard, an offshoot where the narrow street, Vico Iovia, makes a ninety-degree turn. Beneath their room is a stable, where their neighbour sleeps with his mule and an elderly nanny goat. Ettore picks up the wooden pole with which the double door is barred at night, and uses it as a crutch. There's no water for Paola to wash their clothes, but she hangs what spare things they own out on a line anyway, to try to air them. Flies settle on the stiff fabric, like they settle on everything else. Paola comes along the alley with a basket of straw on her hip — fodder she collects for their neighbour's goat, in return for a cup of her milk now and then. She opens her mouth to scold him but Ettore forestalls her.

'Did Valerio find work today?'

'I don't know,' she says.

'And yesterday — he was with the shepherd, yes? How much did he earn?'

'He stank of sheep, so I suppose that's where he was. He wasn't back until after dark, then he slept, and said nothing to me. He . . . ' She pauses, repositions the basket on her hip. 'His cough is worse. Always worse.'

'I know.' Ettore sets off in the direction of the castle.

'Where are you going?'

73

'To check he's earning, since I'm not, and not busy pledging yesterday's wages on wine.'

The castle looms over him as he emerges from Vico Iovia. Crows line its rooftops, bickering and looking down at the mess of life at street level. It looks out of place, almost ridiculous. There it sits, empty, a monument to one man's wealth and power; and to the peasants of Gioia, who live sometimes ten, twelve, fifteen to a room, it's hard to think such things were built and belong in their own world, and not in some fairy land. Ettore's leg throbs harder and harder. It sounds so loud in his own ears that he starts to wonder if other people can hear it too. It begins to bleed again, and leaves a trail of drips so that a stray dog comes to follow him with its nose twitching. When it gets too close Ettore flails at it with the wooden pole. The dog has a hungry, speculative look in its eye. On the Via del Mercato is a bar, a simple place with stools in front of a pitted countertop, and big barrels of wine behind it. It's the first one Ettore tries, and he curses when he sees Valerio at the far end of the room, sitting there stooped and unshaven, playing *zecchinetta* with a man who looks considerably happier than him.

Ettore limps over and slams his hand down flat on the bar in front of them. Neither man is startled, so he knows at once that they're drunk. The playing cards are yellow and dog-eared; there are sticky rings of spilt red wine all around them, and the scent of it sour and pervasive in the air. Valerio looks up at his son, and Ettore sees that he has drunk so much he can't keep his face straight. It veers from shock to guilt to anger to resentment, all in a few seconds. Valerio swallows, and finally settles for a sort of sickly, listless expression.

'Something you want to say, boy?' he says.

'Yesterday's money? Is there any of it left?' says Ettore. He sounds cold and hard to his own ears, when what he feels is a kind of debilitating urge to surrender waiting to swallow him — a deep black well of it, like the hole at Castellana, into which he might fall and never emerge.

'*My* money, you mean? My money, boy.'

'Mine now, in truth,' says his companion, who Ettore has never seen before. The man grins a mouthful of gappy brown teeth at him, and Ettore would like to knock them out of his mouth. He sees at once that this man is nowhere near as drunk as his father.

'He has lost it all to you?' he says.

'What he hasn't tipped down his throat,' says the barman, who has run the place for as long as Ettore can remember. 'And he still owes me twenty-eight lire from the winter.' Twenty-eight lire, in summer, is a good month's wages.

'Why aren't you working?' Valerio says then, glaring at his son.

'I cut my leg. I'll work tomorrow though . . . why aren't *you* working? What will Paola eat tonight, since you've pissed it all away?'

'Don't *accuse* me, boy! Mind your own damned business!' Valerio thumps his fist on the bar and nearly slides off his stool. Raising his voice makes him cough.

'Ah, leave your old man alone, why don't you?

75

Pleasures in life are few enough for you to deny him a drink and a game with an old friend,' says the brown-toothed man. *Your old man.* Ettore stares bleakly at his father, stooped and sunken and coughing; his hair is salt and pepper, grizzled; there's dirt in the bags beneath his eyes. He is an old man indeed. He is forty-seven years old. Ettore takes the man's wine glass and drinks it empty.

'You're no friend of his. And if I see you with him again, you'll wish I hadn't,' he says.

That night, as Valerio snores on his ledge, Ettore is woken by the movement of Paola getting up from the mattress beside him. She's as silken as a cat when she wants to be, but he is sleeping fitfully, with the way his leg itches and thuds. He hears her finding shoes, shawl, knife and matches. He almost asks her where she's going, but since he wouldn't like the answer, he stays silent. When she's gone he reaches out, softly, softly, until he finds his nephew's sleeping body beside him. He rests his fingers lightly on Iacopo's ribs, and feels the reassuring flutter of air in and out, in and out. It seems faster than it should be, but he's still so tiny that Ettore isn't sure. His cheeks are a little rough — some rash or irritation. That Paola has not taken the baby with her tells him where she might be going.

While he waits, because he can't sleep until she's back, he lets himself conjure Livia. Her father brought the family to Gioia six years ago, from a village in the *marina* — near the sea — where they had once worked on a vineyard that was then eaten whole by phylloxera bugs.

76

Livia came with her parents and two brothers, to face the hatred and the resentment of the Gioiese workforce, who had no time or goodwill for people coming from beyond their own borders to take work. For over a year they lived in the street, camping out beneath the ancient arcs of Gioia, or the portico of a church, or the canopied doorways of the rich and absent, until Livia's father finally made some friends in the peasants' union and got enough work to rent a room. Ettore first saw Livia when she was eighteen and he was twenty-two. Just two years ago, but he can't seem to remember what his life was like before she walked into it; just like now he can't quite work out how he's supposed to carry it on without her.

Livia had waves of deep brown hair — a dark chestnut colour, not true black — that matched her skin tone and her eyes almost exactly, creating a harmonious whole, a sort of soft blurredness that was irresistible. She had a dimple in her chin that was his undoing. She would sit in the market place with her mother and the other women with a bucket between her knees and knife in her hand, scraping the husks from nuts, or shelling peas or fava beans, or grinding coffee — whatever was needed. In times when farm work was slack, in November, and January through February, Ettore would steal moments to watch her, and the way she smiled that gave a glimpse of her lower teeth, and the upper ones that were in a strange formation — the canines and premolars longer than the incisors — that gave her a slight lisp when she spoke. It wasn't that she was the most beautiful, or had the best figure or a provocative way of walking. Ettore couldn't say why, exactly, but to him she looked like how heaven might be, and he didn't dare approach her in case he was wrong, and got woken from his dream. Her heart-shaped face had an intelligent expression, her eyes were bright and she had a way of cocking her head to listen that reminded him of a bird; some small, rounded, self-contained bird — a woodcock, or a golden plover.

Pino made him go and talk to her, finally, and the last thing Ettore wanted was to have his friend at his side when he introduced himself — tall, beautiful, devastating Pino. But he never would have done it without Pino's elbow in his ribs, and as it turned out Livia only looked at Ettore. Only at him, right from the very beginning. She didn't blush, or simper, or sneer. She put one hand up to her lips and stared, and said his eyes were the colour of the sea, and reminded her of home; so straight away she baffled him, because Ettore had never seen the sea. Nor a mirror. He found out quickly that she only ever said what she actually thought, and had no guile, no patience for games or dissembling. In the time he'd spent watching her he'd never seen her talking to a man, so he'd assumed she would be shy of him, and afraid of what he wanted. But in the end it was she who kissed him first, with all the simplicity and directness he soon came to expect. And she never did spoil the idea that she was like heaven. She had the power of life and death over him from that first exchange.

＊　＊　＊

When perhaps two hours have passed, Paola
returns. There's a slight grunt from her, and a
thump as something heavy hits the ground. She
pushes it under the bed and Ettore smells blood,
and not from his own leg. She lies back down
beside him in silence, and he listens as her breathing steadily slows. The smell of smoke clings to
her, bitter and strong. She has joined a poaching
raid on a *masseria*, he knows then. They have
stolen, they have killed livestock, they have torched,
and she has her loot under the bed — meat,
some of which they will eat, most of which they
will sell to buy other foodstuffs. He feels nothing
about this other than guilt, because it's his fault
she's taken this risk, his fault that she's this worried about their survival. For a second he's furious
with her, because she could easily be killed, or
arrested, and what would become of Iacopo then?
The guards open fire freely at thieves and raiders,
and then there are the dogs, too. People frequently
die, trying to take what they cannot buy. But his
anger only makes the guilt worse, because Paola
knows the risks, of course, and nobody worries
more for her child than she does. But still she
went. Ettore lies in the dark and his frustration
grows until it's harder to bear than the wound in
his leg. When his sister shakes his arm to wake
him he still has not slept, and he snatches the
limb away in fury, ignoring her offended expression. They do not speak of her absence, of the
meat under the bed, the smell of smoke, or
the frank exhaustion on both of their faces.

In the piazza Ettore avoids the Masseria Vallarta overseer, who knows of his injury, and tries to find work elsewhere. He drops his improvised crutch and balances with both feet on the ground but the weight only on the whole leg, and is hired with a group of men to a smaller farm. But he can't even begin the walk without the pole to lean on, and is promptly dismissed. When all the overseers and workers have gone he finds Valerio, also unemployed, sitting on the steps of the covered market with an unreadable face. Ettore has no idea what to do with his day. A kind of itching desperation means he can't go home, he can't rest. He sits next to his father for a while, as the sun rises and floods the piazza and the temperature soars. He thinks that once threshing starts he might have more luck — a job where he can stand rather than walk, feeding the machine or swinging a flail, using the strength of his arms rather than his legs. His body feels tremulous and broken. The sun roars down at them both but Ettore starts to shiver as his father starts to sweat. He keeps thinking he can hear the hum of a scythe swinging, but that can't be right. He shakes his head doggedly, to be rid of the sound.

'If Maria was alive she would fix that leg,' Valerio says suddenly. 'She would fix this cough too.' He sets great store by the memory of his wife's healing skills, though one time Maria Tarano made a poultice for a neighbour's wound and that wound turned black, the skin around it shiny and fat, and the unfortunate man soon died of it. After that Ettore lost faith in her magic, in her infallibility. He saw from the way she shrank back when others came to her for help that she had lost faith too. But her efforts earned them payment in kind, so she kept them up. And she could not heal herself, of course, when cholera came for her eleven years ago. 'I still miss her, Ettore. Sorely, I miss her,' says Valerio, and Ettore suddenly sees that grief is a thing they have in common, he and his father. It saddens him that he hasn't thought of this until now.

Paola sells cuts of her stolen meat — a sinewy shoulder of mutton — to various neighbours and strangers, by hushed word of mouth. The peasants keep such things to themselves, but the police and proprietors sometimes send out spies to watch and listen, to find out who suddenly has something they ought not to have. For three days they have bread and beans and olive oil to eat, and even a little wine to go with their meals. Paola cooks the beans in a *pignata* by the fire, makes a thick stew with the mutton bone and adds handfuls of black pasta and pecorino cheese. They eat together from one large dish, much cracked and stapled, that has served their dinners for as long as Ettore can remember; sitting on stools around a tiny, wobbly table that is the envy of many less well-furnished neighbours.

'Did you hear about Capozzi?' says Paola, as they eat. Ettore nods. She is normally his eyes and ears in Gioia, when he is in the fields all day; now he is about town in the daytime he sees and hears as well.

'What of him?' says Valerio.

'Arrested again. Beaten as well, I heard. Badly. He was trying to prevent the removal of men from retaken common land, and the burning of what they'd planted there. He was only speaking, but they charged him with disturbing the peace. Disturbing the peace!' The three of them share a steady glance, and Ettore knows that Paola is waiting for them to express their anger, their outrage, their fear.

Nicola Capozzi is a Gioia man who founded the local branch of the socialist party there in 1907. The workers have no real understanding of the politics behind their strikes and their riots — they need no such understanding, but they know that Capozzi speaks for them. That he is their man. Since the new branch of the fascist party was formed in Gioia recently, with the full support of the *signori* and proprietors, there's no doubt as to which side the police are on. There never has been. The men now wait to hear of Capozzi's murder. Assassination, it will be called, and nothing will be done about it as and when it happens. Not via official channels, in any case.

'There'll be a rally. There'll be a strike until he's released. I'll find out today when it will start,' says Paola, holding her brother's eyes. But all the outrage, all the fear and anger at the dinner table comes from her alone. Valerio carries on eating as though he hears nothing; and without Livia Ettore can't find that feeling any more. He can't find his will to fight.

★　★　★

For three days, all is well. Being well fed keeps Ettore's shivers to a minimum, and he feels better even though he doesn't feel right. Then, after three days, the food runs out and Valerio is coughing so hard he can be heard right across the piazza, and Ettore stands square before the overseer of Masseria Vallarta at dawn, with his weight on both feet, and declares himself fit for work. His cut leg beats like a drum; the bone screams silently at him. He can feel the overseer's eyes on him as he joins the group for the walk to the farm; he grinds his teeth together, so hard that his jaw cramps, but he does not limp. Halfway along the dusty track out of Gioia he feels the warm trickle of fresh blood as the wound reopens. It goes down into his boot, and makes his foot slide around. Pino is not with him; he was hired elsewhere, and Ettore looks around at the other faces to see if there is a friendly one, one he knows, who might carry him back to town if he can't walk. He sees Gianni, one of Livia's older brothers, and makes his way over to him.

Gianni looks down at Ettore's leg but says nothing. He's older than Ettore by two years, but seems much older still. His face is hard, his expression grim. If Livia was a golden plover, then this brother is a black kite, silent and watchful. He doesn't moderate his pace to make it easier for Ettore to keep up.

'Gianni. How is your family?' says Ettore. Gianni shrugs one shoulder.

'Surviving. My mother still pines for Livia.'

'As do we all,' says Ettore carefully. In truth,

pining isn't something he can imagine Gianni doing. Pining needs softness; pining needs a heart in which to feel the wound. 'Have you heard anything?' He can't help but ask, though he knows Gianni would have sought him out if he had. Gianni shakes his head.

'It's impossible to overhear the guards when we harvest.'

'I know.' This is something else that might be easier once threshing starts. With the cutting, and the men scattered all over the fields, there is less talk, less gossip. Less opportunity to eavesdrop on the guards and the other *annaroli* — those with permanent jobs on the *masserie*. There will be no other way to find out who did the things to Livia that Ettore is careful not to think about, because it's unbearable in a way that could drive him mad. There's no other form of justice for the peasants than the personal settling of scores; that has always been the way. Ettore has heard guards boasting of their various exploits and misdeeds, at other times, and he always made a note of the man's face, if he didn't know his name, and passed on what he'd heard to those that wanted to know. He trusts that, sooner or later, someone will do the same for him. But it has been six months, and not even a whisper about it. About her. About who would attack a young girl out alone, walking back to town with a bundle of foraged firewood in her apron. Ettore is confused, worried. It's a source of steady shame, but violence towards wives, daughters and sisters is everywhere in Puglia. The downtrodden men, harried by failure

84

and desperation, often lash out at the only targets they have, even if those targets are innocent, even if they're loved; even if he loathes himself all the more as a result. But such violence stays in the home, and is nobody's business. A deliberate attack, outside the family and of such savagery, is everyone's business.

'I always ask. I always try to find out,' says Gianni, as though Ettore had accused him otherwise.

'I know,' he says again.

'We will find out, one day.' Gianni stares along the road ahead, his eyes narrow though the sun is not yet full up. His certainty reassures Ettore. One thing not in doubt is that, when they find him, they will make the man pay with his hide. They walk on in silence, and soon Gianni has drawn ahead, and Ettore is left behind. Gianni is not a man who needs or wants friends. Ettore feels despised for his weakness.

The day is a long and agonising grind. Too late, Ettore uses one of his bootlaces to tie his trouser leg closed below the wound, but the dust and dirt have already found their way in, and the cloth that's tied around it is the same one he's had since the beginning, and it has started to smell. At least, he hopes it's the cloth that smells, and not the wound itself. He is tying sheaves instead of wielding the scythe; it's easier in some ways — no tool to carry, no twisting, less shifting of weight from leg to leg. But more bending over, more stooping; and every time he leans down Ettore's head swoops giddily, queasily, and he fights for balance. When lunchtime comes he stares at his chunk of bread and wonders why, though he knows his stomach is empty, he doesn't want to eat. He puts the bread in his pocket to take back, and swallows his water in three gulps. The flies won't leave him alone. By afternoon he's shivering again, though the day has been one of flat, white heat, and he can tell from the way he's stared at that he doesn't look well. A man he doesn't know claps him on the shoulder and tells him he's earned his rest that day, but his touch makes Ettore recoil. His skin feels like needles and pins; his guts are juddering.

On the walk home he finds himself alone, because he's slow and stops to rest often. The sun is setting and the sky has turned the palest turquoise, a colour so pretty that Ettore sits down on the stone wall beside the road and stares at it for a while, not quite knowing where he is or how he got there. He rolls up his trouser leg and peels off the sodden cloth over the wound. The gash has gone black, the skin of his shin shiny and fat. Ettore grins at it, a baring of his teeth that has nothing to do with mirth. Painfully, he stands and walks on, and it seems only moments until full dark descends. He can see lights up ahead and he thinks it must be Gioia, but he can't seem to get any closer. He legs won't do as he tells them any more; it's a weird feeling — the sudden loss of something taken entirely for granted, like forgetting how to breathe.

He takes another rest, this time sitting with his back to the wall and his legs stretched out in front of him. He wants them as far away from him as he can put them, but the smell of the wound is too strong to escape, and it reminds him of the trenches. Against the far grey sky bats twist and flutter in silence, and tiny stars are winking alight. Ettore stares up at them and can no longer remember where he was going, or why. Then there's a growing sound, a rumble, a crunching. A motor car speeds into view, coming away from Gioia with its headlights dazzling. It's deep red; it kicks up a plume of pale dust behind it, ten metres into the sky. It flashes past Ettore without pausing, and in the instant that it does he's sure he can hear laughter beneath the sound of its engine — a high peal of female laughter. He stares after it in amazement. The proprietors can't get petrol for their tractors or farm machinery, they say, but at least one rich man has a laughing car and enough fuel to make it fly.

He rests his head back on the wall. The night is cool but still the air seems hard to breathe, like it's too thick, and sticks to the sides of his mouth and throat like dust. For a while he focuses on drawing this unhelpful stuff into his lungs, and pushing it out again, and he has no idea if this while is seconds or hours. When a figure emerges from the dark and crouches down beside him, Ettore has no idea what it might mean.

'*Porca puttana!* Ettore — what is that stink? Is that you?' it says, and puts a hand on his shoulder to rouse him. Ettore frowns, rounding up his thoughts and eyes and tongue, which stray away from him like wilful cats. He can see a black outline, a mass of curly hair that seems to move like snakes.

'Pino?' His friend seems enormous, a gigantic version of his normal self. 'Why are you so big?'

'What? Paola sent me to look for you when you didn't come back. Is that your leg that smells so bad? Can you get up? Come on.' Pino's arm is around his ribs; he wraps one of Ettore's arms around his neck and heaves him up. The movement is too much, and Ettore retches in protest, bringing up nothing. He suddenly thinks that if he dies without avenging Livia, his own rage will burn him for eternity — he will have his own personal hell, and he will never see her again. Some other lucky ghost will find her in heaven, and claim her. Ettore hasn't cried since she died, not once, but he starts to cry now.

He doesn't understand much of anything else for a while. He feels as though he's floating, and at times it's quite nice. At other times it starts to feel like drowning. He thinks he hears Valerio and Paola arguing about a doctor, about a druggist, about what to do; he thinks he senses Pino, still huge, waiting to find out what they decide. He wonders how they can carry on talking when the air is hotter than flames. He is inside a building, then he is outside, and then inside again, somewhere different. The sun comes up, and the light hurts his eyes. He is carried, and it is giant, snake-headed Pino who carries him; sweating, the breath puffing in and out of him. From time to time Paola's face hovers in front of him, and her features swim about as though they're melting — her eyes are drips of molten wax, running down the candle of her skull; she's terrifying, and when she speaks she makes no sense.

Ettore is carried for a long time. Then there are walls around him, a place he can't understand. He feels himself righted, feels the ground under his feet although he can take none of his own weight, and can't even clench his hand to hang on to Pino. Only Pino's grip on his wrist, keeping his arm looped around Pino's neck, keeps him upright. There are voices, and the babble of them swells to a deafening crescendo in his ears, louder than summer thunder. He thinks his eyes are open but what he sees can't be real, so he isn't sure. He sees sparkles of light, white skin and golden hair: he thinks he sees an angel. He frowns, struggling with this, because it reminds him of some other thought he had, somewhen. Could it be Livia? Could this mass of impossible, painful brightness be Livia? He stares harder, tries harder. The sparkles of light are eyes, and they are fixed on him; they seem to blaze. He wants to stretch out a hand and know by touch what he can't make his eyes decipher, but his arm won't move and he feels himself sinking, and all the light is gone.

# Clare

In the morning Leandro says that he and Boyd must talk business. Boyd has some preliminary drawings for the villa's new façade to show him, completed in the days before Clare and Pip arrived, and he vanishes into Cardetta's cavernous study with them under his arm, visibly tense at the coming judgement. A pair of sharp parallel lines appears between his brows at such times, and Clare wishes he could conceal his anxiety better — like she conceals her own. He gives too much away. Leandro catches her eye as he shuts the door, and there's a knowing look in it that she can't decipher. But she doesn't trust it; she doesn't know if this man knows how Boyd can be. How breakable.

'Oh, don't you worry,' says Marcie, as Clare turns away from the study door. 'Leandro's a pussycat really — and I know he loves Boyd's style. You should hear him go on about that building of his in New York.'

'Really?' That building of Boyd's in New York, the one he designed half out of his mind. Clare can't see a picture of it without a creeping feeling of dread.

'Of course! He's got nothing but praise for your husband's talents. He could have had any architect in the world come and design this new front, you know. But he chose Boyd — didn't even consider anyone else, as far as I'm aware.

But that's my Leandro, you know? He knows what he wants. Now, what say you and me and Pip go out for a bit of a walk?'

It's mid-morning by the time Marcie has chosen an outfit, and the shoes to go with it.

'Really,' she says, as they leave the house for Via Garibaldi, 'whoever would have known that New York clothes would be so unsuitable in Italy? And that there'd be nowhere — I mean, *nowhere* — to buy any others once I got here?' She's wearing an outfit not dissimilar to the one in which she breakfasted — the lime green of spring leaves — but with high boots laced up her shins. 'Ready, Master Pip? You shall be our champion against the wild Italians,' she says, flashing a smile.

'Had you always lived in New York before you came here, Mrs Cardetta?' says Pip.

'It's *Marcie*, please! Yes, born and bred. And I love it, but I jumped at the chance to move to Italy. Of course, I thought Leandro meant Rome, or Milan, or Venice. That's how he proposed to me, you know — did Boyd tell you? He said he wanted to go home, to Italy, but he wouldn't go unless I married him and went with him. He said I was the missing piece — isn't that just the sweetest thing you ever heard?'

'It sounds very romantic,' says Clare.

'Oh, devastatingly so. Who could say anything but yes? But then, I always did find proposals hard to resist. Got myself into a few fixes that way,' she says. The hare-lipped man who drove them from the station opens the street door for them, to a drench of white light. He watches

91

Clare again, just as he did before, even as he nods to Marcie in apparent deference. 'Thank you, Federico. Whew — it's going to be a hot one today.'

'You were engaged before, then?' says Clare.

'Oh, two or three times.' Marcie waves a hand and then pauses on the pavement, looking right and left as if she can't decide which way to go. 'Like I said, I was a little wild. But I always managed to escape in the nick of time!'

'Mr Cardetta said there was a castle,' says Pip hopefully.

'You'd like to see it? It's an ugly old thing. Well, then, follow me, if you're sure. But I should warn you, it's right in the middle of the old part of town. That's where the peasants live and I must say, it's not always pretty.'

The narrow brim of Clare's hat doesn't cast enough shade over her face, and the sun is relentless on the eyes. She can feel it smarting on the back of her neck, and she's soon sweating. There's the same hush on the streets as she noticed before, the same strange absence of the bustle she'd expected; there are more people around at this hour, but they keep their voices down, and they don't seem to hurry. There are men too, leaning against walls and in doorways, or glimpsed through the door of a bar, drinking in spite of the early hour. The party of three goes at a measured pace, because of the heat and the need to keep an eye on the dirty pavements. The sky is so bright that glimpses up at the architecture must be taken quickly, judiciously, before the eyes are seared.

'The castle's off that way, but we're taking the long route because I wanted to show you Piazza Plebiscito first,' says Marcie, as they come into a large open space surrounded by the shuttered windows and symmetrical façades of houses Clare guesses to be eighteenth and nineteenth century. There are ranks of balconies looking out over the square, each with neat iron railings; a low covered market building that reeks of spoilt vegetables; a raised octagonal bandstand; a beautifully gnarled medieval church, crouched beneath a tall bell tower; and globular street lamps suspended from elegant scrolled poles. Marcie talks them through everything they see. 'That's the old Benedictine monastery. Isn't it just darling? This is where the men all meet every morning to sort out who's working where. This is really the hub of things — processions, political meetings, that kind of thing. We must go to the Chiesa Madre as well, of course.'

There are men who aren't working in Piazza Plebiscito as well, standing with their shoulders stooped and their gazes steady; smoking, talking now and then. They have the patient, intransient look of people with nowhere to go and nothing to do. Many of them turn to watch the two blonde women walk by, with their awkward young escort and their clothes so different to the dark, enveloping attire of the Gioia women. The men all wear black or brown or charcoal, and their eyes are uniformly dark, uniformly ambiguous. They squint at the world through veils of cigarette smoke, and their scrutiny somehow makes Clare feel precarious, less real in the world. She's not a guest there; she's a temporary anomaly. Like water on waxed cloth, she feels that she could stay on the surface indefinitely, and never sink in. And, equally, she could be removed without consequence. It's nothing like the other places she has been to in Italy, where foreigners are a common sight. She feels like checking over her shoulder — she does so several times. The streets of Gioia feel poised, as tense as a pent breath; like the whole town is waiting to exhale, and that exhale might be a roar. Clare thinks of the quick look that Marcie and Leandro exchanged when she first suggested going out for a walk. She checks Pip, but he's swinging his arms and looking around, oblivious.

Only on Via Roma, which they walk down to look at the vast *palazzo* of a prestigious family called Casano, do they see any better-dressed, apparently upper-class people, invariably walking and not loitering. Marcie smiles and greets them but receives only the merest acknowledgements in return. Her smile loses its glow but she won't let it drop. Clare walks closer to her, in solidarity.

'It must be hard to make friends in a new place when you don't have the language,' she says. Marcie takes her arm gratefully.

'They call me his American whore, you know,' she says, in low tones so that Pip won't hear. But he does hear — Clare can tell from the way he stiffens and looks away across the street as if the sight of the water spout, and the queue of women waiting at it, are fascinating to him.

'Small towns breed small minds.'

'Amen to that. Do you know, almost none of the men who actually own the land around here

94

can be bothered to live here? And none of the nobles — well, there's one count who has a big palace outside of town. The rest just have tenant farmers to manage their estates, while they swan around in Naples and Rome and Paris. Anyone with enough money to live elsewhere does exactly that. Except my Leandro, of course. So what's left is a snooty bunch of not-quites, who make themselves feel better by indulging in delusions of grandeur.' Marcie is still smiling but even she can't say all this without sounding angry, and sad.

'I'd never heard of Gioia del Colle before Boyd called me to say that's where we were going,' says Clare.

'*Nobody's* heard of Gioia del Colle, sugar. Give it a few days and you'll understand why.'

To get to the castle they turn onto a narrower street that runs right through the middle of the old town. There are large houses on this street too, but they look more run-down and less fashionable than those on the peripheral streets, and off to either side are tiny alleyways, crowded in with dilapidated stone houses. Windows are clouded with filth; steps run up and down to wooden doors gone jagged and toothy with rot. The gutters are choked with rubbish and muck; there's a stink of sewage, and they are more careful than ever where they put their feet. Clare has the growing impression of smart newer streets surrounding and curtaining off a seedier, far poorer centre.

'Smells like the drains are a bit blocked,' says Pip.

'Drains? Oh, Pip, they don't have drains,' says Marcie.

'Oh.' Pip frowns, and clearly wishes he hadn't mentioned it. 'Don't people get ill?'

'Of course they do. They even get cholera now and then. You're fine at home with us, of course — all our food comes from the *masseria*, and the water's bought in so I know it's clean. Here on your left we have the house that Napoleon built for his little brother when he was in charge here. And if you look up, you'll see the castle.'

Clare and Pip do as they're told, and see three high, square towers with broken tops; the fourth having presumably collapsed. The walls are vast, vertical, indomitable; perforated here and there by small windows and arrow slots.

'Can't we go in?' says Pip. The huge doors don't look as though they've opened in a decade. 'Who owns it?'

'Oh, some noble old *marchese* or other,' says Marcie, with that wave of her hand that's almost a tic. 'I've never seen it open. There's a ghost, though. Do you believe in ghosts?'

'I don't know, really. Probably not,' says Pip, but Clare can hear he's interested. 'Who's it supposed to be?'

'A girl called Bianca Lancia. She was one of the wives of the king who built this place hundreds of years ago — the most beautiful of his wives — and he locked her up in a dungeon here when he heard a rumour she'd been unfaithful to him. So you know what she did to prove her love for him?'

'Threw herself off the battlements?'

'Close. She cut off her . . . well. An important part of a girl's anatomy. Both of them.'

'And did the king love her again?'

'What, when she'd chopped off the things he probably liked best in the first place? Well, he rushed down here to be reconciled with her, but she died. So what was the point of that, I always wonder?'

'Well, she regained her good name,' says Pip pompously.

'A good name's no good to a corpse,' says Marcie, with sudden feeling. 'Stupid girl, that's what I always think when I hear that story. She should have found another way. Or another man.'

'Maybe she *had* been unfaithful, and she wanted to punish herself?'

'Even stupider, then.'

Clare wants to divert them, since the subject's not appropriate for Pip, but beneath the wall of the castle she suddenly can't think quite clearly; she's distracted, and feels vulnerable. She looks up at the looming fortress in case that's where the danger lies — those crushing stone walls, threatening to fall; she looks over her shoulder again, and then turns on her heel, but there's nobody close by. Just then a man in a hurry emerges from an alleyway opposite the castle, and Clare's gaze lands on him, and catches there. He's hampered by a lame leg and has a wooden pole as a crutch, but it's just a wooden pole, with no easy means of gripping it, so he must use both hands and twist awkwardly to do so. He sets off to the south, as quickly as he may,

97

not looking left or right but only straight ahead. He is thin, black-haired; he has knots at the corners of his jaw where his teeth are clenched. A stray dog trots across the street then lowers its head, sniffs, and turns to follow the man, and there's something in its posture that Clare doesn't like; she almost wants to warn him about it. He moves away along the street and disappears behind a wagon piled high with scrap metal and spools of rusty wire.

'What is it, Clare? Who did you see?' says Pip.

'Nothing. Nothing at all,' she says. The sun is moving towards noon, and there's no shade in the street or at the foot of the castle walls. She suddenly longs for London; for the quiet little street they live on, the green smell of the air and the predictability of everything there.

'Well, shall we go back? I don't know about you but I need a cold drink and a sit-down,' says Marcie. They all have a wilted look; the kind of deflation that comes from setting out on an adventure but finding only mundane things — hot feet, thirst, and the discomfiting feeling of being unwelcome.

When they get back to the house Federico opens the door for them, and Clare, instinctively now, doesn't meet his eye. It bothers her that he might think it's his deformity that makes her look away, when in fact it's his scrutiny, which is like a constant question mark; whatever it is he wants to know, Clare doesn't want to answer. He has that look — of one trying to puzzle something out, and something about that makes her not trust him. As they come into the courtyard Leandro calls down to them from one of the upper storey verandas.

'Come up, come up! We're having a pre-lunch drink.'

'Oh *good*! We're *gasping*,' says Marcie. Boyd and Leandro are in cane chairs around a low table. There's a square of vivid cerulean sky above the courtyard, but the terrace is in shade. Boyd reaches out for Clare's hand as she sits by him, and squeezes it. His smile looks genuine, and she's reassured.

'Well, what do you think of our Gioia?' says Leandro. He's wearing a stone-coloured suit with a deep purple silk tie, part colonial gentleman, part dandy; he leans back in his chair and smiles, all ease.

'There are some truly beautiful buildings here,' says Clare. She opens her mouth to say something else, but can't think what. There's a pause, and Marcie shoots her a startled glance. 'It's charming,' she says but her voice is rather thin and unconvincing. She has never liked to lie, and prefers silence. Leandro smiles again, and his eyes slide away from her, and she knows she's insulted him. She daren't look at Boyd. 'Tell me, why do the people wear so much black? I'd have thought it would be terribly hot for them,' she says.

'The peasants, you mean?' says Marcie. 'I guess they like it because it doesn't show the dirt. They don't seem too keen on washing all that often.'

'Marcie,' Leandro rebukes her, gently enough, but his eyes are hard. 'It's not an easy life. These people are poor, they haven't enough to eat; they can't afford doctors. Their children don't thrive. And now, so soon after the war . . . they wear black because they are in mourning, Mrs Kingsley. Most of them have lost somebody.'

'I see,' says Clare, and senses Marcie's discomfiture beside her. She makes a point of not looking at her.

After lunch Leandro takes Pip down to the courtyard, and the big coaching doors swing open, and another car pulls in with its engine coughing and growling. Leandro stands with one hand in his pocket, his shoulders in a comfortable slouch. He watches Pip, and Clare sees his delight in Pip's reaction — the way Pip asks to see the engine, and runs his hand over a leather seat, and stands back, head cocked, to admire the overall proportions of the machine. She herself can see no real difference between this car and the other, apart from that this one is black, and the other red.

'Would you like to drive it, Philip?' says Leandro. Pip's face breaks into incredulous joy, and Leandro laughs. 'I can take that grin for a yes, I think?'

'Isn't that rather dangerous? He's really not old enough,' says Boyd.

'Not dangerous at all. I'll drive us out of town, where there are fewer things to run into, and then he can have a go. Well, lad — are you keen?'

'Absolutely!'

'Then let's go. But — gently, to begin with. If you crash into any trees or walls, I'll patch up the damage with your hide.'

'I won't crash,' says Pip eagerly. He waves to them as he climbs in, and Clare wonders at the ease with which Boyd's note of caution was swept aside, his permission not sought. As the car pulls away Boyd's cheeks turn an angry red.

In the silence after the engine noise there's the creak and thump of the doors as Federico closes and locks them again. Clare turns her back to him before he finishes the task, and goes back up to the veranda with Boyd. There's a small sofa and Boyd sits down beside her so that their shoulders and hips and thighs press together, in spite of the heat.

'Mr Cardetta likes your designs?' asks Clare, and Boyd smiles, and the tension of the moment before disappears. He rests his elbow on the back of the couch, trails his fingertips through the hair at her temple.

'Yes. I think so. He wants something more, though . . . I'm not quite sure what. He told me a lengthy tale about an abandoned castle near here . . . '

'The one in the centre of town?'

'No, another one, called Castel del Monte. But it was built by the same man. It has eight towers, each with eight sides, around an eight-sided courtyard. It has no kitchens, no stables, no discernible function . . . and yet it has obviously been designed with tremendous care and attention, using rare and expensive stone. It's high on a hill so it can be seen from miles and miles away in clear weather. But there's no sign of anyone ever having lived there.'

'It's a folly.'

'It's an enigma. And that's what he wants.'

'He wants octagonal towers high enough to be seen for miles around?' says Clare playfully, but Boyd barely smiles. He is thinking now, his mind has gone back to the problem.

'He wants symbolism. He wants people to look upon his works, and wonder.'

'But whatever for? Isn't it enough to be fashionable, and . . . display his largesse?'

'He wants something that will make all those people in town who think they know everything about him think again.' Boyd shakes his head.

'To show that he's different to them, and not afraid to be so?'

'I suppose so, yes.'

'And can you do that? Can you design him an enigma?'

'Let's hope so,' says Boyd, and he presses a kiss to the side of her head. 'Or we'll be here an awfully long time.' He smiles, and Clare laughs a little, but they know without saying that he's only half joking. There seems to be no question of refusing Leandro Cardetta anything he asks for.

They sit for a while, and the only sound is the occasional rattle of a passing cart, the clop of hooves and fall of booted feet. Boyd sighs, and curves his body towards her. He puts his hand on her knee then runs it higher, to the top of her leg, the outside edge of his little finger touching the crease between her thighs. With his other hand he tips her head back and kisses her neck. In that position it's hard to speak, but when Clare tries to lift her head he holds it there, with one hand on her forehead, her throat as bare as any sacrifice. Just for a moment. She has a sinking feeling, and shuts her eyes to ignore it.

'Darling,' she manages to say. 'Not here. Someone will see.'

'No one will see. The servants have all gone to rest, like Marcie.' His voice is deep, and his hand on her thigh grips tighter. Such ardour in the daytime is unlike him and she wonders if it has its origins in someone or something beyond herself. In the corner of her eye she catches a movement, down by the courtyard doors. She's up in an instant.

'That servant is watching; the driver,' she snaps, and changes her tone when she sees Boyd's face fall. 'Really, there's no privacy here.'

'Of course there is. But we'll go inside, if you like,' he says, standing up. 'Who do you mean — the fellow with the harelip?' He takes her hand, glancing over his shoulder at the empty courtyard. 'Are you sure?'

'Yes. I'm not sure that I like him. He . . . ' But she can't say why, exactly. Only that the thought of him watching them together curdles her stomach. Boyd loops his arm around her waist and pulls her closer. 'Anyway, darling, I'm not sure I'm in the mood,' she says, in a rush.

'But it's been such a long time, Clare.' The difference in their heights makes it difficult to walk so close together; their steps mistime. 'Haven't you missed me?'

'Yes, of course I have.'

'Well then. What's the problem?' Clare smiles and shakes her head, and some small part of her loathes the readiness of her capitulation.

Through glass doors off the veranda is a library, with a large desk at its centre that Boyd has been using for work. His pencils and pens are all there, lined up neatly in their boxes. Clare goes to look, to run her fingers across them, and the hard leather of the desk top. She does this sometimes — touches things before sex, to waken her senses. From behind, Boyd holds her, kisses her, pushes hard against her. She tries to mirror his passion but she can only think how strange it is that it's daylight, and they are not shut away where they should be. But when he puts his fingers into her, and his tongue deep into her mouth, and he undoes her blouse and pulls her bra down over her nipples, she clings to his shoulders and arches herself towards him, because this is a different kind of love-making to their norm, and that's at once alarming and welcome. And perhaps it is this kind of love-making — spontaneous and urgent — that makes a child, and they will look back in years to come, when that child does something silly, and smile fondly and joke in private that the baby was bound to be wild, since it had such wild beginnings. But Boyd stops with the head of his erection not quite touching her. Almost, but not quite. He shudders between her thighs; his eyes are rapt and he's breathing hard, but he stops.

'Wait here,' he says, as he hurries to do up his trousers. Then he leaves the room.

Clare is left with cold touches of his saliva and her own arousal smudged here and there on her skin. She crosses her arms over her chest and listens to her pulse slowing down. He has gone for the rubber sheath, and when he comes back he finishes the act with the barrier between them, and with all traces of her own passion lost Clare suddenly notices the thinning of his hair as he hunches over her, and the way the desk cuts into the backs of her thighs, and that he keeps his eyes tightly shut the whole time. He climaxes without a sound; she only knows it's happened because he stops breathing for the space of three heartbeats, or four — her slower heartbeats, not his rapid ones.

Afterwards, Boyd insists that they go and rest in their bedroom, though Clare wants to dress and sit outside in the shade. He uses water from the ewer to rinse the sheath in the wash bowl. Clare used to hate the sight of the thing. Once she thought about sabotage — she held it between her fingers, pinching it, assessing its strength and noting how easy it would be to put a few holes in it with the pin of a brooch. Now she feels that that would be cheating. If she's to defeat the thing, and be rid of it, she must do so fair and square, by convincing her husband. But she has less and less heart for the fight — the fire has gone out of her hatred of it; it's more a kind of detached dislike now, a resigned antipathy. The implications of that aren't lost on her, and they worry her. She doesn't want to be ready to give up yet. She pictures life at home with Boyd, in years to come, when he has retired and won't go out to the office every day; when Pip has left home, and will call when he remembers to. She pictures the slow march of time like this, and the terrible weight of her impending solitude. Letting these thoughts coalesce steels her to speak up again.

When the sheath is hanging next to the linen towel, drying, Boyd comes to lie beside her, like spoons.

'How do you find Gioia, really?' he says.

'It scares me,' says Clare. 'It felt like we shouldn't be here. Like it's no place for tourists.'

'We're not tourists.'

'What are we, then?' she says, but he doesn't reply. 'Marcie hates it here,' she adds.

'You think so?'

'I'm certain of it. Boyd,' she says carefully, 'will we never have a child? I so very much want to have one.'

'We have Pip, don't we?'

'Yes, but . . . it's not quite the same. Not for me. I'm not Pip's mother.'

'You're as good as a mother to him. You've raised him.' He kisses her hair. 'And made a splendid job of it.'

'You know what I'm asking, Boyd.' She takes a steady breath to keep hold of her nerve. 'Why don't you want us to have a baby?'

'Haven't we been over this, darling?'

'No, not really. You've told me you're afraid — but what's to be afraid of? I've waited and waited . . . I thought in time you'd be ready. But it's been ten years, Boyd. I'm almost thirty . . . There's not that much time left for it. You can't still be afraid, surely?'

'Clare, darling . . . ' He trails off; she waits.

'Did . . . was Emma damaged by childbirth? Is

106

that it? Did she . . . not quite recover from it?'

'No.' His voice is rough with strain. 'No, she was never the same afterwards. It was never the same afterwards. I . . . I started to lose her the day Philip was born, and I . . . I couldn't bear to lose you in the same way.'

'I'd be fine, I know I would. And I — '

'No, Clare,' he says, and now his voice has a hard edge. 'No. I just can't allow it.'

'You can't *allow* it?' she echoes desperately. But Boyd says nothing else.

Through the closed shutters Clare stares at incandescent bars of sky, and it seems wrong to banish the day. With a sudden itch of claustrophobia, she longs to be outside, even in the heat and the sunshine, because the air in the room feels stale and used up. She's hot beneath Boyd's arm; sweat blots her blouse in the small of her back, and his breath on her neck is stifling. She worms away slightly, shuffling her head across the pillow, but Boyd's arm tightens.

'I think I'll go out for a walk. Just a short one,' she says.

'A walk? Now? Don't be silly — it's the hottest part of the day. You can't.'

'But I don't feel like lying down.'

'Nonsense. You need to rest.' He kisses her hair, tugging a single strand that sticks to his lips. 'Why did you marry me, Clare?' he asks. This is another of the things, heard a hundred times before, that she wishes he wouldn't say. There's self-loathing underneath it, which turns the question into an accusation. She knows the answer she must give and says it quickly, to have it done,

107

because silence won't do.

'Because I loved you. I loved you straight away.'

Perhaps it's only half a lie, really. She did fall in love with him — a tall, handsome, older man with an air of sadness, and a hunted expression. At once she wanted to ease his pain. She wanted to be a reason for smiles, and optimism. Her parents introduced them at an afternoon tea in the back garden of their modest Kent home, on a fecund late June day when the borders were alive with bees and white butterflies; she'd already been told about Emma, and warned of his grief. As though that was the only thing about him worth mentioning. It seemed to Clare that he was a man who had lived one whole lifetime already; a man with a wealth and depth of experience that made him steady, and safe. His age reassured her. He struck her as kind but sad, and she wanted to make him happy; and in making him happy, she would make herself happy. His grief was proof of sensitivity, and she wanted to mend his broken heart. He was not overtly demonstrative but she came from a family of undemonstrative people, and she admired the quiet restraint of his grief, and the tender way he looked at her. Her father told her that Boyd wanted a young woman as his second wife; he wanted somebody untouched by grief, unscarred by life. Someone clean of heart and mind with whom to start afresh.

She hadn't found out about Pip's existence until after Boyd had proposed and she'd accepted. When she was told that Emma had died in childbirth, she'd assumed that the child had also been lost. *You needn't have anything to do with him, if you really don't want to,* said Boyd. *I'd understand; and he has his nanny, after all.* Clare had been so terrified at the idea of instantly becoming a mother that she hadn't time to be upset with Boyd for not telling her about him sooner. She thought about pulling out of the wedding, though it had already been announced in the newspaper; she suddenly, and for the first time, had the feeling of being rushed into something, of careering headlong with her eyes shut. But when she met Pip, sitting down to tea in a hotel in Marylebone, all her fears vanished. Aged just five, Pip said nothing, kept his eyes on his cake and ate it a crumb at a time. Clare had been certain he would hate her on principle, but there was none of that. He looked so frightened and lost that on instinct she reached under the table and took his hand; his expression mirrored exactly what she herself was feeling. She simply couldn't bear the thought that the small boy should be afraid of her, or of what her intrusion might mean for him. Pip didn't snatch his hand away, he looked at her in silent confusion — and immediately she wanted to stay with him; with them. She felt an instant affinity with him, and also sensed the gulf between him and his father, and she decided that she would bridge that gap. It all clicked into place, and she relaxed.

★ ★ ★

Later on, after dinner, Clare finds Pip in the very library where she and Boyd made love that afternoon. She's glad he's chosen a chair and isn't sitting at the desk, which she can't quite bring herself to look at. There was no shame in what they did, only impropriety, but somehow shame is what she does feel — shame not at the memory of them together, but of the minute she spent there alone, bare-breasted, while Boyd went out of the room for the sheath. She's ashamed of the controlled way he was able to stop himself in the midst of the moment, and of her own dispassion. Pip has an illustrated atlas of birds open across his knees, and is flicking through it without paying much attention.

'All right there, Pip? Are you bored to tears?' she says. He has already caught the sun, and in the lamplight he has a subtle glow. Beneath his shirt his shoulders and elbows are sharp angles.

'A bit. But this afternoon was the *best*. Leandro says he'll teach me to drive while we're here. Properly, I mean.'

'That's Mr Cardetta to you.'

'But he says to call him Leandro.'

'Even so . . . ' She's about to say more when a sound from outside stops her. Shouting, and the sudden clatter of footsteps. She and Pip share a quick look and then go together to the window that looks over the street.

Clare tilts the shutter slats flat and they peer out through them. There is more shouting, one voice louder than the rest, in words she can't understand.

'Open them properly, Clare, or we won't see a

110

thing,' says Pip. Clare does as he suggests, and they lean out to look along the length of Via Garibaldi, and down to the stone-flagged road. A loose column of men is marching along it, wearing the customary black, but no jackets. The sleeves of their shirts are rolled up; some of them have guns on belts around their hips, others carry short, sturdy wooden clubs. There are flashes of light where a badge or an emblem reflects the light, but they are too far away to make out. A man at the front has a peaked cap, like a policeman, and this is what Clare thinks at first — that they are police. She can think of no good reason why a police procession would be going on at night, and why the men aren't in uniforms, just dressed to identify with one another, to be seen as a group. The sight of them makes her uneasy. Their faces are mostly young, clean-shaven; their eyes have the feverish look of boys doing exciting things. 'Who are they, Clare?' asks Pip, loudly enough.

'Hush!' she says, though the chances of them being heard are small. She's suddenly absolutely certain that she doesn't want any one of the young men to look up and see them watching. 'I don't know,' she says quietly. There's more shouting, angry words, and figures flit here and there in the shadows on the dark side of the street, in the mouths of alleyways. The column keeps marching, and only changes direction when a rock is thrown — Clare thinks it's a rock — and lands with a loud smack and a scattering of dust at the leader's feet. The man in the peaked cap raises his arm to halt them, then

111

points; the men swerve suddenly, as one, and vanish into a side street. They make Clare think of a flock of birds, or a swarm of insects, homing in on something to eat.

Pip is uneasy now, too. They wait in silence, though there's nothing more to see except a woman in a long skirt, hair covered by a scarf, who hurries over to stand on the corner and peer cautiously after the armed marchers. A while later there's a loud, repeated banging, the sound of glass breaking, and a woman's scream. There's more shouting — one voice again, a man's, loud and aggrieved. Then he stops, and there's nothing else. Clare realises she's been holding her breath, and craning too far out of the window.

'Come in, Pip,' she says, grasping his sleeve. She closes the shutters again, latches them, checks that she's done it properly. Pip's eyes are wide and his face is blank with disquiet.

'What was all *that* about? Were they the police?' he says. 'Shall we go and ask Leandro? He's still up, I saw him go across the courtyard a little while ago.'

'It's Mr Cardetta, Pip, and no, let's not bother him now. It's probably nothing. Most likely nothing at all.'

'It didn't look like nothing. And it didn't *sound* like nothing,' says Pip huffily. Clare raises an eyebrow at him and he scowls but goes with her towards the bedrooms. But she can't blame him because he's right. It didn't look or sound like nothing. Clare suddenly thinks of the way she felt earlier, by the walls of the castle — the same way she felt just now, when she thought she might be seen by the marching men. *We shouldn't be here*, she thinks.

★ ★ ★

For two days, Clare thinks about the column of men all in black, but says nothing. For two days she thinks of the insistent way Boyd made love to her, and his refusal to give her a child, but says nothing. She's suddenly more aware than ever before of all the things she doesn't say, and she has that same prickling feeling as when Boyd's breath on the back of her neck was too hot, and his arm around her wouldn't loosen, and he wouldn't let her get up from the bed. It's a feeling like something building up, something gathering. Nobody else seems to notice, as the days settle into a pattern of sorts, and suddenly the thought of spending the whole summer that way makes Clare worry that the feeling could grow into something worse; into something like hysteria, or panic.

Boyd spends hours at the desk in the library, drawing and erasing and drawing again, frowning at his work but completely immersed. Pip has more driving lessons with Leandro, and in between he finds an old bicycle in one of the shady downstairs rooms that the servants inhabit, and rides it around the courtyard, in and out of the colonnades, like a little boy. When it gets a puncture Federico finds the hole using a basin of water, patches it and pumps the tyre back up. Clare sees them exchange a few words

113

and smile. The servant's cleft lip is less noticeable when he smiles — it evens itself out, and he keeps his mouth shut, as if ashamed of his teeth. When the bike is fixed the two young men shake hands before Pip remounts, and Clare wonders if she's being unfair in disliking Federico the way she does.

She spends a good deal of time reading. The library is stocked with works in Italian that have faded spines and dusty tops; they clearly came with the house and haven't been read in a generation. There are only a few books in English, which came with the Cardettas from New York, and Clare wishes she'd brought more with her. When she runs out of things to read, the hours will be even longer, her sense of suffocation harder to ignore. Marcie sews her clothes into new shapes, and writes long letters to friends in New York, and chatters and laughs; her smile flits from room to room like a nervous cat, and Clare wants to soothe her, somehow. But she doesn't know how to soothe a person who is outwardly joyful, and laughs at the merest thing.

'Tell me about London, go on,' says Marcie one afternoon. 'I've never been. Is it wonderful? It must be.'

'Well, I like it very much. The place where we live — Hampstead — is very quiet and green, nothing like the centre of London. There's a huge hill you can walk up, to get a view of the city to the south. There are lots of little teashops and places to eat lunch; the children go on donkey rides and splash about in the swimming

114

ponds. It's lovely . . . '

'But don't you go into the city? Don't you go dancing?'

'Well . . . yes, we do. Not very often — Boyd spends all day there, you see, at work. He likes to come home to the peace and quiet. And he never was much interested in dancing. We go to the theatre quite often.'

'And shopping? There must be wonderful shops.'

'Yes,' says Clare. 'Yes, there are.' She doesn't elaborate, though she can see Marcie's frustration at her reticence. She doesn't want to say that the wife of a modest architect shops rarely, and then in small ladies' outfitters, not at Liberty or Harrods.

'But what do you *do* all day, Clare?'

'Well, I . . . ' Clare pauses. Her first impulse is to defend their quiet life, but then there are the murmurings of panic she feels at the thought of Pip leaving home — of not having him to look forward to; of being alone with the serene slide of the afternoons, waiting for Boyd to come home, and the amorphous disappointment of the evenings once he has. At the thought of being alone during one of his bad spells, when his silence and self-destruction might drive her mad. 'I suppose it can be a little dull,' she says. 'But for the most part I'd rather have dull than frantic.'

'Would you? Golly, I'd far rather have frantic!' says Marcie. 'But then, when you love your husband there's always fun to be had — the best kind. Am I right?' She smiles wickedly, and

115

winks at Clare, and Clare can only nod, embarrassed, because fun isn't a word she has ever associated with Boyd.

The days are uniformly hot and bright. Clouds sometimes gather in the afternoon, but they slink sheepishly into the night as it falls, and are gone by morning. As to how exactly Leandro Cardetta fills his days, Clare can only wonder. He comes and goes, and is rarely in one room for long. On the third afternoon, as the sun begins to mellow, Leandro suggests they join in the *passeggiata* with Gioia's *signori*. Marcie declines with a headache, lying across a long couch in the shade like a fallen leaf; Boyd looks up from his desk when Clare goes to fetch him, and shakes his head.

'I'm on to something here, darling. You carry on without me,' he says.

'Please come, Boyd. I really don't want to go on my own.'

'Don't be silly. Of course you must go, if Cardetta's asked you to.'

'But I just . . . don't know him all that well yet. I'd far rather you came too. Won't you?' The thought of being alone with their host unsettles her; though he's only ever solicitous and polite, still there's something arch and knowing about him.

'Not now, Clare. Take Pip with you, if you need company.' Clare goes back down to where Leandro is waiting, and he smiles as though he can sense her reserve.

With Pip, they stroll along Via Garibaldi first one way and then the other. People are not quite as ready to snub Leandro as they were Marcie.

When he greets them it's with a subtle positioning of his body that makes them stop walking; he stands just enough in their way that brushing past him would be obvious and rude. Clare can almost follow their conversation in Italian, but the southern accent is strange to her; some words elude her, and as she chases after them she misses what comes next. Pip's face mirrors incomprehension, but when Leandro introduces him to someone, he shakes the men's hands with a confident *buona sera*.

'This is one of our distinguished doctors here in Gioia, Dr Angelini,' says Leandro, as Clare shakes the hand of a short, fat man whose face and grey hair shine with grease. 'Well, I say distinguished doctor, what I really mean is revolting quack. This man fleeces the poor of Gioia, selling fake medicines supplied to him by his brother, the druggist; and he examines the women far too enthusiastically — I'm sure you don't need me to elaborate. I don't believe he ever even graduated, and he's the first to flee his post for Rome when cholera breaks out. Don't worry, he can't speak a word of English,' he says, all in the same convivial tone, as Dr Angelini smiles and tilts his head obsequiously. Clare struggles not to show her surprise, and Pip gives a quiet guffaw before he can help himself. The doctor's eyes narrow suspiciously, and Cardetta says something to him, evenly and with no trace of inappropriate humour. The man inclines his head again, but glares at Pip as they part.

Clare steals a sideways glance at Leandro Cardetta as they walk on, and his smile is roguish in response.

'That was so funny!' says Pip, and Clare almost hushes him censoriously, then realises that to do so could be a slight to Leandro.

'You didn't approve of my introduction, Mrs Kingsley?' he says.

'I was just a little . . . caught unawares,' she says. They're walking west into the glaring sun, and her eyes are fighting the light.

'I'd hoped you'd find it refreshing. Unpleasant people deserve to be mocked, after all.' He shrugs. His way of speaking is unusual; the New York accent is quite soft for one who learnt English there, and the imprint of Italian intonation is on every word.

'Why trouble yourself to know them, if you dislike them so?'

'Ah, alas, Mrs Kingsley, in order to be somebody, you must know everybody.'

'What kind of somebody do you want to be?' says Pip. He has become far too familiar with their host since the driving lessons began. And yet Leandro Cardetta doesn't seem to mind at all, and Clare wonders then if all her misgivings — about Gioia del Colle, about Federico and Leandro — are only in her mind, brought on by the tension she senses in Boyd. Jumping at shadows.

'I want to be listened to, Philip,' says Leandro Cardetta. 'I am no idealist. I know that for a *terrone* like me, their respect will always have to be bought. But however I must get it, I *will* get it.' Clare says nothing, and he glances at her again. 'You don't approve, Mrs Kingsley?'

'Oh, I'm sure I know little enough about it.' His smile turns a little stiff.

'Ah, I sense that old British maxim, hovering on your tongue — that respect must be earned to be of value,' he says. 'Your husband has said the same thing to me before, but it isn't always true. If the people I have to deal with only understand money and power, then that's the path I must take with them. I learnt in New York there's a way to get to everybody, you only have to know how to find it. And I didn't work my way up from nothing over there to be dismissed by people who've done nothing in life but sit and squander it, growing fatter and lazier and stupider all the while.'

'But why come back, then, if you'll be forced to be friends with people you don't like?' says Pip.

'Friends? Oh, I have no friends here. But this is my home, in spite of all of it. I remember these streets from when I was a tiny child. This stink . . . ' He takes a deep breath. 'The taste of it. Can you know what that means, Pip? Perhaps you're too young yet. I lived in America for a long time, but every day — every day — I thought of coming home. Now I'm here, and I'm not wanted. Well, too bad. I'm home. And home I will stay.' There's no room for manoeuvre in this whatsoever. Clare wonders how often Marcie has come up against the same brick wall, and feels sorry for her.

'What business were you in in New York, Mr Cardetta?' says Clare. 'Will you pursue the same business here?'

'Waste disposal.' He smiles at her, pleased by her surprise. 'Not what you were expecting? There's a hell of a lot of people in New York, creating a hell of a lot of garbage. And no, those days are over. There's almost no rubbish in Gioia — haven't you noticed? What the poor don't eat, the dogs do.'

They walk on a little further, and pass a group of three men as immaculately dressed as Leandro, standing at a corner with their waistcoats buttoned up and gold watch chains catching the light, and no dust on their shoes. Leandro stiffens; it makes him look taller, stronger.

'*Buona sera, signori*,' he greets them, inclining his head but not stopping. Clare starts to smile but stops in the face of their blatant hostility. One of the men spits, off to one side rather than at them, but the insult is clear.

'You've no right to speak to us, *cafone*,' that man says, darkly, in English. 'You've no right to wear those clothes, or live in that house.'

'You look well, Cozzolino. The season agrees with you,' Leandro says mildly. Once they've passed Clare feels the men's eyes glare after them, and she daren't look back.

'That man was so rude . . . what's a caffoney?' says Pip.

'*Cafone* means peasant riff-raff. Don't look so horrified, Mrs Kingsley. Cozzolino doesn't deserve to be respected, let alone feared. He's the worst kind of Gioia *signori*. He thinks his rank is God-given, and excuses all and any excess. But it'll catch up to him, sooner or later.'

120

'I don't know how you can stand to be spoken to that way. It was horrible,' says Clare.

'Sooner or later, they'll have to get used to me. I mean to give them no choice.' He glances at her again as they walk back towards Piazza Plebiscito. 'I never thought a Briton would be so shocked to see class prejudice in action, I must say.'

'There's no excuse for bad manners. And I suppose I . . . I've never . . . '

'Been at the sharp end of it?'

'Yes. I couldn't stand to have to associate with such people.'

'You would stay away, and let them win? I have a thick skin, Mrs Kingsley — it's impossible to get anywhere either here or in New York without one. But I don't forget these slights.' He taps one finger on the side of his head. 'One day Cozzolino might regret talking down to me the way he does. Or perhaps you think he's right? You think high society is no place for an *arriviste* like me?'

'No,' says Clare, nervous of the edge in his voice. 'No, I don't think that at all.'

'In a small place like Gioia, this is how politics works, Mrs Kingsley. It's all about who you know, and who you pay. Imagine if I ended up in city hall one day! Then I could really make a difference here. But it'll only happen if I make myself one of them, at least outwardly. It'll be a long process, and perhaps a distasteful one, but every game has a set of rules.'

'Ought democracy be a game?' says Clare.

'I didn't make the world.' Leandro shrugs.

121

'Politics was ever a dirty business.'

'Then I think I'd rather not be involved at all.'

'But, Mrs Kingsley, that's no solution! Women may vote in your country, now — isn't that so? Don't tell me you don't exercise that right?'

'Once I turn thirty, I may vote. But I won't have the first idea who I should vote for. I suppose I'll take Boyd's lead on it. Politics has never really interested me, truthfully. Better that I leave it to those who understand it,' she says. Leandro grunts. He walks with his hands linked behind him, studying his fancy shoes for a while.

'For you, politics is something that happens in the newspapers. Decisions made at a distance to you, which have no obvious effect on your life. Is that not so? Easy to ignore it, then. Here in Puglia, politics is something that happens on your doorstep; it's something that happens *to you*, whether you're interested or not. Politics can take food out of your mouth, and impoverish your family. It can make you unemployable, and land you in prison. It's not possible to ignore it, to be uninterested.' Feeling his rebuke, Clare says nothing; the silence is awkward.

'I hope you do get to be mayor,' says Pip, and Clare is grateful. 'Then that man won't dare to be rude to you.' Leandro chuckles.

'Wouldn't it be funny, watching him try to be civil?' He flashes Pip his lupine grin.

Just then there's a commotion in Piazza Plebiscito, immediately up ahead. They are at the edge of the square and a loose ring of people have stopped to watch; they shift on their feet, nervous, uncertain. Wearing the peasant black, these could be the same aimless men Clare noticed before; one or two of them call out words in the dialect, but the men they're watching don't pay them any attention. These others are three men in black shirts, with batons in their hands, standing every bit as poised but with none of the uncertainty of the onlookers. A fourth is putting his shoulder to the door of a house that opens onto the square; his teeth are gritted, snarling, and he grunts each time he drives himself into it. With the other people whose evening strolls have brought them unexpectedly on this spectacle, Clare, Pip and Leandro stop still, paused in the act of turning away.

'Are they the police? Are they going to arrest somebody?' says Pip.

'We should go,' says Clare, and finds that her throat has gone dry, but Leandro neither moves nor speaks. He watches the scene with an unreadable intensity. So Clare and Pip watch too, and she's sure that whoever the men are, they're not the police. With a crash of splintering wood the door gives way and the men are inside. Somewhere above, a woman shouts incomprehensible words; there's the scuff and thud of footsteps on wooden stairs. The ring of onlookers take an involuntary step forwards, as one, but again, something stops them. They are afraid, Clare realises. They are horribly afraid. *We should go.*

Thirty seconds later the men in black emerge, bringing another man out between two of them. The man is middle-aged, his neat beard shot with grey. He has round, wire spectacles; he's slightly built, and they have messed up his hair so that it flops onto his forehead. He walks with a certain reluctance but offers no real resistance. He is dignified, and Clare exhales a little, thinking the worst is over.

'Do you know who that . . . ' she begins to ask, but then words abandon her. Once they are clear of the house the man's arms are released. He reaches up and straightens his spectacles with the index finger of his right hand, then one of the men in black raises his baton and strikes him viciously around the side of his head. It makes a horrible sound, meaty and oddly hollow. The man's spectacles fly off as his head cracks around; Clare hears them rattle as they hit the ground. The man falls down, boneless; there's a spray and spatter of blood. His left eye socket looks odd and collapsed but he must still be awake because he curls himself up and tucks his elbows in, as if that will protect him as more blows fall, the four batons rising and falling, again and again, clenched in white-knuckled hands. They kick him too, driving their booted feet into the soft parts of his body for a long time after he has stopped moving; they are breathing hard when they finish. Clare doesn't see them go — she doesn't see if they saunter, or run away like guilty men. She can only see the crumpled, broken man on the paving stones, and his ruined little spectacles next to him. And then she sits down, without blinking, as if she owes him her undivided attention, and Pip throws up beside her.

* ★ *

Boyd wakes her hours later, with darkness outside the shutters. He turns on the bedside light and it sends a stabbing pain into her skull.

'How are you now?' He takes her hand in one of his and brushes the fingers of the other over her cheek.

'I want us to go.' Clare sits up carefully. She's finding it hard to think because the world is a different place than it was before — it's dangerous and unknowable; there are killers in the shadows. She suddenly knows, in a way she didn't before, how breakable she is. How easily she might die. She's still wearing the clothes she had on for the *passeggiata*, and when she looks down she expects there to be blood on them. A shudder courses through her. 'All of us, you, me and Pip. I want us to go home.'

'Clare — ' Boyd shakes his head.

'Please, Boyd. There's something terrible going on here, and I don't want to be here while it happens . . . I don't want Pip to be here! For pity's sake, Boyd — your fifteen-year-old son just saw a man beaten to death!'

'He's not dead, apparently. He was still alive when he was carried — '

'Is that somehow supposed to make it better?'

'Doesn't it?'

'Well. If he lives, then . . . then I'm glad. But it changes nothing, Boyd. We don't belong here.' She wishes she could stop shaking but the tremors seem to come from the very core of her, rattling up from her bones implacably.

125

'We can't leave, darling.' Boyd shakes his head, calmly regretful. The lamp lights him from below, and puts deep shadows under his eyes. He sits down on the edge of the bed, his spine a long curve, his shoulders collapsing around him. Clare wants to shake him, the way she has been shaken.

'*Why* not? You've had time to get to know this building . . . You could work well enough from Bari, or Rome. Or from London — from *home*, Boyd.'

'That's just not possible.' He stands up and drops her hand; walks to the end of the bed and then back again.

'But why?'

'Because I've given my word, Clare! Leandro asked me to come out here and work with him on this, and I agreed. I can't go back on that.'

'Why can't you? I'm sure he'd understand — any reasonable person would understand!'

'It's not *possible*, Clare!' he cries, standing in front of her, looking down, clenching his hands into fists. Clare stares for a long moment. She doesn't understand him; just then she feels she hardly knows him. When she speaks it's almost a whisper.

'Why are you so afraid of him, Boyd? Whatever happened between you, in the past? Something did — something happened in New York, didn't it?' Boyd stares down at her, and tears spring up, shining in his eyes.

'Nothing,' he says roughly, and they both know it's a lie. 'That's enough. You're my wife and I . . . need your support. I have made my decision.'

'But Pip and I don't need to stay — I never gave my word to stay, and Cardetta can't possibly expect us to. Come with us, Boyd,' she begs.

'Clare, no. You may not leave. I can't bear to be here without you.' Clare can feel the erosion of her resolve — the precise way in which it crumbles, from the edges to the core — but behind it is the thought of staying in Gioia for the rest of the summer, which causes a sickening lump to form, low down in her throat. She fights against her fear of standing her ground, of meeting him head on, unbalancing him.

'I'm . . . going to go and see Pip.' She stands gingerly, half expecting the floor to break beneath her feet, and leaves him there by the bed, buckled in on himself. She goes barefoot to Pip's room.

Pip is sitting in the window again, wrapped up with his dressing gown pulled tight around him, as if he's cold. There's an untouched supper on a tray by the bed, and a cup of milky coffee that has dried into a saggy skin across the top. Pip's face is ashy white, and Clare goes and hugs him, holding his head to her shoulder, until after a moment he puts his arms around her and she feels a single sob rock through him.

'He wasn't even trying to get away,' he says, muffled and bewildered.

'I know, darling.'

'Why did they attack him like that, then? Why didn't the police come?'

'I don't know, Pip. I don't understand it either. We'll be home soon, I promise. We won't stay, you and I. All right? We'll go home.' There's a thrill as she says this; she's never disobeyed Boyd before.

'All right. Good.' Pip nods, and pulls away from her, and Clare runs her hands through his hair to straighten it, and tries to smile. His eyes are enormous.

'I felt like I was part of it. I felt like I was as bad as them, because I just watched and didn't do anything to help. That poor man. He wasn't even trying to get away. Do you think those were the same men we saw the other night? Do you think they were on their way to do that to someone else when we saw them?'

'Shh . . . Try not to think about it too much, Pip. There was nothing we could have done. It was . . . awful. It was just awful, I know. We'll go soon, I promise.'

'You promise?' he echoes, too upset to be embarrassed about the tears streaking down his cheeks. Clare nods, kisses her fingers and presses them to his forehead. 'You're shaking,' he says, and Clare smiles.

'I can't seem to stop. I'm like a bowlful of jelly,' she says.

'I threw up on Mr Cardetta's shoes,' he says tonelessly. 'You know, the black and white ones, with the fancy stitching?'

'Whoops-a-daisy,' Clare murmurs, and is rewarded with a tiny glimpse of his smile. But her throat feels itchy and hot, and she's aware of her heart beating, harder than normal, tight against her ribs.

* ★ ★

In the morning Clare has coffee in her room, near the window so she can see the sky. She doesn't want to go downstairs or eat, she doesn't want to see Leandro Cardetta, and when Marcie comes to flutter around her, fussing and cooing in her fragile way, she is all but unresponsive. She can't seem to find the energy for more because she keeps hearing the rattle of wire spectacles hitting the ground, and Boyd has sunk into the silence that she dreads, and she knows that she's the direct cause of it. But she can't bring herself to say she'll stay; she's as afraid of upsetting Boyd as she is of staying in Gioia. She's torn, and hoping for him to tell her she can go home. She reads without absorbing a word, and jumps every time there's a noise from the street. She was witness to a crime, so the perpetrators have reason to come after her — her and Pip. But then, there were plenty of witnesses. If witnesses were a worry to them, they would not have gone in broad daylight to batter the slim man with the wire spectacles. They had *wanted* people to see them at their work. Clare lowers her book as she realises this, and nearly drops it when there's a knock at the door. She doesn't answer, but a second or two later it opens anyway, and Leandro walks slowly over to where she's sitting.

He stands and watches her for a moment or two, and Clare wishes she could read him better. She struggles to hold his gaze, when her own wants to slide away from him and hide.

Eventually he sighs a little, and shakes his head.

'Mrs Kingsley, I am so sorry.' He waits, as if she ought to fill the pause, but she has nothing to say to this. 'I'm well aware how distressing it must have been for you, and the boy, to witness such a thing.'

'Thing? Mr Cardetta, that was not a thing. That was a murder.' Her voice wobbles on the final word.

'The man lives — '

'For now, and by pure chance.'

'I understand that you're upset, but please, don't be so quick to leave — not when you've barely arrived.'

'It seems entirely inappropriate that we're here at all, Mr Cardetta. There's clearly some kind of . . . crisis going on here. Perhaps nobody wants to acknowledge it, but there it is. Pip and I have no place here, whatever my husband says.' She takes a breath to steady herself; Leandro watches her carefully. 'Who was that man? The man they beat?'

'His name is Francesco Molino. He was — he is — an advocate for the reforms; a key voice in the peasant league.'

'And the men who attacked him?' At this Leandro pauses, and Clare can see him choosing what to tell her, how much to reveal. She holds his gaze.

'Mrs Kingsley, you are quite right. There is a crisis here — in truth, there's a war. Nobody is calling it that, yet, but that's what it is. There is a war going on between the farm labourers and the men who own and run the farms. And I

130

believe the tide is turning. After the Great War ended things went in the workers' favour. There was so much anger and hardship, and the time was ripe for change. But the proprietors have a new weapon now.'

'Those men?' says Clare, and Leandro nods.

'Members of the new fascist party — squads paid by the wealthy to . . . turn the tide back their way. To break strikes, and undermine the socialist movement. You have nothing to fear from them, of course. You're not a part of this.'

'How can you say that after what happened yesterday? And how can they just . . . do what they want like that, with no fear of arrest or censure?'

'This is not Britain, Mrs Kingsley; this is not even Italy. This is *Puglia*. The local branch of the fascist party, begun here only in June, was founded by members of the police force.'

'You mean . . . they may act as they please? They have official sanction — the law is with them?'

'No. They have unofficial sanction, and the money is with them. That's far more important down here.'

From the garden below the window Clare hears Boyd's and Pip's voices, echoing slightly, making a calm sound. Leandro pulls up a chair to face Clare and sits down.

'I have a proposition for you,' he says, lacing his fingers and watching her over the top of them. 'Stay here in Puglia, but not here in Gioia. Not in town.'

'No, Mr Cardetta. I want to go home, and so

131

does Pip. Boyd may even come too, if I can convince him. You have been an excellent host, but I don't understand why my husband can't work on his plans for your new façade from somewhere else. He won't tell me . . . he . . . '
She shakes her head. The trembling has stopped, outwardly, but she can still feel it in her gut, like aftershocks. 'He insists that he must remain here with you, even if he won't explain why. So — please — let him go. Let him come away with me and Pip.'

'Stay, for his sake. Even I can see that he's happier, and works better, when you're with him. We can all see the good you do him.'

'But you just said yourself, there's a war on here! How can you ask us to stay?'

'Stay for his sake, and . . . stay for Marcie's sake. Please. I have a *masseria* outside of Gioia — a farm deep in the countryside, in a tranquil place where none of these troubles will come near you. You and Marcie and the boy can go there, Boyd and I can travel back and forth as we need to. Mrs Kingsley, I know my wife isn't happy here. I'm not blind. If only you could see how much good it's done her to have your company! These past three days she's been more like she was when I first knew her — more like she was in New York — than at any time since we moved here. Please. Go to the *masseria*. My wife needs you, and your husband needs you, and I need your husband.'

Leandro keeps his steady black eyes on her until she feels skewered, and knows that however much she twists there'll be no breaking free. She

132

has that same choking feeling that she knows so well, that feeling of something around her throat. It helps her not to agree; the silence grows until it seems to ring. 'This is very important,' says Leandro eventually, softly, still not breaking his gaze. 'I may not speak freely about everything that concerns me, and I can only ask your forgiveness for that. But I can't allow you to leave yet. I'm afraid I *will not* allow it.' Clare stares at him, stunned mute. She can't quite believe what she's heard, but there's no mistaking that Leandro is entirely in earnest. He is steely with it, too sharp to touch. 'Do you understand, Mrs Kingsley?' In his face, in his tone, she sees the truth. She is entirely subject to his will, entirely at his command; they all are. *When Leandro goes off it's like a volcano*, Marcie said. Clare's pulse flickers in her neck; she has to swallow before she can speak.

'Very well,' she says, and Leandro's answering smile is warm and relieved, and all trace of the threat disappears.

Word is sent ahead to Cardetta's *masseria* — the Masseria dell'Arco — to be ready for their arrival, and they stay the rest of the day in Gioia while Clare and Pip repack their things, and Marcie fills a steamer trunk with clothes and shoes and make-up. She seems as giddy about the change in plans as if they've decided to go on a picnic or to a gala of some kind.

'You're going to love the *masseria*, Pip,' she declares, as they sit down to dinner and Clare has the manic sensation that they're all fiddling

133

as Rome burns. She glances from face to face to see if anyone else senses anything amiss, but they are all acting as though nothing has happened, and she can't work out if it's her who's unreal, or if it's them. Only Pip can't keep his disquiet from showing. He's bounced back from his shock with the resilience of youth, and by sleeping fourteen hours overnight, but he's still quiet and his eyes, when nobody's talking to him, have a far-off look. 'It's like a kind of castle, really. Built to keep out marauding bandits, aeons ago. Lots to explore, and lots of animals too. Do you like animals?'

'Yes. I like dogs — I should like to have a dog.'

'Well, we have plenty of dogs there!' Marcie beams at him. 'Plenty of cows and horses and mules too, but they're far less fun, I know.'

'They're farm dogs, mind you,' Leandro cautions. 'They're not pets, so don't try to play with them until they know you.'

'Oh, darling, of course he won't! Pip's not silly,' says Marcie. 'And the stars! You won't believe the number of stars.' When the food arrives everybody eats, including Pip, but Clare finds that it all tastes of nothing; her tongue seems numb, and even though her stomach feels caved in with hunger, when she tries to swallow it almost makes her gag. Boyd takes her hand under the table and squeezes it with a quiet intensity. She doesn't look at him, and drinks her wine too quickly.

Federico drives the two women and Pip out to the farm in the red Alfa Romeo. The men will

134

follow in a couple of days, and as they leave Clare turns to look up at Boyd from the back seat, so that her last view is of his face thrown into shadow as the car pulls away. He stands with his shoulders slumped, and when he kissed her goodbye minutes before there was something feverish about it, something frantic in the press of his lips that almost made her recoil. The car's headlights lance ahead through the darkness; a plume of dust and fumes trails behind it. Clare thinks of her promise to Pip — that they would go home soon — and wonders if he remembers it. If he will challenge her about it. Right now he seems distracted enough by Marcie and her constant talk. She sits in the front seat next to Federico, and turns back to face them.

'Do you know, there's a raised area in one of the old bedrooms at the *masseria* — it used to be where the bed would have stood, but we don't use that room at the moment because there's a hole in the corner of the roof and bats get in and swing from the rafters — bats! Can you believe it?' She shudders theatrically. 'I'd smoke 'em out, if it was up to me, but Leandro says to let them be. Let them be! We don't need that room! Well, he has some strange notions, sometimes. But — anyway — the platform would make a very fine stage. What say you and I have a few acting lessons together, Pip, and maybe put on a bit of a play? What do you say?'

'All right. That'd be good. What play should we do?'

'Whatever you'd like. We've no texts, of course, but we can do our own version of

135

whatever story you like. We could even write a script ourselves.'

'How about *Dracula*? Then we could use the bats as extra members of the cast,' says Pip with a grin, and Marcie chuckles.

'How about *Macbeth* — we can use real wool of bat for the witches' potion!'

'How about *Antony and Cleobatra*?'

'*The Merry Bats of Windsor*?'

'*The Taming of the Bat*?'

Marcie tips back her head and laughs, and Clare is grateful to her because Pip is laughing too, pleased to have amused her, and he seems to have forgotten what they saw yesterday. Clare can't even find a smile. She feels as though somebody is pressing a knife to her throat; she hardly dares move. She leans her forehead against the cool glass and stares out at the walls and scrubby trees blurring past as the car rumbles along the dirt road, its headlights giving the world a sickly cast. And then they pass a man, sitting slumped against the wall beside the road with his face turned up to the sky. They are past him in a heartbeat, and Clare turns to look back but he has vanished into the darkness. It's late in the evening and they are far from town, and something in his posture makes her think he's not just resting, not just star-gazing — he's in trouble. In her mind's eye batons rise and fall, and she fears for him, takes a breath, and for a moment the words hover on her lips: *Stop the car. Go back.* But she stays silent and he is behind them, and this is one more thing that she doesn't say, and has no power to change. She feels exhausted and afraid. She feels like surrendering but doesn't know to whom, or what her battle is. They arrive at the *masseria* soon afterwards and go straight to their beds. Clare has the impression of massive stone walls and the smell of cow manure. She's so tired she can barely climb the stairs, but then she sleeps only fitfully, skimming through dreams that she knows would frighten her if she could see them clearly.

★  ★  ★

Every wall of the *masseria* is painted white, and in the morning sunshine it's painful to look at. The place is arranged in a square around a large courtyard, its solid, flat rooflines like shoulders hunched against the world, and the only way in or out is via the huge archway that gives the place its name, tunnelling under the full width of the rooms above it, fifteen feet or more, and closed off by wooden doors twelve feet high. One and a half sides of the quadrangle are barns and storage sheds for grain and animals and equipment, with servants' rooms above; these have reinforced gates that open only outwards, not into the courtyard. The dairy forms another side, and then the living quarters rise up three storeys, and only open inwards, not outwards. If the place came under attack, this inner keep would be well protected.

It's early and Pip is still asleep; Clare sits with Marcie, who is quieter before noon, at a table on a partly covered terrace over the dairy, accessed via an exterior stone stairway. The cows have been and gone from milking; Clare heard the soft clatter of their feet, and occasional lows of discontent, sometime soon after dawn. She looks out at the view over the barns, at the parched brown fields and their grey stone walls, and hears the breeze making a low thrum as it rolls along the shallow crease in the land where the *masseria* is situated, and through a forbidding thicket of prickly pear. A dog barks, not far away, and the leathery leaves of a fig tree rattle against the outside wall of the dairy; other than that, the stillness is striking.

'Are you all right, Clare? Did you sleep?' says Marcie. Clare manages to shake her head, but can't speak. For a while she feels Marcie watching her, from one side, then: 'Poor little mouse.' And it might be sympathetic, or an accusation of cowardice.

Clare still can't bring herself to eat, though she knows she should. After two nights of failed sleep the hunger makes her unsure if she's quite awake, or if her eyes are even open, and though she knows Marcie spoke a few minutes ago, she can't quite remember what she said. Something about the weather, perhaps, or about the day to come. When she sips her coffee, she's surprised to find it gone cold. When she looks up to ask Marcie if a fresh pot could be brought, she finds that she's alone at the table, and for some reason this makes her want to weep. She stares out along the gentle curve of the land, squinting into the distance, and tries to think what she ought to do next. She must not be so strange once Pip is up, but everything is different and unsafe and she can't think of a way back to a logical scheme of things, a way back to normality, where she knows what's expected of her, or what to expect of those around her. She has no idea what's happening. There's some commotion down in the courtyard, and the creak of the gate opening, but she pays it no heed. Only when figures appear, directly in her line of sight, does she blink and try to focus.

Two men and a woman stand in front of her, the smaller of the men supported by the larger, who has the face and physique of a movie star. There's a revolting smell with them, a smell of rot and corruption.

'*Signora Cardetta, Signora Cardetta, scusi . . . Ettore . . .* ' the movie star says, and then something else she can't decipher, and Clare shakes her head. They're looking for Marcie, this odd trio. The woman has a raw-boned face and a gaze like a whip crack. Her hair is hidden under a scarf and there are two damp patches on the front of her blouse, over her nipples. *Where is her baby?* Clare wonders. The knees of the smaller man are sagging, and his head lolls on the other man's shoulder, but just then he gasps, his eyes open and they find Clare's. And suddenly she is wide awake. His hair is black and his skin as swarthy as any she's seen in Puglia, stretched tight over cheekbones like razors, but his eyes are electric blue — a ridiculous, unreal blue like a shallow ocean on a sunny day. The colour of them hits her like a slap in the face, and for a few seconds it's all she can see; his expression is at once bewildered and full of wonder, and she longs to know why. And then his eyes roll back and he collapses, and there's a sudden strange expansion inside her head, like something swelling up at speed, and bursting.

The peasants consider love, or sexual attraction, so powerful a force of nature that no amount of will-power can resist it . . . good intentions and chastity are of no avail . . . So great is the power of the god of love and so simple the impulse to obey him that there is no question of a code of sexual morals or even of social disapproval for an illicit affair.

*Christ Stopped at Eboli*
Carlo Levi

# Ettore

Ettore wakes up because he's thirsty. His throat feels torn. When he opens his eyes things swing around his head in a giddy blur that slowly resolves itself into walls, window, ceiling, floor; all of them sunlit with extravagant brightness. He blinks and tries to sit up, and the room tilts again. He hears a soft gasp and movement, and then there are hands on his shoulders; small hands with clean, pale skin.

'Take it easy, Ettore. Lie down. Welcome back to the land of the living, honey.' It takes him a minute to understand — the words are in a language he must pick apart and process, not one he knows in his bones.

'Marcie?' he says.

'That's right, I'm here. You nearly weren't, for a while there. Jesus! You scared us. Why on earth didn't you come for help sooner? Honestly.' He feels the mattress dip as she sits down on the edge of it, and turns to look at her. Her face has lines of concern, and faint shadows under the eyes. Ettore searches in his head for the right words to answer her. The effort wears him out.

'Water? Please. How much time here?'

'Here. Sip, don't gulp.' She hands him a glass of water and he drinks it so quickly he almost chokes. He feels like he could never have enough of it. A cough sends it shooting into his nose. 'Like I said,' says Marcie, shaking her head as

143

she refills it for him. 'That gorgeous friend of yours delivered you here three days ago. What's his name? Penno? Your sister came too but they've both gone back to Gioia now — reluctantly, mind you. Only when the doctor had actually been and seen you, and they were sure you were going to live. Sorry — am I speaking too quickly? I always forget.'

'How much time?' Ettore tries again, when Marcie breaks her incomprehensible babble.

'Three days.' Marcie holds up three fingers, and Ettore nods.

'Leandro?'

'He'll be here tomorrow. Tomorrow — *domani*. Now, please rest. Don't be a man, and try to run before you can walk.' She says something else but Ettore can't hear her. With the water in his stomach he slides back senseless.

\* \* \*

When he next wakes the room is empty but for an orange glow of late afternoon light. The room is not large but it has a high, vaulted ceiling, all painted white like the walls; there are red and white tiles on the floor and windows twice his height in two of the walls, front and back. He stands gingerly and finds that his leg hurts a lot less than it did. It hurts, but the pain is no longer the only thing he can think about. He still doesn't want to put weight on it, however. He's wearing a pair of loose trousers that aren't his, and when he rolls up the left leg to look at his shin, the wound looks wider, but it's dry, and

144

less angry. The trenches smell of it has gone. There's a wooden crutch, a proper one, leaning on the wall by the bed, and he grabs it. With his head spinning Ettore drinks more water, then goes to the front window and steps out onto the little balcony to look out. He knows he's at Masseria dell'Arco, his uncle's farmhouse. At once he feels trapped, anxious to leave. He thinks of the three days of work he has missed; he wonders what Paola and Valerio have been finding to eat. What Paola has had to do for Poete to coax some stolen milk or cheese from him. His hands curl around the balcony rail in frustration, and he stares out along the dirt road that leads away from the farm.

There's a large, walled-in patch of ground to the front of the main buildings, called the *aia*. On a paved area here, threshed wheat is already piled high, drying, waiting to be shovelled into sacks. There's a set of iron gates by which to enter and leave, guarded by a conical stone *trullo* hut where a man sits, night and day, to keep watch. There will be more guards on the roof, he knows, to watch the wheat. Six shaggy, creamy-white shepherd dogs are tied to lengths of chain here and there around the *aia*, and from his vantage point Ettore can see the precise circles they have trampled into the dust at the ends of their chains, each one with a four-metre radius. They wear collars of vicious metal spikes to protect their throats. Ettore stares into the setting sun until it makes his eyes stream. He is fifteen kilometres south-east of Gioia. His leg is better but he feels weak, his muscles wobbly, and he doesn't think he could walk it yet.

Just then a woman walks across the *aia* with a lanky youth at her side; for a second Ettore thinks it's Marcie, but this woman is shorter, slighter. Her hair is a subtler blonde, braided into some kind of knot at the nape of her neck from which wavy strands have escaped to hang down below the narrow brim of her hat. The boy is taller than her, and walks with a slight stoop as if to apologise for the fact. Their footsteps make little puffs of dust rise. For no reason he can find, Ettore has the nagging feeling that he has seen this woman before. That he knows her. They approach one of the dogs and it lunges towards them, barking wildly. The woman puts a restraining hand on the boy's arm, like a mother would, but she looks too young for that. But then, like Marcie, these pale foreigners have artifice and lives of ease that make them look younger than they are. The dog stops barking but wheels about on the end of its chain, back a few steps, around to the left then the right. The boy crouches down and holds something out to it, but the dog won't come near enough to take it. He shuffles closer, and Ettore hears the woman say something in warning. She has her hand on the boy's sleeve, the knuckles white. In the end the boy has to throw his offering, and the dog gulps it down in one mouthful. It paces, and it watches, and goes no closer to them, and Ettore thinks it wise not to trust them.

He finds the rest of his clothes laundered and folded in a chest by the door; he dresses, drinks more water from the pitcher and makes his way downstairs. Marcie is on the terrace over the dairy, sipping *amarena*, eating olives with a tiny silver fork, and making notes on a piece of writing paper.

'Ettore! Dear boy, come and sit down! It's so wonderful to see you up and about. Sit, sit,' she says. Marcie is still beautiful, he thinks, but it's a kind of desperate beauty, teetering on ruin, that's somehow pitiful. Ettore once heard his mother say that beautiful women grow to hate themselves as they age, and he wonders if this is what's happening. If Marcie is starting to hate herself. There's a darker shade, and glints of silver, at the roots of her hair; her smile is a dazzle of red and white; she's wearing silk. Ettore thinks of Paola, and Iacopo, and a wave of anger courses through him. Marcie's smile falters. 'Well,' she says. 'Well. You must eat. You're so thin! How have you gotten so thin in the summertime? I'll call for Anna to bring you something. And of course it won't be long till dinnertime.' She rises and calls through a dark doorway, down stone steps into shadow. 'Anna! Anna!'

'I do not want to eat. I want to go Gioia,' says Ettore, but Marcie seems, or pretends, not to hear. 'Thank you,' he adds, stonily. As she returns to her seat Marcie says, without looking up at him:

'Of course you want to eat, and you need to rest. And you simply *can't* leave without seeing your uncle first. You know how . . . upset he would be. Please, Ettore. Sit down.' She pours him a glass of the cherry drink, and it's the deep,

deep crimson of venous blood. After a pause he takes it from her, and she smiles again.

There are footsteps behind him, on the open steps that lead up from the courtyard, and the other woman and the boy come to the table. The woman's eyes are wide and clear, and there's a strange nakedness to their gaze that Ettore is unsure of; like an excess of transparency. She almost looks stupid, but it's not quite that. The boy, whose face has the nondescript look of something unfinished, studies him with unguarded curiosity.

'Ah, there you are, you two! Come and meet the walking wounded. Clare, Pip, this is Ettore Tarano, Leandro's nephew. Ettore, this is Clare and Philip Kingsley. Clare's husband is the architect designing the new front for the Gioia house, and these two are brightening up my whole summer by staying as guests while he works.' Philip shakes Ettore's hand first, enthusiastically, and Clare follows more reluctantly. Ettore wonders if it's the callused roughness of his hands on her soft skin that she doesn't like.

'Filippo. Chiara. Kingsley,' he says, so that he will remember the names, and the boy grins even more.

'Filippo! Well, of course — I hadn't thought before how fabulous your name is in Italian, Pip! I shall call you that from now on,' Marcie declares. Much of what she says is lost on Ettore, and his face turns hot with frustration. He frowns at his aunt, then looks away; tips the *amarena* down his throat in one gulp. It makes him cough. There's alcohol in it, not just cherries and sugar.

Then Chiara Kingsley speaks in hesitant Italian, and he turns to her, surprised.

'It's a pleasure to meet you, Mr Tarano. I did not know that Mr Cardetta had family remaining in Gioia.'

'Oh! I forgot — how wonderful! You can speak to him in Italian, Clare. I taught him some English last winter but it was hard going for both of us, because I have almost no Italian.' Marcie claps her hands, pleased. Anna, the kitchen girl, arrives with a basket of bread and a plate of cheese, and more olives. The sight of the food makes Ettore sway on his feet, and sweat beads along his hairline.

'Won't you sit?' Chiara says evenly. 'You have been very unwell.' Without speaking, Ettore sinks into a chair. His hand reaches for bread of its own accord.

For a while they drink and they talk, in English, and Ettore is aware of being consciously not watched as he eats savagely, desperately. He despises their tact; he despises himself for sitting there eating when his family in Gioia might have nothing. A shard of bread crust scores his sore throat and he gags, coughing and gasping. Filippo passes him water, which he takes without thanks. Ettore is aware of Chiara leaning towards him, her forehead creased in thought. He knows the look well; she is trying to find the right words in an unfamiliar language.

'The doctor gave you water in a line. In a . . . cord. To the mouth,' she stumbles.

'With a tube?' he says, and she nods.

'That's why your throat is a hurt, I think.'

149

When he doesn't answer her she continues. 'He cleaned your leg with alcohol. He cut away some badness. He has not closed it. It must dry. He comes back to close it,' she says, all in the same careful tone, and precisely over-enunciated. Ettore nods.

'I will pay for the doctor. Please tell Marcie that. I will pay for the doctor and for my time here.'

'Marcie, Mr Tarano says that he intends to reimburse you for his medical treatment, and for his board,' she says obediently.

'Well, rot and nonsense! He's family, for heaven's sake! Oh, why must the peasants be so damned proud? And how on earth does he plan to pay us, anyway, he hasn't two dimes to rub together. Don't translate that, will you dear?' says Marcie. She's had several glasses of the *amarena*, there are two smears of colour either side of her nose and her eyes are sparkling. Ettore understands enough of what she says. He understands her dismissal of his offer, and anger and shame come in equal measures. He stares down at his plate until they begin to talk of other things.

'I want to go,' he says later, quietly, almost to himself. But Chiara hears him; he can feel her half-watching, half-listening, all the time. It's distracting, and he can't tell if he likes it or not.

More food arrives, and he eats but it's too rich and makes his stomach roll. The meat seems to sit in his chest like a fist, the alcohol makes him slow and stupid; he can no longer pick any one word from their rapid English, so he stops trying.

The sky turns to black, and prickles with stars; the white walls of the *masseria* are lit yellow with torches, alive with capering shadows. With the stink from the dairy there's the sweet smell of jasmine, growing up the wall near the table. Knives and forks squeak and clatter against the china; they all chew and cut and spoon. The extravagance of it, the abundance, is like some mad pantomime. Marcie talks and talks and talks, and laughs, tipping back her head so that her teeth shine and the ridges of her throat are exposed. Young Filippo sometimes laughs with her, self-consciously, but Chiara is quiet. She is the one restful corner of the world, absorbing sound instead of making it. When Ettore can't take any more he lurches to his feet, tipping over his chair and shoving the table so that the drinks slop, and it's Chiara who reaches him first, and steadies his arm.

'Come with me,' she says quietly, in words he can understand. She guides him up stairs, through doors, back to his bed.

★ ★ ★

Leandro does not appear early the next day. Without Paola to wake him Ettore sleeps until the sun is high in the sky, and then he rushes downstairs feeling as though he's missed something important, that he is sleeping away all control. He can see the foreigners on the terrace, at breakfast, and it's like they never left the table — like they've been eating and drinking all night, like that's all they ever do. He goes to the kitchen in disgust, asks Anna for some bread and a glass of milk, then goes out across the *aia*, moving faster as he gets used to the crutch. He leaves through the iron gates and goes around to the back of the quad, where there's a complex of large *trulli*, the first buildings to be built in that spot, hundreds of years before the *masseria* was built. They abut and blend into the back wall of the farm, looking like some strange warty growth sprouting from its skin. Here the corporals and other permanent outdoor staff sleep, on wooden platforms above the animals — the stablehand and herdsmen, the dairyman and his wife who makes the cheese.

Detached from it all, a short distance away, is another *trullo* with three large, interlinked cones. These are the private quarters of the overseer of the farm, who manages it day to day, and in his uncle's absence. Ettore pauses. He could go and ask for a half-day's work while he waits for his uncle. He could make a little money to take back to Gioia, but his arm is trembling with fatigue from taking his weight on the crutch, his head aches and his leg is throbbing. He experiments with putting his full weight on it, but the grinding feeling, the pressure, brings tears to his eyes. Just then the door of the overseer's house opens and a man emerges, and all thought of asking for work leaves Ettore's head. This is not the same man who was overseer during the winter, when Ettore last came to stay at the dell'Arco. That man was called Araldo, and he'd been short and fat with a mad red beard. This man is Ludo Manzo. Older, more grizzled, but instantly recognisable. The very same man who once tormented Pino and Ettore, and countless other young boys. Ettore stares, and a violent rush of hatred makes his head throb harder. Ludo sees him there, looks him over lazily, and doesn't recognise him. Why would he? Ettore was just a boy, one of many; as indistinct and unfinished as the boy Filippo. Ludo looks away and carries on walking towards the barns, but Ettore remains motionless for quite some time, with his leg tucked up like a stork.

It's afternoon before Leandro Cardetta appears with another man, tall and hunched, in a car driven by his servant with the deformed face. When Leandro sees Ettore waiting in a corner of the courtyard, leaning on his crutch, he smiles. The tall man must be Chiara's husband, the architect, because he goes to her and hugs her as though he might drown otherwise, and Ettore sees how she keeps her body rigid, supporting the weight of his embrace. Either that, or rejecting it. The man's height and the way he swoops over her make him look like a vulture, like he's devouring her.

'Ettore! It does me good to see you awake and walking,' says his uncle, holding his arms wide as he approaches. They embrace briefly; his uncle's arms have a brute strength belied by his ridiculous suits and the almost jaunty angle of his hat.

'Uncle, thank you for your help, and your hospitality.'

'Don't thank me. Only promise to come to me sooner, when things are so bad. You might have

153

died, my boy. What will my sister say, when I meet her in the next life, if I let her only son die when I could save him?'

'She would say you do not control his destiny,' says Ettore, and Leandro shakes his head ruefully.

'Maria was always proud and stubborn. Too proud and too stubborn, and she passed it all to you with those blue eyes. She wouldn't take my advice and come to New York. She wouldn't take my advice and find a man worth a damn to marry, instead of that waster Valerio.'

'Valerio is my father. You must not disrespect him in my hearing, uncle.'

'Ah, you're right.' Leandro shakes his head, then claps Ettore on the shoulder. 'Forgive me. No man could ever be good enough for a beloved sister. But, pride aside, you must stay until you're fit. I know better than to insist, but at least hear sense, Ettore. You're no good to your sister or her baby if you can't work a day in the fields. You're no good to them permanently crippled or dead. Stay here. Rest. Accept my help when it's freely given.'

'I will not take charity.' Ettore clenches his teeth, repositions the crutch beneath his arm.

'Don't make yourself ridiculous, son,' Leandro murmurs. The two men stare at one another. Leandro's eyes are so dark that nothing can be read in them. They are like black glass, impossible to see through.

The two of them are standing next to the well, a lidded shaft that drops into one of several underground water cisterns around the *masseria*,

154

into which the rain, when it comes, pours like a river. The kitchen girl, Anna, comes to draw water. She has round hips, a nipped-in waist below heavy breasts, and she blushes when she has to approach them. Leandro breaks off his scrutiny of Ettore to watch her, because the weight of the water pail makes her hips jiggle, and then he looks at his nephew and grins. But Ettore does not look at the girl. He has no interest in her, and Leandro's smile fades away. 'You still grieve, my boy. For that girl of yours.'

'Livia,' says Ettore, and with her name, as always, comes a cold, needling feeling inside him.

'Livia, yes. It's terrible to lose the one you love. And to lose her in such a way . . . You still don't know who was responsible?'

'If I did that man would be dead.'

'Of course, of course.' Leandro nods. 'I've found out nothing, I'm afraid. If I do, you'll know it at once. But the men know I am your uncle, you see. I'm sure they guard their tongues around me.' He looks down at his feet, at the high shine on his brogues.

'I'm sure they do. But thank you.' Ettore frowns. 'You have a new overseer,' he says. Leandro's head comes up in an instant.

'Yes,' he says, and there's a warning in the word.

'How can you give that man work, Uncle? He beat you once, did he not? I was little but I remember it. He beat you and then he pissed on you, in front of everybody, for having a handful of burnt wheat in your pocket at the end of the

155

day. How can you look at him, and not want to kill him? How can you give him work and pay?' he says. Leandro's face goes blank and then tightens in anger. Ettore doesn't know if it's the memory or his invoking of it that causes the spasm. Then Leandro smiles, the chilly smile of a reptile. Ettore's sure that smile has been the last thing some men ever saw.

'Ah, Ettore. Yes, Ludo Manzo is an animal. But don't you see? He's *my* animal now. He runs the farm better than anyone else, and what better way to take revenge on a man than to come to rule him?'

'As I would not be a slave, so I would not be an owner of slaves,' says Ettore. 'Your Marcie taught me that last winter. One of your presidents said it.'

'*My* presidents?'

'Her presidents. America's presidents,' Ettore corrects himself, quickly. He may be family, but Ettore knows better than to call his uncle an American.

'I learnt a saying in America too, you know.' Leandro smiles again, and some of the tension goes out of him. 'If you can't beat 'em, join 'em.' He chuckles, and shakes his head. 'Ettore, you of all people should know that this is no place for nobility.' Leandro takes a few steps away, out of the shade and into the hard sunlight, then he turns back. 'Avoid him, if it upsets you to see him. Don't make trouble. And stay, I beg you. Let me do my dear sister that service. If you will not take an easy job here, then at least stay until you can walk better.'

156

Leandro disappears into the house, calling for his wife, and Ettore hears the high bird-call of Marcie's answer, echoing inside. Chiara and her stooping husband have vanished, and the boy is alone on the terrace, reading a book with one foot propped up on the opposite knee, the fingers of his free hand fiddling ceaselessly with the laces of his shoe. Ettore waits to know what to do next. The sun slides slowly across the courtyard, and the breeze that blows is furnace hot, dry as the land. The harelipped driver comes out of the kitchens, swinging his arms. He lies down in the shadow of the water trough, puts his hat over his face, and sleeps. Once he's settled, a few tatty sparrows flutter back to perch along the chipped lip of the trough, dipping their beaks, resting.

Ettore can't leave, and he can't stay. He leans back against the wall. In the winter he was here for weeks because he caught the influenza. There was no work then anyway, so he didn't miss out on any wages, but Paola threw him out of the house in case he passed the infection to Iacopo, or to her. Sometimes Paola weakens, and says he should exploit their rich uncle more; she's too pragmatic to pass up any opportunity of wages when they're starving. But the Taranos and the Cardettas are on opposite sides of this war now, with a gulf between them, and Ettore remembers his mother reading and rereading one of the letters that Leandro sent sporadically from America, sometimes with money in, sometimes without. That particular letter came with a lot of money, and his mother held it in her hand,

157

clenching it tight, while she read and reread. In the end she looked up, her eyes full of sorrow in the failing light, and said:

'My brother has forgotten who he is.'

Ettore stands up from the wall, walks under the arch where the huge gates are, goes through a small door in one wall and climbs carefully up the spiral staircase inside. The steps are steep, and he's clumsy with his crutch. The stairwell is lit by narrow slits in the wall, slits through which once arrows, and now bullets, can be shot. He pauses beside one, and runs his fingers around its rough edge. It's chipped and worn from centuries of use. Ettore takes a breath, shuts his eyes. He sees a bloom of smoke from just such a slot, and a fragment of a second later, hears the crack of the shot. There was a startled gasp at his side, a thump like a fist punched into sand, and a cloud of red droplets as fine as morning mist. Davide dropped like a felled tree beside him, and was dead before he hit the ground. No weapon in his hand; a puzzled expression on his face. Paola's lover; Iacopo's father. It's almost exactly a year since the massacre at the Masseria Girardi. Almost exactly a year since Ettore had to sneak home across country, once dark had fallen, and tell his sister that the second man she'd dared to love was dead. Iacopo was just a smooth swelling under her blouse then, and she'd put her hands underneath it to support it while she howled. She must know how wrong it feels for him to be on the inside of walls like these. Wrong like trying to breathe underwater.

Ettore carries on up the stairs to the roof and

emerges into the light. The guard had been snoozing, sitting with his back to the parapet and his knees drawn up. He struggles to his feet and swings his rifle up, then grins foolishly and waves when he recognises Ettore. He is young, and has a kind face; fair hair, a snub nose. Ettore can't remember his name — Carlo? Pietro? He nods to him and negotiates the pitch of the roof to reach the edge, to lean over and look out. The dry rocky plain of the *Murgia* stretches away as far as he can see — the high plateau that rises inland and runs almost the length of Puglia, north to south, like a giant finger. High enough for the temperature to be lower than at the coast; high enough for there to be snow in the winter, sometimes. But he can see no rivers, no creeks, no lakes. He's above the west wing of the quad, and against the wall below there's a vegetable garden, green with care and water, looking garishly bright against the brown and grey hues of everything else. Little red tomatoes crawl along the ground on their vines; pumpkins too; zucchini; globular aubergines, not yet ripe. There's a path lined with apricot and almond trees, leading to an ancient stone love seat beneath a bower of roses that have shed their petals in distress at the drought. The garden is centuries old; Marcie revived it when she first came, with her fast unravelling dreams of the romance of Italy. The love seat has cracked right down the middle. Slowly, slowly, the land will reclaim it. The air is clear today, as though even the dust hasn't the energy to stir beneath such a sun, and slowly, from the direction of Gioia, a

159

figure swathed in dark clothing walks towards the farm. Long before he can see her face Ettore recognises his sister, and the strutting way she walks with the weight of her son on her back. He hurries down to meet her.

Paola waits for him at the gates, curling her fingers around the bars like a prisoner, and when she sees him walking towards her she grins — fleetingly, but it transforms her face and sends a jolt of joy through Ettore like a kick in the back. It's been a long time since he saw his sister's smile. He pulls her head towards him and presses his lips to her forehead, and they come away with the salt taste of her skin on them.

'You're up. You're well,' she says, and her relief is plain.

'Yes. Soon I won't need this thing.' He smiles and raps the end of the crutch against the gate.

'Don't rush it. Let it heal.'

'Yes, little mother.'

'Don't mock, just do as I tell you,' she says, but she can't be stern. Ettore reaches through and turns her shoulder to see his nephew. The baby is fast asleep with his face rucked up against Paola's spine; his cheeks are marbled red, and he mumbles to himself when Ettore brushes his forehead. 'Don't wake him. He screamed half the night away.'

'Is he sick?'

'No.' Paola smiles again. 'Two teeth are coming through. A few more and he'll be better furnished than Valerio,' she says. Ettore laughs quietly, and for that moment the simple happiness of the child thriving is enough.

Paola's face falls first. She looks past Ettore at the implacable white walls of the *masseria*, and her eyes are troubled.

'Come in. See our uncle and Marcie. You know how she loves to see Iacopo,' says Ettore, but Paola shakes her head.

'She loves it too much. I think she wants to eat him.'

'Don't be cruel.'

'I saw her plenty when we brought you here. Me and Pino. Has Leandro offered you work?'

'Work as soft as I'd like it,' he says, disgusted.

'Take it,' she says flatly.

'No, Paola! Must we have the same argument over and over? This is a war, and you of all people know it. Leandro has chosen his side and we — '

'Poete got caught. They found him with a flask of milk hidden in his coat, and fired him.'

'Damn him . . . Clumsy idiot.' But even though he's dismayed Ettore is also happy that Paola won't have to let the man touch her any more.

'Valerio can't get work. He stands there coughing and spitting and shaking like a leaf, and no bastard will hire him — why should they? He's scarce fit to lift his feet, let alone a scythe or flail. We've *nothing*, Ettore. You must take work here.'

'I can get other work, real work — '

'Don't be a fool! You've one good leg, and if you open that wound again . . . I nearly lost you, Ettore. We can't lose you. Don't be a fool.' Her voice is taut with fear. Ettore leans his head against the hot metal of the gate and feels it cutting into him. He says nothing. 'You must do this, Ettore. Your scruples won't feed my baby. They won't. Please.' He can't bring himself to speak, because he knows she's right. Suddenly the gate is like prison bars indeed, and inside he is not his own man. He has no control. She clasps her hard hands around his for a moment before she turns to go, and he takes a breath. She has iron inside her, like the gates. Nothing will bow her.

'Wait,' he calls, and she turns. 'Wait and I'll get some food for you to take back. If this is our family, let them feed us,' he says bitterly. Paola doesn't smile again, but she looks relieved, and she nods.

★ ★ ★

For four days Ettore does as his uncle suggested, and stews on what his sister told him. She asks of him something she would be unwilling to do herself, but then, her wages, a woman's wages, would scarcely be worth the self-loathing. He rests his leg. He sleeps and eats and does no work, and feels like he's marooned outside his own life. He itches to be away, to be whole and gone. He doesn't eat at the table with his uncle and Marcie and their guests unless he's directly requested to; he says little, letting their English rattle around him, unexamined. The amount of food they put away, the constant chewing, the way some dishes are sent back all but untouched, enrages him in a way that makes it

162

hard to breathe. The muscles between his ribs pull the bones into a tight cage. Whenever he can he fetches his food from the kitchen instead, and takes it up to the roof to eat it, where the guards have got used to seeing him. On the fourth day his uncle returns to Gioia with the architect, and he's left alone with the women and the boy, which makes it easier for him to keep himself away. He can see that Marcie's wounded; he's being an ungracious guest, he knows, but he doesn't feel like a guest. He feels like a traitor. He goes around and around the *masseria* on his crutch, feeling the strength return to his arms and shoulders, the muscles burning, turning hard. The wound in his leg still pulls when he tries to use it — a wrenching feeling deep in the bone — so, since he must heal before he can leave, he doesn't push it. He's not dizzy any more, his body feels strong. He wakes earlier each day, with the voices of the dairy herd as it comes in for milking.

On the fifth day Ettore waits until dusk, until he sees lamplight from inside the overseer's *trullo*, then he steels himself, limps over to the door and knocks before he can think twice. When Ludo Manzo opens it Ettore can't prevent the disgust that jars through him. The overseer's face is deeply scored by years of work outdoors, his top lip is seamed, his teeth are longer and browner than before, but his eyes are as hard and bright as they ever were. He studies Ettore for a second and then laughs out loud.

'I see from your face that you've worked for me before,' he says. His voice is deep and hoarse, like there's grit in his throat. For a hideous moment Ettore is too cowed, too tied up with hate and fear to speak. He nods. 'The boss told me you'd come and ask for work. I guess that's why you're here — not from some yearning for my company?'

'Yes. No,' says Ettore.

'Well, I don't remember you, Ettore Tarano, but I asked in town so I know you're trouble. I guess since you're the boss's nephew, you're my trouble now.'

'I only want to work for a wage. Until my leg is whole and I can go back into the fields.'

'Boy, you're a damned fool. If I had a rich uncle, I'd make myself his right-hand man and get fat and drunk, and laid.'

'I want to work for a wage.'

'I heard you. And I said you're a damned fool.' Ludo stares hard at him, with his mouth twisted to one side as he thinks. Ettore fights the urge to fidget, to turn away, or to hit him. To do anything other than stand there in front of him, waiting, at his mercy again. If he did what Ludo suggested, if he used his uncle, he wouldn't have to do this. He wouldn't have to suffer the likes of this man. 'All right. You can't walk, you can't carry. You can't cut wheat. There's pretty much fuck all you can do, but you can sit on your arse and you can watch, am I right? Take over from Carlo in the *trullo* by the gates at midnight. Keep watch. The rifle stays there — you take it from him, you hand it to the man who relieves you in the morning. Is that understood?'

'Yes.' The effort of staying calm, of staying still,

164

is exhausting. When Ludo nods and shuts the door the breath rushes out of Ettore, and he droops. A guard, with a rifle. Inside pissing out, as his uncle once said to him. And if raiders come from Gioia what then? Will he shoot at them — at people he might know, people he has worked with, people he lives alongside? Ettore limps away.

Until midnight he waits in the vegetable garden, where it's cool and there's a good smell of green things. Out of habit he pulls a few weeds and makes a heap of them; he picks a few little tomatoes and eats them. Bats twist and turn silently along the tunnel made by the fruit trees. When it gets too dark Ettore sits down on the broken love seat and looks up at the sky, and thinks about Livia. She managed to walk some of the way home, after she was attacked. She made it to the edge of town, where she was found, and brought the rest of the way. Bruises the size and shape of a man's fingers on her neck and breasts and thighs; little cuts from the point of a sharp knife, circling her throat like a necklace; bite marks all over her. She was mute with shock; could tell them nothing. It took her two days to die of her wounds, and it was an infection, not the severity of them, that took her. The festering of wounds inside her that her mother couldn't see or clean. She ran a violent fever; her skin was hot, dry and burnished red. She didn't smell right, and when her eyes were open they focused on nothing. *Tell me I'm your sweetheart*, she said, over and over again. *Tell me I'm your sweetheart.* Ettore squeezed her hand tight in

165

his, and kissed her knuckles, and told her that he loved her and that she was his sweetheart, which made her frown slightly, as if dissatisfied. Towards the end she gave no sign of even hearing him, and only repeated her request over and over again. *Tell me I'm your sweetheart.* So he told her, over and over again, that she was his sweetheart, even though that was not a term they had ever used before, and it puzzled him; he told her that he loved her, that he belonged to her, and he pressed his hands to her burning skin as if he might wick the heat away from it. And then she died.

The sound of quiet footsteps jars him back to himself, and he notices that his eyes are wet and itching. He scrubs his face with one hand and then goes still, and hopes to go unnoticed by whatever corporal or servant is passing. But the footsteps turn into the garden, and silhouetted against the light from the *masseria* he sees Chiara Kingsley. She seems to stare right at him but doesn't see him there, deep in shadow beneath the trees. She stops walking, drops her chin to her chest and wraps her arms around her middle, curling in on herself as if she's in pain. He expects to hear her sob, but she makes no sound at all. He can't even hear her breathing. She seems like a person who's trying not to be there; or is trying not to *be* at all. Pale skin and pale hair, with her lightness and her quietness, and her feet bare. To Ettore she looks like thistledown, like something as ephemeral and impermanent as that. Something that the wind will blow right through, even as it carries

166

her along with it. Something that might vanish without trace. If Paola has iron inside her then this English woman has air, or some other intangible stuff. She's not quite real. She's not like anyone he has seen before.

She stays in that odd huddled posture for some time then drops her arms to her sides and looks up at the sky. She seems in no hurry to leave, and Ettore can't stay still any longer. He reaches for his crutch and stands slowly, and hears her quick, indrawn breath.

'Who's there?'

'Ettore,' he says. He makes his way over to stand in front of her, so they are both half-lit and half-shadowed. He opens his mouth to say something else, but nothing comes. Chiara watches him, and her expectation makes him want to walk away.

'You did not dine today,' she says eventually, in Italian.

'I did. Just not at my uncle's table.'

'You prefer to be alone?' she says, and he doesn't answer because though this is not quite right, it's an easy explanation. 'Are you well?' He shrugs, and then nods. He gestures towards the crutch. 'You don't like to be here,' she adds, and it's not a question. Ettore shakes his head, on his guard. His aunt is easy to offend, his uncle even more so.

'I do not like to be kept.'

'Neither do I,' she says softly. He frowns, and doesn't understand her because what is she, what is the wife of a wealthy man, if not kept? 'You are an uncle yourself,' she says. 'I met your

167

sister when she came here with you. I saw that she had a baby.'

'His name is Iacopo.'

'Do you have children?' she asks. He shakes his head. 'Neither have I.'

'Filippo?'

'He is my . . . ' She can't find the word in Italian. 'My husband's son. The son of his first wife.' She starts to smile but it doesn't quite take shape. In the dark her eyes are huge and dazed, like she can't quite see. 'I hate this place,' she says then. 'Is that the right word?' Then she says something in English that he can't quite catch, something bitter and angry.

'You are free,' says Ettore, puzzled. 'You can go.'

'No. I'm not. I can't.' She takes a long breath in. 'Mr Cardetta says the peasants do not speak Italian, only the language of this place. How is it you can understand me?'

'Italian was spoken at school. I have an ear for languages.'

'You went to school?' She sounds surprised, and then looks apologetic.

'A few years, only.'

'And you were able to learn some English from Marcie, over the winter.'

'I must go. I am a guard now.' He can't keep his lip from curling as he says this, disgusted at himself. 'You should not be outside the walls after dark. It isn't safe.' Her eyes go huge again, her arms wrap back around her, shielding her.

'I wanted to run . . . to fly away,' she says.

'Escape.' Ettore gives her the right word, and she nods. That naked look is back — that clarity, that lack of guard. It bothers him, somehow; it snags at him. *Thistledown*, he thinks. 'Go back inside. You should not be out here.' He leaves her there, not waiting to see if she does as he says.

Carlo, the fresh-faced guard he saw on the roof before, grins when Ettore comes to relieve him at the *trullo* by the iron gates. He stands up with a yawn, hands the rifle over and stretches his arms above his head.

'Vallarta had a raid again, three nights ago,' he says, as he passes Ettore on the threshold. 'Three steers taken, and one of the barns torched. Don't fall asleep. The bell is there.' He indicates a large brass handbell in a niche in the wall. 'Make a racket if you see or hear anything, and we'll all come running.' He walks off towards his bed with a jaunty step. Ettore runs his hands along the rifle; the smooth patina on the wood of the butt; the cold, dead, metal barrel. He has wanted to get his hands on a gun for a long time; holding it gives him a sudden wild pang, a feeling of power and reckless violence. In the trenches he felt better with his rifle in his hands; safer and stronger, even though he knew it meant almost nothing, and would likely make no difference. It was a feeling that came from the heart, not the head. He stares out into the darkness beyond the gates, then turns to look at the farm, glowing here and there with lamplight. He doesn't know what it is that he wants to do.

There's no light in the *trullo*, though a lantern sits primed and ready with a book of matches beside it. To light the guard would make him a target, and spoil his night vision; the darkness is

169

where a nightwatchman belongs. Ettore sits down on the stone ledge by the doorway and rests the rifle across his thighs. It presses cold through the fabric of his trousers, though everything else is warm — the stone, the ground, the air. His heart feels cold along with it because he has crossed the divide. To anyone looking on, he has turned his coat. He doesn't know what he will do if raiders come, and he prays that they won't. There are flickers of lightning far off along the eastern horizon. He sits, and he listens to the quiet rustle of geckos hunting, and thoughts of Chiara Kingsley come to him unbidden — the pale weightlessness of her.

He catches himself wondering what her white skin would feel like under his hands, and whether if he held her she would just dissolve, and drift away. She might taste of nothing; might be as flavourless as water. She might be as insubstantial as a breath of air, but then he thinks of the first touch of cooler air that comes in the autumn, drifting down from the north, and how it always wakes him, tingling over his skin like soft sparks of electricity. She's transparent, like water, and he thinks of the first swallow of water after long hours of work, when there's dust in his throat and his eyes and his nose. He would devour her too, just like her stooping husband, if he knew she would make him feel that way. Air and water; thistledown. *I want to fly away*, she said, wrapping her arms around herself. And she ought to. Puglia is a land of earth and fire, he thinks. A thing of air and water will not long survive.

# Clare

The first and only time Clare went to New York was late in the spring of 1914, as the creeping threat of war spread across Europe like an illness. In America the rich were still building, still dancing, still inventing cocktails and laughing the way Marcie laughs now, with excitement and abandon. Clare had been married to Boyd for three years, and she was happy; serene with her own brand of quiet joy. Then Boyd came home from work one day frowning and unsettled; there was a potential new project in New York and the senior partner wanted him to submit designs for it. Clare immediately encouraged him to go, and to take her too, before she remembered that Emma was from New York — that he'd met her there, married her there, lost her there. When Boyd's pained expression reminded her, she stumbled into shocked silence. But after pausing for thought, she hid her embarrassment by pushing on, albeit nervously. She told him it might be a good thing for him to make peace with the city; to lay its ghosts to rest; to see old friends of his and Emma's. At this his head snapped up.

'But I don't want to see any of them! It would . . . it would be too difficult. Too awful.'

'Well . . . well then, darling, it's a big enough city. Nobody need know you're there at all, if you don't want,' she said.

'That's true,' said Boyd. He sounded careful, hopeful, as if he hadn't considered this, so Clare pushed on once more.

'We don't have to go any of the places that you . . . went before. I've never travelled, Boyd; not properly. We can make it our second honeymoon. It would be such an adventure, and, well, it can only be good for you, surely? I mean, workwise.' The month before, Boyd had been passed over for a senior partnership for a second time. He ran his hands through his hair, stood up and paced the sitting room carpet for a while. 'Please let's go, Boyd. I think it would be wonderful.'

'All right,' he said at last. 'All right, we'll go.'

It would be a better honeymoon this time around, Clare decided, since the first had been rife with the awkwardness of two shy people making love for the first time. They'd gone to the Isle of Wight for a week, but her memories were of all the painful little misunderstandings, odd misfires and subtle disappointments. Boyd made the journey to New York first, and had been there some weeks before Clare travelled out to join him, leaving Pip at home with a nanny. He'd started work on his design for the new bank building — not quite a grand hotel, but still something monumental. That was the word the bank used — monumental. Something that people would have to stop to look at, and tip back their heads to take in. He had a design but it wasn't quite there — she heard those words a lot in the six weeks she stayed in the small rented apartment near Central Park. *It's not quite there*. They never mentioned Emma; Clare watched her husband carefully for signs of grief or painful memory, and was relieved to see none.

She'd been a little anxious that the trip might make him worse, not better, but she began to relax. Boyd had spent the first year of their marriage jumping at shadows, and now and then they'd overwhelmed him. Like the time she'd found him holding Emma's silk gloves, cast away in thought. He was the first to check the post every morning; he stiffened whenever the doorbell rang. Clare sometimes found him staring out of a window, or into the fire, hands in his pockets, eyes glassy. Once she saw him staring at Pip as he played with his trains on the nursery carpet, and she went in to them with a smile but paused, because Boyd was looking at his son as if he hadn't the slightest idea who he was. But things had improved since then; the shadows had receded, and he was less distant. Clare spoke about Emma with Pip, but never with Boyd. She wanted her husband to concentrate on the future, not the past, and it seemed to her, in those first few weeks they were together in New York, that he was doing exactly that.

Boyd seemed focused, but happy. He spent long hours studying the Flatiron, and the brand new Woolworth Building, and the St Regis Hotel. He knew the bank had three firms working on preliminary drawings, and that he was the only European. He knew they expected to see something stately and Victorian in style from him, or something *beaux-arts*; something

173

with all the dyed-in-the-wool grandeur of the Empire. Boyd wanted to give them something they hadn't even considered — something they'd never seen before, but that wouldn't shock them overly. A clock tower to break the roofline, with decorations either side after the ancient Egyptian style, and thin obelisks at each corner, like delicate, geometric rock pinnacles. He was secretive, and wouldn't show Clare the drawings he spent so many hours hunched over. Late in the day he'd let her coax him away from them to walk beneath the brand new leaves in Central Park, where the constant city roar was a murmur, and the air smelled of living things as well as food and sweat and burning. The owner of the bank was hosting a party to mark the submission and unveiling of the three designs. The mayor, John Purroy Mitchel, would be attending, and with that news Clare realised, finally, the significance of what her husband was working on. And the day after that announcement came something happened, and Boyd was never the same again.

Clare returned to the apartment from lunch with the wives of two of Boyd's colleagues, and found him at the window in a posture of such unnatural stiffness that she thought at once he'd had terrible news of some kind. Her stomach dropped; she thought immediately of Pip.

'Boyd, darling, what is it? What's happened?' she said, but he didn't move. She went to stand beside him and saw the glass in his hand, and the brandy bottle on the ottoman, and noticed the stink of it all around. 'Boyd?' she whispered, but

174

she might as well have been mute, invisible. He looked dead. His face was grey and had a shine to it; unpleasant-looking, like something was trying to ooze out from inside him. If he was breathing it didn't move his chest and it made no sound. His eyes looked dull and empty. If she'd found him lying down in that state she would have screamed. She tried to take his hand but it was clenched tightly around something, and then she noticed a few white spots against the green carpet. She frowned at them until she realised what they were. Frantically, she prised open Boyd's hand and found his little jar of barbiturate pills, which he took to soothe his nerves and help him sleep. The jar was empty.

At her touch Boyd turned his head slowly towards her and, just as slowly, his face collapsed; his mouth melting open, misshapen, trembling. Clare caught her breath. 'Boyd, *tell me!* Tell me! Is it Pip? Has something happened to Pip?'

'They were here. They came *here*,' he said. 'They knew . . . knew where I was.' The words were so slurred and distorted she could hardly make them out.

'Who knew? *Who* came here? Boyd, I don't understand.' Boyd swayed, took a staggering step, fell to his knees. Clare went down with him and put her arms around him, tried to soothe him. He was heavy, and threatened to topple all the way; she struggled to hold him, and then, with a spasm that felt strange against her body, he vomited. She felt the heat of it spatter her calves, and the stink of the brandy got stronger, and as she tugged and cajoled him towards the bathroom she saw more white pills in what he'd brought up. Many more. He was sick again, and a third time before she managed to get him any distance at all. Everything about him was unfamiliar; his long body was a dead weight, his loose face and rolling eyes had no trace of his personality, or the melancholy dignity of the man she'd married. She left him lying on his side while she called the doctor, so panicked that at first she couldn't remember how to use the telephone, even to reach the concierge.

The doctor was with him for a long time. He gave Boyd an emetic that brought up everything else inside him, until his convulsions resulted in nothing but strands of spittle and horrible choking sounds. Clare went back and forth to the bathroom, emptying the doctor's bowl, trying to clean the worst of the sick from the carpet. The smell of it was inescapable. Outside the window, the sun moved below the rooftops and the sky turned dove grey. Clare watched pigeons bolt across it and noticed how the twilight took the colour out of everything. She felt that these were things that were happening to another person, someone quite other than her. She was detached from them; she didn't understand, and didn't want to think too much about it. She only knew her own fear for what it was when the doctor emerged, and sent her heart jolting madly.

'How many pills did he take?' the doctor asked her, brusquely.

'I . . . I don't know. There were around fifty in

the bottle, I believe, and . . . and a handful were on the carpet. And then, when he was sick . . . ' She swallowed nervously.

'It's very lucky he began to purge when he did. Very lucky indeed. Mrs Kingsley, has your husband attempted to harm himself in this way before?'

'To harm himself? Oh, I don't think . . . I mean, I'm sure he didn't intend . . . ' Clare fell silent. The doctor watched her steadily. 'I'm sure it wasn't that. He takes the pills for his nerves. Sometimes he . . . he can't sleep.' Her voice was jittery.

'It does no good to ignore these things, Mrs Kingsley. I believe he's out of any danger. Let him rest, give him plenty of fluids, and I'll be back in a few hours to check up on him.'

It was a long time after the doctor left that Clare found the courage to go in to her husband. She dreaded to find that grey-faced, boneless stranger; and if he was Boyd again, she dreaded that too. She had no idea what to say to him, no idea what to do. She crept in as quietly as she could; the glass of water she carried shook so badly it threatened to spill. She hoped to find him sleeping but he was awake, sitting up against several pillows with no hint of colour in his face.

'How are you now?' she said, as though he'd had a slight cold. Boyd's eyes glimmered with tears at the sight of her; he squeezed them tight shut, like he couldn't bear it. Clare put the water down beside him and took his hand, gathering her nerve. 'Will you tell me what this is about, darling? Will you please tell me?' she said, as

177

gently as she could. Boyd looked up at her, and took a breath. But after a moment of thought he shook his head.

'I can't, Clare. You of all people . . . I can't. Forgive me. Forgive me.' His throat sounded raw. *You of all people.* She dwelt on the meaning of that for a moment.

'You said before that 'they' had come here. Who did you mean, darling? Was it . . . was it some old acquaintances of yours? Friends of Emma's?' This was all she could think of that might have upset him so — something to revive his grief, and bring it the surface. She'd often felt, since they wed, that he kept too quiet about it. That he kept it from her, so as to never crowd his second wife with the shadow of his first. Perhaps such a storing up of feeling was unhealthy — perhaps this sudden eruption was its only possible outcome. She should have known that sooner or later it would flare up, like a sickness, and knock him down. And she had persuaded him to come to the one place on Earth where that was most likely to happen. Guilt seized her. 'Forgive me,' she said, and kissed his hand. 'I should have let you speak of her more. I should have encouraged it, in fact. You must, if you think it would help; you needn't fear that I'll resent her. I won't, I promise.' Boyd said nothing.

Carefully, uncertainly, life carried on. Clare drew the curtains against the evening, switched on lamps and brewed tea. She tried to ignore the feeling that the ground was fragile beneath her feet. Over the following few days she tried to

178

catch her husband's eye, tried a small smile now and then, but he barely seemed to see her and she felt a little chill in her heart, knowing then that he could never love her as much as he'd loved Emma. But she resolved to love him enough, him and his son, for that not to matter. And he did love her, she was sure of that; even if it was only with the love he had left over after loving Emma. It would be enough. It was three days later, at bedtime, when Boyd finally volunteered to speak, and in the darkness his voice sounded different, and strange.

'I . . . I would die without you, Clare. You're an angel. I would die without you.' Clare smiled automatically, though he couldn't see it. He'd never been as frank before, never expressed such devotion. She smiled and waited to feel happy, and couldn't work out why happiness didn't come. Perhaps because he sounded so sure, so adamant, and she didn't want it to be true — not literally, because anything might happen to her, just like it had to Emma. Sudden sickness, sudden death. She was awake for a long time, too troubled to sleep. She thought and thought, and though her guilt made her replay the events, over and over — what if she hadn't persuaded him to come to New York, what if she hadn't gone out to lunch that day, what if she had coaxed him to express his grief before then — she nevertheless suspected that this crisis had been waiting inside Boyd all along. She suspected that it was waiting there still.

For the rest of their time in New York Boyd was jumpy and distant, worse even than when

Clare first knew him. She found herself watching him, and being careful not to let him notice that she was. She watched, and she saw the tiny blisters of sweat along his hairline, and on his upper lip. She saw the way his fingers fumbled at things, like they were numb. She saw his eyes slide away when people spoke to him, and the way their words drifted past him, unregistered. She saw him sit for hours in front of his drawings and not change a single line. As the day of the deadline and the night of the reception approached, she caught him just standing again, staring. She could think of no way to break the spell, no way to distract him. She felt as though she were on a cliff top, leaning out; her heart careered along whenever she spoke to him. She was no longer sure of anything. She was no longer sure of him.

'We could just go home. Couldn't we?' she said, softly, over breakfast. 'If the drawings are done, couldn't we just go? We needn't stay a moment longer. We needn't go to the party . . . ' As she spoke she was assaulted by a homesickness so powerful it actually ached. She wanted their terraced house in Hampstead with its little square of garden, and Pip home from school, smelling of socks and pencil shavings, asking to be held. She wanted things she understood. Whatever their trip to New York had been, it had been no honeymoon.

'Go? I can't go!' said Boyd, almost shouting. He shook his head manically. 'I can't go home. I have to be there.'

'All right,' she murmured, and in that

moment, again, she didn't know him at all. There was something underneath, something inside him she didn't recognise. 'May I see your drawings?' she said. He took a breath and looked away.

'Yes. If you'd like. They're risible,' he said. But they weren't risible. Boyd had designed a building both grand and graceful; simple yet striking. What it was not was innovative. It was a perfect piece of stone-built, European *beaux-arts*, and wouldn't have looked at all out of place on the Champs-Élysées. There was no Egyptian clock tower, no pinnacles; nothing of the exotic. Clare swallowed her confusion, and something that was almost disappointment. He seemed to neither want nor need her opinion, but she gave it anyway, as robustly as she could.

'I think it's wonderful, Boyd. I think it's just wonderful.'

'Do you?' he said, but he didn't want reassurance. The question sounded scornful, and an affirmation died on her lips.

As they entered the foyer of the Hotel Astor on the night of the party Clare felt tremors running through Boyd; insistent little shivers, as if he was freezing on the inside that warm May night. She didn't care that she wore the least jewellery of any woman there, or that her dress was the least fashionable. She didn't care about being patron-ised, and called *quaint*. She no longer even cared whether or not the bank chose Boyd's design. She only cared about getting away, getting out of New York, going home, with the hope that he would then go back to being the man she'd married. That man had sorrow inside him, but at

181

least sorrow was a thing she could recognise. This nameless terror, this crack in his soul that seemed to be widening, was nothing she knew. He spoke to nobody; he drank with grim determination and his eyes darted from face to face, and into the corners of the room, as though he felt watched.

The young mayor made a speech about their ever-developing great city, and about clearing out corruption. Boyd paled as he listened. He radiated tension, and as the evening grew old he crossed the room to talk to the mayor, who was conversing with two other men. And then it was over. They went back to the apartment, and caught the boat home the next day, and a week later heard that Boyd's building had been chosen, and would be built. He squeezed Clare tightly then, and for a long time.

'Thank you, Clare. My angel, thank you,' he whispered. 'I wouldn't have survived it without you.' By that time, Clare was too exhausted and too bewildered to guess, or to ask what it was he'd survived.

Now she thinks she knows, at least in part, because it can't be a coincidence that they have been called to Italy by a New York acquaintance Clare hadn't known existed, and that Boyd is showing some of the same symptoms of stress that he had in New York. For the first time ever she's angry with her husband for hiding things from her. For leaving her to guess at so many things that he won't talk about. *I won't allow it*, Cardetta said, and there had been no doubting that without his consent, she and Pip could not leave. The anger is as unfamiliar to Clare as the new wakefulness she's felt since Ettore Tarano was brought to the *masseria*. She examines the feeling, noting the way it makes her move abruptly and create more noise than she normally would.

Everything that was muted is loud and obvious now. She's fascinated by the feel of things. She runs her hands over the powdery plaster walls of the bedroom, the smooth dark wood of the bed frame, the rough stone blocks in the stairwell, the hard linen table napkins, shiny from pressing. She rolls splinters of bread crust into powder between finger and thumb; pulls her hands through long lengths of her own hair. The lines of grout between the white and red floor tiles press hard into the soles of her feet; grit gets into her shoes and grinds against the leather insoles as she walks; she hears the changing percussion of her heels on tile, stone, and dusty ground. Before, she could only smell the mess of the dairy cows, the cloying scent of their milk and the jasmine flowers. Now she can smell the stone itself, limey and hard; she can smell the guards' sweat, built up over years in the fabric of their shirts. She can smell her own sweat, and Pip's hair that needs washing again. She can smell Marcie's face powder. She can smell the dust in the tasselled curtains.

Pip is determined to make a pet of one of the guard dogs. He spends two days studying and assessing them, decides which seems the most receptive and names it Bobby.

'*Bobby?*' Marcie echoes, when he tells them

over lunch. 'Shouldn't he have an Italian name, though? It'll be hard enough to tame him if he can't understand you.'

'It's short for Roberto,' says Pip, with a grin, and Marcie laughs.

'You must be careful, Pip,' says Clare. 'Mr Cardetta warned you that they're not the kind of dogs you're used to.'

'I know, but Bobby's different. Come and see, will you? Can I take him the bones from my chops?'

'Oh, sure, whatever you want,' says Marcie. 'Only don't ask me to go and stroke the thing. I've never liked dogs.'

'Bobby's not a thing! Come on, Clare.' The dogs start barking as soon as they appear through the front door of the *masseria*. Their feet churn the dust as they pace at the ends of their chains; their voices are deep and hoarse. Clare had expected lean, sparse, desert dogs to cope with the Puglian climate, like the dogs from the hieroglyphs on an ancient tomb; not these heavy, shaggy, white things. The fur under their bellies is filthy and knotted. Pip leads her to one, which she assumes is Bobby. It cowers and bares its teeth; it snarls even as it wags its tail; runs at them then sidles back. The animal has been driven half-mad by its tethered life and has no idea who or what it is, or how to behave towards a stranger offering food, and Clare both pities and fears it. Its confusion is dangerous; Pip can't know what the dog will do next if it doesn't know itself. She takes his arm, stops him getting too close.

'Careful, darling. Please — I know you like him but it will take him a while to trust you, and if he's frightened he might bite.'

'He won't bite me,' says Pip, but Clare's relieved to see he keeps himself at a prudent distance. Bobby refuses to come and take the pork bones, and in the end Pip has to throw them. The dog stinks; Clare can smell its breath when it barks. Its bewilderment pierces her heart. 'He could be a good dog, don't you think?' says Pip.

'He already is — he has a job to do here, and perhaps it's not very fair to try and interfere with that,' she says.

'I'm not *interfering*,' says Pip, hurt. 'I'm only making friends.'

'I know, darling. Come on — fancy a walk?'

★ ★ ★

Later, when Ettore joins them for dinner, Clare's distracted by nerves. She can't concentrate on the food or on Marcie's chatter. She can sense Pip's curiosity, and their hostess's slight mania; she guesses that there is some family drama concerning Leandro's nephew, yet to play out. Most of all she can sense Ettore's indecision, his desperation. She sits forward, ready, not sure what she's ready for. He gives her the same feeling as Bobby does — that she has no idea what he will do next; that he also has no idea. He eats like he hasn't in a week and she wants to steady him in case he chokes. He is whip-thin, the muscles on his arms and shoulders are lean

185

and hard; there's nothing spare. Below his ribs his stomach is concave. When she speaks to him she hopes she is understood. Their rapid English, which they allow to pass him by, seems like an insult, and she hates it. She thinks hard, searching out the right words in Italian, and when she says them there's the slightest easing of his tension, and she's glad. She wants to know about his unusual eyes, but what can she ask? These things happen; the commingled blood of a thousand ancestors produces strange anomalies, now and then. She wants to tell him he is beautiful, but he wouldn't want to hear it. He's living through a crisis, she can feel it, and she couldn't bear to make herself ridiculous to him.

Ettore keeps himself apart from them. The next day, Marcie and Pip start their acting lessons in the unused room high in the south-west corner of the *masseria*, which has windows looking out across the *aia*, and to the horizon where the sun will set. Clare goes up to watch, for something to do, because her mind is too full and there are no books to read, nothing to distract her, or to keep her eyes from searching him out constantly. The room is empty of furniture apart from a dusty old couch — sagging, dishevelled — which they drag in from a neighbouring room and position facing the dais where a bed would once have been, which will be the stage. On the wall above this platform are the faded remains of a large mural, painted into a shallow, half-moon alcove. There are traces of blue and red robes, the feet of a dog, faces blurred by time and the chalking of

186

the plaster. One perfect brown eye remains, floating in strange clarity in the obliterated remains of a face. It's wide and benign, but still it gives Clare an uneasy feeling, a sense of being transparent.

Marcie and Pip's voices echo back at them from the lofty ceiling; the curtains have been taken down, the rest of the walls are bare. In the corner where the roof leaks there's bat shit on the tiles and a swathe of algae and water stain creeping down the wall.

'So it must rain here, sooner or later,' says Clare.

'Oh, yes. It's long overdue. Mind you, last year was a *disaster* — such a drought! And all the men muttering darkly about the harvest, all the time. Oh, it was grim. This year's been positively soggy in comparison,' says Marcie. 'We had one rainstorm — well, you would have had to see it to believe it. You see the way the ground goes into that shallow gully out front there?' She points out of the window, and Clare nods. 'Full of water. Running like a river. It was amazing! I went a little bit nuts at the sight of it — I'd have paddled in it if Leandro hadn't stopped me. They all just stood there and stared at it — all the farm boys. Like they'd never seen such a thing, and I suppose maybe they never had. It was all gone by the next morning, of course.'

'Oh, look at the bats!' says Pip, pointing up. Along one ceiling beam are a clustered line of dark bodies, silent and unmoving.

'Ugh! Don't!' Marcie shudders. 'It'll be far, far better if I just pretend they aren't there. Now, first things first. Some exercises to loosen us up and make us breathe and project properly. Filippo, if you'll join me.' She steps up onto the dais and shakes out her arms.

For almost an hour Clare watches Pip and Marcie inhaling and *do-re-me*-ing; rolling their heads, shaking their hands, expanding their ribcages. They each recite a favourite poem and then some lines from a play, and Marcie gives tips in the same breath as she praises, and Clare thinks that she would have made an excellent teacher if she hadn't ended up on a remote farm in the remotest part of Italy. The smell of the guano makes her head ache; dust from the sofa makes her itch. It's all she can do to sit still, not get up and run somewhere; she doesn't know where. Then the dogs all start barking at once, the metal gates squeal and they hear a motor pulling in. Marcie pauses, then beams and claps her hands.

'That's a wrap, Pip — here's your pop and my Leandro!' She ushers them out, biting her lips and patting her hair into its neat wave. Clare's hair is unravelling from its knot, as usual; she knows her face is shiny from the heat, and she doesn't care. She doesn't care if Boyd sees her that way, and can't decide if she envies or pities Marcie for her devotion to beauty, and her obvious devotion to her husband. Clare wouldn't want Ettore Tarano to see her wearing make-up. She wouldn't want to accentuate the obvious — that their two lives, their two worlds, could not be further apart. It troubles her, as they go down to the courtyard, to realise that it's his eyes she's trying to see herself through, not Boyd's.

After he's spoken with his nephew, and they've eaten lunch, Leandro insists on taking them on a tour of the farm, and the four of them follow obediently as he shows them around the barns and the dairy and the dusty olive grove that stretches over several acres to the front of the *masseria*. Marcie ties a diaphanous scarf over her hat and loosely under her chin, and flaps her hand constantly at the flies.

'This damned dust gets into everything — you'll soon see, Clare. Just you wait, when you get ready for bed later you'll find it in your chemise,' she says.

'My Marcie is a city girl,' says Leandro, with a smile. 'This is honest dirt, honey. Not like the soot and corruption of New York.'

'I knew where I was with soot and corruption,' says Marcie. 'And there weren't all these bugs.'

'My friend John is obsessed with insects,' says Pip, walking ahead of Boyd and Clare, alongside Leandro and Marcie. 'He catches them and puts them in jars to study them. Then when they die he pins them to pieces of card and keeps them. Even little tiny gnats and thunderbugs. Although, he has to use glue for the thunderbugs because they're too small to pin.'

'Ugh.' Marcie gives a shudder. 'And you're *friends* with this kid, Filippo?'

'Better an odd interest than no interests at all,' says Leandro. 'I'm an oddity, myself. Just ask anyone around here. Many men who leave Puglia for America never come back. And those that do buy a patch of land, and only then remember what farming down here is like, and are broke again in a matter of months.'

At the far side of the olive field is a *trullo* built into a section of field wall, sitting empty with weeds growing all around and inside it. Pip ducks inside the small building straight away, picking his way through fallen stones.

'There's not much in here,' he calls out. 'Lizards and thistles.'

'Watch out for snakes,' says Leandro, and laughs when Pip goes still. Clare gives him an anxious look. 'You should be fine. But mind where you put your feet.'

'They're kind of like igloos, aren't they?' says Marcie. Boyd is walking slowly around the structure, studying the way the stones are laid.

'In the sense that the shape of the blocks and of the cone allows for the entire structure to be stabilised without the need for mortar or separate roof supports? Yes, very similar,' he says.

'Well, sure.' Marcie smiles, flustered. 'That's exactly what I meant.'

'There's a proper chimney,' says Pip, his voice echoing. Clare peers in; he has his head in the hearth.

'They're hovels,' says Leandro, with a dismissive grunt. 'Let's carry on. Much more to see.'

As they walk, Clare finds curiosity overcoming her distrust of Leandro. He is so relaxed, so benign, she can hardly credit her own memory of the way he spoke to her in Gioia.

'How is farming here, then, Mr Cardetta? You said the men who come back from America try to farm but mostly fail,' she says.

'I'm a novelty, Mrs Kingsley, in that I live on the land I own, and run it myself. Most of Puglia is *latifundia* — huge estates owned by rich, ancient families, some of whom haven't actually been here in decades. They let the farms out on short leases to tenants who often aren't even farmers, and have no experience of it at all. They're speculators, with no incentive to make improvements to the land whatsoever. They make what profit they can and then they leave.' He shrugs. 'They use antique ways of farming that exhaust the soil. There's no irrigation, no effective fertilisation, no proper crop rotation. We're on the edge of failure, every year. So a drought like last year? Total disaster. Men starving to death in the streets, in some places. The tenants are working with tiny margins — there's no room for error. They're on the brink of ruin themselves a lot of the time, and the only thing they can control is how much or little they pay the workers. I hope to break this cycle. This is my land, and I want to see it fruitful and stable. I want to pass it down to my sons thriving.' He sweeps his arm across the wide view of dry, rocky ground. 'In whatever limited way it can thrive,' he amends. Marcie loops her arm through his and squeezes it.

'My visionary husband,' she says.

'Most Puglian landlords hate the place and can't wait to leave, but not me. The government posts disgraced officials down here as a *punishment*,' he says proudly. 'But I can take whatever Puglia throws at me.'

191

They have come around in a large loop, and are approaching the *masseria* buildings from the back. As they get nearer they see two or three men standing around a tethered mule, one of them working bellows into a portable furnace, sweat running down his face. The mule's mouth has been wedged open with wooden blocks secured with ropes around its head; its top lip is clamped viciously between the metal bars of a device that looks like a giant nutcracker. Each time the animal attempts to move, a hard-faced man gives a jerk of the clamp, and the animal holds still, rolling its eyes, its ears laid flat back against its head.

'What are they doing to that poor mule?' says Pip, as they draw nearer.

'The animals here get a thing called lampas,' says Leandro. 'The roof of the mouth swells up and hardens, right behind the front teeth. It's because of the rough food they get — straw and coarse stuff like that. It can get to the point where the beast can't eat properly. The twitch, that device Ludo has hold of — that's my overseer, Ludo Manzo — isn't as bad as it looks. It actually helps the animal to relax.'

'It looks evil,' says Boyd. The man who had the bellows has taken a long, ridged iron tool from the coals, glowing red hot at its tip.

'Let's not watch,' says Marcie. 'Come on, Pip, Clare. Let's go inside.' The keen way she says it makes Clare only too happy to follow her, but Pip lags behind, turning his head to see.

Leandro and Boyd turn and start to follow the women, and then the mule starts to scream.

There's a smell of burning flesh, and Pip goes pale.

'Make them stop it,' he says, in a stunned voice.

'Come away, Pip,' says Clare, when she finds her voice. But Pip is frozen in horror and can't seem to look away.

'Cardetta — isn't that dreadfully cruel?' says Boyd. He too looks shocked; his face has paled. 'There must be a better way to treat the poor creature.'

'This is how it's done.' Leandro shrugs.

'Pip, come *on*,' says Clare. The mule's screams are making her wince; she has the urge to put her hands over her ears, to run from it.

'It's horrible!' Pip cries. There are tears in his eyes and he looks panicked. Swallowing hard Clare puts her arm around his shoulders and turns him forcibly. Leandro glances over with an inscrutable expression.

'It is horrible, Pip, but it's also necessary. Like a lot of things in life. It does no good to look the other way. That changes nothing.'

'Really, Cardetta, he's just a boy. And this *isn't* how things are in our life — he's not used to such things, and he needn't become so,' says Boyd frostily. Leandro smiles slightly at Boyd, and for some reason it chills Clare — or perhaps it's the way Boyd recoils from it.

'Really? In my experience there's ugliness and violence in every life. It's only a question of how well concealed they are,' he says neutrally. 'Down here, we don't draw a veil over them.' Clare looks at Boyd but he says nothing more. He turns his back on Leandro and marches towards the farm buildings with his head down, frowning. Pip shrugs Clare's arm off gently and wipes at the tears on his cheeks.

'I'm really fine, Clare,' he says.

'Made of sterner stuff, aren't you, boy?' says Leandro, catching up with them and clapping Pip on the shoulder. Pip manages to nod, though his face is still slack with horror.

For a while they can still hear the mule screaming from inside the *masseria*, and Clare's head starts to throb with faint, imagined echoes of its torture. Pip has gone silent and morose, she suspects partly from shame at his own reaction to the scene, and she wants to tell him that he was right to be horrified, that he was right to cry. It's the nature of boys to want to be like the men around them, but she never wants him to be as callously habituated to such things as Leandro is. She wishes Boyd would go to him and share his disgust, but Boyd has gone just as quiet as his son; he withdraws to a private room, muttering about the need to work. Clare wants to hug Pip and talk to him about it like she would at home, but things have changed subtly here, and with Marcie and Leandro watching she daren't. When he pushed her encircling arm away, as they walked away from the mule, it was the first time he had ever rejected her touch.

★ ★ ★

In their room after dinner she's unresponsive when Boyd hugs her. The anger, which lay still

194

while they were in company, now rises again. They undress gradually and hang up their clothes, and the lamp conjures deep shadows in every corner. Clare finds lines of dirt under the straps of her bra, just as Marcie said she would. In his vest, shorts and socks, Boyd peers into the foxed mirror on the wardrobe door and combs his pale hair, frowning at it as if displeased. It looks just the same after he's combed it — soft, wispy thin, close to his skull. Like a baby's hair. Satisfied with it he comes across to her and kisses her, and she allows him to for just a moment before she drops her chin and turns her face away. He gives her a quizzical look, and when she doesn't smile he moves away and pulls off his socks with a cautious air. He clears his throat.

'Are you all right, Clare?'

'I don't know,' she says, truthfully enough.

'Is it . . . what you saw in Gioia? Is it still troubling you?'

'What I saw in Gioia will trouble me for the rest of my life.' She watches him, and keeps her eyes on him, and he skits about in front of her as if he can't bear her gaze — from the nightstand to the cupboard to the window and back.

'Yes, of course.' He steps into his pyjama trousers, buttons up the jacket, sits down on the edge of the mattress. 'Will you come to bed? I've missed you so much these past few days.' He looks down at his feet as he says this. His toes are long, bony and white, like the rest of him; his stomach is a soft rise behind the jacket, more noticeable than usual. Leandro has been feeding him well these past few weeks.

'I feel wide awake,' she says, and goes over to the window. Their room looks east; nothing to see but a swathe of dark ground, and in the distance the paler shade of a field of wheat stubble, lit by the moon.

'Is it . . . is it something I've done, Clare? You're being very cold,' he says, sounding miserable. At once she feels the familiar guilt, and at the same time the new anger, all of it together, but she refuses to be paralysed by it. She won't be gagged any more.

'I want to know who Leandro Cardetta is. I want to know why we must do everything he says.'

'Clare — '

'Please . . . show me the respect I deserve as your wife, and as someone who has been with you through several . . . crises,' she says, turning to him on the word 'crises', so that he knows exactly what she means. She means Christina Havers. The wife of a London client; the woman Boyd bedded for a time. He flinches and drops his gaze. She has such power to hurt him, power she doesn't want. 'Please tell me truthfully. Who is he?' For a long time Boyd doesn't answer. He swallows, and laces his fingers together, but she won't let him off; she waits.

'Leandro Cardetta,' Boyd says eventually. He pauses, flutters one hand across his eyes. 'Leandro Cardetta is a very dangerous man.'

A shiver runs over Clare's skin; the hairs stand up along her arms. Boyd shoots her a wretched little glance, and she blinks.

'In what way is he dangerous?' she says.

196

'In every way you can think of, Clare,' he whispers, as though afraid of being overheard. From somewhere else in the house comes the sudden, distant peal of Marcie's laughter, and Clare has a powerful feeling of unreality again, when she knows that this is all too real.

'Is he . . . is he a criminal?'

'He . . . yes. He was, when I first knew him. Now . . . I'm not sure. I don't think so. He seems to want to be . . . respectable. He seems to want the farm to work.'

'My God, Boyd . . . my God, what kind of criminal?' Clare whispers.

'What kind?' Boyd echoes, as if bewildered by the question. 'I suppose . . . I suppose you'd call him a mobster.'

'A mobster? What do you mean?'

'Organised crime . . . In New York. I . . . I don't know. Theft . . . extortion . . . I'm not sure. It's a world I don't know, but it's a dark world, and a violent one. I can't say what he's done, or what he hasn't.' As Boyd says this he pinches his eyes shut with the forefinger and thumb of one hand, curls his other arm around his middle. Hiding. Clare stares and thinks and can't speak. 'I'm sorry, Clare. I'm sorry that . . . you're under the same roof as him . . . '

'Is he a killer?' she says. The question appals her.

'I don't know. He could be.'

'Does Marcie know?'

'I have no idea.'

'How . . . how ever did you come to know him?'

'I . . . he . . . ' Boyd murmurs these two words and then goes silent. He shakes his head, and there are tears in his eyes.

Clare doesn't know how to feel, but he looks so dejected that she goes to sit beside him, and leans her face against his shoulder.

'These people . . . once they've got your name, you see . . . once they know who you are, and how they can make use of you, then they'll use any means to do so. They threaten what's dear to you . . . '

'He's threatened you?' she says, and Boyd nods. 'That's why when he wanted Pip and me to come out, for Marcie, you agreed?'

'Yes. I did everything I could to dissuade him, and I said several times that I wouldn't take the commission. I didn't want anything more to do with him, but . . . he insisted.' Boyd shakes his head, perplexed. 'He insisted, and I'm a coward, Clare. He swears that this will be the last time, and I . . . I've seen what he can do. He knows where I work, so he could find out where we live, I'm sure of it. I just couldn't risk alienating him. I'm so sorry. You must believe how sorry I am.'

'Jesus Christ, Boyd!' For a moment Clare almost laughs at the absurdity of it — avuncular Leandro, with his skittish, ebullient wife. 'She can't know — Marcie *can't* know. I can't believe it.'

'Perhaps you're right. She doesn't seem . . . the type.'

'So then, perhaps he *has* left it all behind him?' Clare suggests. 'Now that he has Marcie, and now that he's come home to Gioia

198

. . . Perhaps whatever he did in New York made him rich enough.'

'I never met a rich man who didn't want to be richer still,' says Boyd, and shakes his head. 'Please, *please* do nothing to test him, Clare. Promise me!' He takes her hand and squeezes it hard, and she winces.

'I promise.' She takes a deep breath in and smells that sharp, sour scent, and realises now that it's the smell of her husband's fear. 'But how does he even know you, Boyd? Why would he want *you*, of all people, to come to Italy and design his wretched new façade?'

'I think . . . ' Boyd shakes his head and looks across at her with his eyes still swimming. 'Christ, Clare, I think he just really liked the building I designed in New York.'

They look at one another and then laugh, just for a second. An incredulous laugh, brought on by nerves and adrenalin. It soon passes, and Boyd shakes his head again. 'It's really not funny at all, is it?' he says.

'Not one bit,' Clare agrees.

'What should I have done differently? Tell me. What would you have done?' he says. Clare stands up, feeling light, alert, ready for violence. The feeling is alien to her, and it's troubling but electric too; she feels very alive. She goes over to the window and looks out at the flat ground, silver in the moonlight, and feels so far from everything she knows that she could be on Mars. Just days ago she would have reassured him, even if the words had felt like cotton wool in her mouth. Now, that urge is gone.

'What would I have done?' She folds her arms, running her fingers over the rough gooseflesh of them. 'I've have told him to hang from his damned façade,' she says. 'I would. But you didn't say that. And here we are, you and I and Pip, stuck in a place where some kind of civil war is breaking out, in the house of a mobster and a show girl, and entirely at their disposal. What could possibly be wrong?' She says it lightly but there's no more laughter, no more smiles.

'You're different, Clare . . . what's happened? What's changed?' says Boyd.

'I woke up,' she says softly.

After a long pause she turns to the bed, and climbs in on her side. 'We'd better hope he likes your designs, or perhaps it'll be curtains for us.' Boyd frowns at this and lies down beside her, not trying to touch her. He leaves the light on as if they might talk more, but for a long time they are silent. Clare rolls onto her side, turning her back to him.

'You're so strong, Clare. So much stronger than I am. I'm so lucky to have you . . . I know I am. I couldn't be without you, darling,' says Boyd. 'I don't know what I'd do, if I ever lost you.' Clare lies very still and doesn't answer him. None of it is a question, but all of it begs for acknowledgement. She feels hot, and hard, and tightly wound; she doesn't trust herself to speak. She stares at the heavy door to their room; the vast iron lock, the archaic key that sits in it, ready to be turned. But she is trapped with Boyd already, of course. She has been for years.

Next morning there's a hush at the breakfast

table, as if they're all waiting for something; even Marcie seems to feel it because though she smiles a great deal, words are few. After a while Clare realises that she isn't the only one waiting for Ettore to appear — her hosts are too. The longer he doesn't show, the more strained Marcie seems, and the darker Leandro's expression becomes.

'Perhaps your nephew wasn't feeling very well again when he woke up. Do you think I should go and check on him?' says Pip. All eyes turn to him, and he blushes, and Clare wonders at his intuition. For a second Leandro's hard, black gaze settles on Pip, and Clare's heart lurches, but then his face softens and he shrugs a little.

'I saw him out first thing this morning. Loping along on that crutch he's found. He's fine, Pip, he just doesn't want to sit down and eat like a gentleman.'

'Why not?' says Pip.

'Philip, it's rude to pry,' says Boyd, keeping his eyes on the slice of bread in front of him, the puddle of honey where a fly is trying to land. He is sitting in a shaft of morning sun, squinting; the women have their backs to it.

'Well, my nephew thinks I've sold out,' says Leandro, ignoring Boyd.

'What does that mean?'

'It means he thinks I've betrayed my people — my class — by getting rich, and becoming the owner of this place instead of one of the peasants who simply work on it.'

'I should've thought he'd be happy about it,' says Pip. 'Like now, when he's sick, and he can come here to recover. Isn't he happy about that?'

'Oh, Pip, dear, it's very complicated,' says Marcie. 'The peasants here, they're . . . well, it's like they're from a different country altogether. Like they're a different kind of people, you know? They have their own rules and codes and . . . ' She waves a hand, doesn't finish.

'Am I a different kind of person to the rest of you?' says Leandro. His voice is smooth and even, but the words jolt Marcie.

'No, of *course* not, sugar. I was only trying to explain . . . '

'Perhaps explanations are better left to those who understand,' he says. Marcie smiles and nods, and turns all her attention to her cup of coffee. Pip's cheeks blaze on her behalf, and Leandro smiles when he sees.

'Ettore is happy for me. That is, he was. He doesn't resent my wealth — it's not that. So many men went to America from here, and so few came back. His sister's husband went, and he vanished. They've had no word from him in five years now. I tried to find him over there; I tried constantly, but I never did. The last anybody heard, he was digging tunnels for the subway. Now he could be dead, alive . . . ' Leandro shrugs. 'And as I said before, those that do come back usually spend what little money they saved and are soon back to where they started.

'These are hard times; even the rich aren't rich. The peasants look at a farm like this and they think the man who owns it must be rich. But we're not — not by any measure outside of

Puglia. The yields are poor, petrol is hard to come by, the government took most of the machinery and good animals during the war, it never damn well rains, the soil is ruined from generations of bad farming . . . We can't afford to pay as many workers as want work. We leave some land fallow, because we can't afford to pay the men to work it, and what do they do? They go and work it anyway — their Chambers of Labour tell them they have the right to work, so they go and they work it, and then they come to the proprietor and demand to be paid for their labour! So, at first my nephew was happy to see me, and he thought that because I know what life is like for these men, I would give them work — plentiful work, for good pay, all the year round. But I can't do that, so he tells me I am one of them now, and he hates me.' Leandro spreads his hands and shakes his head. 'I'm wrong to say he hates me,' he adds quietly. 'He's only angry. Angry that I couldn't find Paola's husband in New York. Angry that I can't change the world for him. Angry about what happened at the Girardi place last year. Angry that his woman is dead.'

Clare starts at this, she can't help it. Boyd covers her hand with his but she doesn't look at him. *His woman is dead.* A dry breeze moves through the courtyard, reaches into the buildings and slams a door. The tablecloth flutters. Nobody speaks; they all wait for Leandro's lead, and keep their eyes down, and suddenly Clare hates herself, and all of them, for their cowardice. She looks across at Leandro.

'A serious subject for the breakfast table,' she says.

'The world is a serious place, Mrs Kingsley,' says Leandro. She notices how rarely he blinks. But then he smiles. 'But you're right. These are not matters to be solved over morning coffee. At least the boy is healing; I've no wish to see him ruined. I offer him work here on the *masseria* — I offer it every time. But the *annaroli* are as bad as the proprietors, as far as the *giornatari* are concerned.'

'What's an *annaroli*? And what happened at the Girardi place?' says Pip.

'*Annarolo* means a man who works here all year round, in a permanent job — the overseer and the herdsman, the corporals. And never mind Girardi. Come — let's talk of other things. I'll speak to my nephew again today, and what's between us is for us to untangle. Tell me instead about this play you're devising.'

Clare wants to ask him about the woman who is dead, the woman who belonged to Ettore, but she doesn't dare. Suddenly, it's more important than Leandro's past, more important than his hold over Boyd and the lies she's been told. She concentrates on breathing; she can smell the cattle on the breeze, and a woody, fungus aroma she can't place. She can smell the greasy dogs on their rusty chains. She gets to her feet, knocks the table and causes cutlery to chime against porcelain.

'Clare, are you all right?' says Boyd. She looks down at him, and it feels as though she's looking at him from a long way away.

'I'm fine. I think I'll go for a walk; I need some fresh air.' She knows this sounds absurd, since they're sitting outside, but she doesn't care.

'I'll go with you,' says Pip, also standing and snatching up the last piece of bread from his plate. Nobody else offers and Clare is relieved. Pip is the only one she can be with just then.

'Rehearsals when you get back, Filippo,' Marcie calls as they go. She turns to Boyd and adds: 'I've been wracking my brains, but I honestly don't think that there *is* an Italian version of Boyd, I'm afraid.' Clare doesn't hear Boyd's murmured reply.

Once Pip has stopped to greet Bobby, who barks slightly less but still fidgets at the end of his tether, they walk out through the main gates and around the back, past the *trulli* where some of the men sleep. One or two loiter there, simply standing, smoking. Clare feels their eyes following her and Pip. She looks over defiantly but one of them is Federico, and she looks away again quickly, but not before she catches that same questioning look in his eye, and perhaps Pip notices it too, because he scowls even as he gives them a small wave. The mule that was treated for lampas is standing in the stockade with its head down, a picture of misery. Clare says nothing, hoping Pip won't notice it there.

In the distance the milking herd are grazing in a walled field, so they walk in that direction, glad for something to aim for, something to look at. Aside from the dusty road that leads away from the gates, there are no discernible paths. The road curves away and vanishes behind the shallow hill; Clare has no idea if Gioia lies to the north, south, east or west. She can't exactly picture where she is within Italy, other than south; far south. This realisation frightens her — she is completely lost. Completely dependent on Boyd and Leandro.

'You don't like Mr Cardetta very much, do you?' says Pip, with studied casualness. He picks up a stick from beneath an olive tree and starts to peel away the bark. Mr Cardetta, he says, not Leandro — just as she instructed. Clare wonders how stern she must look for him to suddenly do as she's asked. She tries to soften her face but it's not quite in her control.

'I don't feel I know him well enough to decide yet,' she says, and this seems to trouble him.

'But you like Marcie, don't you?'

'Yes, of course. It would be hard not to like someone like Marcie.'

'That's a reason to like Mr Cardetta, isn't it? I mean, if somebody nice has married a person, I usually take it as a good sign about them. Don't you?'

'I suppose so. Sometimes. But people do change,' says Clare. 'He obviously loves her a great deal.'

'Are you going to watch our rehearsal today?'

'Would you like me to?'

'Yes, of course. Only it might ruin the play if you watch all the rehearsals. I mean, we're planning a surprise ending.'

'Well, I'll watch until you come to something you want to keep secret, how about that?'

'All right.' He swishes the olive stick, makes it

*whoop* through the air. 'Have you seen any other ch — ' He cuts himself off, caught in the act of calling himself a child. 'Young people here? At the *masseria*, I mean?'

'No. I'm afraid I haven't,' says Clare, knowing how lonely and quiet it must be for him.

'Good job I've got Bobby,' he says stoutly. She puts her arm around his shoulders for a moment, and gives them a squeeze.

'Do you know, my aunt's old dog used to go bananas for toast crusts? Especially if there was a bit of jam on them. He'd do anything — turn circles, play dead, shake hands. Maybe toast crusts will be the key to Bobby's heart,' she says.

They stop at the edge of the cattle field and sit down on the wall for a while. Lizards scatter from their feet, darting out of sight; flies appear at once to buzz around their heads. The cows are browsing the wheat stubble and the dark, dirty weeds in amongst it. The herd leader's bell has a sad chime, flat and in a minor key, and they all whisk their tails continually at the flies. A few of them have small calves at their feet, and the calves try repeatedly to suckle from their mothers. From a distance it's hard to work out why they can't seem to manage it, but as the herd gradually comes closer Clare sees the collars the calves are wearing — collars of long metal spikes, even longer than those that the guard dogs wear. Every time the calf gets close enough to reach for the udders, its mother gets jabbed, kicks out and moves away from it. The calves are bony and forlorn, they pick at the stubble while their mothers' udders swell.

'Why aren't they allowed to drink?' says Pip, and in an instant Clare knows the answer.

'So we can.'

'Oh. That's so cruel, though,' he says, and he looks across at them, scowling. Clare wants to get up and walk away from the pitiful spectacle, and try to distract Pip from this realisation, but something stops her. They both drank the milk at breakfast, and ate the fresh mozzarella the night before.

'A lot of what people do to animals is cruel. A lot of what people do to people is cruel,' she says, surprising herself. She wouldn't normally say such a thing to Pip, especially not after the brutal spectacle of the mule the day before. Not every cow has a calf, and she thinks of the veal they ate back at the house in Gioia. Pip stands up and turns his back to them.

'Well, I think it's completely unacceptable. They're only babies! I'm going to ask Marcie — I bet she could get them to take the collars off.'

'I don't think you should, Pip. This is how the farm is run . . . It's not up to you. It's probably not up to Marcie.'

'You always used to say I should stand up against injustice however I could,' he challenges her.

'Yes.'

'Well then.' He shrugs.

'Pip — '

'You said we were going to go home.' He sounds petulant, younger than his age, so she knows how unhappy he is, and she's hit by a

208

wave of guilt; she puts her hand out to him.

'I'm sorry. It's . . . it's not up to me.' For a moment they're silent. Pip ignores her hand, kicking at a rock the size of his fist, knocking it to and fro. 'You do understand that, don't you? Your father wants us to stay,' Clare says.

'How long for?'

'I don't know. Until he's finished his work, I suppose. Mr Cardetta wants us to stay too, to keep Marcie company.'

'Marcie told me we're the first guests that have come to stay with them here — the first ones ever. Can you believe that?'

'Well, it's no wonder they want us to stay then, is it?' she says. Pip shrugs, and nods. He kicks at the rock and lashes the olive stick to and fro, full of frustration. Clare looks to the horizon, across the vast stretch of land, dry as old bones, beneath a sky like hot metal. She thinks it no wonder that the Cardettas' first guests have been compelled to come, and must be compelled to stay.

After that Clare walks a lot. She walks in the morning and late in the afternoon, when the heat is not as fierce. Even so, her face and arms begin to tan, and freckles appear across the bridge of her nose. Marcie exclaims in dismay at them, and loans Clare a white scarf to drape over the brim of her hat, but it's too hot and Clare can't stand it obscuring her vision, so she carries it but doesn't use it. Boyd insists on accompanying her on one occasion, but after his attempts at conversation founder they walk in a silence that he clearly finds excruciating. Clare doesn't mind it. Suddenly she has nothing to say to her husband, and there's nothing she needs to hear from him. When he holds her hand sweat slides between their palms. After that he lets her walk by herself. Leandro suggests she takes Federico with her and she declines at once.

'It's really not necessary.'

'I'm not sure you're best placed to say if it is or it isn't,' he says.

'I'd far rather walk alone.'

'Then stay within the bounds of this farm. Please, Mrs Kingsley.' He holds her hand in his two as he speaks, and squeezes it, and Clare catches her breath. His hands are large and there's no give in them, like they're made of wood.

'Very well,' she says.

But it's hard to know where Cardetta's land ends and the next farm begins. There are only fields, caught between stone walls, one after the other, on and on and on. Here and there are stunted orchards; here and there isolated *trulli*, some in ruins, some with smoke curling up from squat chimney stacks. Clare avoids them. She changes direction when she sees men working up ahead, ashamed to spy on their labours. Once she stumbles across a group of mounted men, their horses in a loose circle, their eyes down. There's movement on the ground, at the horses' feet, and Clare glimpses the shocking, incongruous flash of pale bare flesh. She stares. A man is on his hands and knees, pulling at the short stubble of wheat stalks with his teeth. He's naked, and has lash marks on his back; he's not

210

young, he could be forty or fifty years old; his ribs have dark shadows between each bone. Shocked, Clare recognises Ludo Manzo, the overseer, as one of the mounted men; he has a long whip in his hand, hanging down like a snake. When they notice her they all look up — the mounted men, Ludo, the naked man on the ground. Clare expects them to stop, to scatter, to be ashamed and try to explain or apologise somehow, but Ludo only grins. He points to the man on the ground and says something Clare can't understand, which makes the other guards chuckle. She looks down at their victim, and his expression of anger and humiliation is a mask over bare bones of despair. There's a churned slick of dust and drool around his mouth, down over his chin. Clare can't stand his gaze, she's almost relieved when Ludo flicks the whip and the man resumes his slow grazing. Then she hurries away, sickened by them and by herself, and tells nobody of the scene. She has no words to describe it.

Returning from one walk as the sun is setting, Clare finds Federico in the courtyard; he's rubbing the red car with a rag, and where he's taken off the dust the sunlight roars on the paintwork. When he sees her he grins, and again she notices the way his mouth flattens itself out of its unusual shape when he does. The divide in his top lip is still there, his front teeth are twisted, but the smile is foremost. Clare smiles politely in reply and makes to walk past him but he reaches out and stops her with the tips of his fingers on her arm.

'*Signora, prego,*' he says. Clare looks down at something he's holding out to her. Flowers — a small posy of spiked thistle flowers, pretty and pale blue amidst their thorns. She stares at them. 'For you,' he says, in heavily accented English. He makes her a small bow, still smiling, and Clare's hand rises even as she feels a rush of unease. That look of his, the one he gives her. She still can't decide if her aversion to him is wise or unfair. She lets her hand fall again.

'Thank you,' she says, in Italian. 'But I'm afraid I can't take them. I'm a married woman.' At this he grins even wider.

'I won't tell him,' he says. She looks closely at him, trying to read him. Then she shakes her head.

'Thank you, but find a different girl to give them to.' She turns away and goes inside, and doesn't look back even when she thinks she hears him chuckle.

Before Boyd leaves for Gioia again he hugs Clare tight, and presses kisses onto her forehead.

'I'll see you soon,' he says, sounding hopeful rather than sure. Just then his lost look, his uncertainty, pricks at her. She thinks of Francesco Molino, dragged out and beaten in public, and reaches up to touch Boyd's face. The hard, vulnerable ridge of his eye socket.

'Get those designs finished so we can go home. And be careful, Boyd,' she says quietly. 'Do be careful.'

'I will,' he says.

'I mean it.'

'So do I — and the same goes for you. Why

212

not let the servant walk with you? He can walk behind if you don't want to talk to him.'

'No, no. It would feel like being stalked. There's no danger here — how can there be when I almost never see a living soul?' Clare waits with Pip and Marcie as the two men climb into the back of the car and Federico drives them away. And she's relieved — in one way or another, she is relieved to see the back of all three of them. When they're gone and before the doors close behind them, Clare runs her eyes around the *aia*. She returns to the courtyard, looks up at the upstairs windows, the terrace. There has been no sign of Ettore Tarano that day.

'He might come out of hiding now Leandro's gone,' says Marcie. Clare stops looking, glances questioningly at Marcie. 'Our Ettore, I mean. I think he was just trying to make a point by keeping away. Men! Their pride is their own worst enemy, don't you think?'

'Pride is better than some other things I could think of,' says Clare. Marcie gives her a quizzical look, but doesn't ask.

Before dinner Clare goes and lies down in the still and quiet of the bedroom. She leaves the windows open, though flies buzz in incessantly. She stares at the shadowed ceiling and wonders how long she will be able to stand it — being trapped, being lost, being so awake, and having the maddening presence of Ettore nearby. Outside the dogs bark a few times, like a scattered reflex reaction rather than a real alarm. A door closes sharply; not long afterwards she hears footsteps rushing towards her room.

'Clare!' Marcie shouts, her voice muffled by the door. Clare sits bolt upright, heart racing. 'Clare!' Marcie calls again, rapping on the bedroom door even as she opens it. 'Oh, do come, Clare! It's Pip!'

'What is it? What's happened?' says Clare, grabbing at Marcie's fluttering hands. The blonde woman's eyes are frantic and there is a smear of blood on the front of her shirt. They rush out together. 'What's happened, Marcie?'

'That damned dog! I should never have let him go near it,' says Marcie, and Clare's stomach clenches.

'Has Bobby — has the dog attacked him?'

'It was bound to happen — bound to! I should have put a stop to it! I'm so sorry, Clare!' Clare can't speak any more. She runs into Pip's room with dread clutching at her chest, to find him sitting up on the bed watching the kitchen maid, Anna, bathe his hand in a basin of water. The hand is shaking visibly, even though his arm is resting on a pillow. There are two deep puncture wounds in the heel of it, dark and constantly welling blood.

'Oh, Pip!' says Clare, and rushes over to him. 'Darling — are you all right? Oh, your hand!' she cries.

'I'm all right, Clare — really. It wasn't Bobby's fault . . . ' Clare sits down alongside him, and feels the way he's shaking, just like she herself shook after the beating in Gioia. His face is sickly white.

'Pip — '

214

'I took him some crusts and jam — just like you suggested — and he loved them! He came to take them right from my hand. But then one of the other dogs barked suddenly, and he got scared . . . '

'Oh, *Filippo*! You're being altogether too brave — look at your poor hand!' says Marcie. 'Ought I call the doctor, Clare? Should they be stitched?'

'I'm not sure.' Clare watches as Anna dribbles water into the two deep holes. The water in the bowl is a merry red, berry bright. The sight makes her dizzy — that it's Pip's blood, and there's so much of it. 'I don't think so. I think . . . just a tight bandage.' She swallows, fights to keep her voice even. She holds Pip's head close to her, and kisses his hair.

'Clare, I'm really all right,' he says, embarrassed, but there's a catch in his voice. He might cry from the shock, if it weren't for Anna and Marcie watching. It's only pride that stops him, this new need to be manly.

'You have to stay away from the dogs, Pip,' she says.

'But it wasn't Bobby's fault, Clare, it was — '

'No, Pip, I'm sorry. He bit you — whatever the reason was! You must keep away. Promise me,' she says. She pictures the heavy dog — the muscles beneath the shaggy fur, the mad, bewildered look in its eyes. If it got a proper hold of Pip it could tear him like paper.

'But, Clare — '

'*No*, Pip! Just do as I say!' Pip turns away from her, glowers at his hand. At the foot of the bed Marcie hovers and wrings her hands. She

215

can't look at the wound.

'Well, thank God you're all right, Pip, that's all I can say. How about a brandy to soothe your nerves, hm?' She smiles anxiously at him, and turns to go, and Clare hasn't the heart to object even though Pip is far too young for spirits. When Marcie brings the drink he sips it in a dignified manner, and staunchly refuses to cough when his throat objects.

Clare stays until Pip is asleep, with his fat, bandaged hand resting on his chest. She turns the knob on the gas lamp until it stops hissing and darkness rolls into the light's wake. The floor is warm beneath her bare feet; she crushes a mosquito against her forearm, and rolls it through the tiny hairs there. She can still smell Pip's blood. Anna has taken the gory water away but its metal tang lingers at the back of her throat. There's a red spot on Pip's bandage, and as she watches it gets bigger by tiny increments. She thinks of the naked man, being forced to graze like an animal; remembers the raw look in his eyes when he glanced up at her. She has such a sudden strong sense of the violence all around, the possible and the actual, that she has to grind her teeth together. It's like an electric charge in the air; the hum before a lightning strike. She feels that everything is breakable, and will break; that anything could happen, and will. She wants more than anything to be somewhere else, *anywhere* else.

With steady, silent steps, Clare goes across the courtyard, from shadow to shadow between the pooling light of the lamps. From the kitchens, where the house staff are eating, come voices in the dialect, loud and mocking. She has to insist before the guard will unlock the front door for her, and in the *aia* the nearest dog growls with gut-deep menace. The *aia* is in darkness, a deep black for the dogs to hide in. Clare pictures teeth sinking into Pip's flesh, cutting easily through the soft, elastic skin and the delicate red underneath. She thinks of Boyd leaving her naked in the library in Gioia, as shame washed out her arousal, and how now when they touch she can't feel a single thread of a bond between them. Not since she saw Francesco Molino beaten near to death; not since she saw Ettore Tarano.

She's running now, along the front of the *masseria* because she doesn't dare cross the *aia* past the dogs. Her feet are almost silent without shoes. She feels the dust flying up between her toes, the prickle of stalks and stones. For a wild instant she thinks she could run away altogether — disappear into the night and never see her husband or Leandro Cardetta again. Back to Gioia and onto a train, to Bari, Naples, Rome, home. She turns blindly to begin this escape, taking the first few steps away from the *masseria*, but at once she's surrounded by darkness so profound she can't even be sure there's ground at her feet. Everything vanishes. When she looks up there are no stars, and no moon. The light coming from the building behind her can't penetrate it; the night is like a wall. She stops. A few paces — that's what her flight has amounted to. A few paces, and she's given up already. She hangs her head, defeated, and every nerve in her body feels as sharp as glass shards, so that when she hears movement in front of her, she gasps. Even as she asks who it is she realises that she knows, and there's a subtle change in the way she feels — a change in the tension, which neither lessens nor increases but takes on a different tone: reaching out rather than coiling inward. She strains her eyes to see him but he's merely a wraith until he's standing right in front of her, with the weak light from the walls describing shoulders, hair, drawn-down brows. Ettore's eyes look clouded and sore. Clare wants to tell him everything, and in the next moment finds she's got nothing to tell.

Only when it seems like he will walk away can she speak and ask him how he is, ask about his sister's baby, about his English. She sounds like a fool to her own ears, but she wants him to stay there in the vegetable garden so that she can work out what she's feeling, and what it means. Why her eyes seek him everywhere, why the impossible vibrancy of everything she sees and smells and tastes is causing her to panic. She tells him that she hates it there, and that she wants to run away. The words are out before she can stop them, and though they're honest she regrets them. She can't find the right word and he provides it for her.

'Escape.' He says it in a low voice, and for a second she thinks he will ask her to explain, that he wants to know more. But then he tells her to go back inside, and he sounds impatient, and Clare is dismayed. She sees herself through his

218

eyes then, truly, and sees that she's ridiculous. She's nothing, and could never understand him. It's torture, and it gets worse when he leaves her there, limping past her on his crutch. He smells faintly of sweat, and of clean linen. She holds her breath to hear every last sound he makes, further and further away, until all she can hear are crickets in the foliage, faint sounds from within the *masseria*, and her own pulse, loud in her ears. She does not do as he tells her; she stays outside for a long time, in the dark, trying to know her own thoughts.

★ ★ ★

Ettore comes to breakfast the next morning; he's already at the table, waiting, when Clare and Pip come down. His eyes look bruised, the whites all bloodshot, and Clare, who has not slept, recognises the fatigue in the slow drag of his gaze. Marcie beams when she sees him.

'Well, good morning, Ettore. Dear boy, you look shattered! What on earth have you been up to? Are you ill?'

'He's working as a guard now — I think he was on the night shift,' says Clare, remembering something he said the night before. The urge to look at him is so strong that she's careful not to give in to it. She's worried she might not be able to look away again. The skin of her cheeks is tingling, and threatening to colour.

'He's working? Oh, that's wonderful! Fantastic, Ettore! I'm so pleased you've come around,' says Marcie, so loudly that Ettore winces. He

219

looks questioningly at Clare, and she takes a quick breath.

'She's happy you have agreed to work,' she tells him in Italian. Ettore frowns, and looks down at the table. He nods once.

'Oh dear — he doesn't seem too happy about it. Maybe I shouldn't have said anything — me and my big mouth! Well, let's change the subject. How's the hand, Filippo?'

'Oh it's fine, really. Thank you for asking. Just a bit sore,' says Pip, but it's his right hand that's bandaged, and he's struggling to eat breakfast with his left.

'Shall I spread that jam for you?' says Clare, reaching for his plate, but he shakes his head vehemently.

'I can do it, Clare.'

'All right.' She sits back, stung.

'What happened to his hand?' asks Ettore, nodding at Pip. The sun makes him squint until his eyes are the narrowest slits, the skin around them scored with lines; his irises are a glimpse of iridescence between his black lashes. When he speaks he has the same slow intonation as Clare, each word considered and chosen. She has to remind herself that Italian is not his first language any more than it's hers.

'He was playing with the dog and it bit him,' she says.

'With what dog? With the dogs here in the *aia*?' He shakes his head when she nods. 'Lucky it did not kill him. I have seen one kill a boy before. It took him by the throat,' he says, and grasps his neck to demonstrate. His hands are

220

nut brown, rough with scars and calluses; the nails are wide and broken off. Clare's own hand goes to her throat, mirroring him involuntarily.

'These dogs here? It happened here?' she says, breathlessly. Ettore nods.

'He was coming to ask for a mattock to use. The mattock he had was broken. He didn't know . . . where to walk.'

'I simply *must* know what you're saying,' says Marcie brightly.

'He says . . . he says that the dogs have attacked somebody before — somebody who went too close by mistake. That a boy was . . . killed.' She looks at Pip as she says this, not sure if she should translate it. He fiddles with the frayed ends of his bandage, tucking them in, and there are knots in the corners of his jaw.

'*What!* Oh, I'm sure he's mistaken — I never heard of anything like that happening here! Wouldn't I have heard about it? He must mean on some other farm,' says Marcie.

'He says this one,' says Clare.

'You're only making it up to scare me, and stop me going near them,' says Pip.

'I am not,' Clare says quietly, shocked. 'Pip, please — '

'All right! I get the message!' He struggles up from the table, hampered by his injured hand, and stalks away towards the stairs.

'Oh, *Filippo*, honey,' Marcie calls after him, but he carries on out of sight with his head down and his right arm tucked in to his midriff.

'He is scared now?' says Ettore. Clare shakes her head.

'No. He is angry with me. It's my fault we are here — he thinks so. He was trying to make the dog his friend.'

'He must choose friends more carefully.'

'He hasn't many to choose from, here.'

'Why are you here?' he asks, and she can't tell if he's curious, or if he resents their presence. She wants to explain but doesn't have the right words. She doesn't know the Italian word for *hostage*.

'I do not know,' is all she can say. 'Only your uncle can say.' At this Ettore nods slowly and looks at her steadily.

'You are honest,' he says, and Clare has nothing to reply.

'Now, what we need is to lighten the mood around here a little,' says Marcie. 'Ettore, do you think Paola would come for tea, and bring her little boy? I'm afraid I can't ask your father — Leandro would hit the roof.' She doesn't wait for Clare to translate or Ettore to answer before she carries on. 'Music, that's what we need. An evening of music and a bit of fun, to cheer up poor Pip and stop you worrying so, dear Clare. I'm going to find a gramophone if it kills me. Where shall I find one? There *must* be one in Gioia we could borrow, or buy. And we could make the doctor bring his wife and daughter, and have dinner with us. What do you think, Clare? How old is Pip? I think their daughter is sixteen, or is she older than that now? Anyway, far closer to Pip's age than any of us. They could dance together! Do you think his hand would be up to it? Perhaps in a couple of weeks when it's

222

had more of a chance to heal. Music! I haven't heard any for the longest time. I used to sing as well, you know; as well as acting. I could sing us some show tunes if only there was a piano or something to accompany me . . . '

Marcie talks on while Ettore drinks his coffee cut almost half and half with hot milk, and eats slices of fresh white cheese on crusty bread. He eats more slowly now, without the panic and fixation of when he first arrived. Clare is suddenly reminded of something.

'Marcie, has Pip said anything to you about the collars that the calves wear?' she says, interrupting the vocal march of Marcie's train of thought.

'About their collars? Oh, aren't they just *vicious*? I do hate the sight of them. Of course, they get taken off sometimes during the day, so they can drink, but not within three hours of milking or something like that. Poor little darlings! But no, Pip never said anything. Why?'

'He said he might, that's all. I told him it wouldn't be up to you, necessarily.'

'Oh, it isn't up to me at all. Ludo is the man with the power, and he reports right to Leandro. Tell Pip not to look — that's my advice. If you can't bear to see it, don't look. Ludo, Ludo — I do love the sound of that name, don't you? Tell Pip not to go near the cattle, if it upsets him. I'll tell him.' She waves a hand. When she says the name Ludo, Ettore's gaze hits her in an instant. Marcie looks over at him and smiles, but neither she nor Clare understands the black expression that fills Ettore's face. He looks so bitter and so

223

hard that nobody speaks for a long time afterwards.

Later on in the day, after Pip has had his acting lesson, or rehearsal — Clare isn't sure which it is — with Marcie, Clare goes to find him in his room. He's lying on the bed, on his side, reading. She sits down on the mattress near the small of his back, and knows he's still angry when he doesn't roll over or sit up, or turn his head to look at her. She isn't sure what to say to him, so for a long time she says nothing. From outside the window comes the clanking of the cow bell, and the muted clatter of cloven hooves as the herd come in for the afternoon milking. Eventually Pip lowers his book and sighs.

'It's hard to concentrate with you sitting there,' he says, making a play for an offhand tone of voice.

'Sorry, Pip,' she says. After a moment he turns his head and looks at her, and then props himself up on his elbows.

'Are you all right, Clare?'

'Yes. I . . . I just wanted to see whether you were. Are you angry with me about the dogs?'

'It wasn't your fault. You told me to stay away from them and I didn't. You don't have to keep checking up on me, you know. I'm not a little boy.'

'I know you're not, but . . . you're not the only one who's lonely here, you know. I wanted to come and see you,' she says. At this, Pip frowns in thought.

'Marcie was talking about having a music evening, and inviting some other people,' he says.

'Yes. That could be fun, couldn't it?' says Clare. Pip shrugs.

'James has gone camping in the Alps with all his cousins, and with Benjamin Walby from school. *That* would have been fun.'

'I know. There might still be time for you to go and do something like that with your friends when we get back. I think your dad has nearly finished the designs for Mr Cardetta.'

'I bet he hasn't. I bet there isn't.' They're both silent for a while, and Pip fiddles with his bandage again.

'Do you think Emma would have liked it here? What do you think she would have said about the poor calves, with those awful collars?' says Clare. Pip sighs and rolls away from her, opening his book again.

'My mother's dead, Clare. I have no idea what she would have said.'

\* \* \*

The next day, Clare is far from the *masseria* when the sky begins to curdle. Clouds fill the sky from the north and west; indigo blue and deep, deep grey, the colour of fresh bruises. Lightning flickers in amongst them, and the breeze is suddenly cooler, so much so that after two weeks of the constant heat, Clare shivers. The change is so dramatic that she climbs onto a low stone wall and stares up at the spectacle, letting the air stream through her fingers and the full brooding power of the storm steal up on her. Her feet are sore, the skin rubbed raw from walking in her

225

sandals, which let in the dust and grit. There's an ache between her shoulder blades, a hard knot of tension that has turned the muscles hot with exhaustion. When thunder rolls, echoing along the empty ground, Clare remembers what Marcie said about the water running like a river when the rain finally came. She's tempted to stay out in it, and see it, but the growing darkness is alarming, and she turns her back on the storm, turns towards the *masseria*. Without the hard Puglian sun everything suddenly looks dead, flat, unreal. Her eyes have got so used to the onslaught of light that she blinks repeatedly, and can't focus. She can feel the storm rearing up behind her, and now she almost wants to run from it. *It's only weather, you fool.* There's another roll of thunder, louder, closer. She walks faster.

The olive orchard is the only other place for her to shelter before the farmhouse, but though she hesitates, she carries on through it, thinking she can make it. When the first drops of rain land on her arms they are surprisingly cold — she'd imagined a tropical rain like bathwater; imagined tipping her head back to let it run into her eyes and sluice the dust out of her hair. But the rain feels like splinters, and the next bolt of lightning is so bright it seems to bypass her eyes and sear the inside of her head, and it makes the air smell burnt; the thunderclap comes almost at once, and goes deep into her bones. With a gasp, Clare grabs at her shoulder as something hits her, hard. Hail is falling — hailstones the size of walnuts. One lands square on her head, and the pain is a shock. Clare runs. Head down, heedless, she runs for the nearest shelter as more nuggets of ice hit the ground all around her, and one catches her face, on her jaw to one side of her mouth, making her cry out in alarm. She sees the gates, held open for her, and an open doorway beyond, and she aims for it, careering inside to stand, gasping, in sudden darkness. Her hair is hanging in wet rats' tails around her shoulders, her legs are spattered with mud, her shoes are ruined. She wipes her hands across her face and winces — there's a small cut on her jaw where the last hailstone hit her. Then she realises she's not alone in the hut and turns to find Ettore grinning at her, and she laughs, slightly hysterical with relief.

He takes off his hat and flaps ice from it onto the floor. For a minute they stand side by side, looking out at the storm. She has run into the guard hut by the main gates, and the roar of the hail on the stone roof drowns out thought, and any possibility of speaking. The ground is turning white with ice, the air is a grey blur and it's dark, dark as though the sun has set, and darker still inside the hut. The storm is the only thing in the sky — clouds like vast sculptures carved into it, filling it. Then Clare feels Ettore watching her and her heart seems to convulse in her chest. She turns to him; he puts his thumb to the cut on her chin, and she feels salt from his skin stinging in the wound. It's a small gesture, but it breaks her. It erases the last doubt she has about what she feels, and any possibility that they will not be lovers. She knows herself at last, and whoever she believed she was before, she was wrong. That woman seems like a stranger. She wants Ettore in her bloodstream. His gaze is intent but she can see that he's waiting, and it makes her throat tighten. She takes his hand and lifts it to her mouth, and tastes her own blood on his thumb. Ettore leans forward and puts his mouth over the graze, pressing his tongue into it, and the heat of it is incredible. The sensation sinks through her like a stone through water, to settle low down in her body. Her heartbeat there, between her thighs, is louder and harder than in her chest. She throws her arms around his shoulders, her legs around his hips, and kisses him. The kiss is hard, bruising. Not loving but something visceral, an embodiment of need and want. Her weight throws him off balance on his lame leg; he stumbles and turns, jarring her back against the wall so hard that the breath rushes out of her chest, and he's inside her so quickly that there's pain before the rush of pleasure, felt in her bones like the thunder, like the hail. She can't help shouting out, but the sound is lost in the roar of the hailstorm, and she can only tell from the rumble of Ettore's chest, from the vibration where his mouth is locked on hers, that he is shouting too.

The quiet when the hail stops is so profound it rings in their ears. Clare straightens her clothes and waits to feel ashamed, or guilty. She waits to feel afraid of what she's done, but she feels only happiness. She feels safe. She knows that Marcie and Pip will be worried about her being caught out in the storm; Marcie might even send men out to look for her now that the onslaught has stopped. Ettore stands close to her, facing her with his head resting on her shoulder, the bridge of his nose tucked into her neck. She isn't sure if his posture is one of tenderness, or if he doesn't want to look at her. The smell of him is instantly familiar, instantly beguiling and desperately dear to her. The parts of her he's touching are warm, the parts he isn't are chilly.

'I didn't know it could be like that. It's never been like that,' she says. Ettore says nothing. Gently, reluctantly, she pushes him back. 'I should go inside. They will want to know where I am.'

'No. Stay,' he says, in English. He takes her hand and holds it, and she smiles.

'I must go. I'm sorry.' And she is. She wants to stay with him. 'Ettore,' she says, just for the feel of his name on her tongue.

'Chiara,' he says, and it seems fitting that he should give her this new name, since she is not *Clare* any more, not the person she thought she was at all. It sounds almost like a sigh as he says it: *kee-ahra*. She presses her cheek to his, just for the feel of its contours, the roughness where he hasn't shaved, the hard bones beneath. 'Will you come again?' he says.

'Yes. Soon.' Clare's hand is the last thing to leave the *trullo*, held in his, reaching out behind her. He only lets go in the last instant before his own hand might be seen.

Clare walks across ice towards the white walls of the *masseria*; it splinters under her feet. When she enters the sitting room Marcie leaps up to greet her.

'Oh! Thank goodness! You found shelter? That was a real humdinger. But look at you — you're soaked! And cut!'

'I'm completely fine, Marcie, really — just this one nick where a hailstone caught me,' says Clare, when really her body is a secret map of bruises and aches and tender places.

'But how did you avoid being cut to ribbons? Where on earth were you hiding?' says Marcie, and a sudden sparkle of warning makes Clare hesitate.

'I . . . In a . . . what do you call it.' She waves her hand, buying time. 'In a *trullo*. One of the old, empty ones.'

'Oh, good thinking — how lucky you were near one! I'll get Anna to run you a bath. *Anna!* And then come and sit with us and have a cool drink to restore you — look! Look how we do it in Puglia!' And Marcie laughs delightedly as she drops a smooth, round hailstone into her *amarena*.

# Ettore

When Ettore's shift ends he goes to watch the men shovelling the hailstones in the *neviera*, the snow cave; a stone-lined chamber sunk into the ground behind the *masseria*, where in wintertime snow is packed in thick layers, with straw in between, and will stay frozen for weeks, even months, to be used to keep meat and milk fresh as the weather warms. The hail won't last anything like as long — it doesn't pack down in the same way, and now, in the height of summer, the air is too warm — but for a few days Anna will be able to churn ice cream for Marcie and her guests.

At the thought of them, at the thought of Chiara, Ettore feels the watching eyes of the windows behind him. He feels everything watching him, from the evening sky, clearing now, to the low trees and the men, the dogs and the sparrows washing themselves with manic abandon in the puddles of meltwater. It's like hands pressing down on him, and he knows that really it's Livia he can feel watching; she's the one scrutinising his guilty face and his every guilty move. And the thing that shames him is not that he made love to another woman, but that for a short while he surrendered to her completely; and for that short while he was happy. She was just as she had seemed she might be — a drink of water in a drought; a relief. A

231

complete relief. And he had promised Livia that he would not rest until the man who had raped her to death was dead himself. His anger with himself grows until it includes Chiara as well, and when she doesn't come to find him later that night, he is angrier still. Angry that she hasn't come, and angry at how badly he wants her to.

Ettore can't sleep during the day, even when he's been awake all night, in the *trullo* by the gates. His shifts rotate with Carlo and one other man, so that one night shift is followed by two day shifts, and he can't find a rhythm to it, so that by the end of a night shift he has been awake for twenty-four hours. He lies up on the roof, in the shade of the parapet, or else in his room with the sunlight streaming in through the curtains and the angry buzz of flies, and the slamming of doors and the footsteps and shouts of the household all making it impossible to think, or stop thinking. His anger simmers, and doesn't cool, and his thoughts are sludgy with sleeplessness. He doesn't eat with them again — he can't stand the thought, the pretence. He only went at breakfast, that morning after his first night shift, to see her. To see Chiara Kingsley, and look at her more closely; and now he doesn't think he could look at her without hitting her. Or kissing her again.

The second day afterwards he emerges from the *trullo*, crosses the *aia* and goes under the archway to find the *annaroli* milling about near the kitchen steps, pestering Anna and demanding food from the cook, Ilaria. He can hear Ilaria's boisterous protests from within.

'If one more of you deadbeats comes into my kitchen to ask me what is for lunch and when you will have it, you won't have it at all! It's that simple!'

'What's going on?' Ettore asks one of the corporals, a man he doesn't know, who has an apron of fat hanging over the front of his trousers. The man shrugs, then spits.

'The shit-eating peasants are on strike again — they want some communist bastard or other let loose from jail. So we've nothing to do but cool our heels till it's sorted out. Or till the starving starts.' He has a *marina* accent — he's not from Gioia — and he clearly has no idea who Ettore is. In an instant Ettore has him by the front of his shirt; his crutch clatters to the ground, and there's laughter from the onlookers.

'You'd do better to keep hold of that stick, boy, and use it to batter the man,' says Ludo Manzo, standing up from a shady spot against the wall. He speaks without taking a thin cigarette out from between his teeth, and squints at Ettore. 'You'll have no luck trying to knock that fat pig down with only one leg on the ground.' The fat man bridles but knows better than to say anything. Ettore releases his shirt, hops back and bends to pick up the crutch. 'Watch your temper, Ettore Tarano. I don't care if you're the boss's nephew; if you make trouble I'll whip you myself, same as any other one of these men.'

'Try it,' says Ettore, through clenched teeth. 'Go on and try it.' Ludo grins at him and chuckles. He puts one hand on Ettore's chest

233

and shoves him, quick and hard. Ettore stumbles back, fighting for balance. But he doesn't fall.

'You see that, men? That's the goddamned peasant urge to protest, and not to know they're beaten. That's what we're up against here. But sooner or later they'll learn. They'll learn or they'll die. One or the other.' He keeps a steady, hard eye on Ettore, who doesn't look away or move. 'Change is coming, Mr Tarano, and that little shindig at the Girardi place last year was just the start. Soon if you and your friends want work you'll know to be grateful for the work that's offered, on whatever terms.'

'You're right about one thing,' says Ettore. He stands straighter; the violence in him makes his jaw ache. 'Change is coming. Maybe not the kind you're hoping for, Manzo, but change, all the same.' He spits and turns his back on them. There's a chorus of whistles and curse words and jeering.

He'd expected Paola to come back to the *masseria* to collect money from him, or more food, and when she didn't he'd assumed Valerio had found a wage from somewhere. Now he knows there's a strike, most likely for the release of Capozzi, he worries more. There will be demonstrations in Gioia for the duration of the strike, rallying calls, a dangerous air of rebellion that could boil over into rioting as easily as a dropped match could start a grass fire, and Paola would be in the thick of it, like as not with Iacopo strapped to her back. Not knowing what's going on is intolerable. Once he's out of sight, up on the roof, Ettore puts his left foot down on the ground, gingerly. The ache is intense, the pulling feeling still there, but it's bearable now. Keeping hold of the crutch but not using it, he takes a few small steps. If he shortens his stride to minimise the movement of muscles in that leg, he can manage it, and it gives him a flash of triumph.

'Bravo, bravo!' calls Carlo, from his watch place at the parapet. He grins good-naturedly at Ettore, and Ettore smiles back at him. 'See how fast the body heals with rest and food in the belly?'

'The sooner the better,' says Ettore. 'I have a home to go to.' But before very long his calf muscle is trembling, and then cramp knifes through it and Ettore must stop and sit abruptly, screwing up his eyes at the pain. He rolls up his trouser leg and sees a string of red beads forming along the stitches of the wound. He smears them with his thumb but they grow again at once. His heart sinks.

'Easy does it, though,' says Carlo, and Ettore nods. If he tried to walk back to Gioia now he would ruin it. He wonders if he could manage fifteen kilometres with the crutch yet. He wonders if he could borrow a horse — Marcie would let him, Ludo would not. Of those two he knows who would win. Marcie would flap her hand in distress, and take Ludo's word as law. He wonders about taking one without asking, but knows at once that if he was seen he would be shot first and questioned later. He wonders whether, if he left the *masseria*, he would be able to forget about Chiara Kingsley.

In the night Ettore skirts sleep, and his leg

235

throbs with pain where he disturbed it. He watches the shadows the lamp casts on the ceiling; he leaves the shutters open so the dawn light will wake him, and moths come in to circle the light, hitting the glass, leaving little puffs of dust from their wings. Her knock is as soft as the sound the moths make; he isn't sure he's heard it until she sidles in through the door, closing it silently behind her. Her face is alive with some emotion, something pitched halfway between fear and happiness. When she sees that the shutters are open she gasps and turns, reaching for the doorknob again.

'Wait!' he says, louder than he should. He winces as he struggles up from the bed.

'I can't be seen here! Please close the shutters,' she says, in rapid English that he can barely understand. She keeps her face turned to the door, as though with her back turned she might be mistaken for somebody else. Ettore almost smiles.

'There's nobody awake to see you,' he says. The guards on the roof will all be facing outwards, not in through a courtyard window. But he limps across to close the shutters, barely touching the floor with the toe of his bad leg. Looking out, he thinks he actually does see movement in one of the other windows — a quick, furtive blur high up in an unlit room but he can't be sure, and though he stares at the spot there's nothing more. He latches the shutters then pauses, realising that his heart is thudding far too fast. Fast enough to make his fingers shake. His own weakness infuriates him, and when he turns to Chiara

236

he sees her flinch at his expression.

She takes one step away from the door and then hesitates, her face falling. She conceals nothing; her every thought marches openly across her face. Ettore doesn't know how she can survive in this world, being so visible, so transparent. He wants to warn her.

'Do you want me to go?' she says uncertainly, remembering to speak in Italian now. He doesn't go to her. He sits back down on the bed and he tries to remember his anger, but though he can recall the feeling, he can't actually feel it. Not with her standing there. The twisted length of her fair hair hangs over one shoulder; she's wearing a long white slip which must be her nightdress. He pictures her darting silently along dark corridors to his room, in fits and starts, just like a moth. He shakes his head. For a moment neither one of them moves, but then he raises his hand and holds it out to her, and she walks over to take it without hesitation.

'Why did you not come sooner than this?' he says. He can't help asking even if the question shames him. A spark of the anger returns. He will not be her plaything, to pick up and put down.

'I . . . I couldn't. The guards will see me if I go to the *trullo* in the night, or in the day. The dogs will . . . cry . . . shout?'

'Bark.'

'Bark. They will bark. I came to your room before, but you weren't here.'

'The boy must not know? He would tell his father?'

'Pip must *not* know! He must not,' she says vehemently. 'It would . . . He would not understand.' She looks stricken as she says this, and Ettore nods. He understands her feeling of guilt, of being watched.

'But you want me,' he says.

'Yes I do. I want you,' she says.

'Why?'

'I . . . ' She has no answer right away, and suddenly what she says next is very important. He will not be a tool to shame her husband; he will not be a distraction, a cure for boredom. 'I don't know exactly. Only . . . nothing here seems real. Only you do. Nothing here seems . . . ' She searches for words. 'When I saw you, I woke up. For the first time.' She stares at him, to see if he understands. 'There's so much danger here, so much ugliness . . . I've felt afraid ever since I arrived. Except when I'm with you. Then I feel safe.' A thread of tension in him snaps, and its loose ends unravel. He puts the back of his hand up to her cheek and she turns her face into it, and the sweetness of it is almost unbearable. He hardly dares to feel for her. 'Your uncle said . . . Leandro said you lost somebody. Your sweetheart,' she says, so quietly that he hardly hears. Ettore drops his hand and nods.

'Livia,' he says roughly.

'What happened to her?'

'She was killed. She was violated. She was taken from me,' he says, and can't look at Chiara. His sorrow settles onto him almost as strongly as when she first died; a wave of heat surges through him, the caustic taste of hate is in

238

his mouth. He can hear Chiara breathing, fast and shallow. The rise and fall of her ribs behind the thin silk looks so vulnerable, so breakable. He knows too much of the ways women can be broken.

'When?'

'At the year's head.'

'And the one who did it?'

'I will find him, and I will kill him.' He sees her assimilate this, and not dismiss it as an idle threat, but she does not fear or despise him for it. She nods carefully.

'I know I am not her. I know about . . . being second. I know I am not Livia, and I know you love her,' she says, and because she knows it Ettore feels her take half the guilt from him, half the responsibility for what they will do, and he's grateful to her.

As he lays her down he studies her, as he did not have time to do before. The whiteness of her skin is astonishing, and it's flawless — no scars, no bruises, no blemishes. He has never seen anything like it, and such perfection brings the temptation to destroy — he's torn between wanting to preserve her as she is and wanting to mark her in some way. Mark her as his. She's thinner than he likes; her breasts are small, soft circles against her ribs; her hips curve only slightly more; her bush is the same golden blonde as her eyebrows. Three small moles march diagonally across her stomach, in perfect alignment, like the constellation in the south-western sky. She smells clean, neutral, just like water, and he's startled by how quickly he loses himself in her again; how healing and compulsive the feeling of being inside her is. He can't be slow or gentle, however much he tries. When he makes the mistake of looking into her eyes he climaxes too soon, and uses his mouth and his hands on her instead, and she turns her face into the pillow to stay silent. Afterwards he falls asleep with her long hair in his face; it's too hot and it tickles him but he doesn't want to brush it away. He knows he shouldn't like her too much; that he shouldn't like lying in a bed, curled around her, with an ache in his balls that tells him he'll want to make love to her again by morning. He knows it can't last, this sudden feeling of safety and calm.

★　★　★

Ettore doesn't wake when Chiara leaves, and in the morning when he sits up and puts his head in his hands, he can smell her on his own skin. He holds his head over the washstand basin and pours the whole contents of the jug over himself, gasping at the coldness of the water. He can't pin his thoughts to any one thing, to any one need or wish or action. He feels stupid, vacant; hollowed out by her and frustrated with lust. He shaves messily, cutting himself, then dresses in trousers, shirt, waistcoat, and goes to find Marcie. He tries the sitting room first, and then goes to knock at the series of private rooms she shares with Leandro. After a pause she opens the door rather than calling him in, and he remembers something his mother once said, about never

240

trusting a person who did that. About the multitude of things that could be hidden in the interim.

Marcie smiles when she sees him, and then laughs lightly.

'Ettore — did you shave with a scythe, honey? You're all chopped to hell!' She touches her fingers briefly to the dried blood on his chin, so that he understands what she's laughing at. He shrugs and follows her into the room. She's dressed and made-up but hasn't done her hair yet — it's messy, not set in its perfect wave, and somehow the disarray makes her look both older and younger at once. There are blue damask curtains, lifting gently in the breeze, and a matching counterpane on the bed. Marcie has made a dressing table out of an old carved console — there's a folding mirror on top, and all her make-up, perfumes and hairpins scattered over it on silver trays; her jewellery too. The huge diamond in the engagement ring Leandro bought her sends little rainbows flickering up the wall. She has gold chains too, and earrings that sparkle like the ring. He steps on something slippery and looks down to find his cracked boots dirtying a glossy, buff-coloured cowhide. He thinks of the room in Gioia he shares with Paola and Valerio. He thinks of Livia and her family, sleeping under an archway for weeks, months. His heart ices over.

'What's eating you?' says Marcie. She sits down at her dressing table, facing towards him. He can see her long back in the mirror behind her.

'I am going,' he says.

'Going?' Her eyes widen. 'You can't mean *going* going?'

'To Gioia. I take the money to Paola. So they eat.' He stares hard at her, until a little shame comes into her face.

'If they'd just come here, if they'd just be a bit sweet to Leandro, he'd take you all in — you know he would! Then they'd eat.'

'And Valerio?' he says brusquely. Marcie looks down at her hands, examines the nails, pushes at a cuticle.

'But you can't walk properly yet — you can hardly do a day's work, can you?' she says. 'In fact, how will you even get there? We've no car here.' From this Ettore can pick enough of the salient words.

'I walk. I come back tomorrow.'

'Oh, good!' says Marcie. 'It's just a visit then — I understand! Listen — don't try to walk, for heaven's sake. I'll send Anna on some errand in town — go with her in the trap. And Leandro will be back tomorrow with Boyd Kingsley, so you can come with them in the car. Do you understand? Oh, where's Clare when I need her? Go with Anna, Ettore. Don't try to walk.'

'Yes,' he says at last, thinking of the blisters on his hand that the crutch would give him during the fifteen-kilometre journey.

'And, here,' she says. 'Wait a moment.'

Marcie takes something from a trinket box, gets up and goes to the wardrobe. She's wearing a tubular dress of fine white linen that almost reaches her ankles, and shortens her steps; it

242

rests on her hips with a belt stitched all over with turquoise beads. Ettore wonders what she sees when she looks out at the dry ground and the starving animals; the filthy, starving people. He's not at all sure. She kneels to unlock a metal strongbox in the wardrobe, and Ettore glimpses what's inside it. He stares. The box is piled high with money; tightly wadded stacks of notes. Thousands and thousands of lire. The sight gives him a strange fluttering in his gut; he has never seen anything like it. Marcie looks back over her shoulder.

'Ridiculous, isn't it? Leandro says he doesn't trust the man who owns the bank — that Fiorentino fellow. And why not? I said. He still uses the bank in New York, after all, for all his business dealings there. But he only shrugs, and I think I know the answer — he doesn't trust rich men. He *is* a rich man but he still doesn't trust them. In his heart, he's still the poor peasant he was born. And if you let on that I let you see this, he'll skin me. You understand?' She smiles, and Ettore says nothing. He swallows; he can't tell what he feels. Marcie peels off several notes and presses them into his hands. 'Don't tell Leandro I've given you this — let me, it would be better. Take this for Paola and the baby. I know how worried you are. Take it.' She pushes his hands away when he tries to give it back. 'Just take it! Damn it, Ettore, don't be so proud! Take it.' He knows the word *proud*; she often uses it to describe him, to berate him. She can't grasp that pride is all he has, sometimes. But he takes the money, even though it makes a

243

mockery of him. It's ten times what he's earned as a guard in the past week, and she hands it over like it's nothing, and smiles at his obedience.

Anna waits for him in the courtyard, sitting decorously in the little trap with a rein in each hand and her hair tied down beneath a scarf. She eyes him warily as he climbs up beside her. The mule's knobbed hip bones and scarred knees speak of years of hard labour. It stands with its ears back and its eyes diffuse, entirely disengaged from its surroundings, not even flicking its tail at the biting flies that crowd it. Marcie waves down from the terrace as they move away, and on the far side of the archway, Chiara stands with Filippo beside her, holding her hat by its brim, coming back from a walk with dust up to her knees. She stares up at him and he can read her incomprehension and her hurt. If he could he would tell her he's coming back but there's no time and no way to, so he sets his expression and lets his eyes linger on her for just a second. Filippo waves with his non-bandaged hand and Ettore waves back at him. The dogs chorus them out of the gates, straining at their chains to get at the mule; the mule ignores them completely. All trace of the hail and its meltwater are gone, the only signs of the deluge are subtle: a greener colour to the fig tree leaves; a clarity to the air which will soon be taken back by the heat and dust and the sun's flat glare, which will build and build until the next storm.

Ettore feels better as soon as they are clear of the *masseria*, and the road to Gioia is laid out in front of them; he's on edge, but for different reasons. He looks around him for signs of workers in the fields they pass, but it seems that the strike is holding. The mule slopes along with flat strides that cover the ground, and before long they're in the outskirts of Gioia del Colle. Ettore's mood lifts further. He knows where he is in these streets; he knows who he is, and what he should do. He knows his place.

'Let me down here,' he says to Anna before they reach the centre, and she tugs on the mule's mouth to halt it. Leandro's buggy is modest enough but he still doesn't want his neighbours to see him arriving in it.

'You're coming back with me later? How long will you be?' says Anna.

'No. I won't go back today; don't wait for me.'

'All right.' She nods and flicks the reins, and moves away. Ettore takes a deep breath and notices, in a way he normally doesn't, the stink of Gioia. Sewage and rotting vegetables; sickness, unwashed bodies, horse shit and cigarette smoke. It's familiar enough to be almost comforting, but at the same time it sticks in his throat. He heads towards Piazza Plebiscito, moving almost as quickly on the crutch as he could have walked normally. The square is crowded with people — all the workers, not working; a throng of black dotted here and there with the paler blouses of women. Some young men have climbed the lamp-posts to see better, and the bandstand is hung with socialist banners. At the edges of the square are groups of men who stand tight together and talk to each

245

other rather than listening. They have the tense, watchful air of men who are waiting, and they give Ettore a warning prickle of unease. Some are in police uniform, some in the remains of army officer uniform; some wear black shirts, with insignia stitched or pinned onto them. Ettore stares into the crowd but there's little hope of finding Paola in amongst it.

He makes his way around the outside, looking, just in case. The speaker is an old solider himself, but an infantry man, like Ettore was. Like all the peasants were. His voice comes through a loudhailer, with a metallic echo.

'We asked them, why should we fight for Italy when we may not own even the smallest part of it? Why should we fight for Italy when we have no rights within it? When we are treated worse than the cattle? When we are reviled? Why should we go and die on the orders of men who despise us?' the speaker shouts. His voice resounds in every corner of the square, and causes a stir of outrage in the listeners. When they are on strike, when they are not working, the men are restless to begin with; now they are hard, wound tight with stress. They are the dry grass into which a match might fall. Ettore can feel it coming, like a loud noise far away but getting closer, and closer. He moves faster, searches harder. 'But Cadorna still sent us forward at Isonzo, again and again; still he watched us die in misery. Still he lined up entire regiments and shot each tenth man if we dared to disobey. My brother was one of those men — and he was the bravest of his unit. Shot like a dog. Like a *dog*!'

246

The crowd mutters in outrage, and the mention of Isonzo halts Ettore. He waits for a wave of horror to subside, as the word crowds his mind with a remembered terror so great it almost drove him mad. Twelve battles were fought at the Isonzo front, against the Austro-Hungarian army. Twelve battles over two hellish winters, that left three-quarters of a million soldiers dead in the frozen mud, and yet the lines did not move an inch. Ettore was drunk almost all the time. To be sober was to be too terrified to breathe, too hungry to live. To be sober was to risk madness; to risk opening a permanent crack in the mind. Drunkenness was the only way to survive those trenches, and Valerio isn't the only one who's tried hard to stay drunk ever since. Ettore thinks briefly of Leandro, safe in New York all that time; rich and dirty enough to buy his way out of the draft.

He takes a deep breath and carries on around the square. The speaker's voice is laden with bitterness and anger. 'And all the while the gentlemen shirkers stayed here at home, safe and protected on their farms. Why should we fight? We asked them, and they answered. You will have *land*, they said! You will have the respect and love of your country! You will be able to feed your families, plant your own crops, and work for the future! You will not be hungry any more! You will not be crippled by the winter's debt, or robbed for the rent on an infested basement room a year in advance! I ask you, my brothers, have we got any of the things they said we would be given? Have we?' Almost as one, the crowd

247

roars out: *No!* 'In Russia, they have taken what they were promised. Brothers, the time has come for us to take what we were promised!' In the cacophony, Ettore hears his name called.

'Ettore! Ettore!' He spins about, searching, and sees Pino pushing towards him through the throng.

'Pino! My friend, it's good to see you. Are you well?' They hug roughly, pounding each other's backs.

'Well enough, but how are you? It does me good to see you home, and walking! Are you back? Are you fit?' Pino eyes the crutch doubtfully.

'Not fit enough yet, but soon. I've come back to see Paola; I have money for her. Have you seen her?'

'She was here but she went back — she didn't want to bring the baby, and she didn't want to leave him for long. Come, I'll go with you.'

'How long will the strike last?'

'I don't know. It's been forty-eight hours . . . the men are hungry, and angry, and nobody dares patrol the farms for blacklegs any more, because of the squads. More squads all the time, Ettore. But if the proprietors want the harvest in and threshed, they must capitulate . . . and they must be getting frantic. But Capozzi and Santoiemma are still in jail, so . . . ' he says, with a shrug.

'This meeting could go bad. Can you feel it?' says Ettore, and Pino nods.

'Best you get away before it does, with your leg still weak.'

248

They go into the small, ancient alleyways that lead to Vico Iovia, and the speaker's ringing words and the answering roar quieten behind them. A mishmash of houses, built and rebuilt and patched and added on, crowd in on either side, close enough to touch; stairways and downspouts and crooked shutters, and here and there the stone flowers that let air into the rooms within, napped with age. The shadows are deep and there's filth in the gutters.

'Pino, I must thank you,' says Ettore.

'Must you?' Pino grins at him.

'If you hadn't taken me to Masseria dell'Arco when you did, I might have lost this leg. Or died. Thank you.'

'I didn't do it for you, brother,' says Pino seriously. Ettore glances over at him. 'It was the smell — Mother of God, the smell! I couldn't stand it a second longer. I had to get rid of you,' he says, and Ettore chuckles.

'Well, thank you, Pino,' he says, and Pino gives him a slight shove that nearly knocks him off balance.

'Stop thanking me for something you would do for me, just the same. In fact, just stop thanking me. It makes me nervous. So, how is it there? Is your aunt still living like a queen?'

'Yes. It's . . . incredible. It's like she can't see what's around her. Like she looks out and still sees New York, and so she lives just as she must have done there.'

'Maybe not quite as she must have done. Perhaps she doesn't want to see. After all, what can she do to change it?'

249

'Nothing. But she could at least acknowledge it . . . It insults us all, her deliberate obtuseness. I can't work out if she's stupid or just . . . ' He shrugs.

'What?'

'Crazy, I guess.' He pauses, releases the crutch and stretches out his fingers to ease the ache in the heel of his hand. 'She's got her jewels out on display, for anyone to see — gold and diamonds. And there's a strongbox of money in the wardrobe — more money than you or I have ever seen, Pino! She says my uncle doesn't trust the bank. So it just sits there. She gave me this from it.' He takes the folded notes from his waistcoat pocket. 'Handed it over like she was giving me pocket money. Pino, I think she's crazy.'

'Jesus!' Pino swears, his eyes going wide. 'Still crazy about you, perhaps. Don't flash that around, for God's sake. Someone might carve out your liver for that money.'

'I know.'

'Maybe she's not so crazy. She lives in a house with walls fifteen metres high, surrounded by dogs and guards. Why shouldn't she wear diamonds? What good would it do us if she hid them away?'

'She could sell them. Then perhaps Leandro could pay better wages, or hire more of us,' says Ettore bitterly. 'All through this harvest he's sung the same tune as the others, Pino. 'I am on the edge of ruin, I am making no money from this harvest, it costs me more to hire you than I will make selling the wheat.'' He shakes his head. 'Yet he sits there with enough cash to buy Gioia

250

and everyone in it. And Marcie said he still has money in New York — business interests. I suppose his sons are working for him there.'

'A rich man has a different idea of what being poor is than those of us who are really poor.'

'But this is Uncle Leandro, Pino! *He* knows!'

'He knows, but he's a rich man now, Ettore. It changes a man. Perhaps we would be the same if we became rich.'

'No. Never. I could never forget, as he has forgotten, where I came from and what I have seen. Or how it feels to eat nothing for four days in a row . . .'

'Calm down, Ettore!' Pino smiles. 'What should he do, give away all his money and be poor again himself? What would that accomplish?'

'Perhaps he would get his soul back.'

'Are you a man of God, now?' says Pino, and Ettore smiles sheepishly. 'One step at a time, and don't walk uphill unless you have to. Today, you have money. Today, those you love will eat. Be pleased about that.'

'Take this,' says Ettore, thumbing two notes from the roll and handing them to Pino.

'No, you keep it. You have more mouths to feed.'

'I have more than enough. Take it for you and Luna, and don't argue.'

'Thank you, Ettore,' says Pino humbly.

'Don't thank me for something you would do for me, just the same,' says Ettore.

Just then shots are fired, cracking across the sky and along the alleyway to the two men; they crouch down immediately, covering their heads

251

with the instinct of old soldiers, and in the silence afterwards they look back the way they've come as if they might see the bullets, or the enemy. Ettore sees his own instinctive fear mirrored in Pino's eyes. *We're not soldiers*, he thinks. *We never were. We wanted to be farmers.*

'It's starting,' says Pino. Ettore stands up, grabs his crutch and sets off down the alley.

'It started a long time ago. Come on, move!' Behind them more shots are fired, in quick succession, like a fistful of gravel thrown hard against glass. There are shouts, a rising roar of voices and pounding feet, coming closer. Ettore and Pino rush further into the tangle of alleys, and then into the dead end of the tiny courtyard where Ettore lives.

'I should go home. Luna is alone,' says Pino, breathless.

'Yes, go! I'll see you afterwards, before I go back,' says Ettore. Pino claps him on the shoulder and then jogs away down the alley.

Ettore struggles up the steps to his own door, bursts through it and pulls up short. The tip of a blade hovers a hair's breadth from his throat; he blinks in the darkness and sees his sister's eyes boring into his.

'Paola!' he says, in a strangled voice, and with the rushed release of a pent-up breath Paola lowers the knife, her shoulders sagging.

'*Madonna*! I almost cut your throat, Ettore!' she says, putting her spare hand over her eyes.

'I noticed.'

'I heard the shots — I thought you were a looter! Or one of those blackshirt bastards.' She hugs him briefly, not letting go of the knife, and Ettore feels the hardness of her bones beneath her clothes. She smells sharp with anxiety and baby sick.

'Is Iacopo well? Are you?'

'Yes, he's fine. He threw up all over me this morning, but then he laughed about it.' She shrugs, her eyes going automatically to the wooden box where her son sleeps. Ettore looks around his home. After the light and space of the *masseria*, it's like a hole in the ground. In the darkness across the room, on his habitual stone shelf, Valerio coughs weakly.

'And our father?' says Ettore quietly. Paola shrugs again, her face pinched with worry.

'Weaker and weaker. He hardly eats, not that there has been much to give him. He has a fever, I think. Just slightly, but for several days now.'

'You two, stop talking about me as if I wasn't here,' Valerio grumbles. Ettore goes to stand over him, and Valerio looks up blearily. There's grey stubble in the cavernous hollows of his cheeks, brown rings around his eyes.

'Should I fetch the doctor to see you, Father? I have money — from Uncle Leandro.'

'Him!' Valerio's eyes blaze. 'He gives us charity now, that arrogant son of a bitch?' The effort of anger makes him cough again.

'I worked for it. Well, for some of it,' says Ettore. 'So, shall I fetch the doctor?'

'What's the point? He'll do nothing but send you to his brother to buy drugs that don't work. Leave me in peace, if you want to do something for me. Or better still, go and buy me some wine

253

with that money of his. But I know you won't do me that kindness, will you?' Valerio stares listlessly into the shadows. His breathing is a shallow whistle that barely moves his ribs. Ettore grits his teeth.

'You'll just give up and die then, will you? When I am away from home, and there's no one to help your only daughter and your grandson, no one to earn money to feed them? No one to protect them?' he says. Valerio's gaze goes to Paola, who stands with the knife still gripped in her fist.

'My daughter has always done better for herself than I could ever do for her,' he whispers, and though there's pride in the words, there's self-pity too. With a sigh, Valerio shuts his eyes.

Paola flinches a little, and says nothing for a while. She puts the knife down at last, goes to Iacopo and touches his cheek.

'You have money, you said?' she says.

'Yes, plenty. I — ' Ettore breaks off at the sound of a shot close at hand, and running feet. There's an angry shout, and the wrenching of a door against its hinges.

'They're close!' Paola hisses. She rushes to the door and peers out through a crack in the wood.

'Should I go? Would you be safer?' Ettore's heart thumps hard in his chest, in fear, in anger.

'Perhaps . . . perhaps.' Paola turns to him and her face is the same as his — full of fear and fury. 'You picked a ripe time to come home, Ettore! If they come in here I will cut their throats, by God I will!'

'No, Paola! Not unless you have to. Not unless

254

it's you or them, or they'll kill you for sure. I'll go — I'm going.'

'You mustn't be out on the streets! Go down to the stable and hide there. Go, go! Be quick. And don't be tempted to come out and fight. Promise me! They'll shoot you as soon as look at you.'

'Who are these men?' says Ettore, as he reaches for the door.

'Who they've always been, brother, and they want what they've always wanted — to trample us, because they hate us. Now go.'

Ettore rushes into their neighbour's stable, below the room he and Paola live in, and pulls the rickety gates shut behind. The reek of ammonia is almost too much to breathe. The bony nanny goat who lives there eyes him, turning her head this way and that on her stiff neck, weaving anxiously. Her eyes are alien and without sympathy, and she bleats low in her throat, coming towards him in case he has food. Ettore crouches down, looking out through the split planks of the doors. For a few minutes nothing happens. His breathing returns to normal, the goat nibbles at his shirt, and he feels foolish. Then a knot of men, six or seven of them, march into the little courtyard with orderly purpose; led by a man who has twin ammunition belts criss-crossing his chest, a pistol on each hip, and a silver badge in the shape of an axe in a bundle of sticks at the throat of his shirt. There's something familiar about him, his black curling hair and soft outline, but viewed through a crack and from the side, Ettore

255

can't place him. Not until he raises his fist to halt the men behind him and turns to go up the stairs, and Ettore sees his handsome face marred by a cleft palate and an expression of ugly excitement. Federico Manzo; Ludo's son, and Leandro's servant. Sudden rage grips Ettore; he feels it squeezing him, crushing out the breath and the thought and the reason. His fingers curl around the edge of the door and only at the last instant does he stop himself pulling it open and rushing out to confront the man. He forces himself to remain still; it takes every bit of his will.

Federico Manzo bangs hard on the door.

'Ettore Tarano!' he says loudly. Ettore holds his breath; the goat rumbles in its throat again.

He hears the door squeak as it opens, and Paola says, 'What do you — ' before she is pulled down the steps by her arm, and shoved towards the waiting men.

'Hold her, and watch out for this one — she's a whore and a mean bitch,' says Federico, grinning at Paola's furious expression. 'She's probably got a knife in her cunny, and from what I hear, she'll use it. Where's your brother, whore?'

'At his uncle's farm, where he's been for the last two weeks. As you know,' she says coldly.

'I think you're lying.' Federico smiles, and carries on into the room.

'There's nobody in there but my baby and my sick father! Leave them alone!'

'Shut your mouth,' says one of the men darkly. 'Unless you want to cause trouble? We'll be gone once he's checked. You needn't fear for your virtue — if you have any. I like my women to have breasts,' he says, grinning at her, and his fellows laugh. One of them puts out his hand and grabs at Paola's chest, making her wince.

'I have bigger tits myself!' he declares, to more laughter. Inside the room there's a thump, and a muffled exclamation, and then Iacopo howls. Paola rushes forwards but is grabbed, held back.

'*Iacopo!* If you touch him I'll kill you! I'll kill you!' she shouts. Ettore can't keep his breathing even, his whole body shakes with adrenalin; he silently begs Paola to be still. He hears, but can't see, Federico speak from the top of the steps, and from the sudden clarity of Iacopo's cries, it's obvious he's brought the baby out with him. A new thrill of fear goes through Ettore.

'What a shithole. No wonder your brother likes it at the *masseria* so much. Tell me where he is,' says Federico.

'Don't hurt him! Don't hurt my baby, you son of a whore!'

'Tell me where your brother is, or I'll drop him off these steps.'

'He's at the *masseria!* If he's not, I don't know where he is! I haven't seen him since he went there. Give me my baby! Give him to me!'

Slowly, Federico walks down the steps and Ettore sees that he has Iacopo cradled in one arm, jouncing him gently enough as he crosses to where Paola is held, a man on each of her arms. Federico smiles at the expression of mixed terror and hope on her face. 'Give him to me,' she says again. Federico looks at her with his head on one side.

'He's a beautiful baby. You must be proud of him,' he says, in a conversational tone. Then he sighs, pulls one of his pistols and puts it to Iacopo's head.

'No!' Paola cries. 'No! No!' Ettore can't move; he can't breathe. *Get up. Get up*, he orders his body, but it won't obey him. These men mean to kill him, that much is clear. No man would put a gun to a child's head merely to make an arrest, or give a beating. *He won't do it, Paola*, he sends her the silent reassurance. *He won't do it — Iacopo is Leandro's blood.*

'Where is he, Paola? I know he came to Gioia today,' says Federico. Paola stares in mute horror at her son, and the gun pointing at him. She shakes her head.

'I . . . I don't know,' she says, barely a whisper. Ettore shuts his eyes in sudden agony. He knows then that there's no one in the world braver than his sister. Federico watches her for a moment longer, then shrugs and holsters the gun.

'Perhaps you don't, after all. Perhaps he stayed at the farm — he will if he has any sense. We can't get at him there. Not yet, anyway.' He nods at his men and they release her. She grabs Iacopo from Federico's careless hold, and cradles him as they march out of the courtyard.

'Bye for now, whore,' says the one who grabbed her breasts as he passes. 'I might come back to see you later.' But Paola cradles her son, pressing her lips to his head, and ignores the man. For a while the only sound is Iacopo howling, and Ettore wonders if he will ever have the nerve to leave the shit and piss reek of the

258

goat stall. If he will be able to stand the shame.

Eventually, Paola goes back inside without looking at the doors to the stable. Ettore doesn't move until he hears her call for help, and then he goes in, stinking, silent with hatred, to help her pick Valerio up off the floor.

'Paola . . . ' he says, but he's got nothing to say.

'Go back to the *masseria*, Ettore. You heard him — you're safe there,' she says, tucking the blanket back around their father, pressing her hand to his gleaming forehead.

'I can't go back tonight — I've no means to. Anna will have left when trouble started. Paola, listen, he . . . he can't hurt Iacopo. Leandro is his boss . . . '

'I know. I knew it — that's why I kept quiet.' Her voice is leaden with exhaustion. 'What does it mean, Ettore? What does it mean when our own uncle's servants may come here and threaten us? He would have killed you. Why? Have you done something to anger them? What does it mean?' Suddenly there are tears in her eyes, the first Ettore has seen since Davide, Iacopo's father, was killed. He can't bear to see them; he folds his sister into his arms, rests his chin on the top of her head, and she lets him, for once. A tremor goes through her.

'I don't know,' he says. 'I don't know what it means. But I will find out.' Paola pulls away, wipes at her eyes.

'You can't stay here. They might be watching; they might come back to look again. Go to Pino and Luna.'

'They know Pino's my friend.' Ettore shakes his head.

'Go to Gianni and Benedetto then; go to Livia's family. But don't stay here.'

'All right.' He gives her all the money he has and she takes it without a word. 'Paola,' he says, squeezing her hand with the money in it. He finds it hard to speak. 'You have the heart of a lion. You have twice the heart of me.'

Everywhere in town are sounds of trouble, clashes. There are several fascist squads on the streets, and many groups of Gioia's working men, greater in numbers but weaker, and unarmed. The squads attack unionist buildings, and the homes of known agitators; the workers attack the police headquarters, the town hall and the new fascist party offices. Livia's mother, Bianca, opens the door to Ettore with her face full of fear, and her eyes pinch when she sees him. He can't tell how she feels about him, but she has been cold towards him, distant, since Livia died. He thinks perhaps she blames him for not protecting her daughter, and he accepts that blame. He blames himself, after all, and now he has more guilt — the guilt of a new lover. He wonders if Bianca can sense it on him — the traces of another woman. Perhaps since Livia was killed by a man who wanted to take pleasure from her, she now hates all men who ever thought of her that way. All men who ever wanted to make love to her.

'Can I come in? Men are looking for me,' he says.

Bianca hesitates for a second before she nods

and steps aside to let him into their room, which is every bit as cramped and dank as the Taranos'. She returns to her place on a three-legged stool in front of the stove. She looks twice her age.

'You weren't followed?' says Gianni, a watchful presence in a shadowed corner.

'No. I would not trouble you but they have been to my house once already, and they mean business.'

'They are attacking anyone who's ever been a spokesman, or led a strike, or been at a rally,' says Benedetto, Livia's oldest brother, a bear of man with gnarled shoulders and a mass of black beard. 'Anyone whose name they know. Come in, of course. I heard you were at your uncle's.' Space is made for Ettore, though there's nowhere for him to sit but on a straw-filled mattress on the floor in the far corner of the room. He winces as he sinks onto it, noticing the pain in his leg from all the movement of the afternoon.

'We've only a little black pasta for dinner, with some anchovies,' says Bianca, poking at the contents of an iron pot on the stove.

'I'm grateful . . . ' says Ettore. Then he hesitates. His stomach is rumbling and hot with hunger, though he ate a hearty breakfast at the *masseria*, and he realises with shame that he has got used to being full. 'But in fact I've already eaten, earlier. I would not take from you what I do not need.' Gianni nods and the atmosphere lightens just slightly.

'All right,' says Bianca, sounding relieved. Hospitality dictates that guests be fed, but nobody welcomes an extra mouth to feed.

Far into the night there are sporadic gunshots and shouts of anger, defiance, amusement, scorn. Ettore can't sleep, because when he shuts his eyes he sees Federico Manzo holding a gun to Iacopo's head, and the naked terror on Paola's face. At one point he gets up and looks out through a crack in the shutters, and the sky is orange with burning, and full of smoke. Gioia is built of stone and fire rarely spreads, but equally there is scant water to extinguish it. When a building catches fire, it usually burns itself out. Ettore watches the shifting orange glow for a long time, as sparks spiral up through it, twisting, quick with inhuman life. It strikes him as peculiar that destruction should be beautiful like this.

His mother, Maria, had believed in the three angels that appeared at sunset to guard every home — angels like sprites, like fairies, unrelated to God. She would never leave rubbish right outside the house at night, in case it offended the angel that guarded the door; she made a small bow to the one that sat at the table before each meal; she thanked the one that watched over the bed every night before she slept. Come morning these spirits would dissolve into the sunrise, but Maria Tarano slept soundly in the knowledge that no evil spirits or curses could come upon them in the darkness. For a while, as Ettore watches the burning, he wonders what happens to these angels when a house is ablaze. Do they take fright and vanish, or slink away in shame from their failure, or do they stay and try to fight the flames? Is it their anguish he can see in the swirling sparks, the tortuous coils of smoke? The night is long, and Ettore is glad, for once, that his mother isn't around to have seen today. He feels so lonely just then that it's like an ache in his bones, and he wishes he was back at Masseria dell'Arco, curled tight around Chiara Kingsley with her hair in his face and the warmth of her skin on his, and the soft bump of her heart against the arm he would wrap around her.

In the morning Ettore waits for Gianni or Benedetto to bring news, and it's Gianni who returns first, his hawkish face heavy with care.

'We're going back to work tomorrow. Capozzi and Santoiemma will be released today, but . . . the Labour Exchange is gone.'

'Gone?' says Ettore. Gianni nods.

'Gone up in smoke, and three men dead trying to defend it. All the registers, all the rosters, all the contracts the proprietors signed — gone. We're back to where we were right after the war.' Ettore's heart sinks wearily.

'New offices can be found, new rosters drawn up. Di Vagno will see to it,' he says, and hopes that he's right, and that Gianni will agree with him. Di Vagno is their deputy, their member of parliament, and a socialist. Gianni eyes him with some disgust.

'Keep your dreams, if they comfort you,' he says gruffly. 'Any fool can see which way the wind is blowing here in Gioia. In Puglia.'

'Would you lie down and let them march over you, Gianni?' says Ettore quietly. Gianni's expression blackens.

263

'We fight and we fight but we always lose, and I'm tired of pretending it can be otherwise. It doesn't matter how many speeches Di Vittorio makes, or how many deputies like Di Vagno we manage to elect. None of it matters. I want to work, and I want to eat. That's all.' He goes to lie down on the mattress. Ettore thanks them, and gets up to leave. Their hopelessness is infectious; he can feel it seeping into him like the numbness of a January day, and he doesn't want it. He wants to get his hands on Federico Manzo, and his father Ludo. He wants to punish them. He can't let them win.

This desire for violence charges him, sharpens him, as he makes his way to Leandro's house on Via Garibaldi. He has to pause before knocking at the street door, to breathe, to contain himself. The peasants have long known better than to take their troubles to the police, and the police are more partisan now than they've ever been; if he attacks Federico, Ettore will be the one prosecuted, and nothing that went on before will count in mitigation. So when Federico opens the door to his knock, and grins at him like they're old friends, Ettore must let the anger wash through him and stifle it. It's like eating ashes.

'Mr Tarano. What a pleasure,' says Federico, and makes him a small bow, the perfect servant. 'Your uncle will be pleased to see you.' Ettore walks past him into the shade of the archway, keeping his eyes fixed on him. He's dressed in dark trousers, a grey shirt and a faded but serviceable waistcoat; no sign of the gun belts or insignia. 'It was a troubled night here in Gioia. I think he was worried for you, when he heard you'd come back to town.'

'Perhaps he has more cause to worry than he knows,' says Ettore. Federico smiles again.

'Perhaps so. But you're safe within his walls. Your uncle is a powerful man, after all.'

'That he is.' Just then he hears Leandro's voice from one of the upper terraces.

'Is that my nephew, back safe?' he calls.

'Yes, sir,' Federico calls, and as he turns to go back into his little room by the door, Ettore stops him.

'If you go near my sister again I swear I will cut out your tripes,' he whispers. 'Don't doubt my word.' Federico's smile vanishes; his face writhes in anger.

'We'll see,' he says. Then he steps past Ettore and vanishes inside.

'Ettore! Come on up, talk to me,' Leandro calls. 'Why on earth did you come back to town at such a time? Anything you want taken to Paola, I can have taken. I can send one of the servants.'

'We have no word at the *masseria* of what is happening here in Gioia, and I wanted to see them myself, Uncle.' Ettore climbs the stairs to the terrace. 'My father is very ill, Paola has no help.'

'Ah,' says Leandro, nodding regretfully. 'She was always a wilful and resourceful girl, mind you. If any woman could take care of herself . . . ' He spreads his hands.

'That she can doesn't mean she should have to.'

265

'Then let her come here and work in the kitchens, since she will not be kept as family.' Leandro says this lightly, because he knows Paola won't agree to it.

'Perhaps she might, if Valerio . . . ' Ettore feels disloyal even as he says this; treacherous for envisaging the time after his father's death. Then he thinks that the first thing Paola would do if she came within these walls would be to slit Federico's throat in the night. He shakes his head. 'For now, I'm all she has.'

★ ★ ★

The sky is flat white as Federico drives them back out to the *masseria*; there's a thick blanket of cloud that traps all the heat, and it's so still and so stifling the air seems to have clotted. Seven magpies perch in the contorted branches of a dead olive tree, and they watch the car pass with eyes like lead shot, not even crouching to take wing. They have no fear, but also no energy, no animation. They look dead, and Ettore, still thinking of his mother, takes them as a warning of some kind. He'd been thinking how he would approach his uncle regarding the Manzos, how he would ask about Federico's role in the squads, and whether Leandro is aware that Ettore, his own nephew, is on their hit list. Whether he knows that the well-fed young man driving them that day had, the day before, put a gun to his great-nephew's head. If the magpies are a warning, they're warning him against saying anything, but he's not sure if he can heed it. Mustn't his uncle choose blood over politics? Mustn't he choose his own people over those who have persecuted them for countless generations? *My brother has forgotten who he is*; so said Ettore's mother. Ettore holds his tongue and looks at Chiara's husband instead.

Boyd Kingsley sits hunched in the front passenger seat, with his knees folded sharply and his head ducked down. He has a flat leather case cradled on his lap, and his fingers fiddle constantly with its buckles. He looks profoundly uncomfortable, but then, that seems to be how he always looks. Ettore can only see the side of his face — one slightly pendulous ear, a thin neck with rough skin like a plucked bird, wisps of colourless hair as fine as a child's. He must be fifteen years older than his wife, at least. Ettore thinks of the way he engulfed Chiara in his arms when he first came to the farm, as if he hadn't seen her for weeks, and it makes him slightly queasy. She's his wife; of course he's screwed her. He has every right, and Ettore has none. But once the thought of it is in his head he can't get rid of it, and by the time they turn into the gates at dell'Arco, Ettore despises both men sitting in the front of the car equally; one rightly so, the other unfairly. He wonders if Chiara will come to see him with her husband in residence, and then curses his own stupidity. Of course she won't. Perhaps she only used him in her husband's absence, to flatter her, to fulfil her. Picked up and put down, like a toy. Whatever empathy he thought he sensed from her, whatever resonance there seemed to be between them, he might only

267

have conjured out of grief and loneliness. Ettore's jaw goes tight. The Masseria dell'Arco is not the real world, and neither is Chiara Kingsley.

Because he can't say any of the things he wants to say, he says nothing. He walks inside with Leandro because he doesn't want to be out on the farm where he might run into Ludo or Federico; he doesn't know what he would do. The three men, Leandro, Boyd Kingsley and himself, go into the long sitting room on the ground floor of the *masseria*, where the high ceiling helps to keep it cool, and white voile curtains go some way to keeping out the flies. They sit down on an overstuffed sofa, decades old, and Ettore doesn't listen as the others talk in English. When the women appear in the doorway he watches Chiara carefully, though it's Marcie who makes all the noise, fussing him about his leg, and for news of Iacopo. He wants to see which of them Chiara will look at first — her lover or her husband; which of them she will look at the longest. He can tell himself that he doesn't care, but it's not true. She keeps her eyes carefully away from him, and as if she can feel him watching her, and his anger, she blushes. She greets her husband with the trace of a smile, and he clasps both of her hands to stoop and kiss her. She offers him her cheek. As they sit back down she glances up at Ettore and meets his eyes for a broken second. A darted glance like the sudden startling of a bird, but in it he reads desperation, and something else. Could it be joy he sees? Joy at his return? Something inside him unclenches. She picks a thread from her sand-coloured skirt, sweeps her hands along her thighs to smooth the fabric, and keeps her eyes down from then on.

Anna brings in a tray of cold drinks, with salvaged hailstones tapping at the glasses. As she puts it down she looks at Ettore with such a stiff, nervous expression that he immediately starts to wonder, and then guesses that this girl is how Federico Manzo knew he'd gone back to Gioia. Federico seems to have a way with women, even if he's disfigured; he flatters them with extravagant words and gestures. Or perhaps he's simply paying her. Ettore takes note not to trust the girl. He watches his uncle saying something in English that he punctuates with expansive hand gestures. Hard to believe that this man, in his new light blue suit with the waistcoat buttoned up in spite of the heat, this man with his chauffeur and his wife gleaming and laughing and dripping jewels, is the brother of his mother, Maria Tarano, who believed in curses and angels, and fought her poverty every day, and taught her children that money you didn't need was a poison. By increments, Ettore feels less and less as though this man is his blood. *My brother has forgotten who he is.*

Ettore leans forwards abruptly, interrupting the conversation he has not been following.

'Uncle, do you know what happened in Gioia yesterday? What actually happened?' He speaks in the dialect; there's incomprehension on all faces but Leandro's. 'Do you know that these squads are attacking ordinary people in their

269

homes now? Do you know who is commanding them?'

'Ah, Ettore.' Leandro shakes his head and sighs in apparent regret, but his eyes are stony. 'It's a nasty business. You should remain here, out of it.'

'Are the proprietors paying for their weapons, and the food in their bellies?'

'I have made it my business not to enquire.'

'I don't believe you, Uncle,' he says, and Leandro thumps his fist onto the low table in front of him — so hard that the glasses jump, so quickly that his arm barely seems to move. The others fall silent; Ettore feels their nervous eyes on him.

'This is my house, Ettore,' says Leandro, softly. He points one finger at his nephew for a moment. 'You will not be a guest here, so you are an employee. If that's the way you want it, so be it. But you will be respectful, or you will leave. Those are your choices. I didn't drag my ass out of the New York gutter to come back here and be insulted by you. Do you understand me?'

'Your driver put a gun to Iacopo's head. Federico Manzo — he leads one of the squads. Have you chosen not to enquire about that as well? He was looking for me, and he *put a gun to the baby's head*,' says Ettore, through gritted teeth. Leandro says nothing for a moment. He sits back, sips his drink. His hands are completely steady; Ettore clenches his own to hide how they shake.

'I knew he'd joined the fascists — most of the corporals have. But I didn't know they'd marked

270

you.' His tone is soft now, dangerous. 'I will speak to the Manzo boys.'

'But you will not dismiss them?'

'What good would that do? What control would I have over them then?'

'I can't work for that man, or near his son. I can't be around them.'

'Then leave.' Leandro is composed again, his black gaze steady and implacable. 'It's my duty as your uncle to offer you what help I can, what help you will accept. But I will not be told what to do by you, Ettore. Do not insult me.'

Ettore rubs one hand across his mouth, grips his jaw hard between his fingers. There is so much he wants to say, so much he wants to shout. He wants to stand and kick the table over, and break every glass. He wants to roar. But he doesn't. Marcie titters nervously, and they all begin to talk again; the stilted, self-conscious conversation of people who sense something grim in the room but can't acknowledge it.

'Why do you have these people here, Uncle? These English. Why do you keep them here at such a time? It's not safe for anybody,' says Ettore.

'I have my reasons,' says Leandro. 'What makes you think they're kept here?'

'The woman speaks Italian.'

'Ah! So she does.' Leandro nods. 'And she told you as much? I didn't think the English spoke so openly. That's not their reputation. Least of all this one, brave as a rabbit.'

'Does her husband owe you something?' says Ettore.

271

'Owe me? Well, perhaps. Not in the usual way, maybe, but . . . Let's just say there is something I need to find out from him, before I can let them go home. But don't worry — they are quite safe here, I'm sure. My guards are loyal, and I keep their guns loaded; and if you like the money then stay on here as one of them. It's that simple. But don't make trouble, Ettore. And don't make me tell you again,' says Leandro. Ettore scrapes his hands through his hair, and feels the dust of Gioia on his scalp. He mutters a vague apology and leaves the room.

He goes to find Ludo Manzo; he has no choice, if he wants to start work again. Federico will stay at the *masseria* as long as Leandro does, ready to drive him, and Ettore hopes he won't find the two of them side by side. He couldn't stand their gloating unassailability. In the end he has to ask where to find the overseer, and then sets off on a long walk to one of the furthest fields, where the last of the wheat still waits to be cut. He goes part of the way without the crutch, only using it again when his leg starts to cramp from the uneven, hobbling way he has to walk. The dust swirls in his wake then resettles slowly. He sees the corporals on their horses, and the small work crew labouring under their bored gaze; the rhythmic swing of scythes, the bent backs of the men tying the sheaves. This is the last of this work; soon the men will spend days and days feeding the threshing machines — on those farms that have them, on those farms that have fuel for the machines. Otherwise it will be done by flail, as it has been done for hundreds of years. By the end of July, the grain should be stored, or sold; the straw baled for animal feed. August is the ploughing month; blades dragged through the rocky soil behind mules, oxen, work horses, rare tractors. Then there's sowing, weeding, rock-breaking, the repair of damaged walls. Then by the winter there is nothing at all; no way for the men to earn a wage. The hands of this timeless clock turn inexorably, and Gianni is right — they have fought and fought, and made only fleeting changes.

Ettore pauses when he sees how closely Ludo is watching a pair of young lads at work, one hand on the bullwhip coiled at his hip. It's like no time has passed since those two lads were Pino and Ettore, checking the broken stones for ancient shells, with this same man nearby, a figure from a nightmare, trailing fear into the world when there was hardship enough already. He walks over to him.

'Tarano. You're back safely then,' says Ludo, with his sharp twist of a smile.

'Why wouldn't I be safe?'

'These are troubled times. But here you are, tucked back beneath your uncle's wing.'

'And in your care, Manzo,' says Ettore sarcastically. The overseer laughs.

'I've never been accused of caring for my workers before. Ask these feeble wretches.' He nods at the toiling men. Ettore looks over them; thin and bent and dirty. He frowns, and studies each face. Not one is familiar, and there are subtle differences in their clothes and the shapes of their hats.

'These aren't Gioia men!' he says. Ludo glances down at him.

'You can tell that by looking at them? Jesus, you all look the same to me. We hired these in Basilicata. What's a man to do, if the local men don't want to work? The harvest can't wait.'

'You broke the strike? These are *blacklegs*?'

'Was there a strike?' says Ludo, all innocence. 'I just thought you Gioia scum had taken a holiday.'

'You . . . you can't! The treaty . . . Leandro signed — all the landlords signed. The Chamber of Labour . . . '

'Last I heard there was no Chamber of Labour any more.' Ludo can't hide his amusement. He rests his forearms on the pommel of the saddle, leaning forward to the comfortable creak of leather.

'You may have the police with you, but Di Vagno will see the agreements honoured! You can't run roughshod over the law — '

'There's only one kind of law here in Puglia, same kind there's always been. The sooner you lot realise you're beaten, the better.' For a moment Ettore can't speak, and because he can't unleash his anger it threatens to choke him.

'I want guard duty again,' he manages to grind out.

'Then fuck off back to the *trullo* and take the night shift. And keep out of my way.' Ludo straightens up, turns away, dismisses him.

As Ettore approaches the archway of the *masseria* the red car slithers past him, too fast, billowing dust from its wheels as it skids into the bend. He squints through the clouds and sees young Filippo at the wheel, concentrating hard but grinning, and Leandro in the passenger seat, laughing, holding tight. They roar away towards the gates, which Carlo scrambles to open in time. Ettore is left with dust in his eyes and on his lips. He wipes his face, spits. Clare is alone on the terrace when he reaches the inner courtyard; just sitting, not reading or drinking. Ettore stands in the middle of the empty space, not caring who sees him, who wonders; he stands there in silence, alight with rage, until she sees him. Her mouth opens slightly in surprise, she leans forwards as though she might get up, but then she hesitates. Ettore lifts one arm and points up and behind him, to the window of his room. He waits until he sees her understand, then he turns away and goes indoors. He stays on his feet inside his room; he stands and faces the door and waits, and has no idea if she will come or not. But if she does not, he decides right then, he will never look at her again. Moments later, she slips in through the door without knocking and carries on towards him, not pausing until she is close enough for him to feel her nervous breath on his mouth. She's so bold, so sure; her certainty surprises him, and it's he who falters.

'Where is your husband?' he says. She puts her fingers on his cheek, low down, near his mouth, as if she wants to feel it move when he speaks.

'I don't care,' she says.

After they have made love the things he must think about, the problems he must solve, drop

275

back into Ettore's mind like stones into water, each one sinking fast, each one ruining the perfect calm, the perfect clarity, the perfectly empty head that sleeping with this woman leaves him with. He doesn't want to let them back in. He opens his eyes and stares at her white skin, and runs his stained fingers over it; he breathes in the smell of her sweat and her hair, the human smell under the fragrance of soap. Chiara is awake; he can tell from the way she's breathing. He lies with his face resting on her chest, breathing in time with the rise and fall of her ribs, but when his thoughts get too much and he can't stay still, he props himself up on one elbow and looks away, and feels her watching him. A breeze from the open window caresses his back; outside, the white light is softening to grey. The dairy cows are calling out to be milked, making their way nearer to the milking parlour, and then there's the sound of an engine. It gets louder and louder, comes thundering into the courtyard below, and dies. Leandro and Filippo's voices echo up to Ettore's room, happy and relaxed, and he realises again that this is not the real world.

At the sound of the car and their voices, Chiara tenses.

'I should go. Pip might come looking for me,' she says.

'I didn't think you would still come to me when your husband was here,' say Ettore. Mention of him makes her restless, and she draws in a long breath, fidgeting.

'Yes, I will still come. I will still come. My

276

. . . lie? My traitorness . . . ?'

'Betrayal.'

'My betrayal does not feel like a betrayal. To be married to him . . . to Boyd, feels like the betrayal.'

'But you are married to him. *This* is the betrayal.' For some reason he wants her to acknowledge it. He wants her to feel guilty, because he does — now that the peace has gone, and thought has returned. But he likes what she says. He likes that he has the greater claim. 'My uncle takes the boy driving?'

'Yes, he's teaching Pip how to drive. And Marcie is teaching him now to act. Between them he is kept quite busy. He doesn't need me any more; not like he did.'

'You're sad about that?'

'Yes, I . . . ' She draws up her knees, wraps her hands around them and rests her chin, turning to look at him. 'When I am not with you I am alone. When you go . . . Now, even with Pip I feel alone. That makes me sad.' Her gaze has barbs and he recoils, gets up and moves away, reaching for his shirt.

'I won't be here for long. I will go when I can. And you will go when my uncle lets you. With your husband and your boy, back to . . . ' He realises he has no idea where she lives, no picture in his head of what it might look like. What her life might look like. Not like his, that much is certain. 'Back to your real world.'

Ettore goes to the courtyard window. Federico is sitting on the water trough, smoking idly, watching Anna as she draws water. The sight of him causes a hard jolt of violence. Ettore grips the window ledge, stepping back when Anna goes inside and it seems like Federico might look up. Just then, Filippo appears on the terrace across the courtyard and pauses. Looking for Chiara. Ettore turns back to her and she has not moved, or dressed. She looks closed in, shrunken, and he knows he's hurt her.

'My uncle told me he needs to find out something from your husband before you can go. Do you know what that could be? You could go sooner if you told him.' There's nothing but silence from the room. 'The boy is looking for you,' he says.

'Yes. I'll go. But I don't want to. I don't want to go back to my real world, with my husband. I don't love him.'

'Why did you marry him?'

'I was just a girl. I was eighteen when we met, nineteen when we married. I'd just finished school . . . and my parents introduced us. He seemed . . . he seemed the right person to marry.'

'For money?'

'No, no. Not for money. For . . . safety, I suppose. For a life that was the way life was supposed to be. The way I had been brought up to think it should be. And for Pip. I also married him for Pip.'

'Because you loved the boy?'

'Yes. He was so little, and so lost without his mother. And I loved Boyd . . . That is, I thought I loved him. Now I think . . . I think perhaps I had no idea what love was. No idea how things could be between a man and a woman.' She

278

looks up at him quickly, uncertainly, like she's said too much. Ettore stays quiet. 'But how could I have known? I was so young . . . ' She shakes her head, seems to want him to absolve her of her mistake. 'I was a schoolgirl, and then I was Mrs Boyd Kingsley. That's all I knew how to be, until now.'

'You're still Mrs Kingsley. You still have your life to go back to — the one you chose. The one that is how it should be; the one you *will* go back to. This is life. Full of things we must do whether we want to or not,' he says harshly, and wants to feel angry with her and her naivety, but can't. She takes a quick breath, like a gasp, and then hurries to her feet and starts to dress, but her hands are shaking and she can't manage her buttons, the clasp of her brassiere, her hairpins. Ettore finds he can't bear it; it's like a little knife in his own heart, the ease with which he can hurt her. He goes to stand behind her, puts his arms around her, tucks his face into the crook of her neck. For a second he wants to tell her that she is like a cool drink at the end of a hot day, but he doesn't.

'You're not going yet,' she says, the words blurred. 'Your leg is still not strong enough. You're not going yet.'

'Not yet,' he agrees, but in his head he's already back in Gioia, in the small room where his father is determined to die and his sister nurses her son with a knife in her spare hand. He is in the fields with the men he has always worked alongside; he is in the *piazza*, he is in the ashes of the Chamber of Labour; he has Livia's

279

murderer beneath him, and rocks in his fists; he is a blaze of outrage.

★ ★ ★

For a week he works. He uses his leg whenever he can and the wound no longer opens when he does so, and he can no longer feel it pull in the bone. The ache of it is manageable, and no worse than the fire in his back after a day with the mattock or scythe. The Gioia men return to work and threshing starts; the thump of the machine out away from the house is a constant background noise, like a giant, restless heartbeat. Leandro Cardetta, it seems, has no trouble procuring fuel. Ettore waits for Chiara; when he is not on duty he goes away from the *masseria* and waits. They meet in ruined *trulli*, the abandoned homes of poor men, peasant men, dead men. He avoids company inside the *masseria*; he still itches with impatience, but when he sees her coming towards him with that rapid, light, marching way she walks, he finds himself smiling. They learn each other's bodies, and how they like to be touched; the pattern of their love-making is like a dance, learnt and instinctive at the same time. And he finds that his mind returns to it, to her, more and more; at times when he should be thinking of leaving, when he should be thinking of finding Livia's killer, when he should be thinking of Paola, and home, and the war they are so clearly losing. One more time, he thinks, each time she goes. Just one more time.

One stuffy night he's on duty in the *trullo* by the gates. The dogs whine and mutter to themselves as they settle down for the night; geckos cheep at one another as they wriggle across the warm stones, pausing to mark Ettore with the black spheres of their eyes. He sits with the rifle on his knees and lets his mind wander. There has been no sign of raiders or thieves since he arrived at dell'Arco, and the mood of the guards is relaxed. Twice Ettore has been to the roof and found Carlo fast asleep; once he castigated the young man mildly, and only afterwards realised what he was doing — warning him to be ready to attack Ettore's own people. Then he was so appalled with himself that he almost laughed. One by one the lights go off inside the *masseria* until the darkness is complete, and Ettore's eyes stretch and strain as they adjust. A soft sound gives his skin a prickle of warning; he's on his feet in an instant, his finger on the trigger, heart lurching. The nearest dog growls with quiet menace but then there's silence and he thinks he's imagined the sound, until a face appears at the gates, not two feet away from him. With a gasp Ettore swings the gun up, knocks the barrel against the metal with a clang that makes the dog yip in excitement. Then he lowers it again, shutting his eyes in relief.

'Paola, Mother of God! Don't sneak up like that!' he whispers, and sees her fleeting smile.

'I stayed downwind of the dogs,' she says, pleased. 'Quiet when I want to be, aren't I?'

'Quieter than a shadow. Why are you here?'

281

'I wanted to tell you something, and ask you something. When are you coming back?'

'Soon.' He puts the gun down, glances back at the farm. 'Soon. What's going on — is it Valerio?'

'No, he actually seems a little better. I wanted to tell you . . . there's a plan.'

'A plan?'

'Yes. A plan to fight back, but properly this time. No more strikes that they simply break with blacklegs. No more political debate. If this is a war then let it be an open one.' In the near dark her eyes are huge and they shine. He can read nothing in them but conviction, and it makes him uneasy.

'What is this plan?'

'Well,' she hesitates, choosing her words. 'Well, brother, you're not going to like it.'

But when, after infinite endurance, they are shaken to the depths of their beings and are driven by an instinct of self-defence or justice, their revolt knows no bounds and no measure. It is an inhuman revolt whose point of departure and final end alike are death, in which ferocity is born of despair.

*Christ Stopped at Eboli*
Carlo Levi

# Clare

The more Clare speaks to Ettore, the more time she spends with him, the better her Italian becomes. The latest word she's learnt is *tradimento*. Betrayal. She was so sure that Boyd would guess at once that for the first few days fear chafed at her every time she saw her husband. She'd been sure he would see it in her eyes, or smell it on her — smell Ettore on her — but he's said nothing, and shown no signs of suspicion. Since he told Clare about Leandro Cardetta and his strange, precarious relationship with the man, Boyd has been diffident with her, cautious, as though he's not quite sure what she'll do. Perhaps this distraction is what keeps him from noticing that nothing is how it was before — that the world is not what Clare thought it was, that they are not the same people, any of them, and that to this new version of herself, Ettore Tarano is as necessary as breathing. She fears the speed with which Ettore is healing, his leg strengthening; she dreads his departure from the *masseria*.

One afternoon she goes directly from Ettore's room to the quiet chamber where Boyd works, at the back of the *masseria*. She goes with her hair dishevelled, her blouse untucked from the waistband of her skirt and sweat drying along her hairline, but these could be symptoms of the heat, nothing more. Boyd starts as she comes in, his body curved over his work, the desk covered in papers and pencils; he looks up and the sight of her wipes away his frown of concentration, leaving pleasure and hope in its place. The room smells faintly of him, and of wood and ink, like a schoolroom.

'Hello, darling,' he says, and he smiles. Clare's pulse flutters in her throat; she's alive with nerves, and yet a part of her almost *wants* him to guess, even if the thought of what would happen then terrifies her. She wonders if it was this same impulse that made him confess everything to her about his affair, the year before, with Christina Havers. Clare hadn't guessed anything; she hadn't seen or sensed anything different, until he broke down and wept, and made her sit while he knelt before her and confessed it all. Had he come home with traces of Christina on his body? Had he wanted her to guess, and felt this same frustration when she hadn't? *Nothing has changed.* He said it over and over. *Nothing has changed, my darling, I promise.* But he'd been wrong about that, because Clare took a quick look into her heart and couldn't even find an echo of what she'd felt for him when they wed. She doesn't think it was his affair that made it vanish, but that gave her cause to examine her feelings. And because there was no love there was no injury, there was no anguish. There was nothing much at all.

The affair with Christina showed Clare a side of her husband she'd never seen before. Since their trip to New York she'd known there were things about him she didn't understand, and perhaps never would. She would never know how deep his grief for Emma went, because it seemed fathomless, like his love for her. She knew there were things from that past life that he would not, or could not, put into words. But the way he rounded on Christina Havers — the young, bored wife of a client — after their affair, was a revelation. Christina had thick, dark hair, lazy eyes and bee-stung lips. She was about the age Clare had been when she'd married Boyd — eighteen or nineteen. There was still a layer of puppy fat on her figure; her big, round breasts nestled between soft arms. Boyd said she'd seduced him — got him drunk at a drinks party and came on strongly. He called her a whore, a slut, a trollop, spitting out these ugly words as if they tasted bad; he clearly hated her with a passion. But he hadn't only slept with her once; somehow he'd found himself at her mercy four or five times before guilt and loathing overwhelmed him, and made him throw himself on his wife's mercy.

Clare had believed his remorse — it was impossible not to when he'd worked himself into such a lather. His utter abjection made her think of New York, of the vomit and the white dots on the carpet, and the terrifying way he'd seemed like a stranger — completely, in that moment, and partially ever since. So she followed her instinct to calm him, to reassure him. She believed that he loved her, hated what he'd done, couldn't explain quite why he'd done it, and was terrified she might leave him because of it. But she also believed his hatred of Christina, and

287

that was what bothered her the most. She wasn't sure what it meant; she didn't know how he could make love to the girl and then blame her entirely, and hate her. Making love had required both of them to be there, and willing, after all. Troubled, Clare said very little on the whole subject, and Boyd took her silence as a dignified toleration of his transgression that might soon lead to forgiveness, and life returned to the way it had been before. *That bitch*, he called little Christina, his lips white with the word, tears shining on his rumpled face. *That whore*.

Now, Clare finds herself wondering what it would be like to hear those same words from Boyd directed at her. She can't imagine it — not when he has only ever told her that he couldn't live without her, that she is an angel, that she has saved him. But that was the Clare before Ettore. Boyd holds his hand out to her, and with the thrill of wondering if this will be what gives her away, if touch will be the sense with which he sees clearly, Clare crosses the room and takes his hand.

'How's it coming along?' she says. Dry mouth; shallow breaths. Boyd turns back to look at his drawings and shrugs slightly.

'Well, they're almost ready to show him. As to how he'll react to them . . . ' He looks up at her with mute appeal. 'I can only hope he'll be happy, and we can go home.' Panic bubbles up in Clare. In the space of two weeks her goal has turned on its head, and now she doesn't want to leave. She remembers what Ettore said — that Leandro wants to find something out from Boyd

288

before he will let them go. It could simply mean that Leandro wants to see these finished designs, but it could mean something else. Something more. As soon as Ettore told her she'd thought of New York, and it's on the tip of Clare's tongue to ask, to speculate, but she stops herself. If he doesn't know already, then she doesn't want Boyd to hear that this missing information is what's keeping them there. He might clear the matter up in minutes; their visit might end there and then. There's unease behind all this silent thought — she can't imagine what information Boyd could possibly have that Leandro might want.

Boyd squeezes her hand for attention. 'Well, what do you think?' he says. Clare has been staring at the drawings for a minute or more without really seeing them. She blinks, and concentrates. The new front Boyd has drawn for the house on Via Garibaldi has *trulli* along the roofline. Four small, stylised *trulli*, built of interlocking stone just like the real things, but with regular-sized cut blocks, put together precisely, so that the sides are almost faceted and they are halfway to being pyramids rather than cones. Each one is topped with a tall spike, like that of a small minaret, and the rest of the front is plain, elegant, almost austere, with four Doric columns flanking the large street door. Clare has a sinking feeling inside.

'It's just . . . wonderful, Boyd,' she says honestly. 'It's so different, and yet it won't jar with anything around it . . . It's understated, but it's striking. I think it's one of the best things you've designed. Cardetta has to be pleased.' Boyd sags visibly in relief.

'I am so glad you think so, darling. I was hoping . . . that is, the building seemed to take shape as I drew it — it seemed to know how it ought to look. That's always a very good sign. The *trulli* are such iconic buildings of this area. I'd never seen anything like them before I came here. I think they represent Mr Cardetta rather well, don't you? As emblems, I mean. They're peasant dwellings, after all, but they can stand for hundreds of years. He came from the peasantry but has constructed a far grander life, and a more lasting one, by being steadfast and adaptable.' Boyd pauses, scrutinising his work with an anxious gaze. 'Never mind quite what he has constructed it upon,' he murmurs.

'Indeed,' says Clare, and there's a loaded silence while they both wait to hear what will be said next.

They haven't quite settled this between them yet — the tone they will take when discussing Leandro Cardetta, his past, his designs for them, the kind of man he is, and that Boyd has brought them here at his behest. It bothers Clare that she still doesn't know how her husband came to meet Cardetta in the first place; that he has still never answered that question. Boyd picks up a pencil and starts to sharpen it with the small paring knife he keeps on his desk. Clare moves away from him, ostensibly to study a painting of St Sebastian on the wall, head thrown back in agony, bristling with arrows. *Tradimento.* Here they are talking as though nothing has changed, as though they are a team, when there is so much they don't know about one another.

'When will you show him the drawings?' she says, at last.

'Soon. I don't know . . . soon,' says Boyd. He frowns at his work again. 'I want to make sure they're perfect.'

'Nothing is ever perfect. You've said before that you tend to overwork things sometimes.' Clare hears her own words, incredulous. She should tell him to delay, to wait, to spoil the drawings. She should do whatever she can to prolong their stay. But then she thinks of Pip, and his sullen unhappiness, and she is torn, bewildered.

'You're right, my darling,' says Boyd.

Just then, a strange sound comes from some far-off part of the house, and Clare listens for a moment before she can make it out. Then, unmistakeably, she picks out the three-time rhythm and shrill strings of a waltz.

'Is that Strauss?' she says, and Boyd smiles.

'I forgot, I was meant to tell you — Marcie's looking for you. She said something about a party.'

'I'll go and see.' Boyd opens his mouth as though he will say something, ask something, but he hasn't time to before Clare leaves the room. She goes up to the bat room, the rehearsal room, the spare room — it has these various names — the music getting louder with each step she takes, echoing along the stone corridors, and it's been so long since she heard any that Clare is drawn towards it. It's so profoundly out of place

291

here at the *masseria*, here in Puglia. It's music from another time, another place; it's music from another world, and sounds alien in this sparse land, with these hard people. But it's Marcie, of course; she doesn't belong in Puglia any more than Clare does.

Clare opens the door to twirling figures; they are waltzing across the floor — Marcie and Pip. Pip is awkward and slightly out of time but Marcie doesn't seem to mind and follows his lead, however halting. She keeps a beautiful frame, her neck arched back, eyebrows high and haughty, smile serene. She's slightly taller than Pip in her heels; he has his chin up to compensate, and is concentrating hard.

'Clare!' Marcie calls when she sees her standing there. 'You'll never guess what, but Federico has only managed to fix this old gramophone! I thought it was dead and gone — it's been in the junk room for months.' The waltz is getting slower and slower as the gramophone winds down, so Clare goes over to wind the handle and tighten the mainspring.

'Lord, now it's too fast for me!' says Pip, struggling to organise his feet, and Marcie laughs, and they dance faster, turning around and around until Clare is dizzy watching them. She's suddenly awash with all her love for Pip, and all her pride in him, and the fact that he's dancing when everything around him is so strange and so dark. Her eyes swell with tears and her heart with guilt, because it's him she's betraying too, of course, not just Boyd. Where can her love for Ettore lead her, apart from away

292

from Pip? She has a sudden clear premonition of agony ahead.

'No more! I'm dying!' cries Marcie, breaking off her hold. 'My mama told me a lady should never perspire, but in this heat who could help it?'

Clare lifts the needle out of the groove and quiet fills the room.

'We could have carried on,' says Pip. 'Clare, don't you want a go?'

'Well, we need to save what needles we have for the party, Filippo,' says Marcie.

'You and I will dance then,' says Clare. She wipes her eyes with her fingertips. 'You looked very elegant, Pip. Any young lady would be proud to dance with you.'

'Are you *crying*?' Pip smiles.

'Oh, Clare, whatever's the matter?' says Marcie.

'Oh no, don't worry — you should have seen her at my last school play. She cried all over the place,' says Pip, lightly, but there's something else underneath his words, almost like a tinge of contempt. It jars Clare, so that she clears her throat, reorders her face, and tries not to show her pain.

'I've sent Federico out with the invitations. Ilaria will cook up a feast, and we'll drink too much wine and dance until dawn! Oh, I can't wait,' says Marcie, coming over to Clare and gripping her arms. Her face is flushed beneath the powder, her eyes slightly frantic. 'I wonder if Ettore would come? There must be precious few parties in his life right now. It'd do him the world of good.'

'I'm not sure his leg is ready for dancing,' says Clare.

'Oh, have you seen him lately, then? I hardly even lay eyes on the kid when Leandro's here.'

'I saw him . . . on guard duty, I think. And he's hardly a kid, is he?' Clare fiddles with the gramophone handle, her fingertips feeling both raw and numb, like the rest of her — unbearably self-conscious.

'Oh, they all get that weathered look down here in Puglia. Ettore's only twenty-four though — you wouldn't think it, would you?'

'No.' Clare can't breathe for a second. She thought he was older than her; he seems it in so many ways. Suddenly she understands how young he must have been when hardship began its march over his body and face. 'Will you be performing your play at the party as well?' she says tightly.

'Oh, heavens, I don't think we're ready, are we, Pip? Are we? No, I think that'll have to be a bit later on.'

'Well, I can't wait to see it. Can't you even say what it's about?' says Clare.

'Oh, we don't want to ruin the surprise, do we, Pip?' Marcie aims a flash of her bright smile at Pip, and he smiles, closed-lipped, and shifts his feet.

'That's right. It's supposed to be a surprise,' he says. Clare gazes at him for a moment, because the expression on his face is one she hasn't seen before.

★　★　★

294

The next day is one of heavy cloud and brooding humidity; stillness so complete that not a single leaf nods on the fig tree, not a single blade of the dry grass twists or bends. Clare goes for a walk after lunch and fancies she can feel the air parting to let her through, and closing gummily in her wake. She meets Ettore in the broken-down ruins of a *trullo*, its roof open to the blank sky. They make love first, and talk afterwards, like always. There's little room to think of anything until their initial physical need is sated, and after a day, two days, sometimes three days, that need builds and snaps like a static charge. Clare is left with a graze on her spine from the rough stone wall, which stings, and an overwhelming sense of safety, surety.

'You're only twenty-four, Marcie told me,' she says. Ettore nods. They sit side by side on the stone ledge outside the door of the *trullo*, and Clare thinks of all the people who have sat there before them, down the centuries: men smoking, thinking, watching; women resting, talking, hulling beans. Other lovers, perhaps, who've needed a hiding place and a hard stone bed on which to lie.

'And you?' he says.

'Twenty-nine,' says Clare, ashamed of her fresh face, and that she has no scars, by how untouched she is, how unmarked by the world.

'You have never been hungry,' he says.

'No. No, I have never been hungry.' Clare takes his hand and winds her pale fingers through his dark ones.

'I can't imagine that,' he says, giving her a

wondering look, with no rancour.

'I can't imagine your life. Your world,' she says sadly.

'Don't try. Be happy you don't need to.' Ettore frowns.

'But I want to. I want to know . . . to understand.'

'Why? How can you? What good would it do you?'

'Because it's *you*. It's who *you* are. So I want to understand,' says Clare. Ettore looks up into the heavy sky and doesn't reply.

'It will rain soon,' he says.

'You don't think I can, do you? You don't think I can understand,' says Clare. It's a sad statement rather than a question, and Ettore turns to look at her, smiling slightly. His eyes, glowing with colour, are the brightest things she can see.

'Nobody from outside could. It's not your fault.'

'I want . . . I want to make you happy.'

'You'll only make yourself unhappy.' He shakes his head. 'We should stop this.'

'I don't want to stop it.'

'But we should. Sooner or later somebody will guess, and then your husband will know. We should stop,' he says, and Clare holds her breath until she's sure he doesn't mean now — doesn't mean *right now*. He brushes his thumb over her cheek, and kisses her.

When the first heavy drops of rain start to fall Ettore pushes Clare up and propels her away towards the *masseria*. She starts to walk but the sound of an engine sends her running back to the cover of the *trullo*, as the red car rolls past in the distance, also heading for the farm.

'I didn't know the road was so close!' she says. Ettore hasn't moved a muscle. 'Do you think he saw us?'

'He might not have if you hadn't bolted like a rabbit,' he says, and smiles briefly. 'Nothing looks more guilty.'

'I'm sorry. I couldn't help it. I hope it was the servant driving on some errand, not Pip, or Leandro.'

'If it was Pip there would have been more swerving, more noise and dust,' says Ettore, and Clare smiles. 'Rabbit. My uncle called you that, a while back, but he was wrong . . . you might be frightened but you don't let it stop you. That's courage, in fact.'

'He called me a rabbit?' says Clare. The insult hurts unexpectedly. 'And Marcie called me mouse, once. That's what they think of me — a weakling. A coward.'

'What does it matter what they think?' He smiles lopsidedly at her. 'We know better.'

'I'm so tired of . . . ' Clare shakes her head. She can't put her finger on it. 'I'm so tired of doing what I'm told to. Of being expected to follow where I'm led.' Ettore frowns at her.

'Yes. It gets under your skin, doesn't it?' he says softly. 'When you are shown no respect; given no control over your own life.'

Clare lowers her eyes, ashamed.

'I'm sorry. I have no cause for complaint, I know. I must sound so spoilt to you . . . It's my

297

own fault, anyway. People lead me because I've always let them,' she says. Ettore lights a cigarette and blows the smoke high above his head, and says nothing. Clare is crouching with her face close to the ancient *tufo* stone wall, her fingers braced against it. She stands up and goes to sit next to Ettore. There are ants crawling around her ankles and she bends to brush them away; their bites are spiteful little pinpricks. In the distance, the last dust thrown up by the car resettles. 'Even if it was that servant driving, we should be careful. He seems quite friendly with Marcie. Federico, that's his name. Perhaps he'd say something to her, if he knew about us.'

'He's scum,' Ettore snaps. 'If Marcie knew what was going on, if she opened her eyes and looked, for once, she wouldn't have him near her. Not for a second.'

'Why, though? What's going on? Your uncle told me there was a . . . crisis, a war,' says Clare. Ettore pauses, thinking before he answers. He always does, and Clare loves the way he only speaks once he's found exactly what he wants to say.

'It is a war, Chiara. We've been fighting it for decades; it ebbs and flows, as these things will. Now we're coming to the final act.' He takes a long pull on his cigarette and shakes his head. 'There'll be more bloodshed before this summer is out. You saw a man beaten in Gioia, you told me. Attacked by a blackshirt squad.'

'Yes. Yes, I saw it. His name was Francesco Molino.' Clare recoils from the memory.

'Federico Manzo leads one of those squads.

298

He is one of them; a fascist. There is a great deal of violence in him, I've seen it. The same that's in his father Ludo Manzo — violence that doesn't need a cause, only an excuse.'

Clare stares at him. His words have turned her cold. She thinks of the posy of pale blue flowers Federico offered her, and the sweetness of his smile not quite matching the knowing look in his eyes. She thinks of him mending the bicycle puncture for Pip, and the gramophone for Marcie. She thinks of a man's broken and bloody spectacles falling to the flagstones in Gioia, and yet again she's assailed by the impossibility of all these things being true at once, by the unreality of this place, these events.

'He tried to give me flowers,' she murmurs, in English.

'*Che cos' hai detto?*' says Ettore. *What did you say?* Clare gives a small shake of her head.

'Does your uncle know about this?'

'Yes, he knows.'

'Then . . . ' Clare swallows. 'Leandro is one of them, too? He's a fascist?'

'That is something I'm trying hard to find out,' says Ettore grimly. 'Nearly all of the other proprietors are, of course. They hire the squads, feed them, arm them, shelter them. They're mounting an army to wipe out the likes of me, and my family. But Leandro is also my family.' He shrugs one shoulder. 'Or he was. Many landlords would not even negotiate with the peasant leagues. Did you know that? Not until they were forced to — and some not even then. They said that farm animals belonged in the fields, not at their tables. They said we had no right to speak. That's how they see us — as animals,' he says. Clare stares, shocked.

'But . . . your uncle can't think like that. He *can't*. I saw how he was treated in Gioia, by the other rich men. He was . . . snubbed. Scorned. He can't possibly think like they do.'

'What my uncle thinks is a mystery to me these days. He wants to be accepted by them. I don't know how far he would go to be accepted.'

'But . . . to fight against these squads . . . Can that be the way? People will die . . . you could be hurt. There *must* be another way.'

'Chiara,' says Ettore. He tips his head back against the wall to look at her, as if suddenly exhausted. 'The question is, what should we do when they leave us no other way?'

'I don't know,' she says meekly. 'But I can't stand to think of you in danger. Is there no . . . political solution?'

'We are *all* in danger.' He drops the stub of his cigarette into the dust and grinds it with a chunk of stone. 'And politics? Let me tell you about politics. In 1908 we had an election in Gioia. If we elected the socialist candidate we could start to make our voices heard, but Nicola De Bellis won by a unanimous vote. De Bellis, who believed he was king, and we were all his serfs. A *unanimous* vote, Chiara. Anyone who might have voted against him was beaten, killed, arrested, or barricaded inside. And, just in case, De Bellis made sure he owned the vote counters too. *That* is how politics works here in Gioia. So if you can think of another way, please tell me.'

He turns his head to look at her; his face is tense, eyes narrowed, but her defeated silence seems to calm him, and he relents. 'You should go, before the rain really starts. I'll follow a different way,' he says, and Clare nods. Without having seemed to move, the white clouds have turned to grey, low and solid; fat raindrops explode in the dust and leave dark, uneven craters. Clare wants to say to him, *I love you*, but somehow she knows she shouldn't; she knows he wouldn't want to hear it, and also that he knows it already.

It's pouring by the time Clare arrives back at the front gates, and the young guard, Carlo, lets her in with an amiable grin and water drizzling from the brim of his hat. This is the warm, wetting rain she'd hoped for before; no thunder or hail, just a steady downpour connecting heaven and earth, which plasters her hair to her shoulders and runs down her calves into her shoes. The dogs crouch beneath their meagre shelters, looking out with mournful eyes. They hardly bother to bark at Clare any more, they've got so used to her scent. As she walks past the raised hump of the cistern in the *aia* she can hear the water thudding into it below ground level. She walks a slow loop around the *masseria*, listening to the sluice of water in the gutter, the music it makes as it rushes along stone gullies, unseen, beneath her feet. She pauses in the vegetable garden to hear it battering the almond tree leaves, and pattering on the broken love seat. When she looks up she sees some of the guards on the roof standing out in it as she is, letting it soak them. In England people would run out of this rain, not into it, but here it's a rarity like snow at home — something almost miraculous. But it isn't enough to make a stream run between the fields, even for a little while. After half an hour the rain stops, like a tap turned off with a single twist, and minutes later a bloated sun emerges from the clouds and everything starts to steam.

Federico is in the courtyard, drying the red car with a leather rag. At the sight of him Clare is even more affected than before — physically repelled, like there's a hand on her chest, shoving her away. She takes an involuntary step backwards and keeps her eyes lowered after taking one look at his face beginning to smile. But there's no way to go inside without passing him, so she folds her arms, looks at her feet and marches by. As she does she hears a noise — a hissing, low and rhythmic, full of startling menace. She glances up and it's Federico, hissing at her through the gap in his twisted front teeth, and his smile has turned sour and leering, and his eyes are mocking, and she knows then, absolutely, that he saw. That he knows about her and Ettore. He doesn't stop hissing now that she's looking at him. He wants her to see. Clare turns away and hurries inside, revolted; humiliated at the same time.

She goes into the long sitting room on the ground floor and finds it empty. She climbs the stairs and goes out onto the terrace but there's no sign of Marcie, or Pip. She checks the bat room; the door is open, the room bright and

302

empty. Crossing to the window with the soft sound of her footsteps echoing, Clare looks down into the courtyard. She watches Federico polishing the car, his brows furrowed against the sunlight, his arm working in rhythmic circles. He's rolled up his shirtsleeves and the muscles of his forearms are taut ridges, and she thinks of Francesco Molino — the way he curled against their kicks and blows, after his glasses flew off, the wrong shape of his collapsed eye socket. There's acid at the back of her throat, hot and sour. She can't believe Federico has this normal life, that he looks like a normal man, not like a monster; it seems an outrageous dissembling. She's appalled to have been near him when he had such a secret, and she's frightened of him now, not just uneasy; she wants to tell somebody, to denounce him somehow. But Ettore said that Leandro already knows, and she can't think of anyone else to tell.

Clare feels unsettled and restless, and doesn't want to be alone. She goes to Pip's room but that, too, is empty. The room has been made up by one of the maids — sheets stretched tight, the carafe of water on the nightstand refilled and covered, his copy of *Bleak House* and the photograph of Emma neatly arranged. A soft wash of air nudges in through the window, fresh and warm after the rain, and Clare goes to stand at it, looking out through the back wall of the *masseria*. She sees Pip on the far side of the overseer's *trullo*, standing with Ludo and Leandro. He is slighter than either of them, but almost as tall. He stands with his shoulders

303

pulled back, in discussion about something and pointing to a lone olive tree not far away. Clare watches, curious, even though she doesn't like seeing him in their company, until she sees that they are holding guns — Pip included. She catches her breath, turns at once and goes back to the stairs. She doesn't want to recross the courtyard but there's no other way, so she walks fast and doesn't look at Federico. He stays silent this time; he keeps working, but she can feel his eyes following her.

By the time she reaches Pip he's standing with his legs wide apart and his arm extended, squinting along it. The sight of the pistol in his hand gives Clare a nasty jolt, like he's holding a live snake — she wants him to drop it and step away. There's a splash of white paint on the trunk of the olive tree, and Ludo is at Pip's side, steadying his hand, looking down along it, adjusting his aim. Leandro catches her arm to stall her as she hurries towards them.

'Wait a moment,' he says. 'He's about to shoot.'

'I don't want him to,' she says automatically. Leandro hushes her gently, and keeps hold of her arm. After a moment Clare pulls it away, but she stays at his side. The sight of Ludo Manzo schooling Pip is almost as abhorrent as the sight of the gun. Stepping back, Ludo checks the target once more and gives a curt nod. His eyes are narrow and sharp; he doesn't flinch when the gun goes off, and Pip's arm jerks back wildly before he can stop it.

The bullet smacks into the stone of the wall

two metres to the left of the olive tree, there's a cloud of dust, a shower of grit, and Ludo grins. He says something and then chuckles, and Pip's cheeks flame. He's breathing hard, his eyes are wide with excitement.

'Ludo says the first time he fired a gun he gave himself a black eye, so you did good, Pip,' says Leandro, and Pip turns to smile at him. He seems surprised to see Clare there, but pleased as well.

'Did you see that, Clare?' he says.

'I saw it,' says Clare, but she can't smile.

'You don't approve?' Leandro murmurs.

'He's still a schoolboy. He doesn't need to know how to fire a gun.'

'You never know when it might come in useful,' Leandro demurs. 'Especially out here.' Clare glances sharply at him, but Leandro walks forwards before she can ask him what he means. He puts a hand on Pip's shoulder and gives it a squeeze. 'Now you know how it kicks, so you'll know to be ready for it. Try the shot again. Squeeze the trigger gently, and brace your arm for the recoil.'

'All right,' says Pip. Clare draws breath to speak but doesn't know what she wants to say. Pip is enjoying himself, and she doesn't want to spoil it for him, but she thinks of the naked man grazing the stubble at Ludo's feet, and the way he grinned then, too. She thinks of Federico leading a squad in Gioia, and of Leandro, refusing to let her leave. She's surrounded by men of violence, and she doesn't want the least trace of it to touch Pip, or linger on him, or

305

shape him in any way. The brutality is like a poison, like a sickness, and the thought of Pip catching it is appalling.

His second shot carves a ragged tear in the bark of the tree trunk, still wide of the target but far closer.

'Bravo!' says Ludo, nodding. Pip smiles, shrugs modestly.

'I can do better, I'm sure of it. I just need to practise more. Will you tell him for me, Leandro?'

'Of course. And of course you'll improve — a farm is the perfect place to practise. You'll be a crack shot by the end of the summer.'

'But perhaps that's enough for now?' says Clare. She too has gone closer. She wants to catch Pip's eye, she wants him to sense her unease so she won't need to speak it.

'But we've only just started!' says Pip. He still has the pistol in his hand, held awkwardly and half extended away from him, like he doesn't quite want it to touch him. 'I need to practise more. Then Ludo's going to teach me to shoot the rifle as well, and then I can go and shoot at rats in the barn.'

'Well, be warned — they're devilish hard to hit,' says Leandro. 'You won't believe the speed of them. If you can shoot rats then there's not much you won't be able to hit.'

'I don't see why you need to shoot *anything*,' says Clare, almost pleading. But Pip doesn't seem to hear it.

'I'm good at archery,' says Pip. 'I think I could be good at this, too.'

'A gun is just a tool, Mrs Kingsley,' says Leandro calmly. 'On a farm it's just a tool, like a scythe or a mattock.'

'Pip's not one of your guards, Mr Cardetta.'

'It's really fine, Clare. Father said it was a good idea,' says Pip, stepping away from her, raising the gun again, staring down its sights. 'There are brigands, you know. And packs of rebels. This way I can defend us, if I need to.' He screws up his eyes, tilting his head to take aim. Clare stares at him in shock.

'The boy has been upset by some of the things he's seen here,' Leandro says quietly, for Clare's ears only. 'This is how to make him strong; unafraid.'

'No. This is how to inure him,' she says shakily.

'That's how we get strong.' Leandro shrugs. 'No harm will come of it, I give you my word.' Clare watches for a minute more, and knows she's defeated. She wants to say to Leandro, and to Ludo, *you can't have him.* But Pip is no longer a child, and he was never truly hers. Ludo glances up and meets her eye, and this time there's no grin, no amusement; just a cold, steady scrutiny. Clare leaves them, and as she goes Pip's third shot rings out. The sound makes her ears hum, and then she hears Pip's delighted laugh, and Leandro clapping.

★ ★ ★

A day later, Clare sits out on the covered terrace with Pip, playing rummy with a deck of yellowed playing cards that he found in an empty bedroom. Clare is still tense; she feels full of things she wants to say to him, but when it comes to it she doesn't know how to phrase any of them, so she stays silent. She can't explain to him why it bothered her so much to see him learning to shoot a gun with Ludo and Leandro; or why she distrusts both men so deeply. For the first time ever, the silence between them feels awkward. This is another thing she wants to object to, but to acknowledge it would only make it worse. When raised voices echo out across the courtyard they exchange an anxious look and their game stalls as they listen. It's simmering hot again, but the sky is a deep blue and there's a gently cooling breeze. It seems an altogether too beautiful day for such an explosion of anger. It's Leandro's voice — instantly recognisable — and there are pauses in his tirade as if somebody else is answering him, in a voice too quiet to be heard. It could be one of the servants, it could be Marcie, or Boyd. There's a hiatus during which the whole *masseria* seems to bend its ears towards the absence of sound, then Leandro shouts:

'Is this a goddamned *joke*?' There's a bang of a door slamming and then quiet, and the sparrows in the courtyard, as though they'd been holding their breath, start to hop about and chatter again.

'What do you suppose *that* was all about?' says Pip nervously. He's always hated shouting, raised voices, any kind of confrontation.

'Perhaps I should go and see . . . and make

308

sure everything's all right,' says Clare, getting up. 'You'll stay put?' she says to Pip, who nods, reshuffles the cards and starts laying out a game of solitaire.

She goes down to the long sitting room. Somebody left in high dudgeon, and slammed the inner door, but she has no idea if that person was Leandro or the object of his wrath. Peeping around the threshold Clare sees papers scattered over the central ottoman, curling gently in the breeze from the open doors. She sees the back of Leandro's silver head, his sloping shoulders and solid ribcage, and catches her breath. She's about to slip away again when she realises that the papers in front of him are Boyd's drawings. Her fingers curl tightly around the doorframe, her nails making a minute scratching noise that turns Leandro's head at once.

'Mrs Kingsley,' he says sombrely. His face has a dragged-down look. 'Do come and join me. You must have heard my little outburst. I'm sure they heard it in Gioia.'

'Is everything all right, Mr Cardetta?' she says pointlessly. She sits down uneasily, on the edge of a couch opposite him.

'In a way I suppose it is, in fact. I fear I've given your husband a pasting he didn't quite deserve. Perhaps he meant nothing by it. A misunderstanding, nothing more. I can't imagine him being the type of man to goad another deliberately.'

'Certainly I can't imagine him ever goading *you* deliberately, Mr Cardetta.'

The proprietor delicately rearranges some of

the drawings in front of him, using only his fingertips; he frowns at them in thought.

'We all have our weaknesses, Mrs Kingsley,' he murmurs. 'Mine is my temper. I have such a store of anger in my heart, you understand.' He taps his chest to show her. 'Such a store of it. Nobody could be born poor here and not grow up to have it. It doesn't matter what you do later, or what changes. It never goes.'

'You . . . don't like the designs?' says Clare. Leandro looks up at her sharply, as if even now suspecting mockery. He shakes his head.

'You can't see it either, can you? That rather confirms Boyd's innocent intentions.' Leandro makes a sweeping gesture over the drawings. '*Trulli*. He has designed it after *trulli*. I have worked and worked; I have done things you couldn't imagine, Mrs Kingsley, to pull myself up to where I am. Still, my peers here treat me as peasant scum, and there's nothing I can do to stop them. And now look — after all of it, your husband would put me back in a *trullo*!' He laughs suddenly, loudly. 'In case!' He wags a finger at her. 'Just in case anybody should forget, and mistake me for *signori*!' He laughs again, a self-mocking chuckle that soon peters out. Clare swallows nervously; the thought is there at once that if the designs aren't right, Boyd will have to stay longer. She will have to stay longer.

'I'm . . . I'm quite sure Boyd had absolutely no intention of insulting you, Mr Cardetta.'

'Ah, you're probably right.' Leandro sighs and leans back in his chair. He runs one hand across his mouth, grips his jaw; the same gesture Clare

310

has seen Ettore make. 'Perhaps I should scrap the whole idea and save my money. Chances are the place could get ransacked anyway, before this trouble is done.'

'Then . . . you don't want him to redraw them?' she says breathlessly.

'You must be ready to return to your home?' he says. 'Perhaps this whole thing was a mistake,' he adds softly, and she isn't sure which thing he means.

'No, I . . . that is . . . ' Clare can't for the life of her think how to answer. For a mad second she almost asks him what it is he wants to know from Boyd.

She looks up to find him watching her speculatively.

'You are not at all what I expected you would be, Mrs Kingsley,' he says. 'The British are often so set in their ways. So rigid in their thinking. You seem, if you don't mind my saying, to be just the opposite of that. In fact, most of the time I find myself unable to put my finger on what it is you do think.'

'I find the same thing myself, sometimes,' she says, and Leandro smiles.

'Your husband has told you something of my former life in New York, I can tell.' He says this lightly, and Clare is instantly on her guard. She doesn't trust any levity in him.

'Yes,' she says. Leandro grunts, nods.

'You demanded to know, I'll wager. I can't imagine him volunteering the information. And may I counsel you not to credit everything you've heard, Mrs Kingsley? Your husband and I

311

have a . . . complicated past. I know he would never tell you all of it. Perhaps he should have told you none of it.'

'Will you tell me?'

'Me? Christ, no.' He chuckles again. 'But I will tell you this. In the course of my life I've had to do things that no man in his right mind would be proud of. I've been on the wrong side of the law — so far on the wrong side I forgot there was a right side, sometimes. I forgot there was a law. I've left that behind me now; I'm not that same man any more. But it got me to where I am, it got me to where I wanted to be, and how many men can say that? Do you know what I used to dream of when I was a little boy, Mrs Kingsley?' He leans forward keenly, elbows on his knees. 'I used to watch the *signori* going into the Teatro Comunale in Gioia in the evening. I used to look at their fine suits and the dresses and jewels the women wore, and the carriages they came in, all lit up with lamps. Their horses were sleek and spirited, not broken-winded, or worm-eaten. I used to dream of being one of those men — of walking along with them with a beauty on my arm, and laughing about whatever it was the rich found to laugh about, and spending an evening well fed, watching a play. I didn't even know what a play was, really. I couldn't picture it — there I was, all bones and dirt, a starving, snot-nosed rat like the rest of us. And I watched them, and I dreamed. Do you know how old I was the first time I worked a full day in the fields, Mrs Kingsley?' Clare shakes her head, mute. 'Eight. I was eight years old,' says

312

Leandro, and his face drags down again, remembering. 'You've no idea of the things I've done, and the shit I've waded through, to put myself where I am. And I will cut down any man who tries to take it from me. I will *cut him down.*' He says this with total calm, total conviction, and Clare feels her legs twitch, the instinctive urge to run.

Suddenly, Leandro smiles. 'I've lost the thread of my story. Forgive me.'

'I can't imagine what life must be like for the very poor here. I can be told, but I can't imagine it,' says Clare.

'None of us can walk in another's shoes, not truly. But don't let it distress you, Mrs Kingsley. Soon you'll be back in London, with your husband and your son, and it will be as though none of this ever happened. You need never spare a thought for poor Puglia again. Isn't that what you want?' She looks up sharply because the question has an undercurrent of unspoken meaning.

'I won't ever forget coming here,' she says.

'No. I don't suppose you will,' he says gravely.

'Will you tell me what happened at Masseria Girardi?' She takes a chance in asking, since they're speaking plainly. 'You said Ettore was angry with you about it.'

'Angry with me about it — no. Although, perhaps he ought to be. No, my nephew is just angry about it. He's angry about so many things. Of course he is. He was one of those starving brats, same as I was, and he's never managed to change it at all.'

'But what was it?'

'It's a hard story, Mrs Kingsley.'

'I want to hear it.'

'It was just over a year ago now, and all this . . . violence was just beginning — rumours and whispers. The harvest was a disaster — farmers were torching their own crops because the insurance money was worth more than the wheat! *This* is what the peasants don't see!' Leandro thumps one fist into the opposite palm. 'If they drive us out of business, there'll be nobody to pay them whatsoever! But the workers were starving, and they had the *right* to work — that's what changed after the war. They believed they had the right, and *masserie* that refused to hire were attacked. The Girardi farm had been raided, stolen from. Then the men came and worked Girardi's fallow fields and demanded pay, and Girardi says he saw amongst them the face of at least one man who'd been in a raiding party. And so he hit back. He filled the farmhouse with his neighbours, and with his own guards and *annaroli*. They all brought their guns. And when the workers came at the end of the next day, to return the tools, and Nettis — the man who spoke for them — asked to be paid . . . they opened fire.'

One of the dogs out in the *aia* barks, and there's the sudden stutter of wings as pigeons in the courtyard launch up in fright. Clare has a hollow feeling beneath her ribs.

'They opened fire on unarmed men?' she says. Leandro nods heavily.

'A shameful thing, but Girardi would say he

314

was driven to it. It was a situation with no resolution . . . no good outcome.'

'How many men were . . . killed?'

'Six. Only six. Which is miraculous, really. Many, many more were injured. They fled on foot, and the guards chased after them on horseback. The youngest to die was sixteen; the oldest seventy. It was an evil day. A sad day for this country.'

'And Ettore was there? He was one of the workers?'

'He was there.' Leandro nods again. 'He wasn't injured, but he lost friends. He lost his friend Davide, who was his sister's lover — Paola's lover. They'd have wed if they'd had any idea whether or not her husband was still alive. But New York swallowed him up.'

'And the men who did it? The men who opened fire?'

'Nobody knows for sure who was inside the *masseria*, except those that were there. Some have been arrested, some are on the run. Some were lynched by the *braccianti* in vendetta. Then men from the lynch mobs were arrested . . . '

'The peasants know who was there?'

'They think they know. They thought they knew well enough to seek revenge. Ludo Manzo knows; I'm sure he was there. I can see him itching to say something about it to me, in an offhand way, as he loves to do, but he's not wholly sure where my loyalties lie, you see. Not completely sure. I pay him handsomely to keep this place running but he still sees a *cafone* when he looks at me. He hasn't the wit to realise that I

own him now. Him and his son. There are so
many scores to be settled here, Mrs Kingsley.
We'll be picking away at this mess for
generations.'

Clare turns to look out at the perfect blue sky
and the sunlight glaring on the high white walls.
She half expects to see some sign of the violence,
like smoke in the sky. She half expects to feel the
ground shudder with the ponderous footsteps of
sorrow, hatred, death.

'I should be afraid to be here. I was afraid,
after what I saw in Gioia,' she says softly.

'And you aren't now?'

'I don't know why not. I feel powerless, I feel
weak. But not afraid. Not for myself, at any rate.
Perhaps that's a surrender of some kind.'

'You're safe inside these walls, Mrs Kingsley.'

'Marcie's planning a party. We're to drink, and
dance, and be merry.'

'Marcie is frightened. I shield her from what's
happening here as much as I can, and she
chooses not to look at the rest. All I want is her
happiness. I'm helpless, Mrs Kingsley. Helpless.
She has my heart — every last part of it. I'm not
blind — I know she married a rich man first, and
Leandro Cardetta second. But I married for
love.' He smiles wistfully. 'Like a fool.'

'Then why don't you take her and go? Go
until this has passed? Go somewhere safe!'

'No man and no circumstance will take this
from me, Mrs Kingsley. I may hate this place, I
may hate its people — those who've done
nothing to improve themselves for ten generations; those who scorn the poor from positions of

316

ease that they've done nothing to earn — I may hate it all, but I belong to it. There's nowhere else I belong. Nothing I've done would have any meaning elsewhere.'

'And Marcie?' says Clare, bewildered. 'What of where she belongs?'

'Marcie belongs at my side,' says Leandro intransigently.

'How can it end, a war like this? How can it ever end?' she says. Leandro shrugs.

'We may be about to find out, Mrs Kingsley.'

★ ★ ★

Boyd is back at his desk, stooped and miserable, but since all his drawings are still in the sitting room he's stooped over nothing. Pencil shavings and his paring knife, and the slotted shadows falling from the window. This time he doesn't look up when Clare comes in behind him. He runs his thumbnail along a crack in the wood, gouging out a twisted worm of the dust and dirt of ages.

'He's calmed down now,' says Clare, staying where she is by the door. For some reason she can't go any closer, she can't touch him. He doesn't seem like anyone she knows. *Your husband and I have a complicated past.* 'He knows you weren't trying to insult him.'

'Good. That's good.' Boyd's voice is strangely hollow, hopeless. Clare has the sudden urge to shake him. Shake something out of him. 'But I'll have to start again. It could take weeks. *Weeks,* Clare.'

317

'He told me he might not bother.'

'He what?' Boyd turns to her; his cheeks are mottled, his thin hair limp in the heat.

'With all the trouble in Gioia, he said he might postpone the project. He said we might be able to go soon,' says Clare, and wonders what Boyd might make of her dispassion. But his face lights up, breaking into radiant hope.

'Oh, I hope so! That's wonderful, Clare . . . ' He blinks rapidly, casts his eyes around the room and smiles. 'If only I'd known at the start that all I had to do was produce a design he *didn't* like . . . We could have gone weeks ago.'

'Perhaps we should wait to see what he decides before we start packing,' she says coolly. 'He's the boss, after all. In more ways than one, it would seem.' Boyd looks crestfallen.

'Clare, what is it? What's wrong? There's a distance between us that was never there before — '

'Is there? Wasn't it?'

'Clare, please — talk to me!' he says, still wretched and hunched at his desk. 'Please don't withdraw from me. I . . . I need you so terribly much.' The sight of him is somehow unbearable — she wants to pity him but even that urge makes her restive, irritable. He's like the ant bites around her ankles that she wants to scratch. She can't explain the feeling; she doesn't know if it's him causing it, or if it's taking her over of its own accord.

'I've nothing to say. Really,' she says quietly. She leaves him there, shutting the door behind her and gripping the handle for a moment, as if she might keep him inside that way, away from her.

★  ★  ★

Some nights Clare leaves her husband sleeping to slip through the dark hallways to Ettore's room, letting fear burn out the somnolence of all the sleep she's missing. The risk is huge, but so is the reward, the feeling she has with Ettore that everything — the world, her life, herself, *everything* — is better, and will be well. They are quiet during these night-time meetings; there are few words. She doesn't think about what she will say if Boyd is awake when she returns to their room. She doesn't think about what she will say if she encounters anybody on the way there, or on the way back. She doesn't think of them at all, and usually she sees nobody. So she's wholly unprepared on the one occasion she nearly runs into Pip, coming up from the kitchen with a jug of water, his bare feet slapping gently on the stone stairs. Clare presses herself into a dark doorway and hopes he won't hear her heart thudding. His face is in shadow, his hair, wild with sleep, gives him a strange silhouette. When his door clicks shut she has to wait for two minutes, three, four, before she trusts her legs to carry her; before she's sure that he, the one other person she loves, isn't going to re-emerge. And then the thought intrudes on her again, that these two people she loves are from different planets, and she can never have them both. It stings like the cut of a cold, sharp blade. But she

319

carries on to Ettore's room.

Another time, she pauses at the foot of the stairs that lead up to Marcie and Leandro's room on the third floor. Their voices drift down to her and stop her in her tracks, first with the fear of discovery, then with the irresistible thrill of trespass, of watching unseen. Muffled words, stifled volume, but it's unmistakably a bitter argument; one with its own energy and momentum, that rises and falls in waves as it gets the better of them and then is forcibly hushed. The hairs stand up along Clare's arms. She doesn't want to listen but she does, just for a few seconds. She hears Leandro say:

'Marcie! I've told you, it's impossible.'

'No! What's impossible is that you can expect me to stay here in this godforsaken desert for weeks on end without going *completely insane!*' Marcie replies. Her voice is frayed, like Clare has never heard it before; so ragged with feeling that the words are distorted.

'What would you have me do? Well?' Leandro barks. Then there's something like a wail from Marcie, a thin sound, drenched in misery, almost childlike. With a shiver, Clare moves away, and doesn't hear anything else.

Many days pass like this — days of held breath and waiting, at once transient and ponderous. Sometimes Clare and Ettore meet far out in a distant field where the wheat has been cut and the stubble burnt, and nothing more will be done until ploughing in the early weeks of autumn. One day they hunker behind a wall with a view of the blackened ground, beneath a sky

320

like scalding milk; there's the tired cheep of crickets and the far-off whistle of a kite, and the prickle of smoke in the air. Ettore sits with his back to the wall and his square, bony knees drawn up; Clare curls at his side, leaning into him, and he holds her there with one hand at the back of her neck and the other reaching across to clasp her upper arm in a grip that almost hurts. He doesn't seem to be aware that he's doing it; he is distant, more preoccupied than ever. His thoughts, in their silences, slide away to things she can't know. He no longer needs the crutch to walk; he has a limp, lessening all the time.

'Tell me about Livia. What was she like?' she says. The name makes Ettore breathe in sharply. He blinks, turning his head to look away across the field.

'What was she like? She was . . . ' He shakes his head. 'It's hard to describe her, when it should be easy. It's like talking about a dream.'

'Try. I'd like to know.'

'She was young, younger than me. Full of smiles, even when life was bloody. She was like Pino in that way — such a good heart, nothing could crush it. You know? Do you know anybody like that?'

'No,' says Clare truthfully.

'She had dark hair, dark eyes; not like yours. She had this musical way of talking . . . I always loved to hear her talk, the sound of her voice. She wasn't afraid. She wasn't afraid to be hungry, to go without. She wasn't afraid of what anybody said. She was only afraid . . . ' He pauses, swallows laboriously. 'She was only afraid at the end. After . . . after she was attacked. I think she was afraid to die. I think she knew she was going to die, and was afraid. I wish I hadn't seen her fear.'

'I'm so sorry, Ettore. I'm sure . . . I'm sure she was glad you were with her. It must have been so hard, but I'm sure she was glad. I would be.'

'At the end she barely knew me.' Ettore curls his hand around her head and pulls it tighter to his chest, and Clare isn't sure if this is just a reflex, an instinctive reaction to thoughts of the girl he lost. 'She . . . she had a terrible fever. She hardly knew me.'

'You've suffered such loss. You and Paola. Your uncle . . . Leandro told me that she lost her husband; that he disappeared to America, and then her lover was also killed. Did she love him very much?'

'Yes. As much as I loved Livia, I think. But she's . . . braver than me. Stronger than me. She doesn't let it show. Is that wrong, do you think? Shouldn't a man be the stronger one?'

'No. Not always. I only met her so briefly but that was how she seemed to me — strong. Like she was wearing armour. Perhaps a person can be . . . too hard.'

'Not here. You can't be too hard here. You have to be hard.'

'And she has her son, of course. She has part of her lost lover in him, something to love and care for, and distract her from her pain.'

'Yes, that's true. Many women are waiting — waiting to hear from their husbands or fathers or brothers who have gone to America. Perhaps

322

they still write, perhaps they still send money, perhaps not. Still, they wait. Not Paola. She gave her husband two years, after he went there. Two years to send her a letter, or some sign he was still alive, and if he was still alive, that he still wanted her. Nothing came. So she said to me, 'Life is short,' and she let herself love another. She heals herself; she doesn't . . . let herself sink. I can't seem to stop.'

'It's only been half a year since you lost her,' says Clare gently. She sits up, away from him, and Ettore turns to look at her. He seems tired and vulnerable, like there's no fight left in him, and she wishes she knew a way to sustain him.

She looks away across the burnt land, across the parched remains of wheat stalks; it's a devastated landscape, empty as a broken heart.

'I'm starting to see how strong you have to be to survive here. Why you need to be strong. Working for men like that overseer, Ludo Manzo . . . ' She shakes her head. 'I saw him . . . I saw him doing something terrible to a man. Making him graze from the ground like a sheep.'

'Ludo Manzo likes to humiliate people. Young boys especially, but anybody he can.' Ettore's voice turns hard. 'Any excuse . . . he will use *any* excuse to punish a man.'

'But *why*? How did he become so cruel? And why is he allowed to do such things?'

'He is a product of this place and all the hundreds of years of hate in its blood. There's no other *why*. Many men have tried to kill him, but he has a knack for staying alive. The luck of the devil, some say. Davide — Paola's lover, who was

323

killed at the Girardi farm — once got a knife to his throat in the dark of the night, and yet the blade slipped in his hand somehow, and didn't go deep. Davide said it was like some black magic protected him.' Ettore jerks up his chin, and Clare can't tell if he accepts this idea or scorns it.

'No wonder you are angry.'

'Angry?' Ettore shakes his head. 'Wasps are angry. Spoilt children are angry. What we feel is much bigger. Much worse.'

'Do you think it was Manzo who shot Davide at Girardi? Do you think he recognised him, and . . . shot him deliberately?'

'What are you saying, Chiara?'

'I asked Leandro about what happened at Girardi . . . He said that Ludo was there that day, that he was one of the men who fired — ' She breaks off as Ettore lurches forwards. He pushes her away from him, holds her at arm's length, eyes snapping.

'He said that — Ludo Manzo was at Girardi that day? You're sure?' His fingers are digging into her properly now, painfully. She nods dumbly. Ettore is on his feet in an instant, and stalks away towards dell'Arco without another word.

Clare watches him helplessly, fearfully; she can't go after him directly, and be seen. She waits in agony for a few minutes and then sets off on a different route, frantic with the feeling of having mishandled something fragile, and done irreversible damage. In the end she has no choice but to go to the main gates, even if she is tellingly close behind him. The wall around the vegetable garden is too high for her to climb; the walls around the *aia* are lower but in full view of the *trullo* by the gates and the guards on the roof. And what would look guiltier than scaling a wall, anyway? But just as she has her hand on the flaking metal she hears male voices, raised in anger, excitement; there's a *whoop* like a rodeo cry, and whistling. Clare, compelled by foreboding, jogs around the *aia* to the rear of the complex. The off-duty corporals are all there, gathered, watching. There's a rising cloud of dust, and between the onlookers' bodies Clare glimpses sudden frantic movements.

She edges forwards, already knowing what she'll see. There's a shout from behind her, and she glances up at the guards on the roof who are lined up, watching. At the centre of the dust cloud Ettore is fighting Ludo Manzo. He's astride him, snarling, struggling to free his arms from Ludo's grasp, to be able to hit. There's blood in his teeth; the pair of them are covered in Puglia's gold-brown dirt, barely recognisable. Ludo's face is murderous; a rictus of total fury. On the edge of the circle his son stands watching, arms loose at his sides, fingers twitching with desire. The tendons in Ettore's neck stand out in hard ridges; he claws at the older man's face, leans all his weight forwards and gets his hands around Ludo's scrawny neck, shaking with the strain.

Clare watches with the others. She can't move or speak; there's a clenched fist in her chest that makes it hard to breathe, and the shouts from

325

the others are in the dialect she can't decipher; she feels removed, helpless. Ludo is older but taller and full of vicious malice; Ettore younger but smaller, still weak in one leg, and reckless with anger. With an inhuman growl Ludo throws Ettore off and is on his feet in a heartbeat, fighting for breath, rubbing his throat. He darts forwards and kicks Ettore's damaged leg as he tries to stand; Ettore roars in pain and falls to his knees, and Ludo catches his hair in one hand and lifts his chin to take the full impact of a crunching blow of his fist. Ettore rolls away, gets to his feet but staggers, shaking his head to clear it. Ludo is grinning now, like he's heard a good joke; blood drips freely from his nose, clagged up and gluey with dust.

'I'm going to take your head off for you, boy,' he says, his Italian so contorted with some accent that Clare can barely understand him. He jabs a finger at Ettore. 'Then none of this will bother you any more.' He kicks Ettore viciously in the stomach and puts him back on his knees, retching, heaving for breath.

'Stop!' Clare shouts. Ettore gets back to his feet, still reeling, bent over, off balance. 'Ettore!' She wants him to look up, wants him to see how close Ludo has got to him, how he's coiling himself up, wiry as a snake, to deliver the next kick. Her voice is lost in the din, she tries to push forward but an arm appears across her chest, keeping her back. 'Ettore, look out!' she tries again, but there's no hope of him hearing. But then Ludo freezes.

There's a gunshot, shockingly loud, close at

hand. Before the echo of it has cracked off the *masseria* wall the men have fallen silent and gone still; the fighters included. They stand facing one another, poised; chests heaving, eyes alight with hate. Leandro Cardetta lowers his rifle and points it casually right at them. He walks forwards slowly, and says something in dialect that Clare can't understand. She itches with frustration, but her relief is far greater. She edges back behind the wall of young men, dipping her head, not wanting to be seen. Ludo says something in his hard, emotionless voice, also in the dialect. He jerks his thumb at Ettore, and Leandro asks something of his nephew that Ettore answers, eventually, with a single reluctant nod. Ettore starts to speak, and Clare understands the word *Girardi*, before Leandro cuts him off with a bark. Keeping the rifle trained on the two of them, Leandro asks a question, but neither man will answer. Clare glances across at Federico, and doesn't like the gleeful smirk on his face. Ettore wipes one hand across his face and spits a gobbet of bright red saliva into the dust. He doesn't speak again but turns and walks out of the circle of men, away from his uncle and the huddled, fearful figure of his lover.

He limps away towards the road and doesn't look back, and Clare wants to shout, to tell him to wait, to know where he's going. But she knows already — he is leaving. She can't run after him; she has no choice but to remain amongst the crowd of men, who are deflated now, cheated of the spectacle, and mutter as they move away. Soon she will be obvious, she will be

327

exposed, but still she can't move. She watches Ettore's retreating back, and longs for him to turn. He walks stiffly, one hand pressed to the ribs where Ludo's kick landed, but he doesn't pause. When she's alone, standing pointlessly on the vacant patch of dusty ground, Clare can feel Leandro looking at her. She turns to meet his eye — she can't help it. *I did this*, she thinks. *I did this.* The warm breeze sets to work, erasing the marks of the fight from the dusty ground, and Clare can only tolerate Leandro's hard, questioning gaze for a moment before she too has to turn, and walk away.

At dinner Leandro is subdued, thoughtful, and Clare can't put food in her mouth. The meal glistens on her plate — thin shavings of donkey meat, rolled and cooked in a thick red sauce; focaccia bread oozing oil, studded with nubs of sickly green olive. The mozzarella has wept out a puddle of whey, and the *primitivo* wine smells acid-sour. Anna poured some for Pip at the start of the meal, and he's drunk it all; Boyd puts his fingers discreetly over his son's glass when the girl returns with the jug, and Pip shoots him a rebellious look. Clare would normally be the one to do it but she hadn't even noticed. She glances up now and sees that Pip's cheeks are pink, and his eyes are shining and bleary. But she can't react; she can't find any words to say.

'So he just went off without a word, our Ettore?' says Marcie. 'That's a little rude after all the time he's spent with us . . . But, these Italian men! Nothing if not passionate. Am I right?' She looks at Clare first as she asks this and Clare flinches. But Marcie's expression is simply puzzled, slightly injured. Clare nods once.

'Yes, it would seem so,' she says. Marcie puts her hand over Leandro's and leans towards him.

'Look at my poor husband, so sad to see him go. And to go in high dudgeon like this . . . What on earth were they fighting about, him and Ludo?'

'What the *giornatari* and the *annaroli* have been fighting about for a hundred years.' Leandro flicks his eyes at Clare and it feels like a slap.

'What's the matter, Clare? You look weird,' says Pip. The wine has made him blunt, clumsy.

'Yes, I'm not feeling terribly well,' she says, and as she says it she realises it's true. Her stomach quivers and then lurches up to the back of her throat, as though the terrace is pitching beneath them. The back of her neck feels cold and clammy; saliva drenches the insides of her cheeks; her fingertips tingle. She wants to go somewhere quiet, somewhere dark, somewhere she can be alone to feel this wretched, but she doesn't think she could move without throwing up.

'You have gone awfully pale,' says Marcie.

'Darling, are you all right?' says Boyd, reaching for her.

'Yes, please don't — ' Clare waves her fingers but can't finish the sentence. She shuts her eyes so she won't see all of theirs, watching.

'Is it the heat? Or the donkey meat? It *is* quite rich — I can only stomach a tiny taste of it,' says Marcie, but all Clare's attention has turned inwards; their voices recede into the distance, booming like a far-off sea. She hears the air rushing into her lungs and soughing out; her thudding heart and her blood moving with a seething sound. The world tilts, and goes dark.

★ ★ ★

She wakes to a room lit by a single lamp in a far corner, so that there's no harsh glare in her eyes. She's still dressed, lying on her back on the bed with a strange weight on her forehead. She puts her fingers to it and finds a cool, damp cloth. Pip is in a chair by the bed, and he's finally past halfway through his dog-eared copy of *Bleak House*.

'All right there, Pip?' she says. 'You might actually get that thing finished on this trip.' She pulls the cloth from her head and sits up slowly. For a moment the blood thumps in her ears again, but then it fades.

'I don't know. Perhaps by the time I'm thirty,' he says. His voice is heavy, his eyes hooded. The alcohol has worn off and left him sluggish. 'Don't faint again, will you?' The look he gives her is that of an anxious child, just for a second.

'I'll try not to. Did I make a scene?'

'You took the tablecloth with you when you went.'

'No! Not really?'

'Partly.' Pip smiles. 'You made a bit of a mess. Marcie screamed — I think she thought you were dead.'

'Don't be ridiculous.'

'You did look awful,' he says, and it's almost an accusation. She frightened him.

'Sorry, Pip. I'm fine really. I don't know what came over me. Where's your father?'

'After Leandro carried you up here they went off into the sitting room with brandy. I think they're talking about his drawings.'

'Oh,' says Clare. She knows the decision they might be making, and it causes her a spasm of panic.

'Father was very worried about you, though. He looked very worried,' says Pip, mistaking her tone.

'I don't want him to worry.'

'Why did you faint?'

'I've no idea, Pip.' She smiles. 'Women do, sometimes.'

'You never have before.'

'Then it must have been my turn. Honestly, Pip, I'm quite all right now.' But all she can see is Ettore walking away, bloodied, with one hand pressed to his ribs. Gone, and she knows he won't be coming back to Masseria dell'Arco. She tries not to think about it; she can't let herself break down and cry in front of Pip.

'Is this . . . was it because of Ettore Tarano?' says Pip, sitting back in the chair and rubbing one thumb over the dry scabs of the dog bite on his hand. Clare is instantly afraid of his studied disinterest, the way he pretends the question is idle.

'What do you mean?' she says abruptly, before she can stop herself. Pip glowers.

'You were out for a walk when the fight

happened . . . did you see it? Was it . . . was it as bad as what happened in Gioia?' Clare breathes carefully, and nods.

'Yes — that is, no. It wasn't as bad as what happened in Gioia. I hope nothing ever is. But I did see it. Perhaps you're right. Perhaps that's what it was. It was horrible — they . . . they were in deadly earnest.'

'And then when Marcie started talking about it at dinner it made you think of it again,' he says, and Clare realises he needs to explain what happened; he needs to understand it, so he can know if it will happen again. She nods.

'Yes. That's probably it.'

'This — ' he starts to say, breaking off, frowning down at his hands again. 'This is all real, isn't it? Only it doesn't seem it. Not the way home and school and London seem real. But this is real too. More real and less, at the same time.'

'I know exactly what you mean, Pip. I really do,' says Clare. She reaches out her hand to him, and when he doesn't take it she stands, and bends down to wrap her arms around his head and shoulders. 'We'll go soon.' The words bruise her as she says them; she swallows tears again. 'We'll go soon.' But Pip pulls away, gently but insistently. He stands up and closes his book.

'You should probably rest,' he says, as impersonal as a stranger. 'They sent for the doctor to see you but he hasn't turned up yet.' Clare sits back down obediently, powerless to prevent the ways in which he's changing.

Hours later Boyd enters the room quietly and

comes to kneel by the bed like a penitent. Up close he is all eyes, pale and wide and anxious. His skin has a waxy look and the sour smell is back, faint but unmistakable. Clare shuts her eyes.

'Please don't fuss me, Boyd. I'm fine. The doctor looked most put out to have been called for,' she says, but Boyd doesn't try to fuss her.

'Cardetta wants me to redraw my designs. He's not going ahead now, but he wants the plans ready for when he does. We're going back to Gioia tomorrow, he and I,' he says, in a deadened tone. Clare opens her eyes, hoping he won't be able to read what's in them. 'I'm so sorry, Clare. I asked him to let you and Pip set off ahead of me, but he wouldn't hear of it. He says you oughtn't to travel alone. I suppose he's right. And Marcie has her wretched party next week.' Boyd takes her hand and presses his lips to it. 'We'll go soon,' he says, unknowingly echoing the words she said to Pip earlier, and Clare feels Pip's exact urge to retreat, to pull herself away. 'I promise we'll go soon.' He lays his cheek to her hand and she tries to feel for him what she would once have felt — tenderness, if not love — but it's gone. Only ashes of it remain, burnt out by the fire of Ettore.

'It'll be fine,' she says, because his news has made her happy enough to believe it. 'I'll be fine.'

'You're so brave, my darling. You're an angel.'

★   ★   ★

333

Once Boyd and Leandro have returned to the house in Gioia, Clare waits as long as she can. It's three days, but seems far longer; the hours drag their feet and feel like weeks. She watches from the terrace, from windows, from the roof, even though she knows she won't see what she longs to — Ettore, coming back; the square shoulders from which the rest of his spare frame seems to hang; the economic way he moves, and the limp; his rough black hair and hard face; his astonishing eyes, full of ghosts. She knows she won't see it at Masseria dell'Arco again, but still she watches because there isn't much else she can do. At the end of the third day, when Marcie and Pip emerge from the bat room, she tells them that she's feeling faint again and is going to bed early, and won't have dinner. As firmly as she can without being rude, she refuses Marcie's offer to check on her later, to send up a supper tray, to send for the doctor.

'I think I just need to sleep,' she says, smiling as she lies. There's a specific time she must use, a specific window. It must be while they are both in their rooms, which look out through the back wall of the farm, getting ready for dinner. If she's seen she will say that she changed her mind, and wanted a walk instead.

The key in the ancient lock to her and Boyd's room hasn't been turned in an age. It resists when she takes it out, and when she shuts the door and tries to lock it from the outside she has to use both hands, and strain at it until it bruises her hands. Eventually it turns with a grinding clunk. She puts the key in her pocket, where it swings and weighs her jacket down. She drapes Marcie's loaned scarf over her hair and knots it at the back of her neck. Now when they check on her, as she knows they will, they'll have to think she's locked the door and gone to sleep. She doesn't try to decide what she'll say when they ask why she locked the door, or if the servants let on that they saw her go out, or if she's seen in Gioia. Deliberately, she thinks only about her destination.

Carlo is on the front door and Clare's relieved. He's amiable and obliging; he unlocks the door with a smile and a *buona sera*, and Clare walks across the *aia* with her back rigid and the skin between her shoulder blades tight and tingling, waiting to be seen, waiting for a shout to call her back. The buildings themselves seem to watch her but the dogs don't bark — the one she thinks is Bobby even gives an experimental wag of its tail. Her heart batters her ribs, though her excuses are ready. Somehow, she thinks they'll know at once what she's doing, and that she's lying. She doesn't know the man on the gates; he has a chiselled face, all eye sockets and angles, but since they're used to her walking he lets her out without a word. She can feel his bullet eyes following her as she walks away along the road, but she is out. She is free.

When the road from the farm abuts another, joining it at a right angle, Clare turns in the direction with the most wheel marks in the dust, trusting them to mark the direction of town. She doesn't know how far away Gioia is, but since Ettore's friend carried him all the way to the *masseria*, she hopes it can't be very far. She walks with the sinking sun on her left shoulder, the key to her bedroom bumping against her hip. She walks, and walks. The road is straight and featureless, flanked by low stone walls; there are no men in the empty fields. She walks for well over an hour, until the sun kisses the horizon, flooding the furrowed land with an orange light that glows on every rock, every thistle and weed, every feathered head of grass. Clare stops, hands on hips, thirsty and feeling the first nudge of unease. Night is coming quickly. If she has walked in the wrong direction, she will have to go back to the *masseria* and repeat the ruse again another day. Tears of frustration blur in her eyes. She's sweating under her clothes, and has dust up to her knees. She walks on a bit further then stops again, standing in the middle of the road for some minutes, frozen in indecision. She decides she must have come the wrong way — she doesn't think Ettore's friend could have carried him such a distance, even though he was tall and well built. Clare hangs her head in defeat, turns around and sees a small cart approaching in a cloud of sunlit dust.

It might be one of the dell'Arco servants, sent out to find her. If it is, she will go back quietly and pretend she lost track of time; she will have little choice. Clare steps to the side of the road and when the fat woman driving the cart sees her there she yanks her mule to a halt. The woman's breasts rest on the bulge of her stomach, but there are such hollows in her cheeks that Clare can only think she's lost all her teeth. The scarf over her hair is black, like her eyes. She is no one Clare has seen before, and when she speaks Clare can't understand a word of it. The woman talks at some length, and then laughs, and Clare smiles nervously.

'Gioia dell Colle?' she says, and the woman laughs again, patting the seat beside her.

'Sì, sì,' says the fat woman, and then something else Clare can't follow. She climbs up beside the woman, who whistles the mule back into its shuffling trot. The back of the cart carries a sparse cargo of tomatoes, aubergines and peppers; the woman smells of earth and smoke, and Clare sits mute with relief as, only a short while later, the outskirts of Gioia appear up ahead.

She doesn't know where Ettore will be — at home, or working, or wherever. She doesn't know where he lives, but he once said he lived near the castle, in the tangled streets of the old centre, so she will go there and walk and ask, and avoid Via Garibaldi. The thought of not finding him is debilitating, but as if to make up for her long, anxious journey, a curvaceous young girl walking near the castle walls — only the third person Clare stops to ask — points into the mouth of a narrow alleyway opposite. The girl sketches a right angle in the air with one hand and points to the corner, all the while studying Clare with naked curiosity. There's the same smell of sewage and rubbish as before, the same hush from the people all dressed in black, with their furtive eyes and famished faces, and the women's hair covered with shawls in

337

spite of the warmth of the evening. Dusty and tired as she is, Clare feels too fat, too clean, too pale. Too much of a stranger.

She hurries into the mouth of the alley, into the cover of its deep shade, and feels slightly better knowing she can't possibly run into Boyd now, even if he happens to be out on the streets. When she was at the house on Via Garibaldi he stayed indoors, or in the garden behind. He never wanted to explore; he never wanted to see. Much like Marcie. A knot of barefooted children scurry past Clare, erupting from a doorway like ragged birds. Some of their heads have been shaved, the hair growing back in ugly tufts; they look wiry and feral, swamped by their clothing. They scare up a pair of hens, who shriek and flap and make Clare duck instinctively. There are doors but few windows; flights of stone steps scooped out with wear; iron tethering rings hammered into the stone, weeping streaks of rust.

After a hundred feet or so the alleyway narrows further and then turns a sharp right. At the point of this elbow a small courtyard sprouts off, away from the thoroughfare, and here Clare halts. Twilight has gathered in the corners of the tiny square, and there's a steady silence that seems watchful. From behind a ramshackle wooden gate comes the rumbling bleat of a goat, and Clare jumps. There are two other doors, each at the top of a short flight of stairs. Clare has a sudden clear notion of the risk she's taken, of the encroaching night and her clumsy intrusion into a life she can't know; of her own idiocy. If she doesn't find Ettore she'll be alone in darkness, in a town full of desperate people. Even if she does find him, her disappearance from the *masseria* might have been discovered already — they could already be searching for her, and she might bring as much trouble down on him as on herself. She almost turns and leaves again, as surreptitiously as she arrived, but with the last of her resolve she walks up the nearest steps, to the door above the goat stall, and knocks.

After a pause the door cracks opens a fraction to reveal a face inside, a glimmer of eyes, and for a second of lurching hope Clare thinks it could be Ettore. But the eyes are dark. The door opens wider and she recognises his sister, Paola, who came with him to the *masseria* the first time. Clare smiles, though she's uncertain of her welcome — in spite of it all, she has come to the right house — a rotting doorway in a cramped courtyard; a nook in the maze of old streets. She swallows, and is about to speak when Paola pulls the door open further and says something Clare can't understand, though her incredulity is all too plain. Her eyes are striking in her spare face, set deep beneath black brows; a sensual mouth is the only concession to feminine softness. Clare had thought Paola to be about her own age, but since Ettore calls her little sister she must revise this guess. Paola can only be twenty-two or twenty-three, though there are lines around her eyes, and between her eyebrows, and brackets from her nose to her mouth. She wears a faded grey dress with a high neck and long sleeves rolled up to the elbow, with an undyed canvas apron over it; her feet are in shapeless leather slippers, hair hidden beneath the ubiquitous scarf. When she speaks again it's abrupt, accusatory, and Clare can only shake her head.

'Ettore? I was hoping to see Ettore,' says Clare, in Italian. Paola glares at her, and now she's mystified, and Clare understands that Ettore has said nothing to his sister about their affair. With a click of her tongue and an anxious glance around the empty courtyard, Paola ushers Clare inside and shuts the door.

It takes some time for Clare's eyes to adjust to the gloom. She pulls up short and looks around, confused, because it's just one room — a single room in which a few pieces of furniture are carefully arranged, and a squat stove is making it far too hot. A terracotta jar on the stove top steams slightly, and smells of vegetables. There's one bed, pushed against the back wall, and a single oil lamp on a tiny table with three stools pulled in around it. Clothes hang from pegs around the walls, and there are alcoves here and there where tools and pots and folded cloths are kept. Clare stares around in dawning realisation — that this cramped space is where Ettore lives, with his whole family. The air is rank. Gazing into a shadowed recess in one wall she realises that the dark shape there is gazing back at her. She steps back, startled, and her eyes pick out the creased face of a man tucked into blankets, lying still, not blinking. The man is not Ettore; she doesn't recognise him. Embarrassed, Clare turns back to Paola, who has her arms folded and appears to be waiting for her to speak.

340

'Can . . . can you understand me when I speak Italian?' says Clare, and Paola's frown of displeasure is answer enough. She replies in the dialect, and the only words Clare can pick out are *Ettore* and *Gioia*. 'Where is Ettore?' Clare tries, spreading her hands hopefully. Paola takes in a sharp breath through her nostrils, taps her fingers against the bronze skin of her forearms, and Clare's heart sinks. She's suddenly sure she'll leave again without seeing him; she's not sure that Paola would tell her where he was even if they could understand one another.

There's a long, uncomfortable silence. Paola is in front of the door and when Clare smiles apologetically and takes a step towards it, she doesn't move. Clare has no idea what to do or say next, no idea what Paola is thinking, what she might do, and she can feel the man in the alcove staring, watching, making the hairs stand up along her arms and her throat go dry. Clare does not belong, and she is not welcome. Then there's a high-pitched murmur behind her, followed by a soft, curious squeal, and Clare spins around, spotting Paola's baby for the first time, wedged into a wooden box on the bed.

All that's visible of him are his arms, his hands and splayed fingers, waving in the air above him. 'Oh!' Clare exclaims. At the sound of her voice the baby makes another gargled noise, an inquisitive sound, and Clare goes over to the box. The little boy peers up at her, and she can't help smiling. He has huge eyes, dark as molasses, and a shine of spittle on a tiny red pout of a mouth. 'Oh, he's just perfect,' she murmurs.

341

'May I hold him?' She glances at Paola, whose expression has softened, though she still says nothing. Clare wriggles her fingers beneath the baby's soft weight, lifts him and puts him to her shoulder, surprised by the density of him, the incredible heat his small body gives off. She turns her face to rest against the side of his head, and feels him take a fistful of her hair and pull. Free of the confines of the box, he kicks his legs with arrhythmic enthusiasm. Clare swings him gently, side to side, patting his back. He smells of sleep and milk and the oiliness of his scalp, faintly sour and animal but not the least bit unpleasant. Holding him causes Clare a pang of yearning, hot and painful as a cramp. She looks back at Paola, still smiling. 'He's perfect,' she says again, and perhaps Paola understands this word — *perfetto* — because she can't help but smile too, hesitantly, as if she's not used to doing it.

'He is Iacopo,' she says, in Italian. Softly, Clare hums a small tune, something she can't name, something learnt from her nanny in her own infancy. She's still rocking the child on her shoulder, still singing quietly and being watched with calm bemusement by his mother, when the door opens again and Ettore appears.

One of his eyes is half shut, swollen from his fight with Ludo, and there are other bruises too. He looks more incredulous than surprised, and a question, half begun, dies on his lips as he absorbs this strange scene. His lover, cradling his nephew while his father and sister watch in silence. For a moment he only watches too, and a strange expression crosses his face like a ripple in water, and Clare, seeing herself through his eyes, almost laughs. But then he shuts the door behind him and shakes his head sharply.

'Luna told me you were here but I hardly believed her. Chiara, what in God's name are you doing? Do you have any idea . . . do you have *any* idea?' he says. Paola steps forward and holds out her hands for her son, and Clare gives him up reluctantly.

'I needed to see you,' she says. The recumbent man in the alcove speaks for the first time, something low and hoarse that Ettore answers curtly.

'You can't just come here like this!' he says to Clare.

'Is that what your father just said?'

'It's what *I'm* saying!'

'I'm sorry.' Without Iacopo to hold Clare doesn't know where to put her arms and hands, or how to stand. Three days away from the *masseria* and Ettore looks grimy and tired; she can't tell if the shadow under his good eye is another bruise. 'I wanted to say sorry — if I hadn't said anything about Ludo being at Girardi you wouldn't have fought him, and you wouldn't have had to leave . . . ' Ettore raises one hand to silence her and shoots Paola an anxious glance. Paola looks tensely from Clare to her brother and back, as though something in these words disquiets her.

'Stop. Have you said anything to my sister of these things?'

'No, I haven't, we — '

'Good. Do not.' He puts one hand to his

343

mouth, cups his chin the way he does when he's thinking, worried. 'It was high time I left my uncle's farm. We're almost strangers to each other now. I'd stayed too long.' He looks up at her as he says this, and she can't tell if he's angry or tender. With a sigh Ettore turns, cracks open the door and looks out, then raises his hand to her. 'Come,' he says. 'It's not good for me to be here.' Paola asks him a sharp question, and Ettore gives a soothing answer, but there are no more smiles from her as Clare nods goodbye. She is closed off again, frigid, her squirming son held tight in her arms.

The courtyard is deep grey, lit only by the gauzy evening sky, but it's still brighter than it was inside. There's an argument nearby — two women, shrill with anger, their words an incomprehensible tumble. Ettore takes Clare's elbow and leads her out of the courtyard in the opposite direction that she came in. Their route twists and turns, then passes beneath a stone archway three metres thick, with rooms above it, into a larger courtyard crowded with overhanging upper storeys and stairs and doorways. Ettore tows her into the shadows beneath one overhang, in a far corner away from the street. He turns and holds her briefly, and she grabs onto him tightly, so that he winces. He has a sharp smell of sweat on unwashed clothes; she thinks back and realises he's wearing the same clothes as when he left the farm. There's a tidemark of dirt along his hairline, and ground into his cuticles, and for some reason this brings a lump to her throat.

'Sorry. You're hurt,' she says.

'I think that bastard cracked one of my ribs.'

'Have you seen a doctor?' At this Ettore only smiles, a little sadly.

'You can't come here. You know it's not safe.'

'You didn't say goodbye,' she says, and swallows against the tightness in her throat, the oncoming ache of tears. 'I didn't know when you'd be coming back.'

'I will never go back there. Not until . . . ' He leaves the sentence hanging, shakes his head.

'Then you would have just not seen me again, if I hadn't come to Gioia? It would have been that easy for you?'

'Nothing is easy. Only necessary,' he says bleakly. But then he relents and brushes his thumb across her cheek. 'You knew this was not reality.'

'It could be — I want it to be! I want . . . '

Clare takes a deep breath. She sounds like a child; like a spoilt child when she wants to tell him that she can't imagine not being with him, can't imagine going back to London and living as she lived before. She wants to say that he has changed everything; he has changed her. That everything from before seems as flat and distant as a photograph. She has the sensation of a huge wave building up behind her, higher and higher. She has no idea what will happen when it breaks, and can't put it into words. 'I can't bear it,' is all she says, closing her eyes. Ettore puts his hand around the back of her neck and pulls her head to his chest.

'You can bear it. You have to,' he says quietly.

'When I saw you earlier, holding the baby
. . . For a moment it seemed . . . '

'It seemed like what?'

'Like . . . you belonged there. But you don't.
You mustn't come here again. It's not safe. There
are men here who would kill me if they could.
Do you understand? This is what's real — this
danger. I daren't even stay in my own home, in
case I cause them to come looking there again. If
we are seen together, if they know that we are
. . . close. Do you see? Being foreign will not
protect you.'

'That servant knows. Federico, with the
rabbit's lip. The one you told me was a fascist.'

'Harelip.' Ettore's voice is dead flat. 'Are you
sure?'

'Yes. He . . . he hissed at me. When I came
back from meeting you one day.'

'You listen to me, now. You stay away from
him. Do you hear me? I don't care what you
have to do, you stay away from him.'

'But if he's at the farm, how can I? He's here
in Gioia now, though. Leandro and Boyd came
back here three days ago. They had a terrible
argument over the designs. Your uncle is making
him start again. We could be here for weeks
more, you see,' she says, smiling. But Ettore
doesn't smile.

'Goddamn it,' he murmurs, hanging his head
for a moment.

'Ettore, what is it?'

'Can't you go? Can't you just go home, to
England? You and the boy.'

'Well, no,' says Clare, stung. 'Not until your

346

uncle says so. And I want to stay. I want to be near you.'

'But can't you just *go*? Never mind my uncle.'

'Ettore, what is it? What aren't you telling me?'

'I . . . ' He shakes his head. His eyes are lost in shadows now; she can only see the outlines of his face. 'You are not safe there. At the *masseria*. I don't understand what he's doing, keeping you here. I don't understand at all.'

'Nobody is safe anywhere, from what I have seen. I could . . . I could come back to the house here in Gioia. All I'd have to say is that I was missing Boyd. Perhaps your uncle would allow it? Then we could meet more often, and — '

'No! That would be worse.'

'Ettore, I . . . I don't understand.' Clare waits, but he keeps his face averted and his thoughts to himself. 'Who was the girl I spoke to?' she says. 'The girl who told me where you live?'

'Luna, Pino's wife. I have stayed with them, and with other friends, since I left the farm.'

'Couldn't you stay at your uncle's house here? Wouldn't you be safe there? Why do men want to kill you?'

'Because that's what happens in a war, Chiara!' He gives her a small shake, and she feels childlike again. 'I will side with my uncle no longer.'

'I wish you would. If you're in such danger.' To this he only shakes his head, and watches her steadily, and doesn't try to explain, and she is helpless, hopeless. 'Aren't you even a little bit pleased to see me? Even a little?' Ettore smiles then, a sketch of a smile, more in his eyes than on his lips.

'I could have stayed where I was when Luna told me you were here. I didn't have to come to find you,' he says.

'Then I'm glad I did. I'm glad, if this is to be . . . if this is the last time.'

There are voices and footsteps from the alleyway beyond the courtyard, and behind the wall they're backed against are sounds of life — the rattle of a metal pail; a man coughing; the rustle of kicked straw. But Ettore kisses Clare hard and tightens his arms around her, cinching her ribs, shortening her breath, and she doesn't care if the whole of Gioia stops to watch. They make love in a rush, like the first time, and Clare tries to pretend that it won't be for the last time; that she will see him again, that she will stay in Gioia and live there with him, and be married to him. But she can't believe it, not truly. Not even then, drowning in his touch and the movement of his body, and the smell of him and rightness of it. So she lets her head be empty instead. She lets go of all her thoughts, until she has the feeling of only existing in that single point in time, with nothing in her past and nothing in her future; it's frightening, and it's wonderful.

When they've caught their breath and straightened their clothes it's full dark. They stay for a long time, sometimes in easy silence, sometimes talking disjointedly about things far off and unconnected. They stand close, always touching. Clare has a handful of Ettore's shirt at his waist, and the other grasping his forearm, hard as a bundle of iron rods beneath his skin. Ettore combs his fingers through the sweaty tangle of her hair, and rests it at the nape of her neck, as he likes to do.

'Tell me about your home. Tell me about where you live,' he says, in a languid voice. 'It's very different. It must be.'

'Yes, it's very different. Green — it's very green. It rains a lot. All the time, it sometimes seems. It can be cold in the winter but not too much so. The summers are mild, warm. Compared to here it seems soft. In all my thoughts of it, it seems soft, and safe.'

'And nobody is hungry.'

'Some people are,' she demurs. 'The very poorest, of course. Of course they're hungry. But far fewer people are hungry than here. And . . . perhaps it's easier to find help there. There are charities . . . places the very poorest can go for help.'

'Do the rich hate the poor?'

'No. Not like here. Sometimes they don't think of them at all, and sometimes they pity them, or scorn them . . . but they don't hate them. And people are not only either rich or poor, they can be in the middle. There are lots of levels in the middle — Boyd and I are in the middle. The English are polite, and . . . contained. Everything is done behind closed doors. There are huge trees, and public gardens full of flowers, where anybody can go, and the children can play.' Of all the things she has said, this seems to present the starkest contrast between England and Puglia: a public garden full of flowers, and children playing.

For a while Ettore is silent, as though

picturing this scene. He breathes in, long and slow; Clare daren't ask him what he thinks. If he would ever go with her to England.

'I can see you there,' he says at last. 'I can see you in a garden. In a safe place.'

'Ettore, I *can't* go — '

'How will you get back to the *masseria?* How did you get here?'

'I walked a long way, then a lady brought me in her cart. I suppose I'll walk back.'

'Walk? Now, in the night?'

'There's not much choice, really. I . . . I didn't really think beyond getting to see you, you see,' says Clare.

'Shit and hell, Chiara!' Ettore shakes his head then turns to look out beneath the archway, into the alley they came along. Scraps of borrowed light show up the knots in his jaw as he thinks.

'I'll be all right. I didn't see anybody along that road.'

'Not in the daytime, perhaps. Now, you can't. You'll have to go to Via Garibaldi for the night.'

'No! I told you — Boyd's there, with Leandro. They're not expecting me, and Marcie and Pip think I'm asleep back at the *masseria.* How would I explain to them all? I can't, Ettore! They'd know for certain I was lying. I'll walk back. It'll be quite all right.'

'No, it won't.' Ettore takes her hand and they march back out to the alleyway.

'Ettore, wait — '

'Come on. You shouldn't have come — do you see now?'

'Well I'm glad I did, even if you're not! I'm

350

glad,' she says defiantly. Ettore pauses to give her a helpless look.

'Chiara . . . you are bold. And foolish,' he says.

'You make me both,' she says, and as he turns away she sees the glimpse of his smile again, just for a second.

Ettore leads her through several twists and turns until, though they can't be far from Piazza Plebiscito or the castle, Clare couldn't say for sure in which direction they might be. He stops so abruptly to rap at a door that Clare runs into the back of him, and he loops an arm around her waist to hold her, as though she might try to run. Pino answers the door, and Clare recognises him at once — his beautiful, sculptural face, his unusual height and build. She shivers; the sight of him recalls that violent moment when they arrived at the *masseria* and she first saw Ettore and everything changed. Now he smiles uncertainly at the sight of them on his doorstep, and behind him the pretty girl Clare spoke to earlier darts curious looks out at them. The two men talk at speed — a rapid, incomprehensible exchange that ends with Pino shrugging and coming up with a name. Ettore turns to Clare.

'Did you bring any money?' he asks. Clare shakes her head, and sees him sag. He sighs, pauses, then crooks his finger and lifts the thin gold chain around her neck. 'Is this dear to you?' Clare shakes her head again.

'A gift. From my husband.'

'We'll need it,' he says, his mouth twisting slightly in distaste. Without hesitation, Clare unclasps the necklace and hands it to him.

351

Ettore passes it to Pino, who winds it around his thick fingers and says something to Ettore.

'What did he say?' says Clare.

'He says it's too much, and it is. But if the choice is between too much and nothing . . . ' He shrugs. Luna's head appears around her husband's arm to gaze at the precious metal, her face like a child's at Christmas, and Clare guesses she has never seen gold before. Not up close. Pino closes his fist over it, as if to protect her from it, and Luna turns her rapt gaze onto Clare, so full of questions and wonder that Clare looks away, uncomfortable. Pino says some soft words to his wife, kisses her mouth and sets off along the street. Wordlessly, Clare and Ettore follow.

The two men seem to see better in the dark than Clare; they walk quickly, turning left and right, passing under archways, sidestepping piles of manure and rubbish, as Clare stumbles and dodges along behind them, soon out of breath. Piazza Plebiscito, as they pass along its short western edge, is a blaze of yellow streetlight, but empty. No walkers, nobody taking the air, or killing time, or smoking and gossiping. All of Gioia has the hushed, furtive air of a town under curfew, so much more so than a month earlier, when Clare first arrived. The light of the square only seems to create deeper shadows, deep enough for movement to go unseen, for watching eyes to hide. Clare stays close to Ettore's shoulder, feeling jittery and exposed; like she's walking a narrow ledge above a lethal drop, not across a wide pavement. In spite of everything she has seen and everything Ettore has told her, only now is she afraid. Only now does she actually feel the threat of the place.

Pino leads them down Via Roma, where the town opens out into fields and parched vegetable patches. He turns in beside a squat, handsome villa, glancing at Clare and putting a finger to his lips. Silently, they creep around to the back, to the stable block, and then around to the back of that, to a lean-to with lamplight spilling out beneath its door. While Pino talks to the tiny, elderly man inside, Ettore turns to Clare.

'This man will take you back on the horse, once he's finished pretending that your necklace isn't enough payment. His name is Guido; you can trust him, I've known him a long time — he is Pino's kin.'

'You're not coming?'

'You know I'm not, Clare. I can't go back there.' Behind him, the shuttered windows of the villa stare down blindly. The sky has gone black and is brilliant with stars; the night is warm and kind, and it seems like a ruse. Now, at the moment of parting, Clare feels close to panic. It makes her dizzy, full of dread. She grabs at him, at his shirt, his arms, even as he tries to disengage her. 'Stop. Stop it. You go with Guido. Go back to the *masseria*, and stay there. And try to find a way to leave this place.'

'Ettore, I can't.'

'Do as I say.' He kisses her face, her forehead, the bridge of her nose. 'Please do as I say.' Holding her at arm's length, Ettore seems to think of something. 'Wait here a moment,' he

353

says, and disappears into one of the stables. When he comes back he has something in one hand that he puts into Clare's, warm and alive. She gasps. 'For Pip. A better friend for him, perhaps,' he says, and Clare looks down at the wriggling puppy, as it begins a sleepy examination of her arm — an examination with nose, teeth, tongue. 'Take it back for Pip. Guido will only drown them all, otherwise.'

'Say I will see you again. Say it, or I won't go,' says Clare, her voice fluttery with nerves. Ettore sighs, stares at her for a heartbeat.

'Then I will say it. You will see me again.'

'When?'

'I'll send a message,' he says, and she knows he's lying.

Guido, silent and unsmiling, saddles a tall bay horse, mounts and then kicks his foot out of the stirrup so that Clare can climb up behind him. Pino helps her, smiling and apparently unperturbed. Her skirt tears up the back seam as she straddles the saddle. The horse makes almost no noise on the dirt of the yard, or on the stones of Via Roma. When Clare looks down she sees that its hooves are wrapped in old sacking to muffle them. The puppy, limp and trusting beneath her arm, has gone back to sleep. Between its two pairs of spindly legs its belly is round, distended with worms; the skin shows pink through a smooth, copper-coloured coat. Clare watches the road behind them until Pino and Ettore are barely distinguishable against the darkness, and then have vanished into it. Still she watches, until her neck cramps and her head aches.

354

Once they're out of Gioia Guido clucks his tongue and the horse moves into a jouncing trot. They cover the distance to dell'Arco in a fraction of the time it took Clare to walk and hitch. A baleful moon rises in the western sky, yellowish bright. Clare clings to Guido with one arm, to the puppy with the other, and lets misery smother her, almost corporeal. She feels older; she feels empty and bereft. And she feels sick again, the motion of the horse and the wrench of leaving Ettore are making her stomach judder and roil. She dismounts at the gates onto legs that shake, and Guido turns the horse back without a word, or any acknowledgement of her quiet thanks. Keeping her face as blank as she can make it, Clare ignores the gate guard's black look and slow, suspicious movements. He keeps the rifle in his right hand, his finger on the trigger. Carlo lets her into the *masseria* with no apparent wonderment, and when she asks him the time she can hardly believe that it's not yet even midnight. It feels like a year since she sneaked out in search of Ettore. With a grin, Carlo scruffs the puppy's ears. It wakes up, looks around blearily and yawns — a wet, pink gape edged with needle teeth. Cautiously, Clare looks up at the terrace before she leaves the cover of the archway.

'All are sleeping,' says Carlo, in broken Italian, and Clare shoots him a grateful smile as she sets off across the courtyard.

Up the dark stairwell on feet as soft as she can make them, with the nausea making sweat break out along her hairline and prickle down her

355

spine; with her knees spongy and weak, and all the fear and joy and sorrow of the past few hours making her long for darkness, and silence, and oblivion. Clare glances both ways at the top of the stairs then tiptoes along the corridor to the door of her room, reaching into her pocket for the key to unlock it. Then she halts, her stomach plummeting. The key isn't there. She checks her other pockets, in vain hope. She thinks of the rough, urgent way she and Ettore made love; she thinks of hurrying through the dark to the villa on Via Roma; she thinks of the bouncing trot of the horse, all the way back. The key could be anywhere.

Clare shuts her eyes, sways on her feet. She has no idea what to do. After a minute or two she creeps further along the corridor to the door, with the vague, desperate idea of trying the handle anyway, of the possibility that she hadn't actually locked it. The puppy whines a little, and squirms, and she realises she's holding it too tightly. Her dread is the opposite of panic — her heart seems to have slowed down, almost to nothing; it feels like it's being crushed. Then she stops again. There's a figure leaning against the door to her room, hunched and instantly familiar. She has a puppy she can't explain; she's locked out of the room she is supposed to be in; she's filthy dirty, smelling of sex and sweat and Ettore, and Pip is leaning against the door, staring at her through the dark with angry eyes.

# Ettore

There's only *acquasale* for dinner — boiled stale bread with a little salt and dried chilli, not even any mozzarella now that Poete no longer works at the cheese factory. After the month he spent at the *masseria*, Ettore's stomach contorts and yammers at him, begging for more, for better. The money Marcie gave him, and his wages, have been spent on the settling of Valerio's debts, on a new blanket for Iacopo, new soles for Ettore's and Paola's shoes, their rent arrears and some supplies of dried beans, pasta and olive oil that Paola is hoarding ruthlessly for the coming winter. She eyes him across the tiny table as he guzzles down the thin soup, scraping out every last drop.

'Remembering what hungry feels like?' she says unkindly. Valerio, well enough to rise from his shelf, continues to spoon in his soup with tremulous care, and pays no attention to his offspring.

'I never forgot. Only my belly did,' says Ettore. Paola grunts.

'In a man, mind and belly are one. Mind and body are one. Mind and cock are one.' She curls her lip in disdain and gives the last ladleful of soup to Valerio. Ettore bristles.

'Is that was this is about? Is that why you're being such a shrew?'

'Oh, I don't know. Why should I be angry to

357

learn you've been screwing another man's wife all this time I thought you were working and suffering and in terrible pain? When I thought you were grieving?'

'I was working! I was in pain! I am grieving.'

'No, I don't think you can wear your black band any more, brother. And you were fit enough to fuck her so hard she came all the way into town for more!'

'Paola,' he says, and pinches the bridge of his nose in frustration, embarrassment. Valerio has stopped eating and is staring at him now, his face wholly without expression. 'It wasn't like that.'

'How was it, then? And if her husband finds out? If he doesn't know yet he soon will — if she keeps coming here like that, bold as brass.'

'I've told her not to come again.'

'And you really think she'll do as you say?'

'I don't know, Paola! Stop breaking my balls!' he shouts, and throws his spoon into his empty bowl with a clatter. On the bed, Iacopo wakes and makes a small noise of alarm. He starts to wail and Paola gets up to settle him, shooting a venomous glance at her brother.

'Idiot,' she mutters as she passes.

Ettore turns away from his father's gaze and stares at remnants of the plaster that once covered the walls; centuries old, so flaked and patchy it looks like a rash on the stone's skin. He tries to picture Chiara there again, in that very room, the room he has lived in since he was a boy. It's almost impossible, like it was almost impossible that she had been standing there, holding Iacopo. Hard to believe it was real, then and now, which explains the feeling he got — peculiar and shocked and also quite like happiness. The image of her there, that impossible scene, caused that same little softening he's felt before; that same pleasant sinking, like letting go. And now he has a nagging fear that he doesn't need; there's an extra complication, an obligation he doesn't want, but can't avoid. He is afraid for Chiara. Gingerly, Valerio gets to his feet and goes back to his alcove, where the blankets are rank with the smell of him and his sickness. By the bed, Paola rocks and sings to her son, as his cries dwindle into sleep.

When Paola comes back to the table she's calmer, more yielding. For a while the lamp's steady hiss is the only sound, and its light sculpts itself into the contours of her face. She sighs as she pulls the scarf from her head, undoes her hair and runs her fingers through it. Her hair is long, thick, black, just like their mother's. With it down around her shoulders, softening her face, Paola is a different creature. Younger, more fragile.

'You're beautiful like that,' says Ettore.

'Stop trying to butter me up. You do know she's in love with you? Your pale mozzarella?'

'No, she is — '

'Don't argue. Any woman could see it, plain as day. She is in love with you, and she wants another child.'

'Not another; she has none. The boy is her husband's only.'

'Then it makes even more sense. Do you love her?'

359

'No! Only . . . I don't know. Not love. Not like Livia.'

'Like what, then?'

'I don't know! Anyway, soon she'll go home and that will be the end of it. Don't ask me when, because I don't know.'

'Jesus, Ettore — do you know how much like a child you sound? How much like a sulky little boy? What did she say to you about Girardi? I heard her say something about Girardi.'

'No.' Ettore's jaw goes tense. He's too afraid to tell her the truth. 'You heard wrong.' Paola eyes him suspiciously.

'Luna said she gave you her gold necklace as if it meant nothing.'

'It did mean nothing to her, her husband gave it to her. She doesn't love him.' Ettore can't help that this pleases him; he hopes Paola won't hear it. 'What else did Luna say?' Paola hesitates, looking up at him through the hoods of her lashes. It's what she does when she's holding back, and it makes Ettore uneasy. 'Well?'

'She says you told Pino they have money there. Cash, a lot of it. And jewels . . . '

'No.' Ettore splays his hands on the table and leans back, arms straight, adamant.

'We could buy weapons! We could feed ourselves — all those who would fight! We could buy animals, tools . . . '

'No, Paola. Are we brigands now? Nothing better than thieves? If we raid, we raid so we don't starve; we raid to punish those who've hired and armed squads to set against us; those who have attacked us first. That's how it's always been. Do you see yourself leading a famous gang of brigands, like Sergente Romano? Is that how this looks in your head? This grand plan?'

'Don't patronise me, Ettore! At least Romano *did* something! At least he stood up, and showed courage!'

'Courage or no courage, he was shot to pieces by the *carabinieri*. Who will care for Iacopo when that happens to you? And you would steal from our own family?'

'Spoils of war,' she says curtly, but he see his words unsettle her. 'We mean to *take over*, Ettore! Not simply punish, or find our next meal. No more tit for tat. We mean to take back control! And you said yourself Leandro is not our family any more. He's just one more fat proprietor, and a landowner to boot. One more rich man who feeds and shelters his horses and oxen and mules all through the winter while he lays off the men to starve and die!'

'I was angry when I said that about Leandro, and I am angry with him . . . but he is still our uncle. He is still our mother's brother, and he treats the workers better than some. Better pay, better food. This plan of yours will end in blood.'

'*Their* blood!'

'And ours! Rivers of it,' he says. Paola's face twists in frustration.

'When did you get so afraid, brother? 'He treats the workers better than some'? Can you hear yourself, Ettore? You're talking about a man who employs not only Ludo Manzo but his fucking fascist son as well!'

'I know who I'm talking about!'

'Then why do you suddenly refuse to fight for the rights that are denied to us by all men like him? Is it the mozzarella? You don't want her to get hurt, is that it?' She glares at him across the table, until Ettore is forced to look away.

'You think that if we fight the good fight, they'll have to fall? And the *latifundia* with them? Are you really so naive, Paola?' he says.

'You sound like Gianni and Bianca, and all those others who've given up and are ready to just . . . cower down.' She waves a hand in anger. 'We need a *revolution*, like in Russia. If we stood up all at once we would be unstoppable.'

'Would we? No,' says Ettore, raising his hand to forestall an angry retort. 'I have not given up, Paola, but Gioia del Colle is not all of Italy. It's not even all of Puglia . . . Troops will be sent. More squads will be hired. This is not the way, Paola!'

'It's the only way left, brother.'

'Before this summer is out I will lay my hands on Ludo Manzo again, and his son. I swear it. But a raid on dell'Arco would be *suicide*! Leandro is no fool. The roof is covered in armed guards. The gates are iron, the walls are three metres thick. The dogs in the *aia* would kill anyone they got hold of. It would be madness to try it.'

'Not if we had guns. That's the idea — that's why we strike at Masseria Molino first. The new tenant there is so nervous he's spent all his money on rifles and ammunition and now he can only afford to keep two permanent guards to use them. And he's recruiting for the squads all the time, and arming them, if that makes you feel

362

better. The moron is sitting there on a huge, barely protected arsenal. When we have guns, we can shoot the dogs at dell'Arco, and the guards.'

There's that dangerous conviction in Paola's expression again, that righteous fire, like a hunger eating her away. Inside, Ettore is cold. 'We do this, or we surrender, and nothing will change. We do it, or we starve this winter. You, me, him.' She hooks her thumb at Valerio. 'My Iacopo. Pino. All of us. Those are the choices.' For a long time Ettore doesn't answer. He knows what Paola says is true. But it's a bitter truth.

'It's hard to shoot a guard on a roof. They would pick us off through the slits as we stood banging on the doors,' he says softly.

'No, they won't,' says Paola. Calmly, she gathers up her hair and begins to braid it for bed. 'Not if your mozzarella opens the doors for us.'

\* \* \*

In the night Paola sleeps soundly. Her breathing is steady and even and sure, as if to prove a point to her brother, who is restless and chased around by his dreams. He dreams of the bottomless pit near Castellana, seeping out mists and bats and spectres. But in the dream the fields as far as Gioia start to break and crack open, into jagged fissures through which Ettore can see that the abyss is vast, and right beneath their feet. There is emptiness where there should be rock and roots and earth. Dusty soil dribbles into the cracks and sifts away into nothingness. Fear turns Ettore's bowels watery, scatters his thoughts like blown smoke and brings him to his knees, scrabbling his fingers into the mud in an effort to cling on. He wakes up dried-mouthed and ashamed, and variations of this dream of insecurity mock him until sunrise.

Ettore takes Valerio's hat, a worn-out brown felt fedora, shiny around the band with sweat and grease, and wears it low over his forehead to throw his distinctive eyes into shadow. He wears his father's jacket as well, which is too long in the arm for him; anything that might help him go unrecognised in the opalescent early dawn. His limp is harder to conceal, but many men limp. The piazza is as crowded as ever, and the mood is blacker than the long shadows lurking in the east end of the square. Fear and anger and confusion, violence and uncertainty; the group of men is like one body — one hungry, belligerent, frightened creature keeping its head down when it wants to fight; keeping quiet when it wants to roar. They are on a knife edge, with capitulation on one side and savagery on the other, and it's a sickening choice because death waits in both directions. Ettore wishes he felt as certain about it all as he did before Livia, before Chiara. He wishes he knew which way was best, he wishes he knew which way the others would jump, but most of all he wishes he was far, far away. He wishes for things he doesn't really believe in — justice and peace and fair treatment. Fantasies every bit as alluring as that of a fair-haired woman waiting for him at home, and loving him.

Ettore walks right up to Pino to check his anonymity, and it seems to work quite well. He gets close enough to smell spilt machine oil on his friend's sleeve, and a trace of wine on his breath, and Pino takes a second to notice him when Ettore bumps his arm.

'What's with the hat?'

'It's Valerio's. To give me a chance of being hired.'

'Good idea.'

'Do you tell your wife *everything*, Pino?' he says pointedly. He can tell from Pino's guilty look that his friend knows exactly what he's talking about.

'Sorry, Ettore. I kind of do tell her everything. I forgot that women also tell each other everything.'

'Paola can't get the idea of Leandro's money, or Marcie's jewellery, out of her head. The way she goes on you'd think there was a cave full of treasure over at dell'Arco, which will somehow solve all our problems.'

'Well, it could solve some of them.' Pino shrugs.

'And it's every bit as well guarded as you'd expect. She wants me to . . . to make Chiara open the door for us.' Ettore rubs his index finger across his brow, an unconscious anxious tic. Pino says nothing. 'Leandro would shoot her without hesitation, if he knew, if he saw her. I know that much. Strip off the suits and the American accent and he's the same ruthless bastard he ever was, and his temper's no better.'

'She means something to you then, this

woman?' Pino smiles at him; he has always been in love with love. Ettore is about to deny it, on reflex, but then he nods.

'She does.'

'So, don't ask her.'

'And when my sister joins the raid regardless, and gets herself killed?'

'So, ask her.'

'You're no bloody help, Pino.'

'If I could help, I would.'

'Can you get yourself hired to dell'Arco? Pass a message to her — give it to that young guard with the snub nose, you know the one I mean? His name's Carlo; he's *simpatico*. He would pass her a message, if you said it was from me.' At this Pino looks nervous. He has a ground-in fear of stepping out of line when Ludo Manzo is anywhere near.

'I don't know, Ettore.'

'Just a slip of paper. I'll write it out. I want to tell her to go. To get out and leave.'

'I don't know. Can't you just tell your uncle?'

'Warn my uncle that my sister and my friends are going to attack his farm?'

'Well, no. Perhaps not.'

In the end only ten men are hired to continue the threshing at dell'Arco that day, and Pino isn't one of them. Ettore joins a work gang headed west from Gioia, to a farm only three kilometres away. The overseer refuses to say what hours they will work; he refuses to say what pay is being offered. They are told that there is work; they are told to step forward if they want it. They are told they will be paid at the end of the day, and they must take that on trust. There is to be no negotiation.

'This is not how men are hired any more,' says Ettore, unable to help himself.

'It's how I'm hiring you,' says the overseer stiffly. He has shifty eyes and a mobile expression. He's trying for implacable neutrality but little tweaks of nervous excitement keep spoiling it; little spurts of glee. 'We'll hire at street price, or not at all. Now do you want to work or don't you? Not you,' he says, to one man with sombre grey eyes and shoulders knotted with muscle.

'Why not me?' he says uneasily.

'Because of that,' says the overseer, and he sneers as he lifts his stick to poke at the man's pocket watch. 'I've no use for clock-watchers.' This is what the fascist squads have achieved, already, in so short a space of time — the foremen feel invincible again; they hate the workers all the more for the gains they made after the war, and they are jubilant now those gains are being reversed. Their hatred makes them scornful, and ruthless. Behind each man are thirty more wanting work, so Ettore and his small band of colleagues take the terms, shaken, and start walking.

It was like this before the war — decades before the war — and suddenly Ettore sees how right his sister is. The backward slide towards the bad old days is happening at breakneck speed, so fast that the *giornatari* are bewildered, scrabbling to keep up. It might already be too late, and that thought puts the taste of metal in Ettore's

367

mouth, and makes his hands curl into fists. If they do not resist, what then? He stares at the overseer's back, riding at the head of the men with his meaty arse filling the saddle and his spine in a comfortable slouch. He remembers the moment of simple, primeval joy when he managed to get his hands around Ludo Manzo's throat; he takes a slow breath in and lets this memory pump his blood until it's racing through his body. It feels like waking from a daze in which he's been aware of words and movement around him but has registered nothing, reacted to nothing. More than ever at that moment, Chiara Kingsley seems insubstantial, dangerously vulnerable; he is desperately afraid for her even as he warns himself not to care deeply for such a friable, breakable thing. He can't let himself be crippled by that softness, that sinking. He will not lie down.

The threshing is done by hand on the farm he's been hired to. They use old-fashioned flails — two lengths of wooden pole joined by a metal chain — to beat the grains from the stalks of each wheatsheaf. Bent backs and the circular spin of the flail end, sweat blooming through their shirts at neck and back and belly; the constant sibilant thump of each blow landing, and behind that the rattle of the winnowing machines, each turned by hand by one man who stands in place the whole day long, cranking the wheel around and around. Husks and dust fill the air, getting inside the seams of their clothes and itching, bringing up a rash; the men wheeze and wipe their streaming eyes on their cuffs. The process seems to dry out the insides of their noses, their whole bodies, drawing out the moisture until they're like the husks that blow away, the hollow stalks of straw left behind.

Ettore works the flail with unblinking intensity, with sweat stinging in his eyes and making his hands slide on the wooden handle. He has to hold it with a grip every bit as intense as his focus on the task. The muscles in his forearms scream at him; by noon his bruised ribs have built up an ache that feels like a spike lodged in the bone. The man next to him tells him about three men who died of heatstroke the day before, threshing in full sun. The day is one of the longest Ettore can remember. His time at dell'Arco, on guard duty or just waiting for it, dozing on the roof, eating when he feels like it and meeting with Chiara, have taught his stomach to be full and his mind to wander; he'd forgotten the monotony, the exhaustion, the crushing, mindless drudgery of farm work. Stepping out of life as his leg healed makes him notice its patterns anew, and now he can see the days stretch ahead of him to the day of his death: hard, hungry and unchanging. It's maddening. Lunch is bread and a cup of well-watered *primitivo*. Work doesn't stop until the sun hits the horizon towards seven, and the pay is less than half what it should be. The men take the money and stare at it. Some of them are furious, some are resigned, some are panicky, shocked to have earned so little. But all are silent, so it makes no difference.

By the time Ettore is back in Gioia he can't

remember the exact colour of Chiara's eyes, or the precise feel of her hair between his fingers, and he knows that the part of him mourning the loss of these things must be stifled, and pushed far down inside. Tenderness has no part in what he needs to do. He's so tired, so distracted that he goes home without thinking, forgetting the need to hide. Paola feeds him his dinner in silence. She seems to be waiting. When he's eaten he wets a cloth with a splash of water from the urn and wipes it over his face. He pulls his shirt off over his head to be rid of the prickling fragments of husk trapped in it. He rubs away some of the dust and sweat from his chest and arms, and the back of his neck. He peers down at the bruise on his ribs, which has gone from blue to black in a splayed shape like a handprint.

'When is the attack on Masseria Molino?' he says at last.

'Not tomorrow night, but the next,' says Paola, with no inflection, no surprise or gloating.

'How many men?'

'Twenty-five.' She keeps her eyes on him, unblinking. 'Perhaps twenty-six.'

'So few, this revolutionary army of yours?'

'When we have guns, more will join us. You'll be with us?' she says. Ettore looks over at her, standing straight, evenly balanced, with her arms at her sides and her chin dipped down. A fighter's stance he's too weary to emulate. But he nods in answer to her question, and when he sleeps that night, it's dreamless.

★ ★ ★

Farm raids are frequent, more so since the massacre at the Girardi place. They are normally about stealth, in the black of night; about taking what food can be carried, or destroying something in some outlying part of the *masseria*, away from the guarded main house. A short and ugly act of desperation, hunger and vendetta. Farms where the overseer is cruel and a man has been beaten or humiliated; farms where the wages are lowest and the hours longest; farms where the proprietor is known to hire brute squads — these are at greater risk. But all are at risk when the men are starving. Sheep and cattle might be killed or stolen; barns or grain stores razed; anything movable or edible taken by a handful of men, and a few women too; with no weapons but rocks, cudgels, whatever farm tools are actually owned rather than borrowed each day. Living in sunken rooms with no electricity, and the long pre-dawn walks to work, begun in childhood, have given Gioia's *giornatari* excellent night vision. Their faces and hands are steady when they raid; they are set, even if their hearts race and stumble with the thrill and the danger, all unseen. They dart in and dart out, leaving fire and curses in their wake; corpses very rarely. But this new scheme is something different; something far more dangerous. They will fight their way inside the *masseria*'s buildings; it will be a pitched battle.

Ettore has not been on a raid since Livia died, but even before that he went rarely. He has always said he wants to work, not to take. *And if they won't let you work?* Paola's same argument, over and over, from when they were twelve and fourteen years old. They wear black; she has her knife tucked into her belt, Ettore has the twisted length of olive wood they've kept by the door since Federico's visit. The wood is ancient, sun-baked, as smooth and hard as bone. He rubs his thumb over its knots and close grain as they wait for the midnight bells of Santa Maria Maggiore. Valerio watches them from the alcove, his eyes blank, as though all of this is some staged drama he's not quite following; as though they are someone else's children, and he is far, far away. Before they leave Paola leans over her sleeping son and traces one finger down his face, wearing the expression of hopeless love and care that she wears at no other time. Then the bells begin to strike and Ettore's heart leaps up, thudding at the back of his throat. His sister pours two small cups of wine, bought for this night, and they swallow them down, not breaking eye contact. They tie scarves across their faces, masking everything from the eyes down.

'Ready?' says Paola, and her voice is a fraction higher than normal, a fraction tighter. That's her only concession to fear.

They walk fast, in silence; slipping through the shadows with no lantern. Before long other silent figures are ghosting at their sides, until they leave Gioia to the north, twenty-two men and four women; a pack with one purpose, saying nothing. An owl whistles in alarm at the sudden passage of this grim band, the scuff of their feet in the dust, the muted rush of their breathing, the sloshing of the precious can of kerosene one

372

of them carries. Masseria Molino, named for the ruins of an ancient windmill that sits beside the small complex, is five kilometres distant, a walk of under an hour. They mass beyond the reach of the lantern above its gates, where a single guard stands with a rifle in his arms and a pistol on each hip. Ettore almost feels sorry for him. There's no outer wall or perimeter, there are no dogs. The *annaroli* sleep inside but besides this gate guard only one other is young, and fit. The rest are women or youths or old men; people the tenant can get away with paying the least. The raiders watch for a while, checking for anything out of the ordinary. Waiting for some indefinable right moment. Ettore feels outside of himself, one more anonymous organ of a fighting body. He remembers this feeling from the trenches; this protective disassociation of thought from action, of mind from flesh. He has no fear, only a fatalistic sense of the possibility of death, and underneath this single-minded will to act and not think are the remnants of himself, quiet and distant.

With a quick glance around and a nod, the first man rushes forwards. He is small, thin, bald-headed and rat-faced; he's been chosen for his violence and the quicksilver way he moves. He sprints forward, alone. In a heartbeat he's within the circle of light and the guard jerks as though he's been slapped, swinging the rifle up and drawing in a deep breath as if to shout. In his surprise he forgets to make a sound. The bald man is on him in seconds, taking a flying leap and planting both heels in the guard's guts. The guard drops with a ragged tearing sound as all the air rushes out of his lungs, on the ground he's kicked again, and again. A kick to the head leaves him boneless. The bald man picks up the rifle and both pistols, checks for signs of consciousness and then nods at the waiting darkness. The rest of them surge forwards. Still silent, no cries of attack; they are all business. The pistols are handed out, checked for ammunition. The kerosene is sloshed around the lock of the wooden gates, a match is lit and the darkness boils into orange light. The gates are ancient, the wood tinder dry. The flames burrow hungrily into the wood. Soon there are shouts from within, but by then the wood is weakened. With coats and blankets around their heads and shoulders, a knot of the biggest men rush the gates, ramming their full weight against them, and the lock surrenders with a scream of nails and splintering wood. Then the night erupts into gunfire.

One of the men who rushed the gates drops with a yell, grabbing at his thigh. When the first volley from within is spent the bald man fires his rifle through the gates and the attackers run in behind the bullets, spreading out at once, screwing up their eyes against the smoke. Ettore tries to keep Paola in his peripheral vision but she's gone, darting away like a cat. They all know exactly where they are supposed to be. More guns are fired from the upper windows of the building, and from the arches of a ground-level colonnade around the courtyard. A bullet zips past Ettore's ear and explodes into the stone behind him with a shower of chips and dust; a

374

man rushes him with a snarl and Ettore ducks, swinging the olive wood cudgel. His assailant is shadowy in the smoke but there's a satisfying crunch and a grunt as the cudgel connects. Not waiting to see if the man is down Ettore dodges to one side, through a narrow doorway, and goes up a twisting stair to the roof. The stairwell is pitch-black. He runs hard into a closed door at the top and curses, breathing hard. He can't know for sure how many men are on the other side — it's a curtain wall, narrower than at dell'Arco; a walkway, not really a roof. It would be easy to be thrown off, easy to be shot, and by colliding with the door he's announced his arrival. Ettore puts his ear to the door and hears shots fired close at hand. There's at least one armed man on the other side, and no good way to proceed, so he puts his shoulder to the door, grits his teeth and bursts out onto the wall, into the whistling swing of a rifle butt.

In the sudden quiet stars wheel across his vision — a juddering array of lights careering through his skull, distracting and puzzling him. For a moment he can't remember where he is or what the lights mean, then an obliterating pain crumps through him so he can't react when he feels hands on him, hauling him up, dragging him; there's only room in his head for the pain and confusion, nothing else. He has no idea what's happening to him. He feels hot air on his face, choking smoke and the stink of burning hair. On instinct, he resists. He strains with every muscle in his body and in the next breath he realises that the burning smell is him. He opens his eyes and sees flames, swirling sparks, the dark ground and sky wheeling dizzily beyond — he has lost all sense of up and down, of which way round things should be. The sense of it all is tantalisingly close, but trying to unravel it is exhausting. The fire has a hypnotic beauty; Ettore stares down into it and decides not to bother fighting any more, and suddenly he hears Livia's voice in his ear. *Tell me I'm your sweetheart*, she whispers. Ettore frowns, and tries to answer her. *Tell me I'm your sweetheart.* The smoke fades to pale grey, or perhaps he does. He's in a soft, light place and he thinks he can smell a woman — her hair, her skin, the ready wetness between her legs. A spike of longing shoots through him but then the sense of her is gone. There are no more whispers in his ear, no more tender scents; there's darkness and burning, and the longing turns to ire.

Ettore arches his body violently, shoving back against the man who was about to wrestle him over the wall into the fire below. The pain in his head is incandescent but he shuts it out. He's stronger than his assailant, and angrier. He braces his hands against the hot stone parapet and pushes them both back from the edge, then lets his weight drop to throw the man off balance, and break his grip. Ettore turns, swinging a fist and landing a glancing blow on the man's jaw. The man grunts and it's an oddly high-pitched sound. Grimacing, Ettore hits him, again and again. There's a clatter as his assailant staggers back and kicks the rifle he dropped, spinning it on the stone.

'You should have fucking shot me,' says Ettore. He can hardly hear his own voice above the booming inside his skull. 'You should have just fucking shot me!' He knocks the man's legs out from under him, reaching down for the rifle and wrestling it from his attacker's hands when he grabs for it. But the man's resistance has crumbled; he curls into a ball and covers his face with his hands, and makes a strange noise. Ettore brings the rifle up, his finger on the trigger, sleek black barrel not a metre from the guard's head. But that noise makes him hesitate. High-pitched, familiar, incongruous. Ettore blinks, scowls, tries to organise his thoughts around the pressure building in his skull. Then he bends down and pulls the guard's hands from his face. The man is sobbing. The man is a boy, perhaps twelve or thirteen years old, and he's weeping in sheer terror.

Swaying and shocked, Ettore lowers the rifle. He puts one hand up to the place on his head, near the temple but mercifully slightly higher, where the pain is worst. His fingers come away bloody, and his own touch is intolerable.

'Jesus,' he mumbles, sitting down abruptly next to the boy. Vaguely, he pats the boy's arm to soothe him. 'Jesus,' he says again. 'I almost shot you . . . I almost . . . ' Ettore can't make the thought or the sentence finish. The night is thudding as though the whole world has a heartbeat. From below there's more shouting but fewer gunshots; the fire roars as it devours the gates, and from the barns come the startled noises of animals as they smell the smoke. Ettore

377

tries to gather himself. He looks down at the quivering boy curled, fetal, beside him. He has hair the colour of earth, fair skin and a small mouth, bloodied and contorted with fear; a dark patch of urine is spreading around the crotch of his trousers. 'Boy,' says Ettore. He clears his throat, tries again. 'Boy, enough. It's over. Nobody's going to kill you,' he says. The boy shows no sign of having heard him. 'You fetched me one hell of a crack around the head. Would you really have thrown me over? Perhaps you would. Fear can make us strong, can't it? Well.' He looks down at the prone figure. 'To a point, it can.' With the rifle's help Ettore stands, gingerly, his stomach churning in protest. 'Stay up here. Don't come down until we've gone. And for God's sake don't attack anyone.'

Down in the courtyard the fight is over. The *annaroli* are in one corner, standing in a resigned huddle. Only one of the raiders needs to watch them, with a pistol in each hand — there's no fight in them. Ettore staggers over to where most of his comrades are gathered, in the far corner of the courtyard where an arched doorway leads down into a cellar. They're passing out weapons — rifles and pistols, belts of ammunition, even a few old officers' swords. The drumbeat in his head is still making Ettore slow, but his eyes search out his sister. It's hard when their faces are all covered, but he can tell her by her build and the way she moves, and when she sees him she comes over at once, her eyes bright with worry until she's sure it's him, and that he isn't shot.

'Where the hell have you been?'

378

'I got into a fight with a child,' he says thickly.

'You did what? Is it just your head?'

'Yes — ah! Paola! Don't touch.'

'All right. But I'll need to clean it when we get home. You big baby,' she says, and he can tell how relieved she is that they've both survived. She herself is not only unscathed but seemingly unruffled. The skin of her forehead, the only part of her face that shows, is smooth and clean, with a slight sheen of perspiration, and Ettore marvels at her, even as he feels slightly removed from her. He pictures her as the cross-legged child he once knew, and it's clear that she's transmuted herself somehow; that she's had to. From flesh to iron; from girl to soldier.

There's a shout of outrage from the proprietor as he's disarmed and brought out at gunpoint. He's dragged into the courtyard by a man on each arm, dressed for bed in his drawers and a long linen shirt. A young man, in his thirties; good-looking and well fed, with a rosy pout of a mouth and fine, straight hair. Not a Gioia man; not even a Puglian. The cracked, sunburnt skin across his nose and cheeks is clearly not used to the southern sun.

'Show your faces, you cowards! You pieces-of-shit bastards!' he shouts. There's a low chuckle from the assembled raiders. 'I called for help as soon as you got here. I telephoned for help — the *carabinieri* will be here, and others — I think you know which others I'm talking about. So you'd better give up.' The tenant's eyes are wide, popping out of his head. He looks like he could run to the moon on the excitement.

'You're not in Rome any more, you moron. This farm has never had a phone connected. None of the farms have phones connected,' says Paola, stepping towards him. The man's lip curls in disgust.

'A *woman?* You peasants let your women go out and fight? What kind of worthless *terrone* are you?'

'The kind that are relieving you of these weapons. And advising you to honour the labour agreements you signed, whether the Chamber of Labour still stands or not,' says the bald-headed man steadily.

'You'll be punished for this! Every last one of you . . . you'll be punished! We know who you are, whether you cover your faces or not! I know who you are!'

'Careful now,' says another raider, stepping up to him with a cocked pistol. 'Don't give us a reason to shoot you.'

'You're finished,' the tenant mutters, as though he can't help himself.

'No,' says the raider. 'This is just the start.' The farmer stays silent, breathing hard, his face blanched and contorted. They gag him, and tie an old grain sack over his head.

The raiders take what they can carry from the *masseria*, leave the *annaroli* untouched and march the proprietor out through the embers of his gates, back to Gioia. When he feels paving stones beneath his feet the man starts shouting for help, and is knocked into stumbling semi-consciousness for his pains. Two men drag him all the way to Piazza Plebiscito, where they strip him naked and leave him tied to the bandstand. Then they, like the others, melt away into the dark streets as the bells strike three. Stolen guns are spirited away, tucked under the straw and sleeping bodies of pigs; wrapped in sacking and wedged up chimneys; concealed in piles of firewood. The raiders vanish into their homes, wash the soot from their faces and take to bed. They will be up in two hours and in the square for work, as though nothing has happened — their own safety depends on this. When the police and proprietors hear about the attack they'll be on the lookout for absentees.

Ettore's head is throbbing so severely he's not sure if he'll make it to work. While Paola checks Iacopo he lies down on the bed, not pausing to take off his boots, and immediately begins to drowse. He doesn't even object when Paola cleans up the cut on his head, too tired herself to be gentle. She murmurs to him that it isn't deep, and that a hat, worn low, will cover it well enough in the morning.

'Try to get some sleep,' she says. 'Don't worry, I'll wake you in time.'

'Oh, good,' he mumbles, and hears her quiet huff of amusement. Then sleep has him, so suddenly and so totally it's more like passing out.

★ ★ ★

In the nights after the raid there are more squadrist attacks, more shouts in the dark and sudden scuffles, more evictions and persecution of union men, but despite what the tenant of Masseria Molino claimed, he couldn't name any of those who'd been amongst the attackers, so the reprisals are random, aimed at anybody deemed to have shown rebellious, socialist or ungrateful tendencies. Ettore is forced to hide in the goat stall again one evening, after a tip-off from a neighbour. After that he takes to sleeping on a dusty pew in the tiny church of Sant'Andrea, not far from Vico Iovia; jimmying the rusty lock open, and finding bolts on the inside to seal himself in. The church is like a cave of soft stone and cool shade that has stood for a thousand years or so, and long been without a human incumbent. It will not do for the winter, but now, in the heat of summer, it's comfortable enough. The air is fresher than at home — ripe with the scent of the gently chalking walls, desiccated wood and the brittle, decades-old candle wax that cascades down the walls from niches. There's the musty smell of bird shit from the swallows that swoop in and out through a broken window pane, and have built their mud nests in the rafters. Pigeons roost on the pulpit at night, and launch into their staccato, rushing flight when Ettore startles them. It's been many years since the bell on the roof was rung.

At dawn Pino bashes his fist on the door to wake Ettore on his way to the piazza, but hidden away in this quiet space at the start and end of each day, Ettore feels time sliding to a stop, growing diffuse like the sunlight at evening time. The wheeling cries of the swallows seem to come from far away, and he could be a hundred miles from all the trouble. It's so peaceful he has to force himself to leave in the morning, and it seems to him that his head only starts to ache once he has stepped outside. He remembers hearing Livia's voice in his ear as he dangled, near senseless, over the fire during the raid. *Tell me I'm your sweetheart.* That lisping, musical way she spoke. He loved hearing it but it bothered him too, because it just didn't sound right. It hadn't at the time — sweetheart wasn't a word he'd ever heard Livia use, before those final fevered hours of her life when she'd repeated the phrase over and over. Ettore called her his darling, his treasure, his fiancée; she called him her love, or just Ettore. Never sweetheart. He wonders where she got the word. But all his wondering and all his questioning, and all the promises he'd made to her memory had got him nowhere. He was no closer to discovering who'd attacked her that day, so callously, so ruinously. In the steady peace of the church Ettore stops making his promise to her. He stops promising he will find the man out, and accepts that he probably never will. *Forgive me, Livia. I don't know what else I can do.* His defeat makes him feel small, and tired.

His headache makes him sluggish, and two days in a row he gets no work. Paola says nothing; he can sense her worry in the way she moves, even the way she breathes, as she dips reluctantly into the food she was saving for winter. The tension in Gioia only ever increases; there are rumours amongst the men, guarded carefully from the proprietors, the police and the *annaroli*, of the fight back that's coming, that's already begun. They have a run of cooler days, with a welcome breeze, but there's no more rain. Out of town, vegetable crops are stunted and failing, and fruit grows slowly, hard and juiceless. In town there's not much to buy but bread, and the price of that creeps up and up. Meat never lasts in the summer, but it's still sold even when it's slimy and off colour. The price of barrelled water rises until none but the rich can afford it, and the workers only have their allotted time at the pump in which to draw any. Wages and hours decrease as the rush of the harvest tails off; the streets are more populous with the unemployed, the unfed, and the anxious.

Ettore relies on Paola to connect him to what's going on. She is part of the invisible web of quietly passed words that sustains the raiders in between action. She walks to Piazza XX Settembre, or out along Via Roma, with a covered basket on her hip and Iacopo on her back, and returns with news. Ettore has no idea whom she talks to, and simply waits to be told what will happen next, and when. They will wait a few days until things have quietened somewhat — that's the word she brings. But they can't wait too long: the proprietors are nervous; they're strengthening their guard.

While he works Ettore finds it easier to keep his mind from wandering. But when he's not working, the temptation is to retreat to the empty church and lie in silence inside, imagining himself removed from his life. He tries not to think about Chiara out at dell'Arco, waiting for a message he said he'd send. He tries not to think about her skin or her touch or the taste of her, or what life must be like in her universe. He tries not to think about Marcie, and her blind, hopeful eyes; or Ludo Manzo watching the youngest boys with one hand on his whip and a keen expression on his face. But he can't not think about them, and he can't not think about Federico Manzo, with his cocky walk and his criss-crossed gun belts. He's not sure what's worse — thinking of him in Gioia, perhaps bullying Paola again, or out at the *masseria* near Chiara. *He hissed at me*, she said.

Ettore's stomach gets used to being empty again, his muscles to being weak for want of fuel. He lies in a shaft of dusty sunshine from the derelict window, both present and absent from the world, in one moment drifting listlessly as though none of it pertains to him, in the next beset by fears and anger and doubt and wanting. When it gets too much he clenches his fists until the knuckles crack, and his conscience bothers him constantly about something else entirely, until at last he has to speak.

He waits until Paola is nursing Iacopo. It's a dirty trick, but he has to know she won't run off at once and do something dangerous. The room is full of steam; a small pot of dried beans is boiling to softness on the stove. Paola sits on the edge of the bed to nurse, with a shawl draped over her shoulder and her breast, for modesty's sake. Ettore doesn't tease her about it, though they've had to use the *prisor* in front of each other since they were old enough to sit on it.

Dignity must be enjoyed where it can be got.

'What is it, Ettore?' she says, as he works himself up to speaking. 'You've obviously got something to say. What is it?'

'It's bad, Paola,' he says carefully. She gives him a steady look.

'How bad can it be? Just spit it out.'

Ettore takes a deep breath. 'You must promise me to think before you do anything. Think before you act, once I've told you. You must promise me that, first.'

'Then I promise it,' she says, tension in her voice.

'Ludo Manzo was at Masseria Girardi that day. He was one of the shooters.' He says it in a rush, to have it over with. Paola stares at him for a long time, and a ripple of anguish passes over her face, filling her eyes with tears. She blinks them back.

'The mozzarella told you?' she says at last. Ettore nods. Paola clears her throat and looks down, peeking around the shawl at the baby. 'Why didn't you tell me sooner?'

'Because I didn't want you to get yourself killed for a vendetta. I wasn't going to tell you at all, for just that reason, but you . . . you have a right to know.'

'How did that man get so full of hate, I wonder?' she says softly. 'It must plague him. It'll be a mercy when I put a bullet in him. A mercy to him and everyone else.'

'You won't go out there alone and try anything? Promise me!'

'No, I won't go alone.' Paola detaches her son,

386

calmly turns him to her other breast; her hands and her movements are automatic, deft and tender. 'But you wanted an honourable reason to attack dell'Arco and there you have it — Ludo Manzo is an enemy to all of us. We'll go to dell'Arco next; when I tell the others he was there that day, they'll agree with me. We'll go there next, and if you want to be sure we don't lose anybody you'd better talk to your woman. You'd better get her to open the doors for us.'

'She's not my woman.'

'She *is* your woman. She'd do anything you asked, I saw it.'

From the alcove in the wall there's a sudden slight movement, and they've got so used to there being none that it startles them. Valerio props himself up on one elbow, shaking visibly. He tries to speak, has to clear his throat and try again, and his children watch on in amazement.

'Is this true, boy?' he says to Ettore. 'What that woman who was here said about Manzo?'

'She had it from Uncle Leandro,' says Ettore. Valerio nods slowly, just once.

'Then you must go there, and he must die. This is the way of things. And if that woman who was here can help, then make her. This is a war, and no time for your soft heart, boy.' With another nod Valerio collapses back down into silence, like some oracle that has spoken incontrovertibly, and is spent. Paola and Ettore share a glance, and say nothing more for a long time. When Iacopo has fed himself to sleep Paola wraps him and puts him down in his wooden box.

'Don't be long about it, Ettore. Can you get word to her? Get her to meet you? We must keep the momentum of this; we mustn't let the men lose heart.'

'You need to decide what night we will attack, and at what hour. It won't be easy to get messages to and fro. It won't be easy for her to come here, and I can't risk going there. If she comes here again, I must be able to tell her everything.'

'All right. Send a message that she should come. I'll find out what you need to know.'

★　★　★

In the morning Ettore tears a slip of paper from a mouldy hymn book he finds on a shelf in Sant'Andrea. He has no pen or ink, so he uses a fragment of charcoal to write, in laborious Italian, where he is, and that she must come as soon as she can, then he gives the note to Pino and watches anxiously as his friend shoves to the front of the crowd near Ludo Manzo, and is hired to feed the threshing machine at dell'Arco. The sight of the overseer fills Ettore with a caustic, gnawing hatred. He glances around the square, half expecting Paola to come running out of nowhere and fly at him with tooth and nail. But she doesn't. As he moves away Pino looks back at Ettore and gives him a tight nod, and Ettore can see how nervous he is of the task he's been given; how he curls in on himself when Ludo is near, as delicately as a scorched leaf. Ettore sends a silent prayer to any watching angels for Pino's success, and safety, for if anybody deserves to have a watching angel, surely it's Pino.

The day is long; Ettore gets work breaking rocks to build a wall, and by the end of it there are rings of salt on his clothes and his arms have the tremor of exhaustion. But in the safety of the church in the deep of evening, Pino stops in to see him.

'It's done, brother,' he says, with a smile, palpably relieved.

'You gave it to Carlo?'

'Yes. I said it was a love letter from you — he grinned like a little boy. Nobody saw me do it, I'm sure.'

'Well done, Pino. Thank you,' says Ettore. Pino lingers in the dark doorway of the church.

'She . . . she won't be hurt? The English woman? You'll be sure to keep her safe in all this, won't you?' he says. 'None of it is her doing, after all.'

'I know it's not. And I . . . I'll do my best,' says Ettore, ashamed that his friend feels the need to say this. That he's getting Chiara involved in the raid. Pino has never been on a raid, and would never go on one. There's no violence in him, not even enough to keep watch while others perpetrate. 'I'll do my best. The danger will be far greater if we don't have her help.'

'The danger will be great, regardless,' says Pino. 'Your sister scares me sometimes, you know that?' A quick grin as he says this.

'The times I'm not frightened for her, I'm frightened of her,' says Ettore, nodding. Pino clasps his arm for a moment, and then he's gone.

Ettore expects her to come in the evening again, like the last time, or even in the deep of night, stealing into town like a thief. Instead it's pure chance that he's in the church, far gone in thought, when she appears in the middle of the morning, two days later. He's so distracted that he doesn't react when the door creaks open, and for a moment he stares at her there, golden in the light, unable to make sense of the sight of her. Her smile is uncertain but irrepressible; he can see the breath high up in her chest, her ribs at their widest arc. A swallow flits in and sees her, circles and flies back out, but Chiara only looks at Ettore as he sits up, and it's so incongruous that she's there, and that they have this soft, lucent place to themselves, that he smiles. He bolts the door behind her; takes hold of her without reservation. There's something so inexpressibly poignant in the smell of her hair, warm from the sun, that his heart aches a little, and when he kisses her he's almost reverent, and gentler than he has ever been. Footsteps outside, back and forth past the door; the swallow comes in again and there's the tiny scrape of its claws as it lands, the descant piping of its young — rammed into the nest, fat and silly, ready to fledge. Ettore takes off Chiara's clothes and lets the sun fall, incandescent, on her skin. He turns her this way and that to see, touching her here and there — the notch at the base of her throat where there's a gleam of sweat; the line where buttock joins thigh; the smooth protrusions of her elbows and knees. She has long toes and pale, narrow feet. He examines every inch and he lays her down, and he wonders if the tingle of heartbreak is in the feeling he has, right down at gut level, that this will be the one and only time he will see her like this. Glowing in the sun like one of his mother's spirits; beautiful, untenable, not of this world.

Time passes like this, distorted and dreamlike. Time disconnected from anything outside the tiny church. Later Ettore watches Chiara dress again. She does it in a leisurely way, with no sense of impropriety or indecent haste. Like a woman in her own boudoir; languidly at ease.

'Come here,' he says, when she's finished buttoning the back of her skirt, and the front of her blouse, and her bedraggled stockings into her garter belt. She puts on her shoes before she obeys him, coming to sit beside him on the pew. She sits close; he puts an arm behind her shoulders and lets his fingers rest in the hair at the back of her neck. The width of her neck fits his hand exactly, and it's satisfying. 'My sister says you're in love with me.' At this she stiffens for a fraction of a second, but then surrenders.

'Of course. Didn't you know?' she says.

'I don't know,' he says, but of course he did. He denied it to himself because of the bewildering way it pleased him in one second and angered him the next. There's a hung moment in which she doesn't ask him if he loves her back.

'It doesn't matter if you don't love me back. It doesn't change anything,' she says simply.

'I don't know if I can still love anybody. Or

anything. Not properly. Not as I would wish to,' he says, and this is truthful enough. He can feel his own pulse in his fingertips, resting against the skin of her neck.

'It doesn't matter,' she says.

'How . . . how are you here? How did you get here?'

'Carlo gave me your message the day before yesterday, but I couldn't come any sooner. Then I said I wanted to come and see Boyd. My husband, here in Gioia. Anna brought me in the little cart, and I told her I was going for a walk before I went in to see the men . . . I don't think she believed me.' A defiant jerk of her chin. 'But why shouldn't I go for a walk, to stretch my legs after the ride?'

Troubled by this, Ettore thinks for a moment.

'Anna is close with Federico. You must be careful; she might tell him and he would know why you have really come.'

'He doesn't know you're here, in this church, though. Does he?'

'No. No, that's right. But you must go to Via Garibaldi before you go back to the *masseria*. You must see your husband.' Saying this is like needlessly pressing a bruise.

'Yes. And Pip . . . Pip knows,' she says, in a mournful voice, rich with guilt. She shuts her eyes. 'There was the most awful scene. When I got back from here last time . . . It was awful. He's so hurt. I . . . I don't know what to say to him.' She looks down and a tear lands on her skirt; a small dark mark on the fabric. Ettore almost says *it will be over, soon*, but then he

392

realises it would sound cruel, not kind as he means it.

'Will he tell his father?'

'I don't know.' The words are spoken on a sigh, soused in misery. Something else occurs to Ettore, something possibly more dangerous.

'Will he tell Marcie?'

'What? Why should he?' she says, puzzled. 'And what would it matter?'

'Never mind. Listen to me, Chiara. I have to ask you to do something for me.'

'Whatever it is, I'll do it.'

'Don't say that until you've heard me. It . . . could be dangerous for you.'

There's a pause, and in it Ettore has the choice. He can tell her the raid is coming, tell her to get out of the *masseria*, her and the boy and Marcie, and be far away when it happens. Or he can ask her what he must ask her. He keeps his jaw tight shut for a moment more, a moment in which she is not in great danger, and he is not the cause of it. It's a soft, elastic moment, like the time they spent making love — the luminous space between seconds, impossible to preserve. 'There will be a raid,' he says at last, and the darkness creeps in. 'On Sunday night there will be a raid on my uncle's farm. He is in Gioia, not on the farm, so he will be in no danger, and it will go easier. I . . . I will be one of the raiders. My sister with me, and many others. I need you to ask the guard to open the main door for you, at exactly one in the morning. And then you must go into the main building and lock yourselves in a room — the three of you together, Marcie, the boy, and you. Can you do that?'

He can hear her breathing, high up beneath her ribs again, like when she first arrived. He can sense his words sinking into her, being absorbed, and he waits to see how she will react — if she will panic, if she even understands what he's said. When she looks up her eyes are fearful, but there's no panic, no refusal.

'One in the morning is too late. They would never open the door for me then. It must be earlier. I've never been out after midnight before, and they were very reluctant to open the door even then.'

'Then, you'll do it?'

'If I begged you to be safe . . . if I begged you not to do this, would it make any difference?'

'No.'

'Then I will do it.' She tips her head, lets it rest on his shoulder for a moment, but she's too agitated and lifts it again, fiddling with the frayed cuff of his shirt, running the threads through her fingertips. 'But it must be earlier. And I must hope and pray that Carlo is on the door.'

'What time?'

'Eleven? Sometimes I've walked before bed, to help me sleep.'

'It's risky.' Ettore shakes his head. 'Gioia won't be fully asleep . . . the squads will be about . . . '

'Later would be impossible, even if Carlo is on the door. You won't . . . you won't hurt him, will you? If it's Carlo? He's so young; he's harmless . . . ' she says, and Ettore agrees with her. But he'll make no empty promises.

'Don't stay to see. Do you hear? You run to your room, and you lock it. That's all you do.' Her face clouds at this obvious skirting of her question. Ettore looks away.

'I did not want it to be this way,' he says. 'But they leave us no other way. You must say nothing of this. To anyone.'

'If you're hurt . . . ' Chiara shakes her head; tries again. 'If you're hurt — ' Ettore lifts her chin with a crooked finger and stares into her eyes to press home his command, and make her obey.

'Don't stay to see.'

He keeps her there as long as he dares, after the sun has gone past noon and she's long overdue at the house on Via Garibaldi. He has the feeling that she wouldn't leave at all if he didn't make her; that same inseparable mix of bravery and stupidity he's seen in her before, that same blind urge to follow her heart against all better sense. She would stay with him in that little church, and pretend that they could live that way. At the door she turns.

'You could come to England,' she says; a sudden flare of reckless hope. 'With me. You could come back to England with me. I'll divorce Boyd . . . we could marry. Pip would come around . . . he's almost a man. You could come away from all of this.' He can hardly bear the look on her face, the fragility of her. In the time it takes him to reply, in the time it takes him to frame the only answer he can give, he sees her collapse into herself, and the hope burn out as quickly as it flared. In the end she slips away before he's said anything else, dipping her chin, pulling her hand away from his.

Once Chiara has left Ettore goes to tell Paola that she's agreed to help them, but his sister's not at home; Valerio is alone on his shelf, sleeping soundly. Dogged by restless impatience he walks a convoluted route back to the church, and as he's going in a strange figure comes hurrying towards him, moving in a crabbed way, keeping to the deep shade on one side of the street. Ettore braces himself for trouble, for a fight, but the figure is Pino, and Ettore relaxes for a second before he sees why his friend is walking so peculiarly. He has Chiara in his arms. Ettore stares stupidly, making no sense of this, as Pino barrels past him into the church.

'Ettore! Shut the damn door!' he says, sitting Chiara down on a pew. She curls forwards, her face almost on her knees. Her blouse is torn, her skirt too. There's blood from somewhere, smudged on her cheek and her collar, and Ettore's mouth goes dry. He slams the door, slides the bolt across.

'What's happened?' He goes over to Chiara, puts a hand on her shoulder and feels her shaking. 'Pino! What's happened?' Pino looks away, catching his breath; he seems reluctant to speak, like he's almost afraid.

'She was attacked,' he says at last. He sucks in a deep breath. 'It was blind luck I was passing. Work stopped early — there was nothing left to thresh. Or I wouldn't have been back. I wouldn't have been there to stop it . . . '

'Chiara?' Ettore crouches down and looks into

her ashy face. Her pupils are huge, black, focused on nothing. Her lower lip is split, and blood is smeared over her chin; her hands are bruised, the nails broken. 'Who did this?' he says. She shows no sign of having heard him. Ettore looks up at Pino. 'Was she raped?' The ugly word rasps in his throat, turning his stomach. Pino shakes his head.

'I got there in time. But I think it was his intention,' he says guardedly.

'Whose intention? You saw who it was?' says Ettore. His own hands are shaking now; pressure's building behind his eyes, and in a tight band around his ribs. Just then Chiara takes a ragged breath in and shudders. She says something quiet that Ettore can't hear. He crouches in front of her again.

'Ettore . . . ' says Pino; a note of warning.

'Chiara . . . you're safe here. I'm here,' says Ettore.

'Tell me . . . ' she says indistinctly. She blinks slowly, drunkenly; slides her eyes to look at him. 'Tell me I'm your sweetheart,' she murmurs. Ettore can't breathe. He reels back from her, loses his balance, sits down with a bump.

'Ettore, I saw who it was. It was Federico Manzo. He must have followed her here,' says Pino.

'That's what he said. What he kept saying.' Chiara's voice is hoarse, whispery dry. 'He kept saying, 'Tell me I'm your sweetheart.''

# Clare

Pino and Ettore start to clean her face and brush at the dirt on her clothes, but in the end they realise there's no point. After a curt exchange in the dialect they lead her back to Via Garibaldi, and she goes with clumsy steps, dazed, and at some point realises that the only hand on her elbow is Pino's — Ettore has gone. Pointlessly, she turns to look over her shoulder. When they're at the door to Leandro's house she pulls back. *If you speak of this,* Federico said, *I will tell them where you have been. Where you have been many times. Anyway, you like Puglian men, don't you?* This said with triumphant levity, with one grimy hand clamped over her nose and mouth so she could hardly breathe; a knife in the other, its tip pressed casually into the hollow above her collarbone. *No screaming,* he said, as he took his hand away, reached down for his belt. *Now, tell me I'm your sweetheart.* A lingering kiss, a hideous mockery of tenderness. *Tell me I'm your sweetheart;* more insistently, when she didn't speak. And then, miraculously, Pino was there, and Federico was running away, and the relief was so overwhelming that for a moment Clare forgot how to stand, how to speak or think or move.

Federico Manzo, mending the bicycle for Pip. Federico Manzo, offering her flowers and then hisses — from stately courtship to gleeful menace in a day, when he realised she was no Madonna. Clare looks at the door to Leandro's house. Will Federico open it to let them in? He's had time to get back, to compose himself, but Pino gave him a kick in the stomach that sent him scuttling off, doubled over, so perhaps he won't be back yet. The thought of coming face to face with him brings on waves of clammy dread. *If you speak of this, I will tell them where you have been.* She puts her arms around Pino's waist for a moment, presses the side of her face to his shirt. He smells of sweat and labour, of earth and straw.

'*Grazie*, Pino,' she says. When she steps back he looks pleased, abashed, and she believes everything Ettore has ever told her about this man's good heart. He frowns in thought, searching for a word he can give her in Italian.

'*Coraggio*,' he says, and she nods. *Courage*.

Clare has never seen the man who opens the door before; he's a different servant, older, stooped. She uncurls her sweaty fists. The house is quiet, could be empty. Faint echoes of her footsteps drift around the shadowy colonnades. She goes upstairs to the room she had before, but none of her things are there, of course, so she can't change. Some of Boyd's clothes are in the wardrobe; his shaving brush and soap are on the washstand, and there's an inch or two of water left in the jug. Clare uses his comb on her hair, and redresses it; washes as best she can and changes out of her torn, bloodied blouse, putting on one of Boyd's clean shirts instead. It hangs low and shapeless on her, like a bad imitation of one of Marcie's tunics, but it covers the tear in the waistband of her skirt, the dirt on the seat. In front of the mirror she stops to stare into her own eyes — they have swollen lids and an odd emptiness that even she can't reach into. She tries to think back to when it was that Ettore left her — at what point on the walk from Sant'Andrea to Via Garibaldi. She can't remember. *I'm here*, he said, but then he seemed to vanish, and he'd had a look in his eyes she'd never seen before, hard and hungry. Pino had fidgeted nervously, moving diffidently around his friend as though Ettore was ill, or dangerous. The sunlit hour in the church, before all this, seems to have happened in another age, to another person. And she'd been fool enough to think, for that short while, that she'd never been happier.

A knock at the door and the breath squeezes out of her lungs. Boyd comes in and straight over to her; a hand on her shoulder, a wide, appraising gaze, full of concern.

'Darling, the servant just came and told me you'd arrived. But Anna was here hours ago . . . where have you been? Are you all right? What's happened — your lip!'

'I'm all right, Boyd.' But her voice wobbles treacherously. She doesn't know how to be with him any more; she doesn't know how to act.

'Did somebody do this? Have you been attacked?' His voice has gone high in outrage, in disbelief. Clare shakes her head.

'I . . . I went for a walk around town and I . . . fell down some steps. Silly of me. I just lost my footing.'

'Some steps?' He furrows his brow, not quite believing her. She claws through her memories of Gioia. The town is level, the only steps lead to the doors of upper level apartments. Like Ettore's.

'Yes. The steps from the church. You know, the front steps of the Chiesa Madre?'

'Were you feeling faint again, my darling?' A hand on the side of her face; stooping over her. Clare feels trapped, overshadowed; can hardly stand it. She shakes her head.

'No, not really. I just lost my footing.'

'Why didn't you come here first? I'd have gone for a walk with you, happily.'

'I . . . I thought you'd be working, darling. I thought I'd wait until lunchtime before I interrupted you . . . '

'You mustn't walk around on your own. Please promise me. You mustn't any more. It's not safe, least of all when you've not been well.'

'All right.'

'But why did you come into town at all, darling? Why are you here?'

Clare looks up at her husband. Pale face, scrubbed and clean-shaven; soft, limp hair combed neatly back; his lanky height, thin shoulders slumped so as not to tower over her. For a moment she can't make her mouth open; can't make her tongue move. There are too many things she can't say.

'I . . . wanted to see you,' she says, and the words are so crabbed with duplicity she's sure he must hear it. 'I need to talk to you about something.'

'Oh?' His eyes search her face, worried now.

'Yes, but I do have rather a headache now . . . ' She puts a hand to her forehead, as much to break his gaze as anything, but in truth her head is pounding as though there's too much in it — too much blood and matter, too many thoughts and fears.

'Of course. Leandro wants to see you too, but rest first. I'll have them send up some fresh water and a cold drink for you.'

'Thank you.'

He goes from the room as softly as he came in, moving as he always does — with steady grace, never sudden or abrupt. Sidling through the world as though he doesn't want it to notice him. When the door clicks shut Clare sits down where she is — sinking to the floor with her back to the mirror. She needs a moment to try to think of any one useful thing, any one right thing, and she can't seem to do it while she must concentrate on standing. Pino came. Pino came and saved her. Yet her thoughts are brimming with what might have happened otherwise — Federico's parody of a kiss, one hand undoing his belt; the press of his erection against her stomach, and the tip of the knife at the base of her throat. *I'm here*, Ettore said, but then he wasn't. There's acid in the back of Clare's mouth, cramp between her ribs. She can still smell Federico's breath and feel the odd shape of his mouth on hers, his crooked teeth too prominent when he kissed her. Her stomach swims with nausea; sweat breaks out on her face.

At the end of the afternoon Clare goes

downstairs because she realises that, more than anything, she wants to be out of Gioia. Her legs are unsteady and there's still a strange taste in her mouth, at the back of her throat — a metallic kind of tang, like copper or iron. Almost like blood but different, cleaner. She finds Leandro on the terrace, studying a list of notes and figures in a ledger with a glass of wine held lazily in one hand. There's no outward sign of her cut lip but a thin red line and a gentle swelling. Most of the damage is on the inside — caused by her own teeth when Federico crushed his hand over her mouth. Leandro puts down the ledger but doesn't rise as she comes over to him. He crosses his legs and watches her, so unflinching and so knowing that Clare feels naked. She can't keep her hands from shaking. Leandro sees this, of course, as he pours her wine and she gulps at it; he sees everything. The wine tastes odd — almost musty, but Leandro seems to find nothing amiss with it.

'Somebody attacked you?' he says mildly. Clare shakes her head.

'I fell down . . .'

'The steps of our Chiesa Madre, yes, your husband told me. Wide, even steps, and only a flight of three.'

'I tripped.'

'I would happily take action against the man who did this,' he says, as if she hasn't spoken. Again, she shakes her head.

'Then I hope you'll have the sense not to see him again. And not to come into Gioia by yourself to do so.' Clare catches her breath, poised to defend Ettore before she realises that she can't, any more than she can tell Leandro what really happened. Not without confessing her infidelity, however much she wants to denounce Federico. She can't stand to think of him out at the *masseria* with Marcie, and Anna and the other servants; or in Gioia at night with the *braccianti*'s wives and daughters.

'I came to see my husband,' she says. Her voice is small and tremulous. Leandro grunts.

'As you wish.' He takes a swig of wine, always with his eyes on her. 'I'm beginning to think I made a mistake in bringing you out here, Mrs Kingsley. You and the boy. I did it for a good reason, you must understand. But perhaps I've made matters worse. Perhaps it's time I sent you home.'

'Will you tell me why you brought me here?' she says. Leandro pauses, and behind his unswerving gaze she can see the shifting of thoughts, the weighing up of things. He uncrosses his legs and leans forwards.

'It might be hard for you to understand, or even believe, Chiara, but I brought you here for your own safety. I think you could be in danger.'

'What can you mean? I wasn't in any danger until I came here.'

'Yes, I see that now. Ironic, in some ways. I must tell you, though — ' He cuts himself off as Boyd steps out onto the terrace. 'Downing tools for the day?' Leandro says smoothly, in the exact same level tone, and Clare has the clear impression that whatever he'd been about to tell her had been for her ears only. He shoots her a

404

warning look as Boyd seats himself, and she bites back all the sudden questions she has for him, and all the sudden fear.

Anna comes to ask if Clare will be travelling back to the *masseria* with her that evening, but since she has told Boyd she wants to speak to him, and since he wants her to stay the night, she has to turn the offer down.

'Federico can drive you tomorrow,' says Leandro.

'No!' says Clare, too loudly, before she can stop herself.

'No?' Leandro echoes, watching her closely. When she returns to silence he doesn't press. 'Very well. I'll drive you myself — all of us. We were heading back on Friday, anyway, for this party of Marcie's. A day early won't matter, and we can stay for a few days. I miss the clean air at the farm.' Marcie's party — Clare had forgotten all about it. A party on Friday night, and on Sunday night the farm will be attacked. It seems impossible. Did Ettore really tell her about it, and ask for her help? It has the same cast of dreamy unreality as everything else that happened that day before Federico. Marcie's party; Marcie and Pip waltzing around an empty room; Pip taking the mongrel puppy from her wordlessly, as they stood opposite each other in the dark outside her locked door in that awful, bruising silence. Peggy, he's named the puppy — after its spindly peg legs, and after he ascertained that she was a bitch. Clare's eyes scorch with tears; she excuses herself before the men notice.

In bed, with darkness outside, Boyd curls

405

himself around her. He seems too long, too soft, too awkward. There's something loose but clinging about him, like the stifling drape of a heavy, heavy blanket. He doesn't fit her neatly like Ettore does, and he doesn't smell right. Clare stares into the shadows as he strokes a lock of her hair down over her ear. The shivers it gives her are the wrong kind.

'Please don't hold me so tightly. I can't quite bear it,' she says, and he leans away wordlessly, hurt.

'What did you want to talk to me about?' he says. Clare's thoughts are fragmentary, jarring into the distant past, into recent happenings, into the future; alighting and then skipping on so fast she can hardly follow them. Finally, she chases her unease and all her unanswered questions right back to New York.

'What did you say to the mayor?' she says.

'What on earth do you mean?'

'In New York, when we were there seven years ago. At the party when the three designs were exhibited, by the different architects.' There are three steady beats of silence, a fourth, a fifth. She can hear him breathing. 'You were very nervous. Desperately so. You didn't speak to anybody all evening, not even me, until you went up to talk to the mayor and some other men. Then you seemed better; and then we left. What did you have to tell him?'

'Good Lord, Clare, I really can't remember,' he says; an awkward parody of offhand. 'It was a long time ago.'

'I don't believe you.'

'Clare — '

'I don't believe you! I want you to tell me.'

'Clare, don't raise your voice. You'll be heard.'

'I don't care!' She struggles up from the bed, out of his grasp. The sudden movement makes her head swim. She stands facing him, barefoot, arms around herself like armour.

Boyd sits up slowly. The sheet drops to his waist; he's bare-chested — a soft sag of skin around each nipple, a short run of ribs visible above his rounded stomach, a fuzz of pale hair around his navel. She shouldn't be in bed with this man; it seems wholly inappropriate that he should be so undressed. 'Tell me.'

'It was . . . ' He shuts his eyes, passes one hand across them. 'I had to put in a word for Cardetta. I had to put in a good word for him.'

'Why? For what?'

'He . . . they . . . the city waste management contract was up for review. Leandro wanted it, but there were . . . rumours about him. And the new mayor — the one who seemed too young to be out on his own — was making a point of clearing city hall of corruption. So he was unlikely to award the contract to a known mobster, or a suspected one.'

'So you . . . you walked up to the mayor and told him who to hire?'

'No, of course not. The . . . one of the other men talking to him was to raise the topic, and to mention Cardetta's name. I was to provide a . . . character reference for him. Off the cuff — by chance, it was to appear.'

'And what did you say about him?'

407

'I said . . . I said I'd worked with him on a building project. He had interests in construction as well, for years. I said he'd built for me, and I'd found him to be honest and open in all his dealings, and had delivered an excellent standard of work. I said I believed the rumours about his . . . other business concerns to be malicious ones put about by rivals and xenophobes.' Boyd sounds like he's reading from a script and Clare realises that he has this by rote. Still, seven years after the event, it's imprinted in his mind. She thinks back to their stay in New York, and the sudden erosion of all her hopes for her marriage.

'It was Cardetta who came to the apartment, wasn't it? Or his men,' she says, and Boyd nods. 'I thought it was people who'd known Emma. Old friends of hers and yours, and it had upset you to see them. Thrown you back into grief.' He shakes his head and then hangs it; he looks pale and uneasy.

'But why did you do it for him, Boyd? How did he even know you?'

'He . . . I . . . It was a straight trade, you see. I did this for him, and he made sure that . . . he made sure that my building . . . '

'He made sure that *your* design for the new bank was chosen?' To this there's that hangdog nod again, that reek of self-loathing. 'But how did he find you, Boyd? How did he even know who you were?'

'I don't know. I . . . ' His brows knit in thought, still not looking at her. 'After Emma died I . . . I had a rough time of it. He

408

. . . we . . . ' He trails into silence, gulping in a breath with a spasmodic lurch of his chest.

Clare stares at him. At this point she would normally relent and soothe him. She would be too afraid to push him into a depression that might take him days, weeks, to come out of. But that was the old Clare from before, in her safe, careful, quiet life. It amazes her, now, how frightened she was then, when she had nothing whatsoever to fear. Not compared to now.

'You're not going to tell me, are you?' He glances up at her flat tone, her uncharacteristic mien. She sees a flicker of self-awareness in his eyes, a swift recalculating, and realises how easily he's played on her fears in the past. She takes a deep breath but then he crumples. Anguish stampedes over his face, and it's real.

'I've lost you, haven't I, Clare?' he whispers.

'I don't know,' she says. She feels far out, alone; she feels that there can be no going back from here, or any undoing of these things.

'That was the one thing . . . That was the one thing I never wanted. Never, ever.' He smears tears from his eyes with the thumb of one hand. 'I love you so much, Clare. My darling. You're my angel, truly. You're . . . perfect. I couldn't live without you . . . you must believe — '

'Stop it!' She has no control over her sudden shout. 'I can't bear it when you say those things! I can't *bear* it!'

'Why not?' he says, shocked. Never once in their ten years together has she raised her voice to him.

'Because they're *not true*! And how can I

possibly live up to them — how could anybody ever live up to them? They're tyrannical! And they make me hate myself — you make me *hate* myself!'

The quiet after her outburst seems to roar in her ears; the night's silence returns, steadily repairing the tear she made. They don't speak for so long that it becomes impossible to. They can only wait, with this pounding quiet between them, until one of them makes a move. Clare reaches up and wipes away half-dry tears with the flats of her hands. She feels sick, exhausted, and her head is ringing. Wordlessly, she comes to the bed and lies down on top of the sheet. Boyd stays where he is, sitting up and hunched, and she's too tired to guess at his thoughts, or what they should do next; how things can go between them from now on. She shuts her eyes and pictures herself inside a sunlit church, small and ancient; she pictures the delicate way Ettore touched her, and kissed her; the tenuous, disconnected look of happiness on his face. But however much she tries the image remains distant, already fading. She falls asleep telling herself, over and over, that it was real.

★ ★ ★

Pip comes trotting down the outdoor stairs when he hears the car, and Clare's heart leaps up to greet him; but when he sees her he falters, and when he sees his father he halts altogether. He hasn't seen Boyd since before the night Clare locked herself out of her room and he discovered

410

her lie; she has no idea how he will react to his cuckolded father, or how he will act. She watches as he stops on the bottom step, squinting in the sunlight with strands of his fringe in his eyes. It's been weeks since it was cut. He looks slightly harried and flushed; he has points of colour on his cheekbones as though he has a touch of fever. Clare daren't put her hand to his forehead to check. She hardly dare approach him at all, when all she wants is to put her arms around him and hold him until he can feel how much she loves him, and how she can't bear his hurt, his anger. She watches to see if he'll blurt out her betrayal at once, and expose her publicly, or whether her punishment will be more slow-burning than that.

Peg is under Pip's arm, squirming and mouthing at his fingers. Boyd stretches his back, standing his full height for once, and walks over to his son with a studied ease.

'Philip,' he says, with peculiar formality. They haven't spent much time together on this trip — stilted mealtimes, passing moments at breakfast and dinner, and then only during the times Boyd has been at the *masseria*. They clasp hands, lean in for a brief press of their shoulders, Boyd's left to Pip's; half of an embrace. 'How are things? What on earth is this?'

'This is Peggy,' says Pip. His voice sounds deeper, more adult, than even the six weeks ago that they travelled down on the train. Clare's amazed by how things have changed since then; how many things, and how much. Pip raises his eyes to her, just for a second. A flick of a gaze, to remind her what he knows, and Clare's stomach

411

flutters. Her lip is still swollen, with a reddish bruise spreading onto her chin, but he doesn't seem to notice it. 'Clare found her in one of the ruined huts when she was out for a walk,' he says. This is the story they agreed to tell, when, in the darkness outside her locked door, Pip said: He *gave it to you, didn't he?* And Clare had nodded, dumbly. 'We think her mother must have abandoned her,' he adds. Boyd grunts.

'She's probably the runt. Best not to get too attached to her, son, they often die.' This makes some little spark in Pip fade out, visibly, and Clare wishes Boyd would see. She wishes he wouldn't say such things.

'I'm sure she'll be fine now she has Pip to look after her,' she says, but Pip doesn't react.

'It'll be full of worms — don't let it chew you like that. And make sure you wash your hands with lots of soap.'

'Peggy's a she, not an it,' says Pip.

'Pure Gioia mongrel, through and through,' says Leandro. He smiles, scuffing the puppy's smooth head with his knuckles. Peg twists around and tries to gnaw his hand. 'Tough as old boot leather; smart and loyal too. She'll be a good dog for you, Pip.' When Pip smiles Clare feels the pull of it in her chest, far under her ribs; a spreading warmth like a swig of brandy, swallowed fast.

'Well, she'll have to stay here when we leave,' says Boyd, and Clare hates him for a moment.

'Peggy's coming home with us,' she says flatly. She walks past her husband and up the stairs to greet Marcie, who has appeared on the terrace

412

with fresh powder on her cheeks and fresh red lipstick on her mouth, her hair immaculate.

Clare looks up at Leandro's wife as she reaches the top step, and for a second sees an expression on Marcie's face that she's never seen before — something flat, cold, almost hostile. She falters but the look disappears at once, replaced by that dazzling, indiscriminate smile, and Clare thinks she must have imagined it.

'My dear Clare, what on earth has happened to you?' says Marcie.

'Oh, I fell. I lost my footing on some steps.' They kiss with a light press of each cheek, like the men with their shoulders — the same not-quite embrace.

'Sweetie! Were you faint again?' Marcie takes her hands, drops her voice and her face towards Clare. 'You're not in the family way are you, honey?'

'Oh, no,' says Clare, at once. And then she thinks of her dizziness, her nausea, the odd tastes in her mouth, that she hasn't had her period at all since they arrived in Italy. The shock of it causes her throat to clench, choking out a single stunned syllable. Marcie looks at her quizzically.

'Well, come and sit down, do. How was your little trip?' There again is something in Marcie's tone, some note that could be a warning. But Clare can't tell if she's heard it or imagined it, and she lets herself be led to a chair and seated because a mad buzzing has started up in her ears, and she can't follow what Marcie says next.

Later on Clare helps Pip dose the puppy for worms. They go down into the smoky kitchen

— a cavernous space running beneath the long barn that forms the west wing of the quad, where the low vaulted ceiling is black with generations of soot, and the heat is a solid, tangible thing. There's a huge iron range with a stack of twisted firewood beside it, and pots on every hot plate; a smell of smuts and meat, of yeast and ashes. The cook, Ilaria, has a recipe to purge the parasites; she describes it at length as she mixes it, not seeming to mind that Clare and Pip don't understand a word, and make no reply. She grinds cloves and pumpkin seeds, dried worm-wood with its bitter stink, and some other herb that Clare can't identify. She binds this mixture into a pellet with a glob of lard, sticky and rank. Peggy squirms as though she knows what's coming as Ilaria cranks open her jaws and shoves the purge far down her throat. The puppy gives a little whine of protest, and gags as it goes down. Ilaria wipes her fingers on her apron and gives them a satisfied nod. Job done. They thank her in Italian as they turn to leave.

At the bottom of the kitchen steps Clare puts her hand on Pip's arm.

'Please, wait a moment,' she says. Up above is the bright oblong of the doorway, the blanching sunlight waiting outside, making it hard to hide. Clare wants shadows and quiet in which to speak. Pip bends and puts Peggy down; the puppy gambols between their feet and then settles down to chew the toe of Pip's shoe. 'Pip, listen. I . . . ' But Clare doesn't know what she wants to say, exactly. Only that she must speak. Pip has saved her from herself already — it was he who suggested that they get the master key from Carlo to reopen her bedroom door, when she'd been frantic and stupid with fright and self-recrimination at losing the original.

'Did he do that to you?' says Pip, looking at her swollen lip.

'No! Of course not.' She's not even sure how he knew, or why she didn't deny it. *You've been with him, haven't you? With Ettore?* That was his question, his accusation, in the dark of the *masseria*, outside her locked door. She could have denied it; she could have laughed, or feigned outrage. But she'd felt utterly exposed, and wretched, and she'd needed him, and all she'd had left was honesty.

'Are you going to leave Father?' he says.

'No.' She has a numb feeling, and that buzzing in her ears again, and she knows he's really asking: *Are you going to leave me?* And the answer to that has always been no.

'But you're in love with Ettore.' Pip shakes his head, won't look her in the eye. Clare wonders if he can see this love on her, somehow; then she realises that he simply can't conscience her being treacherous for anything less.

'But I'm married to your father, darling.'

'I'm not a child, Clare! Stop treating me like one! You think you can give me a puppy — a puppy *he* gave you — and that'll make everything all right? That I'll be so busy playing with her I won't notice you lying and sneaking?'

'Ettore meant the puppy to be for you. Pip, please.' She catches his arm again, as he turns to go.

'I want to hear the truth, Clare. I can't . . . I don't want you to lie to me. To hide things.' He's working hard not to cry.

'All right, Pip. All right. I . . . I am in love with him. But I'm not going to leave you.' She can't bring herself to say she won't leave Boyd; she can't make herself imagine what life will be like if she stays with him, for ever. But that is what she promised when she married him. It's like being crushed by a heavy, heavy weight. *Are you in the family way?* If she is, there's no possible way the child can be Boyd's. How can their marriage continue under those circumstances? Yet beneath her panic there's a rising arc of elation. A baby; Ettore's baby. Pip's face contorts and for a moment she thinks he's going to cry; then she realises its disgust.

'How could you, Clare? He can barely speak Italian, let alone English! I bet he can't read or write. He's a . . . a dirty peasant!'

'*Pip*!' Clare is stunned. 'How could you be so hateful? A dirty *peasant*? You sound like . . . ' She searches her mind, because these words are familiar but they don't sound like Pip's. Then she realises — they sound like Marcie's. Clare shuts her mouth abruptly, and Pip's cheeks blaze. He looks stricken, ashamed of himself but defiant.

'Well, anyway, you won't see him any more, will you? You won't keep going to Gioia,' he says.

'No. No, I won't go again.'

'And you still love my father? You always told me it was possible to love two people — the way Father loves my mother, and you as well.' There, in the midst of this frighteningly adult conversation, is a snatch of the childishness that hasn't quite left him.

'Yes, you can love more than one person. And your father is my husband,' she says, and they both know that this is no answer at all. But she can't lie to Pip, ever again, if she wants to keep him.

Pip looks down at his feet, where Peggy is cavorting on her back: a pot belly and waving legs, eyes rolling, ears inside out. Clare waits for some sign from him that this talk has improved things between them. She feels the weight of her promise not to go to Gioia again, dragging at her. It's all so much, so heavy. She longs to lie down and steadies herself against the wall with one hand, noticing the rough cobbles, the film of dust on every upward surface. It's an ancient wall, hundreds of years old, six feet thick, built in another age to keep out raiders and thieves. And now raiders and thieves are coming again, and Clare will be one of them.

'How did that happen?' she murmurs, shaking her head to Pip's questioning glance.

'Is *he* coming to the party tomorrow?' says Pip darkly.

'No. Of course not.'

'Not of course — you know Leandro loves him, kind of. And Marcie's never had a family before — cousins or siblings or nephews or anything.'

'You've become good friends, haven't you? You and Marcie. I'm . . . glad.'

'Well I haven't had much choice, have I? With

417

Father in town, and you . . . ' Pip pauses, looking away again. 'With you busy. Out walking. What was I supposed to do, all that time?'

With this twist of the knife he sets off up the stairs, and Peg scrambles after him. Clare stays a while in the shadows — not in the kitchen, not out of it; halfway between worlds, between lives. She puts the flat of her hand to her middle. There's nothing to feel, of course, it's far too early. If anything, she has lost some weight since they came to Italy — her stomach is almost concave between her hip bones; the skin is taut, smooth, no different to the touch. And yet she *knows*. She is completely certain. And in that halfway place where she can imagine, for a while, that no grief will come of it, she smiles.

★ ★ ★

Clare tries to be wherever Boyd is not. He has his work but he's restive and rises from it often, to pace the sitting room and the terrace, to emerge into the courtyard only to stall there, stock-still, as though he can't remember why he went. Clare tunes her ears to the sound of his steps, and keeps out of sight. She and Pip have spent much longer at the *masseria* than Boyd; they know it far better — its hidden corners and stairs, the way to the roof, the cracked love seat in the vegetable garden. She goes along the corridor to what was Ettore's room, and stands in the white emptiness of it. She lies down a while on the bare mattress. No scent of him, no trace. *The father of my child*. Clare turns the

418

words around in her mind, over and over. Somehow she's sure Ettore will be happy. In a place with so much death, mustn't new life be a welcome thing? She thinks of Iacopo, and the way he is treasured — he is illegitimate, the child of Paola's lover who was killed at the Girardi massacre, and it doesn't seem to matter at all. She's desperate to tell Ettore, and to look into his eyes as she does. But soon the room gets too empty, too quiet, and Clare's thoughts are too loud in comparison, so she roams on.

From outside the bat room she hears Marcie's laugh, and Pip's muffled voice. There's music playing so she can't hear what they're saying, even though she remembers Marcie saying that they ought to save the gramophone needles for the party. It had been when Clare had been about to dance with Pip. She puts her hands to the wooden door and presses her ear to it, shuts her eyes and feels a hundred miles from them, from Pip. She lets the knife turn in her heart — that she has left him so much alone to be with Ettore; that she turned her back on him from the very first moment Leandro's nephew collapsed in front of her on the terrace. When she can stand it no longer she knocks and goes in with a tentative smile, hoping to be absorbed into their fun, hoping to see Pip laugh. She expects to see them dancing again, like before, or up on the dais, but they are sitting side by side on the old couch. Marcie has her feet tucked up like a girl, her arms linked under her knees, her body turned towards Pip. She's listening to what Pip's saying with rapt attention, and for a moment they don't notice Clare there, they haven't heard her come in.

'I hope I'm not interrupting,' she says. Pip breaks off mid-sentence and blushes.

'Clare!' says Marcie, unfolding her legs. Her feet are bare, smooth and pale; her toenails are shell pink. She looks as though she'll stand up, but then changes her mind. Pip doesn't get up either, and Clare is left standing over them, awkwardly, trying to talk from a different eye level. 'We were just . . . discussing the play,' says Marcie. 'Weren't we, Pip?' Her teeth and tongue are stained, and Clare notices two sticky glasses on the floor, and a jug of red wine, dark inside. She can smell it in the air; she can smell it on Marcie's breath. She glances at Pip, searching for the same traces on him, but he keeps his mouth shut and nods to answer the question, so she can't tell.

'Oh. I see,' says Clare. She looks at Pip again, and because he won't look at her she knows he has been drinking too, and doesn't want her to see. 'All right there, Pip? How's it going?' she says.

'All right, I suppose,' he says. The words pitched halfway between gruff and petulant.

'I was thinking about going for a walk — do you fancy coming with me? Protect me from these bandits and rebels I keep hearing about?' She smiles. She wants to grab his arm and drag him from the room, and knows she can't. Not any more.

'Perhaps later on. After lunch,' he says. His eyes flick up to hers briefly, guilty and defiant.

'Yes. It is rather early, isn't it?' says Clare. She

looks at Marcie, whose cheeks and eyes are pink, and whose smile has gone as hard and flat as glass.

'Oh, there are few such rules here. This isn't England,' she says, too loudly, and her tone dares Clare to argue. There's a glitter in her eyes, a simmering anger, and Clare thinks of the row she overheard, deep in the night — the frayed edges of Marcie's voice, the hint of mania there.

'No more it is,' Clare murmurs. She can't hold Marcie's gaze so she looks at Pip again, but he's peering at his hand and running his thumb over the bite marks — dry and flaking, almost gone. 'Well, I'll leave you to it, then,' she says, with a desperate feeling, like she might cry.

'Enjoy your walk,' Marcie calls after her, and though Clare wants to look back and see if this is mocking, or serious, or angry, somehow she can't bring herself to.

From a narrow window, sunshine pouring through, she sees Leandro Cardetta on the roof of the opposite side of the quad. He's standing near the edge with his arms loose at his sides, his chin high; lord and master of all he surveys. The weather is restless and threatening. There's a hot, dry breeze, the kind that spreads fires, and blackish clouds on the southern horizon. The air catches at Leandro's hair and shirt; they are the only things moving in that still scene — the parched ground and stone walls behind him look like a painted backdrop. He stares fixedly into this menacing distance and Clare realises that, despite all the time she has spent as his guest that summer, she can't even guess at his thoughts. In Gioia he had been about to tell her the real reason he brought her and Pip out to Italy, she was sure of it. He'd said she was in danger. But then Boyd had appeared, and he'd cut himself off. What did that mean? That he didn't want Boyd to know the reason, or didn't want him to know that he intended to tell Clare?

She stares at Leandro; is every bit as still as him. In spite of all that has happened to her, all that has terrified her, she hasn't quite got the courage to interrupt him. He is a closed book; stern face, implacable eyes. *Leandro Cardetta is a very dangerous man.* For the first time Clare looks at what Boyd said from a different angle — beyond the obvious fact that Cardetta is a man who'll use his own means to achieve his own aims. Dangerous beyond that — dangerous to Boyd in some specific way? She watches his windblown figure with growing unease until the black car pulls into the courtyard and Federico Manzo climbs out of it. Then she shrinks back to her own room, keeping close to the walls; jittery with revulsion and wishing there was still a key she could turn in the lock.

★ ★ ★

On Friday evening, the night of the party, Marcie comes alive. The furniture in the long sitting room is pushed back to make room for dancing, and the gramophone is set up on a side table. Torches outside the main gates and every lantern in the place are lit to beat back the dark. On the terrace the long table is laid with twelve

422

place settings. For all the invites she sent, for all the expectation and preparation, Marcie has only managed to find seven people, beyond her husband and houseguests, willing to come to Masseria dell'Arco for dinner. In defiance of that she fusses as though the King of Italy will attend, and is wearing her silks and jewels; the light swoops over the shallow curves of her hips, the deeper ones of her chest, and glitters from her ears and neck and fingers.

Clare is dowdy in comparison, and doesn't care. She washes her hair and leaves it loose to dry, so that it hangs without shape or bounce. She puts on clean clothes and the only pair of evening shoes she has with her, but pays no attention to the outfit. She catches sight of her reflection as she's about to go down and only then sees how pale she is — a strange kind of pallor that seems to come from within, since the sun has coloured her skin for weeks and brought out freckles. Beneath the suntan, her face is bloodless. She rubs some blush into her cheeks and puts on a little lipstick, but somehow these touches only make it worse. When Marcie sees her, her face falls. But she takes Clare's hands and squeezes them together.

'Clare, honey. Are you sure you're up to this evening? You look pale, and I know you've been feeling under the cosh lately.'

'Aren't we all under the cosh here? But I'm fine, thank you,' she says. Marcie smiles.

'Tonight's going to be so much fun. We can pretend to be normal wives, leading normal lives. Won't that be grand? Just for a little while,' she says. Her eyes sparkle, and Clare wonders if she even remembers their tight exchange in the bat room. Marcie takes a deep breath; her grip on Clare's hands gets tighter, and tighter.

'Perhaps we are normal wives. Perhaps this is just what life is like,' says Clare. Marcie drops her hands at once and takes a step back, shaking her head.

'Don't say that. Well! Try to enjoy yourself, anyway, Clare. It could be your last chance to before you go home, and the only exciting evening we're likely to get this summer. God, I need a drink.' She stalks away, the high heels of her silver shoes tapping and glinting, and Clare watches after her with a seasick feeling, thinking how wrong she is. A more exciting evening, exciting for all the wrong reasons, crowds the steps of this one.

It's Friday night, and in two nights' time, on Sunday, Ettore will come, the farm will be raided and she must play her part, and play it well, or risk harm coming to him. The thought stuns her, blindsides her, every time it comes into her head. It's like a sudden cacophony that drowns out everything as the other guests start to arrive, and Pip appears from his room in his best clothes, and Boyd comes up from the sitting room with Leandro at his side and a glass of whisky in his hand. The other guests are the doctor who treated Ettore's leg and Clare when she fainted, his wife and teenage son and daughter; a stern man called Labriola, a retired teacher who likes to practise speaking English; and Alvise and Carlotta Centasso, a witless pair from Gioia too

424

dazzled by Leandro's wealth and Marcie's jewels to mind that they are American *arrivistes*. They drink milky, almond-scented *rosoglio* on the terrace and Clare gulps at hers, longing to feel numbed, to feel serene for a time. The drink is hot in her stomach, but doesn't settle it.

'Are you feeling all right?' says Boyd, close to her ear. Clare shrinks from him; she can't help it. She nods wordlessly and moves away towards Leandro, who is grand and groomed in his evening suit, a black silk tie fastened with a perfect knot at his throat. So it's by pure chance that she's standing next to him and not next to her husband when Federico Manzo comes up the terrace and crosses to Leandro to murmur some message in his ear.

Clare is hung; she can't take her eyes off him, or move away, however much she wants to. All she sees now are the muscles beneath his clothes, and the ease with which they overpowered her; she sees his mouth and instantly recalls the feel of its odd shape against her own, and the taste of his saliva; his broad hands, and how just one was wide enough to prevent her breathing. She rocks back on her heels; wants to run but is paralysed. She feels stripped naked, humiliated; the blood roars in her ears and when Federico turns to go he looks at her and the glance is sullen, coldly hostile. For the short moment his eyes brush over her it's like the unwanted touch of his hands again, the intimate press of his body. It turns her cold.

When he's gone she grabs at Leandro's arm without thinking, only needing the support. He smiles down at her and then notices her distress and draws her immediately to one side.

'What is it, Chiarina?' He uses the diminutive of her Italian name with such concern, such warmth it almost undoes her. She swallows tears.

'Federico,' she says quietly.

'What of him?' he says, but Clare can't answer. She looks away, looks down, and can't prevent a shudder going through her. There's a long pause. 'He did this, didn't he?' says Leandro then, in a very different tone; touching one finger softly to her chin. Clare nods. 'But why? I thought it was my nephew you'd fallen for?'

'You *know*?' says Clare, stricken.

'But of course. My dear, not much goes on around here that I don't know about. Tell me — why did Fede hit you?'

'He just . . . I was alone, in town. He must have followed me, and . . . ' She can't finish this, can't say the words. Leandro's face gets that dragged downward look she's come to recognise — his features weighted with anger, black eyes snapping.

'Forgive me. This is my fault,' he says, in a voice flat with fury. 'He attacked one of the kitchen girls last year. Spun me a yarn about how they'd been courting, and how she'd given her consent and was lying about it after the event. I gave him the benefit of the doubt.'

'No. The fault is mine,' says Clare. 'He saw me . . . he knows about Ettore.' She raises her eyes to him wretchedly. 'Don't tell my husband! Please, tell no one. Not even Marcie,' she whispers.

'No, no. We won't speak of it. And Federico Manzo won't set foot here again, I promise you that. I've no need for a man like that — no better than an animal. It's the duty of the men in my household to *protect* the women, not endanger them! I'll go now and see to it. Are you steady now? Here — take another drink.' He passes her his own glass and watches her drink, then steers her by her elbow to Marcie's side, where she can hide in the shadow of his wife's radiance.

'There you are, Clare,' says Marcie, seeming to think nothing of the way her husband deposits her there. 'Have you ever been to watch the horse races back in England? I've never seen one — is it fun? Mr Centasso was just telling me about his new racehorse — a thoroughbred, no less! The *signori* here do love their horse races. Oh, do promise you'll invite me to watch your horse run, Mr Centasso,' she says. 'And I promise I'll bet on it.' Clare watches after Leandro as he excuses himself and leaves the terrace.

A short while later Leandro draws her to one side again, and walks her to the far end of the terrace from which the *aia* and the main gates are just visible. He points, and in the wash of light from the farm a figure is visible, walking stiffly and fast, as if propelled. Clare recognises Federico at once.

'Dismissed. From my service and both of my households. His father will have words with me; perhaps he'll leave as well. But some things are rightly done, even if they make waves.' He pats her shoulder gently. 'You won't see him again.

I'm sorry that harm has come to you here.'

'Thank you,' Clare whispers. Leandro gives a weary grunt.

'Don't thank me. I brought you here.'

'But you are kind. When you told me of your . . . old life, I thought that you couldn't really have left it behind. I thought you must still be that way, and ruthless, and a . . . bad man. But you're a good man, Mr Cardetta.'

'Good?' He shakes his head, almost angrily. 'No, you mustn't say that. You mustn't think that. I don't deserve to be thought of as good.'

'Well, you've been kind to me. You knew of my . . . bad behaviour, and you didn't inform my husband. And now you've dismissed a loyal servant, without question, on my behalf. I will always think well of you.'

'Your bad behaviour?' He smiles. 'When I saw Marcie for the first time, up on stage in her sequins and feathers, she cracked open my chest and stole my heart right out of it. I was married at the time — I'd made promises I ought to have kept. But there are things we can't foresee, and things we can't help but do, where the heart is involved.' He taps two fingers lightly on her chest, against the bone. 'How can love be a sin? Hate is a sin, but love — never.' Clare's eyes are hot with tears. She looks down, struggles to hold them.

'I don't know what to do,' she says.

'Ah,' says Leandro. 'I can't help you there, I'm afraid.'

'Please don't send us away yet. Don't send me away with my husband.'

428

'Sooner or later it'll have to happen.'

'But not yet. I need . . . some more time. I need a few more days.'

'Very well. But listen to me, Chiara. Nothing is set in stone. If you don't love your husband, then don't stay with him. It could be even more dangerous to do so than to leave him.'

'Dangerous? You said that before — will you tell me what you mean?' she says, but Leandro shakes his head.

'Now is not the time — look, they're bringing out the supper dishes. Try not to be afraid. Of any of it, Chiara.'

Anna and another of the kitchen girls have brought out platters of meat and vegetables, cheeses, bread and wine, and the table gleams with oil and silverware. A confusing mixture of Italian and English is spoken, and the red wine dulls their teeth as it brightens their eyes, and Clare feels a million miles from it. She hears herself answer questions directed at her, but minutes later can't remember what she's said. She's aware of quizzical looks aimed at her, as though the guests aren't sure if they're misunderstanding her English, or her Italian, or simply her.

She never questioned, for a second, the rightness of the coming raid. She accepted it as part of the war, and that Ettore would choose to make war on his own uncle didn't really register. But now she must question how well she's repaying Leandro's kindness by aiding the attack; by not warning him. But the choice is simple: she must betray Ettore, or betray

Leandro — so it's no choice at all. She thinks of the massacre at the Girardi place; she thinks of the unarmed peasants, shot down by men hidden safe behind high stone walls. Picturing Ettore in such danger makes her knees ache, her stomach swoop with fear. *He is here in Gioia,* Ettore had said, meaning his uncle. *It will go easier.* But Leandro was at the *masseria,* and still would be on Sunday. The raid would not go easy. When she realises this Clare jolts upright in her seat, wanting to run to Gioia, to warn Ettore, to make him call it off.

After dinner they go down to the sitting room. The music starts and Marcie dances with each of her guests, and with her husband, time and again. She laughs, and flirts, and smiles, smiles, smiles. Such total abandon that Clare finds it bewildering, as though Marcie is a language she can't pick up. More and more, it bothers her. *He's a dirty peasant.* Pip watches Marcie with a cautious kind of smile, and takes his turn dancing with her, and also dances with the doctor's daughter. She's a year older and a head taller than him, but it's the daughter who blushes, and Clare tries to see Pip through her eyes — a handsome young man, not a boy; least of all a child. Surely he wouldn't disappear from her life if she disappeared from Boyd's? Not now, when he is so grown. Not unless Clare stayed in Puglia with Ettore. She has to remind herself that Ettore has made no such invitation, and then she thinks that perhaps he might, when he hears about the child. Her thoughts pace around in this circle, again and again; she's like the *aia* dogs at the ends of their chains, dizzy and tired. The party is a kind of madness; they're laughing as the ceiling cracks, dancing as the ground falls out beneath their feet. *Madness.* Clare declines several invitations to dance until one comes from Pip — a wordless, almost shy extension of his hand, a declaration of peace.

The dance is an old-fashioned waltz, and though Marcie and Leandro are spinning, filling the floor, Pip leads Clare cautiously, holding her as if she might break. His face is flushed from the heat, the dancing and the wine; a stubborn lock of hair has escaped the oil he's combed through it. Clare tips her head back to see him clearly, and then smiles slightly.

'You've got taller this summer, you know. You're growing so fast I can almost see it happening.' Once he would have been pleased, but now he frowns a little. Clare needs to weed out the things she said to him when he was a child, and find a new way to talk to him. 'You made the doctor's daughter blush,' she says, and at this he looks pleased.

'I don't know why, it was only a dance.'

'I think she'd like another,' she says, and smiles again. Leandro turns Marcie too close to the gramophone; she shrieks in dismay as her heel bumps the table leg and jolts the needle from the groove. There's a loud, awful tearing sound, and laughter. Clare flinches from the noise, and then the sudden silence.

'Clare, what's wrong? I mean . . . there's something really wrong, isn't there?' says Pip.

'Oh, Pip . . . ' She shakes her head.

431

'You *have* to tell me what it is — you promised.' He sets his jaw when he's said this, and for a few moments Clare says nothing. The music restarts and the dancing with it. Beneath her hand Clare feels Pip's shoulder sag as the tension, the fake belligerence, leaves him. He takes a deep breath and lets it out slowly. 'I don't understand any of this,' he says helplessly. 'Please, Clare. I can't stand you not saying . . . don't you trust me?'

'Darling, of course I trust you. You're . . . you're my best friend. I want you to know you'll be safe. Whatever happens, you'll be safe.'

'What do you mean, whatever happens? What's going to happen?'

In that moment Clare has another choice — to keep her word to Ettore, and say nothing of the raid, or to win back Pip's trust and keep him safe when the trouble begins. She hesitates, but she has to warn him. The thought of him hearing strange sounds on Sunday night and blundering down into danger is too dreadful.

'Swear to me you won't repeat what I'm about to tell you to anybody. Swear it,' she whispers. Shocked, wide-eyed, Pip nods. 'Swear it, Pip?'

'I swear it.'

'There's going to be a raid. Here, at the *masseria* . . . you know what we saw in Gioia? The gangs, and the beatings? It's a war, Pip, and . . . and Ettore is one of the people fighting it.'

'He's going to attack his own uncle?'

'No, no — he's not leading it. I think . . . I don't think he likes the idea. But raiders will come, and he will be one of them. They don't

432

want to hurt anybody — it's very important for you to understand that.' She thinks of Ludo, of the other guards laughing as he flicked the whip at the naked man, making him graze. Ettore wants to kill Ludo Manzo. 'Not you or your father, not Marcie or Leandro. In fact, Ettore thought his uncle would be in Gioia, out of the way . . . '

'Then why would they attack this place?' Pip's voice is tight with nerves. 'We have to warn Marcie and Leandro!'

'No! No, you promised me, Pip — you *swore* you wouldn't!' She grips his arms so hard that cramp starts in the heels of her hands.

'Ow! All right! But . . . what do they want? If it's not to hurt anybody?'

'I . . . I'm not sure. Perhaps they only want to show that they can do *something*. Perhaps they only want to be heard — and treated better.'

'What . . . what should I do?' He swallows convulsively, fearfully.

'Don't be frightened, Pip, and don't do anything. Stay up in your room. Does the door lock? Then lock it. Don't come down no matter what you hear, and you'll be safe. Promise me you'll do as I say! And please, please, say nothing. If the guards know they're coming . . . ' It's Clare's turn to swallow, because her mouth is dry, her throat in a chokehold. 'If they're ready for them, then people will die. Do you understand?'

Dumbly, Pip nods, and Clare sees him glance around and realise that they've stopped dancing even though the music is still blaring. He looks at Marcie, at Leandro, at the doctor's pretty

433

daughter making eyes at him from across the room. She can see him trying to assimilate what she's said, struggling to continue with real life now that he has this unreal knowledge; now that the stakes have changed so drastically. 'If only we'd gone,' she murmurs, too quietly for him to hear. 'If only we'd gone right after what we saw in Gioia, like I wanted to. Before any of the rest of this happened, and we came to this point.' But though she'd do anything to keep Pip safe, she can't regret Ettore — can't regret loving him; can't regret the child now planted in her. She holds Pip tightly, subtly leading him to the end of their dance, and realises that Sunday night, when she opens the door to the *masseria*, might be the last time she ever sees Ettore. She and Pip dance on, woodenly, disjointedly, as if they can't hear the music.

Late in the evening Clare walks out under the archway to stand by the doors with Boyd and the Cardettas and see off the last of the guests. Pip has gone to bed; he didn't seem to enjoy himself much after Clare spoke to him, even though Marcie jollied and cajoled him, and looked hurt when he didn't respond. The Centassos' little trap pony spooks at the *aia* dogs as it trots past them, and Clare takes a lungful of the night air, which somehow tastes different to that within the *masseria*. There are few stars and no sounds of night birds or insects; there's a preternatural stillness, hunkered down like a stalking animal. Movement catches Clare's eye and she sees a fragile curl of ash, drifting down from the sky like a dirty snowflake; then she notices the tang of

434

smoke, and turns to glance at Leandro. He's staring northwards, where an ugly orange glow is smudged along the sky, and at once they're all uneasy; at the colour of the fiery sky, and the fixed way Leandro stares at it. The fire isn't close, but it's on his land.

'Marcie, take our guests inside,' says Leandro. She's still waving after the Centassos, though they haven't turned to see. 'Marcie!' he barks. She starts, turns to him. 'Go inside.'

'What's up, honey?' she says. But then Ludo Manzo appears through the gates on his horse, cantering towards them. He has his rifle in one hand, his face is streaked with sweat and soot and has a murderous look. When he reaches Leandro he yanks the horse's mouth to halt it and unleashes a violent burst of his accented Italian.

'What's he saying, Clare?' says Boyd, at her side. Clare shakes her head.

'I can't follow it.' Her heart is racing with nerves — that this is somehow related to her, to Federico's dismissal.

Ludo and Leandro talk for a short time, then the overseer wheels his horse around and rides away fast. Leandro turns to them, and his face is set and grave. But he doesn't look at Boyd, or at his wife — he looks at Clare. And Clare goes cold.

'What is it?' she says, not caring if Boyd wonders at her question. Leandro's face twists then; he sucks in a breath. 'What is it?' she says again, with an edge of panic on the words. 'Tell me!'

435

'I must go. I have business . . . ' he says, still looking at Clare. 'Go inside. Stay there.'

'Sure we will, darling,' says Marcie. 'Come on, Clare. And you, Boyd — whatever this is I'm sure Ludo and Leandro can handle it . . . Do come on. It's best to do as he says when there's trouble on the farm.' She's still glimmering in her finery, fluttering her hands to herd them. Leandro turns and starts to follow his overseer, but Clare runs after him. She takes his arm.

'Is it him? Is it Ettore? Tell me!' she whispers. In the distance the sky glows with steady menace, and smoke blooms upwards like some vast tree. Leandro stares down at her; she sees anger, pain and something else in his eyes — something intractable.

'Go inside, Chiara,' he says, so adamantly she has no choice but to obey. Boyd puts his arm around her shoulders when she reaches him. Clare's head feels detached from her body; she stumbles, letting Boyd steer her.

'You understood more of what was said than you're letting on, didn't you?' says Boyd. 'What were they saying, Clare?' The *masseria* door closes behind them with a thump, and Clare can't bring herself to speak. She has never been more afraid.

# Ettore

When Ettore tells Gianni and Benedetto that he's found Livia's murderer, their silence is long and has a solidity that seems unbreakable. But Bianca breaks it; Livia's mother. She's on her stool by the stove, and she makes a little sound like a whimper of fear, but when Ettore looks at her he doesn't see fear. He sees hunger. Fat black flies buzz around in circles, drowsy after dark. The noise of their wings is almost more than Ettore can stand — he feels he could snatch them out the air with his eyes closed. He's so on edge his eyes catch every movement, his ears every sound. The air sits high up in his chest; he can't unknot his shoulders. Not while Federico Manzo walks and breathes and smiles. He doesn't think about Chiara — he can't. Livia is enough, and thinking that the same man has touched Chiara might tip him off this point of fine balance, and break his tenuous grip on control. Images of her distended pupils, her bloody lip, appear in front of his eyes now and then, and he twitches his mind away from them. There's nothing for him to sit on in the cramped room; Livia's two brothers sit on the mattress with their legs out in front and their backs against the wall; Ettore crouches on one knee in front of them to deliver his message, like a supplicant.

Gianni is staring at him as though it's Ettore he would kill. He has always made Ettore feel like a boy, ineffectual as a child, and as he draws breath Ettore thinks Gianni will ask if he's ready for what will come; or tell him to leave it to him and Benedetto. But he doesn't.

'And you are sure of this, beyond all doubt?'

'Yes.'

'It will be hard to get him by himself. It should be done with as little noise as possible. I've no time for a pitched battle with his *mazzieri* scum companions. Can you think of a way? Can you get him to come out of your uncle's house?'

'Not without arousing suspicion.'

'Yes. We must be nameless, faceless,' says Benedetto, in his bass voice. 'It only matters that he knows us, in his last moments. That he knows it's for *her*.' There's a dull fire in his eyes; a gleam of famished violence.

'He goes to and from Gioia to the *masseria*, you say. Does he ever go alone?'

'Sometimes, but if he did so it would be by car.'

'Then it will have to be here, in town. You say he attacked your new woman, so he must go around by himself sometimes. We'll keep watch — one of us must always watch for him, in turn. If the opportunity comes, it must not be missed.' Benedetto rolls himself a cigarette and lights it calmly; the scratch of the match gives Ettore a shiver.

'Yes.' Gianni nods once with the word.

'You first, Ettore. Then Gianni the day after. Then me.' Through the haze of his cigarette smoke Benedetto's face is murky and indistinct.

'I can get a gun,' says Ettore, thinking of the

pistol Paola took from Masseria Molino.

'Forget it,' says Gianni. 'Too quick.'

'But to force him to some quiet place?' he says. Gianni glances at his brother.

'Yes. Let whichever one of us is watching for him keep hold of it,' says Benedetto. The three men nod. Then they have nothing more to say to each other and the silence returns, and Ettore can't stand the buzzing of the flies and the stinging smoke another second. He rises abruptly from the floor and turns to go, and Bianca catches his arm. Ettore looks down into her rabbity face, all scored with years of grief and hardship; her stained eyes are clouding up with trachoma.

'Don't stay your hand, boy,' she says, in her soft, whispery way. 'Think of my girl, and don't stay your hand. She'll have justice no other way.' Ettore pulls his arm free, nods again and leaves. His flesh feels as raw as the rest of him — he can't tolerate her touch.

Keeping to the smallest, blackest streets he can, Ettore makes his way to Vico Iovia, where the lights at home are out and the doors are shut, and only the smell of that morning's spilt sewage betrays that anybody lives there at all. He lets himself in quietly, to not wake the baby or Valerio; lies down on the bed next to Paola and reaches for her hand. When he finds it he meshes their fingers, like he did when they were little and Valerio beat their mother. He squeezes her fingers tightly enough to know it must hurt, but Paola doesn't flinch.

'You spoke to them?' she says, in the lowest of murmurs.

439

'Yes.'

'And?'

'As soon as we can, we'll take the debt from his flesh.' He says this dispassionately, when what he feels is passion, conviction. He has seen soldiers, just boys, blown apart in the war; seen their blood pooling, warm and dark, in pocks of frozen mud. He has seen his fiancée beaten and raped and left to die; his mother killed in two days and a night by cholera — scoured out from the inside. So much death, so many ways to die and no such thing as justice in any of it. Life is not cheap, but death is easy — this he knows. Never before has he actively planned a killing; never before has a killing been so right. His conscience is clear. Murder is just another term, like prosecution, like unlawful, like judicial process, that belongs to the wealthy, not to the peasants. The *braccianti* have always had their own kind of justice.

Paola turns to face him. He can't see her but he can feel her breath on his cheek, and the weight of her plaited hair as it falls against his arm.

'Livia can be at peace once it is done. But can you?' she says.

'Yes,' he says at once. 'That is, perhaps. Perhaps no; perhaps never. But it wants doing, either way.'

'Can it not wait just a few days, Ettore?' she says urgently. 'Just a few days! We should do nothing to put them on their guard before the raid. Afterwards, there need be no such concern. Three more days, only.'

440

'It's already begun, Paola. From this moment, when I leave here, one of us will be watching for him, and if the moment comes I won't let it pass. Any more than Benedetto or Gianni will. Perhaps we'll find him after the raid, perhaps before.' Paola takes a deep breath and exhales slowly.

'So perhaps he will be lynched before Sunday, and the corporals will be twitchy, and we must be at dell'Arco at eleven at night to begin the attack — we'll have to leave Gioia so soon after dark! I don't like it, Ettore . . . there's so much at stake.'

'This is how it must be, Paola. And we can attack dell'Arco later, if you wish. But not with Chiara's help.'

'She'd better do as she says she will.' Paola is angry, anxious. 'If she chickens out I'll skin her myself, and — ' She cuts herself off when Ettore's grip tightens convulsively. He feels the little bones in her hand shifting. 'Sorry. I didn't mean it,' she says.

'She will do as she said she will. She has always done what she's said she'll do.'

'Tell that to her husband,' Paola snorts.

'Enough, Paola. Please.'

'I need you to work! I need your wage. You're no good to us skulking around Gioia, waiting to ambush this man. He's looking for you too, don't forget.'

'One day of three, I will stay in town. The work is drying up, anyway — nobody's being hired all week long. And you keep telling me that after Sunday we'll be rich and well fed. And he put a gun to your son's head, Paola. Have you forgotten that?'

'I haven't forgotten.'

'Then stop! You can't always be the boss of everything. This is the way things must go, and I'm not going to argue with you about it.' There's a long pause; he relaxes his grip on his sister's hand and lets their fingers slide apart.

'All right then,' she says softly. Ettore grabs her plait and tugs it gently, like when they were little. Then he gets up, tilts his hat low over his face and goes back out into the night.

★ ★ ★

He spends the next day moving steadily around town: from the castle walls to the Chiesa Madre; from the Teatro Comunale to the market stalls in Piazza XX Settembre; Santoiemma's wood mill to the bakeries; Via Roma to the station and the slaughterhouse. He talks to a few men he trusts; puts the word in the right ears that Federico Manzo is sought. That he has a debt to pay. The workers know who Federico is — his harelip makes him easily recognisable, and besides, of late he has been prominent, in his black shirt and his emblems. Before that, even, he was famous for being Ludo Manzo's son, and none of the workers have any reason to love Ludo. But no word comes back to Ettore all day. No useful word — Federico has been seen driving Cardetta's black car out towards the *masseria*; he hasn't been seen coming back. Troubled, Ettore asks after his uncle's whereabouts, and hears that Leandro drove the red car in that direction himself earlier the same day, and has

442

also not yet returned.

Febrile with impatience, Ettore walks the same loose circuit of Gioia again and again. Into cobblers' shops and scrapyards and blacksmiths and bars. He's angry, and disappointed — he wanted to be the one to find Federico, and he'd wanted it to be that day. No waiting, no delay; the man should not be allowed to enjoy another day of freedom. The stolen pistol is cool and heavy, tucked into the back of his trousers, concealed beneath his waistcoat. Ettore fantasises about drawing it out and putting the barrel to Federico's head. *Come with me*, he would say. With all of Benedetto's stony depth, and Gianni's emotionless delivery. *Come with me*. And Federico would go with him, and what was coming would come. And after that, he's not quite sure what he'll do with all his thoughts.

As night falls he buys some cheap, end-of-day bread and takes it to Pino and Luna. Luna slices it, rubs it with a finger dipped in olive oil and then the open side of a cut chilli pepper. They eat it with mashed fava beans and dark green chicory, and only water to drink, and Ettore tells them about Federico. Luna stops chewing, and can't seem to swallow. They have stools to sit on, but no table. They eat from cracked bowls in their laps, with their feet tucked beneath them like schoolchildren; tall Pino hunched and folded with the ease of long habit. He has worked all day and has the smell of hard labour on him, and he eats ravenously, regardless of what is said. But when his bowl is empty he clears his throat.

'When you find him, I'll go with you,' he says.

Ettore shakes his head, puzzled. Pino always avoids violence.

'No. Why get involved? It's not your fight — keep your hands clean.'

'I saw him, Ettore,' says Pino, and his face shows his revulsion. 'I saw what he was doing to Chiara. What he would have done, if I hadn't put my boot in his guts. A man like that is like a mad dog — the duty falls on all of us to put him down. Or do what? Wait for him to attack my Luna next?' He casts a glance at his young wife, whose eyes have gone wide in alarm at her husband's words. 'Besides,' says Pino, taking Luna's hand. 'We loved Livia too.'

'We did, poor Livia,' says Luna. She looks at Ettore. 'You *must* keep our Pino safe. You must.'

'Manzo will be by himself. Helpless, like the women he preys on. We will be four strong when we take him,' he says.

'Yes. But still,' says Luna.

Ettore watches the house on Via Garibaldi all through the night; tucked out of sight in a doorway. He sees a gang of blackshirts about their work, armed with pistols and cudgels, but Federico is not with them. The night is long, and mild, and with his eyes fixed on the street door Ettore's mind wanders, skirting the weird and hazy world between sleep and waking. His thoughts turn into dreams and then jolt back into reality, over and over. He has Chiara in his arms; he is in the trenches at Isonzo; he is listening to Livia and the sweet, slight lisp when she spoke; he is a boy, hunting fossils in the dry stone walls; he is falling into the darkness of the

444

hell mouth at Castellana. He's made of stone, but at the same time he's as weightless as the air. He's smoke and smuts, blowing in the breeze, and Chiara is a dream he once had — a dream of longing, of another life completely.

At daybreak on Friday morning Ettore walks back into the old streets of Gioia and hands the pistol to Gianni, who takes it without a word. Then he goes to the church of Sant'Andrea, lies down on a pew and wraps his arms across his face to block out the light. He sleeps for hours, and when he wakes is on his feet at once, restless and hungry. It's dark when Benedetto comes to find him; evening but not yet night. Ettore is in the bar opposite the castle, watching men argue and lose money at *zecchinetta*, when Livia's oldest brother puts his head through the door, catches his eye and nods. Ettore's pulse triples; he has to force himself to walk, not run.

'Ready?' says Benedetto. 'We got lucky — Manzo was walking back towards town, all alone. Gianni was coming back from Vallarta with some others and saw him. He sent a friend back to tell me. He was walking out in the middle of nowhere, all alone! I think God must want him dead, too.'

'He must do. Why walk, and not drive?'

'Who knows — who cares? You want to get a knife? A club?'

'Gianni has the gun? Then no,' he says, when Benedetto nods. 'But I must . . . ' Ettore pauses, about to say he must fetch Pino. In truth he doesn't want his friend anywhere near this — it will be brutal, bloody. It will be everything Pino

445

is not, and with anything like this there's risk. There's danger for all of them, of being discovered, of there being reprisals. But ignoring Pino's request would be an insult to him, and the danger is small if they are smart about it. 'I must go and bring Pino. He was fond of Livia. He wants to help.'

'Come on then, and be quick,' says Benedetto. Spoken *sotto voce*, his words sound like the grinding of rocks. 'I'll go with you.'

They walk out in darkness, along the south road, and turn off about three kilometres short of Leandro's farm to go across country. Climbing over walls, trudging across stubble fields, stumbling over rocks. They don't speak. Benedetto carries a club over his shoulder, as casually as a work tool; Pino and Ettore have empty hands, and none of them speak. Then out of the darkness looms the huge, pale shape of a straw rick, three metres high, waiting to be taken to a barn. With a slight misgiving, Ettore realises that they're on dell'Arco land. Paola will be furious. But at the foot of the rick is Gianni's dark, triumphant form, and in the light from his lantern, face down on the ground at his feet, is Federico. Hog-tied, hands to ankles behind his back, a filthy old rag stuffed into his mouth and a cut above one eyebrow oozing blood. Ettore feels Pino hesitate — a hung moment between steps, a quiet intake of breath. He turns to his friend.

'If you want to go, it's no shame,' he says. 'You should. This is not your problem.' Pino swallows, and shakes his head. Gianni and Benedetto watch him steadily. Then Gianni almost smiles.

He gives Federico a poke with the toe of his boot.

'Stick around. Haven't you ever seen old women watching a riot from up on a balcony? Gossiping and chewing their gums? You can be like one of them,' he says, and Benedetto grins.

'I'll stay. For Livia,' says Pino. Ettore clasps his shoulder briefly. Then all eyes turn to the figure on the ground.

Federico's eyes are mad with anger; he's breathing hard, kicking up the dust under his nose. When he sees Ettore he tries to say something, tries to spit out the rag.

'I think he has something to say to you, Ettore,' says Gianni, crouching over Federico like a hunter over a kill.

'Let's hear it,' says Ettore. Gianni shrugs, reaches around and pulls the rag from Federico's mouth. Benedetto lifts the club down off his shoulder and rests it in the palm of his hand. His eyes never leave his sister's killer.

'You!' says Federico. He tries to spit but has no saliva. 'So this is because I felt up your English whore? Are you in *love* with her?' he asks scathingly.

'I made a promise, nearly every day for the past seven months,' says Ettore. 'Do you know what the promise was?' He feels calm now; the unnatural calm on the far side of crisis. Federico struggles against his ties, breathing through clenched teeth, saying nothing. 'I promised my fiancée I would find out who attacked her, and left her to die, and that that man would burn.' As he says this Ettore realises why Gianni has brought them to this straw rick — he realises that Livia's brother has the same idea. He crouches down, speaks close to Federico's ear. 'You're a dead man, Federico Manzo. How does it feel?'

'You're all dead. *You're all dead!*' Federico shouts, nearly incoherent with anger.

'How many have you raped? How many killed?' says Benedetto. Federico grins hysterically.

'Hundreds! Fucking *hundreds*! I've had more pussy than any one of you limp-dicks will *ever* have. You'd better kill me, *cafoni*! You'd better kill me or you'll all die, and your families with you!'

'Don't worry,' Benedetto chuckles. 'We're going to.'

'So I had your sweetheart, did I?' Federico leers at Ettore. 'Fucked her to death, did I? I wish I'd known she was yours. I'd have taken more time on her.'

'Son of a *whore*!' Pino exclaims. 'Can't you hear yourself? What kind of animal are you?'

'I'm not afraid of you! Any of you — you see that? I'm not afraid of you!' But Federico's eyes say different; his face says different, all twisted up, writhing. Ettore nods.

'Her name was Livia Orfino. I loved her. We all did — these are her brothers, Gianni and Benedetto Orfino.' He points to them in turn. 'You've had this coming a long time, and if you'd been even a little bit sorry I'd have knocked you out cold before this next part. But you're not sorry. You're proud. And you tried to do the same thing to Chiara. So.' He shrugs.

Before Federico can say anything else Ettore stuffs the rag back into his mouth, muffling his stream of curses and threats. Benedetto hoists him up roughly, onto his shoulder; Gianni and Ettore climb up onto the rick and haul Federico up behind them. Then they jump down and step back. Ettore catches sight of Pino's face, bloodless as bone, his mouth slightly open in horror. Benedetto strikes a match and walks right around the rick, setting it alight every few paces. Then he rejoins the others, as smoke starts to rise. They stand shoulder to shoulder, the three of them, with Pino edging back behind them, breathing hard. The darkness gets a flicker to it; a breeze teases the flames, puffs at the smoke. The quiet rushing sound of it gets louder and louder by steady increments. Ettore watches, and feels nothing. This is cause and effect. This is the logical end of this man's life. He feels no pleasure, no satisfaction. It's a thing that must be done, and he's relieved to have fulfilled his promise at last. *Cause and effect.* The night vanishes into a storm of yellow and orange; the minutes tick by. At some point Federico gets the rag out of his mouth, and for a while they can hear him screaming at the heart of the buffeting roar of the fire. Ettore watches, and thinks nothing, and is only half aware of Pino lurching away to one side to throw up.

Once the screams stop Benedetto cuffs Ettore's shoulder to rouse him. He nods his head at the darkness.

'Time to go. They'll be able to see this right back in Gioia,' he says. Ettore blinks — his eyes feel gritted up, stinging from the smoke; he's sweating from the heat of it. He nods and turns to follow. He's the last — Gianni's marching off, Pino's already fifty metres away, at the edge of the fire's glow, about to vanish into darkness. Then there's a sudden strange noise up ahead, and a yell, and a man on a horse comes galloping out of the darkness with an overarm swing of a cudgel that smacks into Pino's head. Pino drops full length, felled like a tree. Ettore hears Benedetto shouting, a massive roar like the bear he is; he sees the big man swinging his own cudgel and bringing down another man from his horse. The horse's eyes are white and rolling, it shies away from the fire and bolts. On instinct Ettore drops to the ground as the man who knocked Pino down rides past him, and the club swings over his head with a whistle. He's up and running before the man can turn his horse.

'Pino! *Get up!*' he shouts. But Pino stays down. There's the deafening crack of a shotgun nearby. Ettore feels something snag his shirtsleeve; there's a sting like ant bites on his arm, and to his right the ground erupts into dust and fragments. He changes course, zig-zagging as another shot is fired, and misses him. He sprints as fast as he can, with stones rolling under his boots. His weak leg wobbles, threatens to give way; it feels like his heart will explode. There are shouts behind him; he thinks he can still hear Benedetto roaring, or perhaps it's Federico howling. But he's reached Pino, so none of it matters.

The cudgel blow has staved in the side of his head, above his ear. The hideous dent is a hand span long, five centimetres deep in its centre; dark with a matted mess of blood and crushed skin. Pino's eyes are half open, sightless. His face is as perfect as it ever was; there's dust in his hair, and the top two buttons of his shirt are missing. It seems entirely impossible that he has this wound, and that he is gone. Ettore collapses to his knees beside his friend. He puts his fist on Pino's chest, at the open neck of his shirt. For a while he can't make his hand uncurl — can't make the hand do what he tells it. The air in his lungs doesn't work; he's gasping and it feels like he's drowning. When at last he manages to unclench his fist and press his fingers to Pino's throat he knows he won't feel a pulse, not with that gruesome head wound. But still he hopes, like a child.

'Ettore! Move!' shouts Gianni, running by. 'More are coming! *Move!*'

'No,' says Ettore. His voice is thick and slow; he sounds idiotic. 'No. I'm staying with Pino.'

'Benedetto!' Gianni shouts over his shoulder, as he runs on, out of the light into the sheltering dark. The firelight is flickering in Pino's eyes and making him look alive. Ettore puts out a hand to close his lids but it's shaking so badly he doesn't manage it on the first try.

'Pino . . . Not you. Not you,' he says. Then huge hands haul him to his feet and drag him along, stumbling.

'Leave him, boy. If we try to carry him back we'll be caught. Move! Take your own weight and run!'

'Wait,' says Ettore, still struggling to breathe,

451

struggling to speak. 'I think . . . I think Pino's dead.'

'Yes, he's dead,' says Benedetto, his rough voice unsuited to being gentle. 'And it won't help if you die too.' So Ettore runs, and the last vestiges of the child inside him, the last part of him that knew how to laugh, stays behind in the dust, with Pino.

★ ★ ★

When he tells Paola she says nothing. Her eyes blaze and her lips press hard together, and for a while she stands as still as a statue. Then, quick as a snake, she grabs the *pignata* full of soup from the stove and hurls it across the room with a screech that sounds like it's tearing her throat. Then she wets a rag and scrubs frantically at the soot on Ettore's face and hands. Traces that could give him away. When he tells Luna she drops slowly to the floor, buckling downwards, falling in slow motion. She curls herself up, knees to her chin, and then she doesn't move or speak. Ettore knows exactly how she feels. He stays with her the rest of the night, and because her eyes are as sightless as Pino's he doesn't have to hide his tears from her.

'We should have left as soon as the fire was lit. But we wanted to be sure Federico didn't escape — roll clear or something. But he didn't. We could have gone straight away. Or just shot him. No need for a fire that the corporals would see. But we wanted him to pay, you see; wanted him to burn, like Livia burnt with the fever he gave

452

her. Pino shouldn't have come with us at all; I should have told him he had no place there. Livia didn't belong to him, like she did to me, like she did to her brothers. He owed her nothing. I shouldn't have fetched him when we found Federico — I could have lied. I could have said I didn't have time to come and fetch him. It's my fault. All of it,' he says, but Luna shows no sign of having heard him. She stays huddled down where she is, threshed out like the wheat, the living heart of her gone.

★ ★ ★

There's no work on Saturday. Ettore can't stay still so he walks around Gioia del Colle, openly, without caution or his hat tipped low to hide his eyes. He watches the world with flat disregard and waits to be stopped, waits to be arrested, since everybody knows he and Pino were friends. But he isn't stopped. Nobody approaches him, nobody seems to have noticed that something utterly, abhorrently wrong has happened, and Pino is dead. He's incredulous; furious. Pino's body is brought to the police barracks, identified and returned to Luna, whose mother takes custody of it since her daughter is still mute and incapable. Ettore is on the street corner when the barrow comes out with Pino's body on it, and a lad wheels it to the mortuary to be laid out. A growing number of people come to walk alongside it, to accompany him. Pino was well liked, well loved. Ettore doesn't walk with them, though the wrongness of that makes him queasy.

He doesn't feel he has the right. The procession goes past him, and the trolley with its creaking wheels. Some of the followers turn to look at him, puzzled, frowning. He welcomes their disapprobation.

Ettore has the sense of being hundreds of years old; the feeling gets stronger and stronger. He is not Ettore Tarano but merely one of a million *cafoni* who have lived and died in Puglia for centuries. He's one of a silent multitude who have broken themselves against the rocks and hard ground, who have starved and toiled and ground a life out of dust, and afterwards have given back their bones for the privilege. Short lives, anonymous lives; lives lived hand to mouth, with their fleeting moments of joy like tiny sparks that flare and are then snuffed out. He's ancient man, he goes back thousands of years; he has worked with stone tools, then bronze, then iron; his eyes, the colour of the Adriatic, have looked out from his dark face and seen ages creep past, never changing. He is the blood and soul of this land, he is its constant march, and he's tired. So tired.

Paola watches him closely, but when she speaks he can't find the energy to reply. He must walk — when he stands still all those millennia pile up around him, crushing him. And yet he doesn't see how anybody can be expected to carry on when they're as tired as he is.

'Ettore . . . ' says Paola, shaking his arm as the light begins to fade on Sunday. He stares at her from far away, then blinks and looks around. He's in Piazza XX Settembre, frozen in the middle of its triangular space, with no recollection of arriving there. 'I need to know you'll be all right tonight. I need to know you'll come back for it,' she says. Her face is careworn; grey hairs have started to thread through the black. For a second Ettore sees their mother.

'Come back?' he says.

'From wherever the hell you've gone!' She smacks the side of his head with the flat of her hand. She sounds frightened.

'I've gone nowhere. I'll never go anywhere — neither will you.'

'In a few hours we go to dell'Arco — are you listening? We will go as planned and we will attack it, and kill Ludo Manzo, and take what we need. What we deserve. Will you be with us? Your mozzarella might panic if she doesn't see you . . . she might cause trouble — sound the alarm, who the hell knows. So?'

'Chiara?' he says, and the thought of her causes a faint sting, quick as a fitful sigh. Paola shuts her eyes. She takes hold of his sleeve, leans her forehead against his shoulder for a second.

'Please, Ettore. Please don't do this. We need you. Di Vittorio has resigned. He's left Cerignola, and fled north. All the socialists are fleeing north. Everything's falling apart . . . I need you.'

Somehow the warm press of her head reaches him, touching some place that's still tender and living. He reaches up, holds the back of her neck for a moment.

'Don't be frightened, Paola,' he says. 'It's all right. I'll go with you.' With a sudden shimmer of unreality, a sudden slipping of time, he remembers saying the exact same thing to her on her first day of school. His sister looks up at him, relieved.

'All right,' she says, nodding. 'All right. Good.' She steps away and smooths out his torn shirt sleeve, bunched up where she grabbed it. There are three ragged tears in it where lead shot winged him on Friday night; three corresponding scorch lines on the skin underneath. 'Don't wander off again. Don't vanish. Go to Sant'Andrea; I'll fetch you in a few hours, when it's time.' Ettore nods, but when he doesn't move she sighs and takes his arm again. He lets her march him; he has no will of his own. He is callused hands and an aching back; he is wounds and bruises; he comes from nothing, and nowhere. He is deep beneath the ground, falling.

★ ★ ★

In the soft darkness of early night Ettore walks at his sister's side, his breath stifling beneath the scarf tied across his face. Faceless, nameless; one of a number. He moves with them and lets them inform him, this gang of thirty-three souls. There are guns amongst them, tucked into belts and pockets; knives, cudgels. Ettore will be the first in; he has a pistol because he might need to use it on the door guard. He is distant and wholly calm until they are at the top of a slight rise in the land, looking across at Masseria dell'Arco with its lights blazing out, shining from the high white walls. It's beautiful and serene, but a fortress nonetheless. Looking down at it, Ettore feels his heart beat harder. He takes a deep breath in, and with a tingling at the back of his neck he feels himself wake up. It's just like in the war, just like at the Isonzo front; drunk and freezing, thought obliterated by fear and the bursting of shells, and yet when the whistle blew, when the firing started, his mind went crystal clear, and he focused, to the exclusion of all else, on doing what needed to be done — on staying alive.

His throat has gone dry but he's steady. They have circled and approached from the south, to be downwind of the dogs. There's some fine timing to be managed. The gate guard will be silenced just before Ettore goes over the *aia* wall at the corner of the quad, and sprints to the doors at exactly eleven, when Chiara will have them opened from inside. Then he will remove the door guard and the others will cross the *aia* as fast as they can, and be inside before the roof guards have got themselves together to fire down at them. The raiders stand, bunched together, silent. Waiting. One man has a pocket watch in his hand; he squints down at it intently.

'I hope you remembered to wind that thing,' Ettore says softly. There's a low collective chuckle, and beside him he feels Paola relax minutely. At five to eleven the man with the watch nods to another, who sets off with a knife in his hand, low to the ground and fast, towards the gates. They wait, listening hard. There's a tiny noise, like a foot dragged through dust. The nearest dog barks furiously for a moment, then growls and goes quiet. They have no way of knowing if their man has been successful; they can only trust. At one minute to eleven, Ettore gets the nod.

He runs on silent feet down to the wall. It's near two metres high but made of huge chunks of rough *tufo*, easy to climb. He's over in seconds, drops as softly as he can and freezes. The nearest dog growls, gargling the sound deep in its throat. Ettore hardly breathes. The dog comes as close as it can to where he is, sunk in the deep shadow of the wall. It strains on its chain but doesn't bark, and he wonders if it's familiar with his scent, if it recognises him at all. He can't trust in that. When he moves, it will have to be like lightning — as soon as he does he'll be within the dog's reach. He waits, the muscles in his legs burning, wanting to straighten up. But he's waiting for a specific sound. The seconds tick by and his heart thumps twice as fast, and he thinks eleven o'clock must have come and gone, and Chiara has not done as she said she would. As clear as day, he sees the end of them all in gunshots fired from the darkness above, in the jaws of these dogs, in swinging clubs, buckling skulls. Then he hears it. The soft, high sound of her voice coming quietly from inside, and the jangling of the door keys. He has a split second to be grateful and then he's up, running with every shred of effort he can find.

The dog snarls and launches itself at him. He smells the greasy stink of it, its meaty breath as its jaws snap centimetres from his face. But he's past it and the small door is opening, swinging inwards, a hand's breadth, then two. He's through it without hesitation, and has the guard back against the side of the arch, the pistol pressed up under his chin. It's Carlo, his pleasant face sagging in shock.

'Open the big doors,' he whispers. He sees Carlo recognise him, feels him relax a fraction. He drags him forward then thumps him back again, harder, gouging the gun into his soft gullet. 'Do it! Now!'

'Wait, Ettore! Something's wrong!' Chiara has her hands on him, trying to pull him back towards the door. 'Go — run! Please!' she says.

'Chiara, go inside! Lock the door — do as I told you!' Ettore hisses at her. He turns his head to her for a second, sees her fearful face and the pale golden glow of her, fresh and lovely as rain. He can't let himself be distracted.

'No, you must listen to me! Your uncle's here and he's been filling the place with guards since this morning. Armed men — I don't know who they are! I don't know what's happening, but you have to *run*!' Her fingers are digging into his arm; her fear is infectious, and her words have turned him cold. But it's too late, because the *aia* dogs have gone wild, shattering the night with their furious voices. Cursing, Ettore knocks Carlo down with the butt of the pistol, snatches up the keys and fumbles to let Paola and the others in.

'Go now, Chiara!' he shouts, but still she hesitates, and then there's the deafening crack of rifle fire, and everything turns to chaos.

# Clare

On Sunday morning Clare comes down for breakfast on the terrace but finds it deserted; the table laid ready. Every other time, when he's been at the *masseria*, Leandro has already been sitting there, peeling a fig or sipping black coffee. Since the fire on Friday night he has been morose, sunk in thought. Clare listened out for him after the party, late into the night. When she heard him return she went down, barefoot, leaving Boyd awake and bewildered in bed. Leandro was dirty, and stank of smoke; he detached her grasping hands to tell her that Ettore wasn't hurt. Two men were dead — a peasant she wouldn't know, who was one of the arsonists, and Federico Manzo — so badly burnt they'd only known him by the cleft in his upper jaw. How and why Federico came to be in the fire hasn't been established, but Clare felt nothing when she heard of his death. No satisfaction, no remorse. She only had room for her relief that Ettore was not a part of it, or if he was, that he hadn't been caught or hurt. When she got back to bed a faint smell of smoke had transferred to her from Leandro's hands, and Boyd's eyes were wide open, watching her. It was too dark for her to see what expression was in them, and she said nothing.

There's something ineffably sad about the empty breakfast table, so Clare goes up to the roof to

460

look out. It's early and the air is still cool. Behind the muck and milk smell of the dairy is a freshness the sun hasn't yet burnt off. The sky is the colour of forget-me-nots; it makes her think of England, but her homesickness is faint, distant. She can't imagine going back to the quiet routine of mealtimes and letter writing and grocery shopping and tea that was her life before. She might not belong in Puglia but she no longer belongs there, either, and she has no idea where that leaves her. There's movement to the north of the complex and Clare turns to watch. His son is dead, but Ludo Manzo is still at work. Clare sees him emerge from his *trullo* and run his hands through his hair before clamping his hat over it. A man she's never seen before is holding the head of a leggy brown horse, and Ludo sets about appraising the animal, running his hands over joints and muscles, peering at its teeth. The overseer's eyes have black rings around them, and his expression is grimmer than ever, but he moves with his same easy precision, speaks with his same clipped efficiency, and shows no outward signs of grief. Clare watches them for a while, then watches the way the sun, as it climbs, obliterates the subtle shades from the landscape — the mauve smudges under the olive trees; the pastel lemon and orange of the ripe prickly pears; the milk-coffee-coloured ground. The baleful sun bleaches them all away. What softness there is here is fleeting, and fragile.

Hearing the scrape of a chair, somebody coming out to the breakfast table below, Clare

461

goes down. It's Leandro, wearing one of his linen suits but no tie. His shirt and jacket are rumpled, and he hasn't shaved. Uneasily, Clare sits down opposite him. He looks up and smiles faintly, but there's something lacking from it.

'No husband or wives yet this morning, it seems. Nor stepsons,' he says.

'I don't think Boyd's sleeping very well at the moment. I didn't like to wake him.'

'And Pip slumbers on, like all boys prefer to. I remember having to rise early at his age. I remember making a silent pact with the devil that he could have my soul if only he'd let me stay in bed.' He isn't smiling. 'But I always had to get up.'

'At least you got to keep your soul, then,' says Clare.

'Only to lose it at a later date, as it turned out.' He takes a sip of his coffee, then pours a cup for Clare and pushes it towards her. Tiny fronds of steam dance on its surface, and vanish.

'Surely not,' Clare demurs cautiously.

'No, you're right. Just an old man, feeling sorry for himself.'

'Mr Cardetta, I don't think I've ever met anyone less sorry for themselves than you are.' At this he does smile a little, but then he looks away and it slides off his face. For a while they sit in silence, listening to the sparrows bickering around the water trough in the courtyard. 'I've . . . I've been wanting to ask you, Mr Cardetta, what it was you had been about to tell me, that afternoon in Gioia after Federico . . . after I'd come to find my husband. You'd been about to tell me why you'd brought us out here — Pip and me.'

'Had I?' He watches her steadily.

'You said I was in danger.' She feels her stomach clench at the memory of his words, and of that time; the memory of Federico's kiss.

Leandro grunts, and looks down at his coffee. 'Perhaps we are all in danger,' he says.

'Please,' says Clare, in desperation. 'Please. I need to know what you meant.'

'You need to know? Perhaps,' he says, looking up at her again. There's something new in his expression, and it gives her a shiver of warning. 'Perhaps we all have bigger and more pressing things to worry about this day. Wouldn't you say?' Clare doesn't dare answer him. He sips his coffee and looks out across the courtyard. 'It seems so peaceful here, doesn't it? So much goes on beneath the surface. Do you know what the fascists call the peasants, and their uprising? The Bolshevik Menace. What do you say to that?'

'What ought I to say?' says Clare.

'Does it seem apt, to you? You've got to know my nephew, and you've been here many weeks. Do the peasants fight for socialist ideals? Do they fight to overthrow the senate, and install a communist state?'

'It seems to me that they fight for the right to earn enough money to feed themselves, and their families.'

'Exactly!' Leandro thumps the table with the flat of his hand. 'And who could condemn them for it?'

'Only . . . those blinkered by prejudice and . . . greed.'

'*Exactly*, Chiarina. Exactly. What then should

the landowners and proprietors do? What should they do when their farms are attacked, their crops burnt, their animals killed and carried off? What should they do when money they haven't agreed to pay is demanded with menaces?'

'I don't know, Mr Cardetta.' He glares at her with a slow, deep anger in his eyes; jabs one index finger at her for a second and then lowers it.

'I make a loss, you know. It *costs* me money to run this place — such is the way of things when a country almost bleeds itself dry on the battlefield; and when it never bloody well rains. I wanted to show that the land could be improved, and relations between farmers and workers needn't be bad. I've paid higher wages than any other man near Gioia. I've been fair to the *giornatari*; they've been well fed and watered in my fields . . . '

'You've employed Ludo Manzo, who beats and mocks them.'

'Ah. Ludo Manzo. Is he the reason I'm attacked by arsonists, then?' Leandro's voice has gone dangerously quiet. Clare swallows. 'Is he the reason I'm lumped in with all the other *masserie*?'

'I don't know. How can I know? But . . . perhaps it's only the case that . . . ' Clare hesitates. 'Perhaps it's only the case that you can't be on both sides at once.'

'Ha! It's strange to hear my nephew's words coming out of your mouth, Chiara,' he says.

'They're my words, Leandro. You said to me, weeks ago, that down here politics is something

464

that happens to you, not something you can choose to ignore. And you were quite right. These are desperate men, and desperate times, so it seems to me. I don't see that anybody can remain on the fence. Not even you.'

For a long time after Clare says this Leandro watches her; he's inscrutable, she can't tell how he feels or what he thinks, yet she senses hostility, a new chill. Eventually he says:

'No, you're right. It's time I came down off the fence.' And the hairs stand up along her forearms. It sounds like a warning. Then the *aia* dogs start barking, their clamour ringing in the still air and echoing from the walls. Four men on horses have arrived at the front gate. There they pause, the horses tossing their heads and stretching out their necks, while one man talks to the gate guard. Then they carry on around to the rear of the complex. Clare and Leandro watch them until they are out of sight below the walls, and Clare feels anxious knots forming in her gut. The men all have rifles across their backs, or holstered behind their saddles. Leandro says nothing; he turns back to his coffee and reaches for his cutlery as Anna brings out a fresh omelette and puts it in front of him. And even though Clare knows she shouldn't ask she can't help herself.

'Who are those men?'

Leandro chews carefully, and swallows, his eyes on his plate.

'An insurance policy,' he says, not looking up.

'*Signora?*' says Anna, gesturing to the omelette. Her eyelids are puffy and red, as they

465

have been since Federico died. Clare shakes her head, and the girl goes. She doesn't even want her coffee. She doesn't dare ask Leandro what he means, but sweat starts tickling along her hairline, and when she thinks of the coming evening — what she will do, and what will come afterwards — she has a cold, creeping feeling of dread.

All day as they sit, or drink, or read, Clare is gnawed by anxious thoughts. This is what they've done every Sunday of the summer, and yet it now seems as though they're faking it, deliberately killing time, stiff in their roles; as if they all know something's coming, somehow, though only Pip does. Clare sees more mounted men arriving, and then six others in a mule cart, who clamber out and stand beneath the *masseria* walls, stretching out their shoulders and backs, some of them joshing each other, some grim-faced and quiet. She paces the roof, watching, powerless. The door creaks and thumps as several of them come into the complex, vanishing into the servants' rooms and storerooms in the front wing of the quad. After lunch, Clare decides she must warn Ettore. Whatever the purpose of these men is, he thinks the *masseria* will have its normal handful of guards, and that Leandro is in Gioia. Her prescience of violence is like seeing black clouds gathering upwind, and knowing there'll be no sheltering from the storm when it breaks. But when she tries to leave, planning to walk into Gioia and warn him, the guard on the front door refuses to let her out.

'The master . . . rules nobody to go,' he says, in tortured Italian. 'Much trouble. To be safer, inside.'

Breathing too fast, and with her cheeks scorching, Clare can only retreat. Her heart sinks. If she gets the same response that night, at eleven, what then? The only possible hope is that Carlo is on the door, and can be persuaded. She feels close to tears; close to breaking. From the terrace she sees Leandro watching her, and she dithers for a while before setting out across the courtyard. His level gaze is like a searchlight, and Clare does everything she can to clear her face of expression. She goes to sit with Pip in the long sitting room as he finishes the last pages of *Bleak House*, running one of Peggy's silky ears between his finger and thumb, again and again. He frowns at the text, and after a while Clare realises that his eyes are completely stationary, and he hasn't turned the page. Time is rushing on too quickly; she wants the sun to stay up for ever, and the night to never fall.

And then, of course, with Leandro and Boyd in residence dinner is later, the whole evening longer. Without them, Pip, Marcie and Clare would likely have retired by eleven, for want of something else to do. Sick to her stomach, Clare barely touches the food. Full dark falls and it is nine o'clock, then ten, and they are all still at the table on the terrace surrounded by sticky little glasses and various bottles of liqueur, with smoke from Leandro's pipe clinging to their skin and hair. There are tremors in Clare's bones — like after Francesco Molino was beaten, like

467

after Federico attacked her — juddering up through muscle and blood, her own personal earthquake, and she can do nothing to stop it. It's half past ten when they finally quit the table and go down to the sitting room, and Clare walks close to Pip.

'Go to your room now,' she whispers to him, and he stiffens.

'Do you really think they're coming?' he says.

'I . . . I don't know. I hope not.' She has the wild thought that they'll somehow have heard about the extra men arriving, or at least that Leandro is here. That they'll call it off. 'I don't know,' she repeats. 'But just in case. Will you go, please? And lock the door. I'll come up and join you soon.'

'All right.' He gives her a look then; a strange, appraising look, quite alien to him. Startled, Clare says nothing else.

She almost gasps in relief when Marcie excuses herself minutes later, yawning conspicuously.

'I'm done in. I think I'll hit the hay,' she says, taking Leandro's hand and smiling as he kisses her knuckles. 'And I'm sure you boys can't wait to be shot of us so you can discuss business and broads. Will you be up for hours?'

'It's not true! And no, honey, not hours,' says Leandro. Clare carefully doesn't look at him. She stoops, gives Boyd a brief peck on the cheek.

'I'll go too,' she says, flushing when nerves turn the words shrill. She wants to take a deep breath, wants to steady herself, but she can't seem to exhale properly. Boyd reaches up and

468

cups her neck gently for a moment, and she's sure he must be able to feel her pulse thudding.

'Good night, darling. I'll be right behind you.'

'Walk me up, Clare?' says Marcie, proffering her arm. 'What's bothering you?' she says softly, as they climb the stairs. 'Come on now, I can see there's something.'

'I . . . ' Clare's mind goes blank. 'I think perhaps . . . perhaps I may be in the family way, after all,' she says desperately. There's a startled pause and then Marcie laughs. It echoes up and down the stairwell, and has a sardonic edge that jars Clare with instant suspicion. 'Is that funny?'

'Oh, no! I mean — well, I'd thought it was something awful!' Marcie gasps, dabbing at her eyes. 'Why should that make you look as though you've the weight of the world on your shoulders?'

'Well, I . . . I'm not sure how Boyd will take the news.'

'Oh, I *bet* you're not!' says Marcie. Clare stops climbing. Beneath her hand Marcie's arm is smooth and slender, but strong.

'What do you mean by that, Marcie?' she says. Marcie's smile lasts a second longer, and then it vanishes. Her eyes are unreadable.

'*Mean* by it? Why, I don't mean anything by it at all. The pair of you haven't had one of your own yet, so I guessed there must be some problem. But we reap what we sow, Clare. Perhaps this baby is your just deserts.' For a long moment the two women stand eye to eye, and neither one speaks. Clare feels the malice of the words, is sure of it; then Marcie smiles. 'For

469

years of waiting patiently, I mean. You do want the kid, don't you?'

'With all my heart,' Clare whispers.

'Well then.' Marcie carries on up the stairs, alone. 'Congratulations. I'm sure Boyd will be delighted.'

★ ★ ★

At five to eleven Clare crosses the dark courtyard with her fists clenched at her sides and the tremors making her teeth chatter. The guard gets to his feet as she approaches, and when she sees it's Carlo she has to fight the urge to throw her arms around him. She sways as she stands there, and her voice wobbles when she speaks.

'Will you let me out? I'd like to go for a walk.' She tries to smile but her face feels frozen. Carlo makes a regretful face, spreads his hands and shrugs.

'Sorry, Signora Kingsley. I am not allowed.'

'You can call me Chiara,' she says. Her mouth is dry; she can feel her pulse in her temples. Outside, one of the dogs growls and goes quiet. 'Please. I know we're not supposed to. I know Mr Cardetta is . . . worried, after the fire. But I must go out, just for a short while.'

'I don't think . . . ' Carlo shakes his head, but she can sense his indecision.

'Please. I'll only be ten minutes, I promise. Aren't we friends? And I'll never tell anyone. Please,' she says. She puts one hand on his arm and manages to smile. Carlo grins at her; he loves that she comes to him, that he has been able to grant favours; he loves the idea of her love affair. He's really just a boy, full of mischief. Clare sends up a silent prayer for his safety.

'Ten minutes. And we never tell,' he says, picking up the keys and unlocking the small door, smiling at her all the while.

For a split second, Clare thinks nothing will happen. She stands there stupidly, looking at the open door, but then Ettore appears, moving fast, pushing Carlo back with a gun to his head. She can hardly believe he's there; can hardly believe the danger he's in.

'Open the big doors. Do it! Now!' Ettore says to the stunned guard.

'Wait, Ettore! Something's wrong!' says Clare. She grabs him, trying to turn him, to make him listen. 'Go — run! Please!' she says. His eyes are avid, his forehead shines with sweat; he doesn't seem to hear her properly.

'Chiara, go inside! Lock the door — do as I told you!' he says.

'No, you must listen to me! Your uncle's here and he's been filling the place with guards since this morning. Armed men — I don't know who they are! I don't know what's happening, but you have to *run*!' She holds him as tightly as she can; wants to shake him, daren't raise her voice when she needs to scream. For a second she thinks she sees comprehension dawning on his face; he pauses and she thinks he'll do as she says, but then the dogs outside erupt, and his head snaps around, away from her. He hits Carlo with a backhanded blow and the young guard staggers back, slumping against the wall. Clare stares in

471

horror as blood trickles down the boy's face.

'Go now, Chiara!' Ettore shouts. He snatches up the keys, fumbles them as he tries to unlock the big carriage doors. She has seconds; they have seconds. She wants to hold him and tell him that she loves him; she wants to tell him about their child. The doors swing open and Clare stands stunned at the sight of dark figures pouring across the *aia*, kicking at the dogs when they lunge for them. Then a deafening barrage of gunfire starts up from the roof; there's a whiff of cordite, voices shouting, and Ettore turns to Clare, his face pinched with fear. 'Run!' he says. And she does.

She sprints across the courtyard and movement above catches her eye — the roof is crowded with men, hurrying into action, reloading. The flash of muzzle fire is blinding in the dark, the sound of it impossibly loud, filling her skull, reverberating in her chest. Idiotically, because it won't save her, she wraps her arms across her head as she runs. Lights are still on in the long sitting room; she thinks she sees movement behind the drapes and dodges away — she can't let Leandro see her. She races up the outside stair and then turns before going in through the door, her eyes searching for Ettore down below. The courtyard is a mass of running figures and the roof is swarming, and several figures have fallen, sprawled, across the stones. Clare stares, bewildered by fear. She can't tell whether any of the fallen is Ettore. A bearded man appears in front of her; she vaguely recognises him as the *masseria* guard who refused to let her out earlier. He has his rifle in one hand and pauses before going down the steps, turning to her, shouting something she can't understand and shoving her in through the door.

Following corridors and stairs familiar from her secret visits to Ettore, on quiet nights so different to this one, Clare hurries to Pip's room. She expects to see his door shut; expects to knock and call out, and be let in. She expects to hug him, and soothe him, and wait it out. But as she turns the corner she stops. Pip's door is ajar, the room inside dark.

'Pip?' she says, too loudly. She pushes through the door. The shutters are still open from the day. Peggy is asleep, rolled up on the bed; it's stuffy and warm but there's no sign of Pip. Clare stands there with the sound of her own breathing deafening her. She has no idea where he can be, no idea what can have gone wrong, why he hasn't locked himself in as planned. Desperately, she checks her own room, though there's no longer a key to lock it, in case he got confused. But that room is empty too. 'Pip!' she calls out pointlessly. Her voice tunnels along the empty corridor, all but lost beneath the battle sounds outside. A door bangs somewhere, and glass breaks; there are other people moving inside the *masseria*.

For a while Clare stays where she is, and hasn't the slightest idea what to do. She racks her brains, trying to think where Pip would go. Then she thinks she knows. She races up another flight of stairs, tripping in haste and splitting her

473

knee open on the stone. But the bat room is deserted and the door to Marcie and Leandro's room, the highest in the whole building, is locked, and when Clare thumps her fists on it and shouts thought the keyhole, there's no hint of movement within. She goes back down the stairs, woodenly, not knowing what else to do or where she should go. She can't hide herself away in safety until Pip is doing the same, and not while Ettore is outside somewhere, maybe hurt, maybe dead. She thinks about going up to the roof, but knows it would be madness; she thinks about going back out into the courtyard, but the idea terrifies her. As Clare dithers, the noise outside begins to dwindle; the gunfire is getting less frequent, and silences form between each shot. She carries on down the stairs that she and Marcie climbed earlier, which lead to the long sitting room. And halfway down she stops, a startled exclamation dying on her lips.

Pip is there, at the bottom, hiding in the shadows outside the brightly lit doorway, peeping through. Clare stares. Marcie is behind him, one hand on his shoulder, also peering round, tentatively. *Have you both gone mad?* The question doesn't make it as far as Clare's lips. There are raised voices inside the room, and though she can't understand a word she knows the voices at once — one is Leandro, the other is Ettore. Her ribs clench in painful relief. They're arguing furiously in the dialect, and outside it has all gone quiet. The raid is over already, and Ettore is safe. Clare comes down another two steps, softly, understanding why Pip and Marcie

474

don't want to interrupt. Then she stops again, bewildered, because Pip has a gun in his hand — a pistol — and she can see that he's shaking from head to toe; he's so vibrant with tension it's like a glow around him, like a rank, feral smell. Clare looks at him, and at the gun in his hand; she looks at Marcie's long white fingers, holding his shoulder. They're both staring into the sitting room and when Clare follows their gaze she sees Ettore, unscathed, his face twitching in grief and rage as his uncle roars at him, flecks of spit flying from his lips. She watches, stunned, as Ettore's arm whips around and he punches Leandro; slamming his fist up under his uncle's chin with a meaty sound. She hears Pip gasp and can't react, can't move a muscle when he suddenly walks forward into the room, into the light, and in the shocked silence raises his hand, points the pistol at Ettore and fires.

The air is dragged out of Clare's lungs. She can't make a sound, can only stumble after Pip with her arms out wide for balance because the ground is no longer flat, no longer solid. She's dimly aware that Leandro has sunk lopsidedly to one knee, with his head bowed like he's praying and his hands clamped around his jaw. Boyd is off to one side, pale and mute. But all she can really see is Ettore on his back, his legs a jumble, a spatter of red droplets across his face and all around him. She collapses next to him and he looks up at her with that same mix of confusion and wonder as when they first met.

'Ettore! It's all right, you'll be all right,' she says, in a voice she doesn't quite recognise. He reaches up and she grabs at his hand. 'You'll be all right.' She peels back the lapel of his jacket. Pip's aim was erratic, he was still raising the gun when he fired and the bullet has gone into Ettore's right shoulder, just above his armpit. There's blood spreading out beneath him, and blooming through his shirt, but Clare chokes up with relief. The wound is nowhere near his heart, or lungs; it ought not to kill him. She struggles out of her blouse, wads it up and presses it gently over the bloody entrance wound. 'Lie still, my love,' she says. 'You're going to be all right. We'll get the doctor back . . . you'll be fine.'

Her vision is blurred, her thoughts scattered. She glances up and sees the gun in Pip's hand, still raised and trembling at the end of his arm, frozen at the point it went off. His face is bloodless, even his lips; his eyes have a look of such blank terror that she wonders if he even intended to fire.

'Pip, what are you doing?' she says raggedly. 'What on *earth* are you doing?' Pip doesn't even blink. Clare feels the heat of Ettore's blood, soaking up through the thin fabric of her blouse and onto her hands. Behind Pip, Marcie comes into the room, her eyes huge in a drawn, stunned face. Clare looks to Leandro but he's still on his knees, shaking his head, dazed. It's Boyd who comes over to them, moving unhurriedly, like he's on his way to fetch a book from the shelf. 'Boyd — take the gun away from him. Take the gun away from him!' says Clare. Boyd stares down at her for a second and then does as she says, prising the pistol from Pip's clenched hand.

476

Clare relaxes, turns back to Ettore and touches her fingers softly to his face. Boyd moves a step closer to them, and Clare knows she's given herself away. But the baby in her womb had done that already — would have done it, sooner or later. She swallows, and looks up at her husband. His face has that melted look she's seen before, slack with grief and fear. His mouth hangs open, his eyes are swimming. He looks just as he did in New York, drunk and drugged, right before he collapsed, and Clare goes cold. Boyd looks down at the gun in his hand; he's holding it by the grip, his finger is curled around the trigger. Keeping his eyes on it he raises it slowly, turning its barrel upwards, towards his own chin.

'Boyd,' says Clare, as softly as she can. 'Boyd, no. Don't.' He freezes for a moment, not even seeming to breathe; the pistol quivers in his hand, he sticks his chin out a little and the barrel touches his skin. He sucks in a breath, a ratcheting sob. 'Boyd, no,' says Clare.

'No,' he says, with a twitch of his head. He's shaking all over and his eyes are fixed on her now, cutting into her. Then he straightens his arm, points the gun at Ettore and fires.

'No!'

For a second Clare thinks she herself has shouted this out, but it can't be her because her heart has stopped beating and her teeth are clenched, impossibly tight. It's Marcie. 'No, no, no!' she screams. Her voice sounds weird and sluggish; the gunshot is ringing in Clare's ears. She can't move. She watches as Boyd repositions his feet for better balance, turns his torso and levels the gun at her face. She struggles to focus her eyes past the perfect black circle of the barrel. Boyd's face, above it, is now so empty that he almost looks calm. But there's a muscle ticking beneath the tears on one cheek, trapped in some mad dance of nervous trauma, and his eyes are furious. They stare at each other and while the moment lasts Clare has no sense of time passing. She looks up at this man and her death, and can't recognise either one. Boyd jerks the trigger and the gun clicks, but doesn't fire. He frowns at it, hesitates, then brings it in to check the cylinder. Then Leandro is on him, knocking him down, driving his fists into him, again and again. The gun clatters to the floor off to one side and Clare finds herself staring at nothing. Then she looks down at Ettore.

Boyd's shot was clean. It has left a perfect dark circle above Ettore's temple, an exact replica of the barrel Clare was just staring into, and his eyes are half-shut, and he's too still, and even though she knows he's gone she can't let herself believe it. She picks up his right hand and puts it at the back of her neck, underneath her hair, as he liked to do. His hand is still warm; she imagines the fingers curling, imagines his grip, pulling her closer; imagines him taking a breath, still with her.

But these are imaginings, nothing more. She kneels there in silence, holding his limp hand; putting it to her face, her lips, the back of her neck again. The weight of his arm is surprising; the skin of his palm is hard and callused; he smells of earth and blood. She can't believe he's gone, and she doesn't know or care what the others are doing — why Pip had a gun, why Marcie is next to her, sobbing brokenly over Ettore's body; where Leandro has gone with her husband. She doesn't care about any of it. She doesn't care when Paola marches in, unarmed but ferocious, with a guard at her shoulder keeping a close eye on her; doesn't care when the girl sees her brother lying there and her mouth drops open, and she emits such a terrifying howl of pain that it feels like a knife in Clare's skull. Paola rushes over to them, grabs Marcie by her shoulders and tries to haul her away. Marcie fights her, snarling through her tears; they jostle Clare but she stays where she is. She holds Ettore's hand, and lets go of everything else.

★　★　★

Sometime later Clare is lifted up and seated on one of the couches; a glass of brandy is held to her lips and tipped into her mouth when she shows no signs of drinking it.

'Come on. All of it,' says Leandro. Clare swallows and then gags, coughing. 'Ah, Ettore! My poor boy. To survive the Great War and this fascist strife, only to be shot by a coward when he was down.' He shakes his head; he's leaden with sorrow. 'I'm too old to expect justice in this world, but still. Some things are far too bad. Drink the brandy. We all need it.' The pistol is tucked into his belt. He moves like an old man; his knuckles are bloody and his chin is bruised. Clare looks down at where Ettore lay but he's not there any more, just the blackish stain of his blood. She can't remember them taking him; far beneath her shock she senses grief and panic, scrabbling for the surface like a trapped animal.

'Why are you crying like that? For *him*?' says Pip. Clare looks at him but he's sitting next to Marcie, and speaking to her. Marcie's face is a ruin; her make-up is streaked and grotesque.

'You weren't supposed to shoot him. Nobody was supposed to *shoot* him!' Marcie gasps, between sobs.

'I was protecting you! Like I promised I would — like you asked me to! But why are you crying like that? It's . . . it's *me* you love! You said so!' he says. Clare stares at him, horrified; Leandro grunts as he sits down.

'You'll find that not much that comes out of my wife's mouth is altogether true, boy,' he says.

'We're in love,' says Pip defiantly. He takes Marcie's hand. 'She's going to leave you! She doesn't love you any more, she loves me. We've been together for weeks.' But Marcie shakes her hand free.

'Shut up, you little idiot!' she snaps at him. Pip keeps trying to catch at her hand. His face is almost comic with hurt and confusion.

'What?' Clare manages to say, but too quietly for anyone to hear her. The brandy spreads out into her blood. She takes another sip and looks around the room. No sign of Paola or the guard, and Boyd is sitting in the corner with his knees drawn up, his arms wrapped around them and his face down, like a child. It's so absurd Clare almost laughs.

The sound of Marcie crying is all they hear for a while. Pip stares at her, abject, bewildered; he keeps trying to take hold of her hands. Clare's head is ringing.

'Do you know how I knew, Clare?' says Leandro. 'Clare, are you listening to me? Do you know how I knew you were in danger, and why I brought you out here? It was to protect you, you see. Isn't that rich?' He swigs his brandy, nods at Boyd. 'I brought you out here to protect you from *him*. I thought he meant to have you killed. He said to me — when he first got out here and I asked about you — he said 'She's an angel. A perfect angel', and straight away I was frightened for you, because that's what he said about his first wife Emma, you see. That's *exactly* how he described her to me, with that same . . . desperation, that same *passion*, when he bought me to kill her. I've got to tell you, Clare, I think the man you married is sick in the head.'

'What?' says Clare. She can't follow him, can't unpick the meaning of these bizarre words. Pip has gone very silent, very still; he's stopped trying to grab at Marcie's hands. Clare doesn't like his colour, or the way his eyes are glazed and shining.

'What else would you call it? The irrationality of it . . . I had nothing but contempt for any of the people who hired me in that capacity — because what were they all except cowards? Hypocrites. Killing but keeping their hands clean. But Boyd was the worst; the weakest. He was shaking like a leaf when he came to find me, and couldn't look me in the eye the whole time we talked — not until I asked him why. I asked him, what had she done? Then he looks up with this sudden calm, this total conviction, and tells me his wife is a perfect angel.' Leandro shakes his head. 'Tells me it like he's *affronted* by the question. So I turned him down at first, I didn't think he was serious; I didn't think he knew what he wanted. But he kept offering me more money, and in the end I took it. I wish I hadn't; God knows I wish I hadn't. But I did and there's no getting away from that.'

Slowly, his story sinks into Clare. She frowns in disbelief, looking over at Boyd's hunched figure as though he might react, as though he might stand up and deny this outrageous accusation. But he's motionless. She thinks of the perfect circle of the gun barrel, the hollow click when he fired it at her.

'No. No . . . Emma got ill and died. She died of a fever. Everybody knows that; everybody said. How can she possibly have been . . . murdered, and nobody know about it? It's ridiculous.'

'It was in the New York papers, for a while.' Leandro shrugs. 'But not on the front page. And Boyd was never implicated — I don't think the police even figured out Emma had been cheating on him, and he did a good job of looking heartbroken. They just thought it was a street robbery. Then Boyd went to England, found new friends and spun them a prettier story — for the boy's sake, he could have told anyone who heard a rumour — and I'm sure all you Brits were far too polite to enquire any further. But believe me, she was murdered. I ought to know.'

'Are you saying . . . are you saying you're an

482

assassin, Mr Cardetta?' says Clare.

'I was, yes. That's how I started out; how I started to get rich. Killing people for money. All of this' — he spreads his hands to encompass the fine room, the *masseria*, the land around it — 'is built on that. So, do you still think I'm a good man, Chiarina?' Clare has no answer for him. 'But Emma Kingsley was one of the last. That was the moment I felt like I'd lost my soul, you see,' he says, sounding sad and distracted. 'Do you remember I said so? It was killing that lovely young woman. Killing her for money, when all she'd done was fallen in love. I knew it was wrong but I told myself it was business, and it didn't matter. Well, it was business, but it did matter. I felt the injustice of it in my blood, like . . . like a sickness. It bothered me. And it bothered me that it didn't seem to bother him at all.' He points a finger at Boyd. 'Perhaps I thought we should both be punished. I don't know. But he's stuck in my mind, all these years. It joined us somehow. We were in it together, him and me.'

Clare sits mute and tries to think. Her mind is slow, everything is languid and unreal, like it's underwater. She's in an alien element, far out of her depth. She thinks back, goes through her memories, tries to fit them into this reality and finds, astonishingly, that she can.

'It did bother him. He was afraid. He was always afraid,' she says, woodenly. 'After you came to see him in New York, seven years ago . . . after you found him he tried to . . . he tried to end it all.'

'Did he?' Leandro grunts and nods. 'Well, fear is a kind of sickness, I suppose, it can drive a man mad. I would have left it at that, if he hadn't called you what he did. 'A perfect angel.' If he hadn't said that, I'd never have tried to intervene.'

'Why did you even contact him again? Why did you even want him to design for you?'

'I'm not even sure myself, truthfully. Moments like that in life — moments when things turn a corner, when you step off the path you're on and go a different way — those are important moments. And he was there with me for perhaps the most important of mine. He was the author of it, and I never forgot him, not completely. After all this time I wanted to . . . I wanted to see him again. I wanted to see how this thing we shared was affecting him. *If* it was still affecting him, like it was affecting me.' He shrugs. 'The urge to find him wouldn't leave me alone. Then he spoke about you as he'd spoken about her and I . . . I *couldn't* let that go. I needed to see how he was with you, how you were with him. I needed to know if he'd changed, or if history was repeating itself.'

'How did you think you could help me?' Clare is still bewildered, fighting to keep up.

'Again, I hardly know. I wanted to warn you, I suppose. Or frighten Boyd so much with the consequences of something happening to you that nothing would. Or persuade him to simply let you go, if it had come to that. And what do you do when you get here? You cheat on him! You fall in love with Ettore, and make

484

goddamned sure he's got cause to kill you! Ha!' Another swig of brandy; he rolls his lips back over his teeth as it goes down. 'There was something about that blue-eyed mongrel, that's for sure. My wife fell for him, same as you did, when he was here with us last winter, although as far as I know the boy held her off. He showed me that much respect, at least.' He fixes Marcie a look, blackly simmering. 'All those English lessons, all that fussing and nursing; always pestering me to make him stay longer.' Finally, Marcie stops crying and starts to look afraid.

'You knew?' she says.

'Honey, I love you but I've got to tell you — you're a bad actress. Really bad.' Leandro runs his hands across his hair and down over his face, like he's wiping something off. 'Things haven't gone quite as I planned them,' he says, to nobody in particular.

After a few seconds of stillness Marcie takes out a handkerchief and starts to wipe her face, as if shocked into propriety. She sits up straighter and smooths down her hair, and beside her Pip watches her every move as if searching for clues or instructions. His eyes are bloated with tears; before long they start to slide down his face.

'Pip,' says Clare. She has the sudden clear image of him standing, shaking, pointing the gun at Ettore and pulling the trigger. She shuts her eyes. 'Pip, come and sit with me,' she says, holding out her hand; but Pip ignores her, like she hasn't spoken. He turns his head slowly towards Boyd.

'Father . . . it's lies, isn't it? Tell them it's not

true. My mother got sick and died. Just tell them!' Pip's voice turns shrill. Boyd shifts minutely, like something's coursing through him, causing a ripple. But he doesn't look up, and he doesn't reply.

'It's not lies, Filippo. I'm sorry for it, and I'm sorry you're hearing it now, but you need to. Your mother didn't deserve what happened to her, not for the crime of falling in love. A man will be angry to be cuckolded, yes.' Leandro glances over at Boyd, who doesn't move a muscle. 'Angry, yes. So divorce her if you want, or cut her off, but accept it. Life's like that; the heart is like that. These things happen and we can't help them — I don't see why women should be expected to resist the strength of such feelings, any more than men.' He looks hard at his wife again. 'But seducing a boy, little more than a child, out of *spite*? Doing it with a cold heart, deliberately to *wound me*?' His voice has risen to a bellow; Marcie flinches. 'That's low.'

'I wasn't trying to wound you, Leandro, I swear, I wanted to — ' she says, and breaks off, flicking angry eyes at Clare.

'You did it to hurt Clare? Why? Oh . . . I see. Because Ettore fell for her, and not for you.' Leandro nods. 'That's still vile, Marcie. It's still vile.'

'You made Pip tell you? About Ettore and me?' says Clare. Marcie glares at her.

'I knew weeks ago, you fool. I saw you two together — I saw you go into his room at night, in your slip. Before he had a chance to close the shutters! I've known all along.'

'You saw me through the window? But . . . your room doesn't look out that way.'

'I wasn't in my room, I was — ' Marcie stops short again, snaps her mouth closed.

'Watching his window from some vantage point?' says Leandro softly. Marcie's cheeks redden. 'Like a love-struck teenager?' He shakes his head, wistful. 'There was a time you held such a candle for me, Marcie. Do you even remember it?'

'You brought me out here and left me to rot,' she says, her voice trembling.

'I brought you out here to love and support me! To be *my* wife!' he shouts. 'Woman, you make my heart sore.' With a small, broken sound Marcie puts her hands over her eyes. Her mouth is a set, flat line and she's no longer crying. Clare remembers her advice to Pip: *If it bothers you to see, don't look.* She wants to tear Marcie's hands away and open her eyes, but she hasn't the will to move.

Leandro levers himself up and goes around with the brandy bottle again, topping up all of their glasses. Only Boyd doesn't have one. 'Drink it. All of you. We need to restore some fucking sanity here.'

'You . . . you killed my mother?' says Pip. His lips have gone ashen again; the skin around them almost blue.

'Drink your brandy, Philip. You look ready to die of fright,' says Leandro. 'Yes, I killed her. A single shot to the head, as she walked home from her boyfriend's house one night; and then I hit the boyfriend too, right afterwards. That's what

487

your father paid me to do. If I was the gun that shot your mother, then it was your father who pointed me and pulled the trigger.'

'Leandro, that's enough,' says Clare. Pip is breathing far too fast; she can't imagine what he must be feeling. She doesn't try to imagine what she herself is feeling. All she knows is that when she's able to feel anything again, she'll wish she can't. When she looks at the folded-up figure of her husband she realises that the nagging feeling she's had all this time was right. She doesn't know him at all.

'The cat's out of the bag already.' Leandro shrugs. 'And since my wife's spent the last month making a man out of the kid, I guess he's grown up enough to hear it.' But he's not, Clare knows. Pip is crying like a child; he can't possibly be taking everything in, it's too much. It's too much for Clare.

Two young men come in from the courtyard, wearing the dark uniforms and peaked caps of the *carabinieri*. They sweep their eyes uncertainly over the room's mixed and broken inhabitants. 'You've rounded them all up?' Leandro asks them in Italian.

'Yes, Mr Cardetta.'

'How many dead?'

'Seven; and twenty-one wounded.'

'And my niece?'

'We have her, unharmed. Shall we take her in with the others?'

'No. Have my men put her somewhere here for now, and keep watch on her.'

'Paola?' says Clare. Some thought nudges for

her attention. 'No . . . her baby. She must be allowed to get back to her baby.'

'In due course,' says Leandro, and his tone brooks no argument. 'I want to talk to her first. But take that one.' He points at Boyd. The *carabinieri* exchange a look. 'Yes, yes — take him! He shot my nephew, Ettore Tarano, in cold blood, for a vendetta. We all saw him. He must be kept in custody, and sent to Bari for trial.'

'Yes, Mr Cardetta.'

'Please — you must at least send someone to fetch Paola's child to her. He can't be left all alone, he's too little,' says Clare.

'Perhaps she should have thought of that before she came here to *rob* me!' Leandro's sudden bellow is shocking, but there's a treacherous sparkle in his eyes. He glares at Clare but she isn't cowed. Ettore is dead; she has nothing else to fear. Leandro relents. 'All right. Have someone go to Vico Iovia; the Taranos have an apartment there, in the courtyard. Fetch her baby and bring him here.' The *carabinieri* nod. 'Anything you want to say to your husband before they take him?' he says to Clare.

The two officers pull Boyd to his feet and he looks across at Clare. His face is shiny and flaccid, he's as colourless as whey, his long body is limp. When he looks at her his eyes are quite empty.

'You were perfect,' he says. She can't make out his tone of voice — it's heavier than neutral; past calm, into somewhere else. 'You were perfect. No man had touched you until . . . until you let that . . . *peasant* . . . ' He swallows convulsively, as

489

though the very thought nauseates him. That's what's in his voice, she realises. Disgust; even revulsion. 'No man had ever touched you. You were pure.' Boyd shakes his head, and Clare understands what he means. Before, she'd wondered if they'd ever made love at all, given the barrier that was always between them. Now she knows they had not, and that this had been his intention — to keep her pure. *That bitch*, he called little Christina Havers, after their affair. *That whore*.

'You dare to look disgusted with me?' she says softly. 'Ettore was twice the man you are. A hundred times the man!' Her voice is rising; she wants her words to scar him. 'I loved him more than I *ever* loved you! And I loved making love to him!'

'Shut up! Shut up, you *whore*!' Boyd roars.

'Enough! Take him,' says Leandro. In silence, the *carabinieri* march out with Boyd stumbling between them. Clare realises that she has referred to Ettore in the past tense, twice; a strange, raw keening starts up in her throat, and for a while she can't stop it. She puts her hands over her mouth but the sound leaks out through her fingers, and she can smell blood on her skin — she has Ettore's blood all over her hands.

★  ★  ★

The sun rises on Masseria dell'Arco as though the new day is the same as any that went before, and Clare wakes with every muscle aching, to the sound of splashing and sweeping. The

490

servants are scrubbing blood from the courtyard stones with long-handled brooms and buckets of water. She looks in on Pip, still sound asleep, then wanders out onto the terrace, barefoot and dressed in her slip, to watch the clean-up. She's still not able to absorb everything she's seen and heard and learnt. That Marcie seduced Pip, and he thought himself in love with her. That Marcie was in love with Ettore. That Boyd had Emma killed, when she wasn't as perfect as he wanted her to be. That Boyd killed Ettore, and that he aimed the gun at Clare, and pulled the trigger. She feels nothing whatsoever about the fact that the chamber was empty when he did. She can't decide if it was good luck or bad, and she doesn't care. Ettore is dead. None of these events, none of these things she's learnt, will settle into a sensible order in her mind; an order she can read, and understand. It's all a dark jumble and every time she feels some small satisfaction that she need never see Boyd again, that she is safe from him, it's followed closely by the raw pain of remembering that Ettore is also gone. It's exhausting. Trying to think it through is exhausting.

She goes back to Pip's room and watches him sleep for a while. The room is full of the soft smell of him — skin and hair and breath. He's sleeping off his shock, his double heartbreak; the trauma of losing his father, of having to rewrite his own history; the strain of sifting the truth from all the lies. To Clare it seems as though he's cocooned himself in sleep — that this stupor hides a metamorphosis of some kind, and she can only wait to see what form he will take when he emerges from it. When she thinks how Marcie used him it kindles a slow-burning anger; she tries not to dwell on it. Marcie hasn't yet come down from the high room she shares with Leandro, to which she retreated at some point in the night, and more than anything, now, Clare wants to be gone, and see none of them again. She wants to take Pip and leave. She thinks of all those hours he spent with Marcie in the bat room, listening to music or supposedly rehearsing a play that will never be staged. She thinks of the dusty old couch they dragged in there, initially for Clare to sit on and watch them. Perhaps it was all a play to Marcie, but Pip thought it was real. *I was protecting you*, he said, after he shot at Ettore, *like I promised I would.* She pictures Marcie playing the helpless, frightened woman, making Pip feel like a man. It's all too easy to imagine. And she knows how word of the raid got to Leandro in time for him to prepare its defence. From Marcie, who heard it from Pip, who had sworn to Clare that he would tell no one. But she has no blame for Pip, only for herself. She abandoned him to be with Ettore; she left him to be lonely and uncertain — left an open wound for Marcie to heal.

Clare can't eat. Not even when her hands start to shake with hunger and black flecks jig around the edges of her vision when she moves too quickly. Carlo is back on duty at the front door as though nothing has happened. His nose is swollen and bruised, split open across the bridge, and his eyes are bloody. When Clare apologises to him he turns his face away and doesn't answer. He tries for a stony expression but he's too young and too sweet; he looks like he might cry instead. Clare asks him where Paola Tarano is and Carlo jerks his thumb at the stairs behind him, still refusing to look at her, and she goes up in silence.

Paola is in a small room high up in the front wing of the *masseria*. There's a little window overlooking the courtyard but Paola has her back to it, curled on her side on the narrow bed with Iacopo asleep against her stomach. These are servants' quarters, and the room doesn't look like it's been used in a while. The nightstand is thick with dust, as is a rickety chair against one wall — the only other furniture. Someone has taken up a jug of water and a plate of bread and cheese, but they're untouched. Paola moves nothing but her eyes when Clare knocks softly and goes in. For a second Clare hardly recognises her because Paola's hair is loose, released from its usual knot and scarf. It reaches down past her elbows, black, and wavy from braiding. She looks younger, prettier, but her eyes are ancient with grief. For a while Clare simply stands there and says nothing, and their shared pain hovers between them. There's some other resonance as well, something else they both feel — it takes Clare a moment to put her finger on it. She can feel her own guilt over Ettore's death seething inside her, and she'd expected Paola to blame her, and be furious. But Paola is sodden with guilt as well; Paola blames herself.

Gently, to not stir the baby, Clare sits down on the edge of the mattress. She takes Paola's hand, and though the girl's black eyes fill with unease, even suspicion, she doesn't pull away. They stay like that for a while. There's nothing Clare can say to explain, nothing she can say to make things better, even if she could make this hard-faced girl understand her Italian. In the end she lifts Paola's hand and presses it to her middle, low down, beneath the waistband of her skirt. Paola gazes at her, confused.

'Ettore,' says Clare. Paola still stares, so Clare points to Iacopo, then taps the girl's hand on her abdomen. 'Ettore's baby. *Bambino*,' she says, and sees comprehension dawn, and as it does Clare's eyes flood with tears, and she can't seem to stop them. She hangs her head and lets them run. 'I never got to tell him,' she says. 'He'll never know.' Paola keeps hold of her hand but says nothing.

Clare stays for an hour or more, unwilling to leave because she's sure that this will be the last time she sees Paola. The girl's kinship to Ettore is a precious commodity now; the tantalising hint of him she has about her is a grain of comfort. When she gets up to leave she stoops and kisses Paola's forehead, before the girl can jerk away, and Paola watches after her with an odd mix of anger and vulnerability. Clare can see how she hates to be cared for; how she doesn't want sympathy, and mistrusts affection. She has a strength in her that Clare can't hope to emulate, but then she thinks that if Paola won't bend she must break, eventually.

Restless, searching, Clare paces the rooms and corridors of the *masseria* like a ghost. She would go out into the landscape but she can't stand the thought of seeing the places where she met Ettore; can't stand the thought of having to return to the *masseria* once she's left it. Perhaps she wouldn't return — perhaps she'd just keep walking, and she needs to be there when Pip emerges. She can't go without him, but there's a kernel of terror inside her that somehow, when he's reborn, the bond between them will have vanished. That Marcie and Ettore will have somehow erased their affinity, that invisible tie they had, which is not motherhood, and could dissolve without trace. He would be justified in blaming her, after all — for all of it. Even for his father being taken away. He might refuse to leave while Boyd is still in Italy; he might want to stay with him. Clare's walk drifts to a halt. Could that happen? Could she be forced to choose between Pip and staying for ever in a place that has begun to feel like a vast prison? It could happen. The idea makes it seem like the air itself is crushing her.

When she walks past the door to what was Ettore's room Clare shrinks back, and doesn't stop. From a high window she sees Leandro on the roof, in the same place he stood two days earlier, staring out in just the same way. For a second her thoughts scatter into wild imaginings of it really being two days earlier — of how she would do things differently if she was given the chance, if she really had walked back through time. How she would force Leandro to let her out, so she could warn Ettore about the extra guards at the farm. How she would rush down the stairs as soon as she saw Pip and Marcie waiting at the foot of them, and snatch the revolver from his hand. How she would take it from him after he'd shot Ettore in the shoulder, instead of leaving it to Boyd to disarm him. How she would refuse to help the raiders by opening the door, so that perhaps they would call it off. She tortures herself with what might have happened if she had not done the things she did, in the order in which she did them; pouring salt into her wounds until she can't take any more. Then she goes up to the roof and stands beside Leandro.

He turns to look at her briefly, his expression unchanging. He looks older, and tired; he stares off into the far distance as if he can see the future there, so Clare follows his gaze and tries to do the same. The landscape hasn't changed, and that seems unreal because it feels as though great seismic shifts have shaken everything to pieces. She expects to see ruins, giant fissures in the earth. But she sees the flat, long land with its brown grass, its burnt stubble fields; she sees the same gnarled olive trees that have witnessed generations of human lives flickering out at the end of their time like the stars at dawn. She sees the dry stone walls and the dusty road; the madly bored *aia* dogs and the *trullo* by the gates where Ettore first kissed her, and they first made love. The breeze rolls softly from the north. It moans over the stone parapets of the complex and the low field walls; it runs through Clare's hair and flutters her shirt against her ribs, filling her ears with quiet noise. It's impossible that all this should still exist when Ettore does not; Clare wonders whether perhaps she doesn't exist either. She feels like thistledown; she's the same weight as the air — she could blow away at any moment, and drift, disperse, vanish.

Leandro's voice, when he speaks, is sombre.

'You want to leave. You must do. Do you want to see Boyd before you go? It could be arranged.'

'No,' says Clare. 'No. Never again. But . . . Pip might.' She must sound afraid because Leandro turns with a speculative look.

'You can't think he'll want to stay here, with his father?'

'I don't know. He . . . he was very angry with me. About Ettore.'

'Jealous of your attention, only.' Leandro shrugs. 'He'll want to be with you. He doesn't love his father like he loves you. I saw that from the start. And now he knows how his mother died . . .'

'I hope you're right.' Clare pauses. 'There . . . there was something you wanted to find out from Boyd before you would let us go home. Ettore told me. Was that it? Was it whether or not he might harm me?'

'That was it.' Leandro nods. 'Killing that girl changed me. Killing Emma Kingsley. It may be hard for you to believe, but she was the only woman I ever harmed and, by Christ, she haunted me afterwards. And I changed; I went into business. I'm not saying I was a model citizen ever after, but . . . but I was never as low and dirty again as I was that night. The night I shot her and her lover. I wanted to see if Boyd had changed as well.'

'But couldn't you tell straight away that he was just the same?'

'Not for sure, and even when I suspected it I wasn't sure what to do about it. How to change things. He . . . it was cowardly, you see. It was cowardly to have her killed, rather than to confront her, or just let her go. It was cowardly not to kill her himself, if that was what he wanted. But why kill her at all, when she had a child that needed her? There was no need. But he's unbalanced; he doesn't think the way I think, that much is obvious.'

'No, he does not. I was a thing to him — an idea, not a person. I think I've always felt it, though I couldn't quite define it. And when you say he's a hypocrite you don't know how right you are. He has been unfaithful to me — with one woman that I know about, and perhaps others that I don't. And yes, he is a coward. I thought he was grieving, but it was guilt. I thought he was afraid to let me know how deeply he'd cared for Emma, but he was only afraid of me finding out what he'd done — of anyone finding out. I thought he was vulnerable, and ultimately kind. But his vulnerability was just . . . weakness, and his kindness was a fraud. I tried to love him but I . . . I never could.'

'Who could love such a man? But you stayed for the boy? For Pip?'

'Yes. I stayed for him. And because I had no idea there could be an alternative. It never occurred to me to look for one.'

'I wanted you to come here for Marcie — that was also true. I could feel I was losing her, and I wanted her to be happy. But after Boyd spoke about you that way I needed to meet you, too. I needed to . . . see.'

'I'm grateful to you. I owe you my life.'

'No. I risked your life,' says Leandro.

'But I'm free of him now, and it's your doing.'

For a while the two of them stand and watch the world, and wait. There's no hurry. Clare breathes in, and breathes out, and feels calmer for being by Leandro's side, and knowing that he is waiting too. Waiting for thoughts to come, and go; waiting for the next moment, and what it will bring. 'Will you write to me and . . . keep me informed as to Boyd's whereabouts? And what happens to him?' she says, at last.

'Yes. If you want me to.'

'Not for me, but for Pip. And I'm sorry, Leandro. I'm very sorry that I betrayed you, and didn't warn you about the raid,' she says. Leandro smiles faintly.

'Ettore gave you little choice. I understand that. And besides, I'm too angry with my niece, and with Marcie, to be angry with you too. I might give myself a stroke if I tried.'

'You're angry with Paola?'

'Of course I am. She was always the firebrand, always the instigator. Left alone, Ettore would have fought with reading and propaganda, with speeches and strikes. He would have fought with his *brain*, you understand? But Paola's as spit-and-claws as they come. She's already told

499

me the raid was her idea — she's proud of it. Attacking her own family . . . '

'What . . . what will you do with her?'

'Do? Oh, nothing much, I shouldn't wonder.' He takes a long breath in, lets it out slowly. 'I only want her to stop fighting. It's over. She must stop being a soldier and start being a mother to that baby.'

'Will you take care of her? She has nobody else now, nobody to support her. Valerio is too sick to work.'

'Yes, yes. I'll take care of her. She'll come and work in my house in Gioia, whether she likes it or not. It's either that or she can go and be tried as a brigand with the rest of them. She won't like it,' he says, grinning sourly. 'So I get to punish her and take care of her at the same time.'

'What about Marcie? What will . . . what will you and Marcie do?'

'What will we do?' He shrugs. 'Again, nothing. We will do nothing. If she wants to leave me, she can, but she'll leave empty-handed. I'm staying here, in this place. This isn't the first thing she's done to hurt me since we came here. I know she hates it here, and I know part of her hates me for bringing her here. But I love her — what can I do? How should I punish her for what she did?'

'I don't know,' says Clare. 'Pip's only fifteen years old. She used him . . . she's broken his heart.' She can't hide her anger.

'None of us emerge from this spotless, Chiarina. Pip will recover, and he'll have learnt something important about this world, and the people in it. In time he'll hardly think about it any more — the young are like that. It will take you and me far longer to mend, I think.'

'I feel like . . . I feel like I shouldn't go on living,' says Clare. Fresh tears are choking her, aching in her throat, but she's sick of them and forces them back. 'This summer has been . . . it has been the best and worst time of my whole life. The best and the *utter* worst.'

'But you will go on living, and you have my great-nephew to think about. Or great-niece. Marcie told me,' says Leandro. He puts one hand on her shoulder for a moment, squeezing it. 'Perhaps in time, when all of this is less raw, you'll let me visit you, and the child? Or you'll come here to visit us? I have precious little family left to me.'

'I'll never come back here.'

'Never? And if Pip wants to visit his father in jail — because Boyd will be jailed, I'll make sure of it — you'll make him come on his own?'

'No.' Clare hangs her head. 'No, I won't make him come on his own.'

'Life is a catalogue of things we must do for the people we love, whether we want to or not. The only way to avoid it is to never love, and what would be the point of anything then?'

They are silent again, letting more time pass. The wind rolls around them and the hot sun is in their eyes, and it seems as though they might ossify, slowly, if they stayed there long enough; they might become a part of Puglia's bones. Clare can see the land's hard beauty, then; the harsh glory of it. It makes her think of Paola; it makes her see that you'd need that stony

501

strength of heart to live there. 'This war is almost over,' says Leandro. 'You asked me how it could ever end and here's the answer — with the rich crushing the poor in an iron fist. The *braccianti* have already lost; in a few more weeks they'll have to admit it, even to themselves. The proprietors have won. We proprietors, I should say. Every time the workers resist, they will be beaten down.' As he speaks, Ludo Manzo rides past the gates on his new brown horse, kicking up dust from its hooves. He rides easily, sitting back in the saddle, holding the reins loosely. 'They may happen to call themselves fascists right now, but there have always been men like that to beat the peasants down, and there always will be,' says Leandro, nodding towards his overseer. 'The Manzos. At least we're down to one of them.'

'Ettore said that Ludo has a knack for staying alive.'

'That he does, more's the pity. His son was the one that killed Ettore's fiancée. Did you know that?'

'Federico? No . . . I didn't know.' Even in her detached state, Clare feels the shock of it.

'Despicable. I'm sure my nephew had a hand in Federico ending up in that fire. He and the girl's brothers; and I don't blame them one bit — he had it coming. The man that was killed that night was Ettore's good friend. The one who looked like a movie star — I think his name was Pino. So I'm sure Ettore was there.'

'Oh, not Pino too.' Clare thinks of Pino's kind face; his young wife peering out past him at their door, and the way he kissed her before he left. She thinks of him saving her from Federico, and searching for the right word to say to her afterwards. *Coraggio.* Somehow his death seems the worst injustice of all. 'This place is horrible! It's *brutal!*' she says bitterly. 'How can you love it?'

'Love it? No, I don't love it. But it owns me.' Leandro turns to her and smiles sadly. 'Whenever you're ready, I'll take you and the boy to the station.'

★ ★ ★

Clare packs her things. She leaves Boyd's clothes hanging in the wardrobe, his shaving brush and soap on the washstand, the rubber sheath in its flat box, tucked into the bedside drawer. She doesn't know or care what will happen to these things. She goes up to Marcie and Leandro's room and finds the door shut, the corridor outside in shadow. She stands at the door for a long time, with the hair on her arms prickling; gripped by such knotted emotions she can't pick one from the other. *You nearly made a murderer of Pip*, she wants to say. *Kind, sweet Pip. You broke his heart out of spite. Or was it simply boredom?* And then she wants to say, *I know you're miserable. I know you hate it here, but you can't leave. I know you didn't want Ettore to die.*

'Marcie?' she says. The word bounces back at her from the wood. Perhaps she imagines it, but the silence inside seems to take on a sentient quality. She's sure Marcie can hear her. She raps her knuckles against the door. 'Marcie? Can I come in?' There's a tiny sound of quick, panicked movement; a rustle of cloth against skin. But that's all. Clare waits for a long time but the door doesn't open and she doesn't knock again. 'We're leaving soon. We'll be gone, so you won't have to see either one of us,' she says. And even though she'd planned to say much more she doesn't, because she can't say sorry, and she can't lay blame; she can't demand an explanation, and her anger is already burning itself out. So she turns her back and walks away, and leaves Marcie hidden there in silence. And then she realises that there could be no greater mark of regret from Marcie, no clearer expression of grief, than silence.

Clare goes to Pip's room and her heart jolts at finding his bed empty, the door ajar and the windows open, blowing out the fustiness of sleep. She takes a deep breath and grips the bedpost until she feels steady. Then she gathers up all his things and packs them into his trunk, and drags it over to the doorway. It only takes five minutes. *We'll leave and everything here will carry on without us. And we will carry on. It'll be like we were never here.* As if in answer to this, as if to deny it, a wave of nausea forces her to sit down on the lid of the trunk, drenching her forehead with cold sweat and her mouth with saliva. She wipes her face and then puts both hands on her midriff. 'I hadn't forgotten you,' she tells the baby quietly, and almost smiles. She knows then that the child will give her back the notion of joy, in time, and that even if the world must think the child is Boyd's, she will tell it about its real father — about his wild blue eyes, and his strength and his gentle heart; how it had felt like she'd always known him, and that she'd loved him instinctively, right from the start.

Time passes and she stays there, on the lid of Pip's trunk, trying to picture what it will be like to be back in Hampstead, back in the house that was Boyd's before it was ever hers. She pictures the slow turn of the hands on the clock in the empty hallway, and the silence that will settle once Pip is back at school, and she knows in that moment that she won't stay there. Not for any longer than she absolutely has to. She will have to find work, and a flat to rent, and she doesn't know what or where she will do or go, but an image of the sea on a summer's day comes into her mind — the deep, deep blue of it, with the mirroring sky above. She longs to have this shade of blue in her life, this saturation of colour.

The thought of starting over, of a town full of strangers, holds no fear for her. Instead she wonders how she can have been so afraid of such trivial things before. Before Puglia, before the Masseria dell'Arco, before Ettore. She realises she'll always be better for coming here; she will always be more alive; she feels like some of Ettore's strength has bedded into her alongside his unborn child. And when enough time has passed she'll be able to divorce Boyd, and cut herself free of him. She doesn't care that she will be gossiped about; she doesn't care what anyone will say. The Kent coast, or Sussex; a small town by the sea where Ettore's child can be born, and Pip can come in the holidays, and the puppy can run about. Boyd's house in Hampstead can sit and wait for him, if he should ever return to it. Clare will not be waiting; she will go her own way.

She finds Pip in the bat room, curled up on the old sofa. His hair is messed and greasy; he's still in his pyjamas. He has Peggy on his lap and the puppy sits up when Clare comes in, staring, perking her ears. Pip frowns at the puppy like she's misbehaved in some way, and as Clare walks across to them she finds herself holding her breath. Her footsteps echo in the rafters; light pours in through the windows and dazzles her. From high on the wall, that one watching eye of the mural stares down, and Clare tries not to think about everything it has witnessed that summer. She comes to stand right in front of the couch and Pip still won't look up, and fear makes her palms clammy. This is the moment when she'll know if she's lost him. This is the moment when she'll know if their bond has survived, or has shattered under the strain.

'All right there, Pip?' she says, and can't keep her voice even. Some emotion clenches his face, and his cheeks mottle with blood. She waits for a moment, in case he'll speak, but when he doesn't she turns her body slightly, towards the door. 'It's time to go, I think. Don't you?' She tries not to let the weight of everything sound in her voice; she doesn't want him to feel it, or have to share it.

'Home?' he says hoarsely, almost whispering.

'Home,' she says. Then she holds out her hand to him, and they can both see it trembling. Pip looks away and opens his mouth, and seems afraid to speak.

'I didn't . . . ' His brows pinch together. 'I didn't mean to shoot him.'

'I know you didn't,' Clare says at once. She waits a while, but Pip stays quiet. 'Coming then?' she says. She holds her breath again, until it burns and her heart lurches in protest. Then Pip gathers Peggy under one arm and takes Clare's hand.

'All right, Clare,' he says.

# Author's Note

*The Night Falling* is a work of fiction. Though the town of Gioia del Colle is real enough, and much of the historical detail is as accurate as I can make it, some events have been omitted, altered or imagined to fit the story, while — I hope — remaining true to the era and to the social and political landscape. I trust that those in the know will forgive this use of artistic licence. While key historical figures including Di Vittorio, Di Vagno, Capozzi and De Bellis were real people, all characters with significant roles in the story are entirely fictitious, including Francesco Molino, the man Clare sees beaten by a fascist squad in Piazza Plebiscito.

In September 1921, the socialist political leader Giuseppe di Vagno was assassinated as he gave a speech in Mola di Bari. His killers were rumoured, though not proven, to have been hired by the landowners and proprietors of Gioia del Colle. By the early months of 1922, two years' hard-won progress made by the peasants' unions and by socialist local government had been almost completely undone by the rise of fascism and its use of violence and intimidation to weaken opposition, culminating in the fascist March on Rome and the commencement of Benito Mussolini's dictatorship in October 1922.

The six workers killed at Natale Girardi's *masseria* on 1 July 1920 were: Pasquale

508

Capotorto, Rocco Orfino, Rocco Montenegro, Vincenzo Milano, Vito Falcone and Vito Antonio Resta. I placed Paola's lover Davide amongst their number for the sake of the story. For a comprehensive account of the incident, I recommend *L'Eccidio di Marzagaglia*, an article by Ermando Ottani, available online. Historical works concerning this era of Puglian history are hard to come by in English. I have found *Violence and Great Estates in the South of Italy* by Frank M. Snowden (Cambridge, 1986) very useful for research purposes. For those who can read in Italian, *La Memoria che Resta*, edited by Giovanni Rinaldi and Paola Sobrero (Provincia di Foggia, 1981) is a moving collection of first-hand accounts of peasant life at the time.

# Acknowledgements

I am hugely indebted to all the wonderful people I met during my stay in Gioia del Colle, who were so generous with their time and knowledge, and who, in several cases, let me snoop around their homes. Particular thanks to the endlessly enthusiastic and knowledgeable Angelo Coluccia; to Nicola Capurso, who arranged for me to be shown around several private *masserie* and shared some wonderful historical insights with me; ai Signori Bianco della Masseria Vallarta; ai Signori Mancino della Masseria Eramo; ai Signori Capurso della Masseria Capo Jazzo; a Valerio de Palma della Masseria La Signorella; al Prof. Pier Giorgio Castellana; e a Vito Santoiemma, for taking me around his incredible collection of historical artefacts linked to every sphere of town and peasant life in Puglia. The collection is available to view by appointment at his private museum, 117 Via Giuseppe di Vittorio, Gioia del Colle. Last but by no means least, my thanks to Bianca Alberelli, my wonderful Italian tutor — grazie mille per tutto!

My thanks to Genevieve Pegg at Orion for her knowledge, skill, and clear-sighted treatment of the manuscript; to my wonderful, wise, indispensable agent Nicola Barr; and to Susan Lamb and the whole team at Orion for their continued support, dedication and expertise. Thanks to my friends and family for always listening, for early reading and constant enthusiasm.

We do hope that you have enjoyed reading this large print book.

Did you know that all of our titles are available for purchase?

We publish a wide range of high quality large print books including:
**Romances, Mysteries, Classics**
**General Fiction**
**Non Fiction and Westerns**

Special interest titles available in large print are:
**The Little Oxford Dictionary**
**Music Book**
**Song Book**
**Hymn Book**
**Service Book**

Also available from us courtesy of Oxford University Press:
**Young Readers' Dictionary**
**(large print edition)**
**Young Readers' Thesaurus**
**(large print edition)**

For further information or a free brochure, please contact us at:
**Ulverscroft Large Print Books Ltd.,**
**The Green, Bradgate Road, Anstey,**
**Leicester, LE7 7FU, England.**
**Tel: (00 44) 0116 236 4325**
**Fax: (00 44) 0116 234 0205**

*Other titles published by Ulverscroft:*

## THE BALLOONIST

### James Long

Running from a troubled past, Lieutenant Willy Fraser, formerly of the Royal Flying Corps, has chosen the most dangerous job on the Western Front — a balloon observer hanging under a gasbag filled with explosive hydrogen, four thousand feet above the Ypres Salient, anchored by a slender cable. Swept across enemy lines after his balloon is damaged, Willy is hidden by Belgian farmers, whom he grows close to during his stay; with their aid, he manages to escape across the flooded delta at the English Channel and return to his duties. But once he's back in the air, spotting for artillery and under attack, Willy can only focus on his own survival — until he is forced to make an impossible decision that threatens the life of the woman he has come to love.

# THE GHOST OF THE MARY CELESTE

## Valerie Martin

In 1872 the American merchant vessel *Mary Celeste* was discovered adrift off the coast of Spain; her crew were never found. A rather hard-up young writer named Arthur Conan Doyle hears of the ship and decides to write an outlandish short story about what took place. It causes quite a sensation back in the United States, particularly for sought-after Philadelphia psychic Violet Petra and skeptical journalist Phoebe Grant, who is seeking to expose Petra as a fraud. Then there is the family of the *Mary Celeste*'s captain, linked to the sea for generations and marked repeatedly by tragedy. In salons and on rough seas, at seances and in the imagination of a genius, these stories converge in unexpected ways as the mystery of the ghost ship deepens. Will the sea yield its secrets?

# THE TWO OF US

## Andy Jones

Fisher is fizzing with the euphoria of new love — laughing too loud, kissing more enthusiastically than is polite in public. How he met Ivy is academic; you don't ask how the rain began, you simply appreciate the rainbow. The two of them have been an item for less than three weeks — and they just know they are meant to be together. The fact that they know little else about each other is a minor detail . . . But over the coming months, in which their lives will change forever, Fisher and Ivy discover that falling in love is one thing, while staying there is an entirely different story . . .